THE
COLLABORATIVE

THE U.S. CONFRONTS ILLEGAL DRUGS & TERRORISM

Ken Berquist

Edited and Proofed by Robert Garofalo.
Edited by Shay VanZwoll, EV Proofreading
Publishing Assistance by V. L. Dreyer
Cover design by Ihor Tureh.

Edition Number: 2.0

I wish to express my appreciation to all of those of whom were helpful in creating this work.

To, Gail, my loving and very patient wife who understands, when I get into the 'writing mindset', it ultimately results in a periodic slippage into hibernation.

"When we go hunting, it is not our arrow that kills the moose, however powerful be the bow; it is nature that kills him."

Big Thunder, late 19th century
Wabanaki Algonquin

"You have noticed that everything an Indian does is in a circle, and that is because the Power of the World always works in circles, and everything tries to be round..."

"The sky is round, and I have heard that the earth is round like a ball, and so are the stars. The wind, in its greatest power, whirls. Birds make their nests in circles, for theirs is the same religion as ours..."

"Even the seasons form a great circle in their changing, and always come back again to where they were. The life of a man is a circle from childhood to childhood, and so it is in everything where power moves."

Black Elk (1863 - 1950)
Oglala Sioux holy man

TABLE OF CONTENTS

CHAPTER 1:
MARTIAL LAW DRUG PLAN

"There can be no letting up in the fight against illegal drug use until the act of drug abuse itself, in America, is a thing of the past." The audience, sipping after-dinner coffee and brandy, began applauding and, like a cresting wave, moved to a standing ovation preventing the President from finishing his speech. The President used this time to organize his thoughts for a dramatic close and to give the TV cameras time to focus on his naturally serious and determined face. With the Republican convention still fresh in the minds of voters and the reelection campaign beginning in full swing, he could use a dramatic closing to garner the NY Times's headlines, the most influential newspaper in the region, if not the country.

President Covey held his hands up, palms facing the audience, asking the audience to let him finish. Slowly, just as he'd planned it, they sat and waited to hear his final words. "Now we come to the difficult part. My fellow Americans, stopping drug abuse won't be easy and it won't be inexpensive, but we all know it must be done and done now, for each day we wait this cursed problem affects our children, our friends, our neighbors, the very security of our nation. Each day we wait will cost an estimated ten million dollars more and take three days longer to cure. The raw cocaine and heroin are produced in countries where Al-Qaeda operations are based and in many cases provided by Al-Qaeda directly. Therefore, Americans that traffic and buy drugs are financing the terrorist groups that threaten America, and they must be stopped." He waited for that to sink into the audience's conscience, watching their faces for the proper timing before taking a deep breath and beginning again. "This is why I have not asked Congress for additional funding. The delays caused by congressional analysis and debate could cost America millions of tax dollars and result in a further weakening of our national security. This is why, as of today, I have declared war on illegal drugs, war on the people who traffic in drugs, war on the people who sell drugs, war on the people who buy drugs, war on the people who use drugs, and war on the terrorist groups that are financed by drug revenue."

He knew this would be the tough part. He could see the heated whisperings of the congressional leaders seated at the front table. President Covey was a seasoned political veteran. He had been through the Boston political training ground, beaten the Democratic stronghold on Massachusetts, lived through the war in Afghanistan as a POW, and knew he could control the fervor he would create in the next three minutes. Raising his finger and pointing toward the audience, but at no one person specifically, he began his closing statement. "As of today, by Presidential Authority, I have declared Martial Law, within the United States of America, with the express purpose of finding, arresting and prosecuting, to the absolute limits of the law, all people and organizations, foreign or domestic, that deal in illegal drugs within the boundaries of the United States of America, and by doing so cut the flow of cash financing many terrorist operations." It was taking on even greater weight now — declaring it to the American public — than even he thought in preparing the program and then the speech. "My singular goal is to make the streets of America safe once again, to restore national security and to cut off the most significant source of funding to terrorist groups threatening our way of life."

Pandemonium. Applause mixed with whistles, screams, cheers, people stamping their feet and yelling "Yes! Yes! Yes!" with their fists pounding on the tables. Some people just stared in disbelief that finally something was being done about the most serious problem confronting America. Still others tried to get close to the big man to shake his hand or just touch the larger-than-life person. Women and men wept real tears, some were speechless. One woman slowly fell to her knees and, clasping both hands, started to pray, praying for what President Covey didn't know.

The TV cameras were panning the crowds, recording the maximum footage for the editors to cut up into small pieces to make the dramatic speech even more dramatic when interrupting regularly scheduled programs for the Special Report.

President William Covey waved with commitment as he left the podium and was immediately surrounded by Secret Service agents and ushered out the side exit of the Plaza Hotel's main ballroom to his sleek black spotless new Cadillac limousine parked and ready on 58th Street.

The heavily armored-plated limo pulled effortlessly out into the lighted street where traffic had been stopped by uniformed NYC police officers, annoying the drivers who had little time to waste. The presidential limo was flanked by two dozen of New York's finest motorcycle police, with two vans in front and two in the rear filled with Secret Service and their latest toys and weapons. The Cadillac made an immediate right on Fifth Avenue and with the help of the escort, a left on 57th heading toward the East River. Security was especially tight, Robert had seen to it weeks in advance, knowing the controversy that the President's speech would incite.

Bill Covey felt that the speech had gone better than he expected. He removed his horn-rimmed glasses, massaged the bridge of his strong nose and leaned his head back to reflect on the evening. Robert Dunkin, his close friend and aid, knew the President well, and could see that he was in a state of introspection and not to be disturbed. He sat back to enjoy a peaceful evening ride to LaGuardia Airport where Air Force One and the rest of his staff sat awaiting the short trip to Washington D.C.

Bill was thinking of the headlines on the NY Times's next edition and was enjoying the inner glow of self-satisfaction when the limited-access secured telephone gave that awful squawk, like a child's damaged video toy. There were only a handful of people with access to this telephone number. One could not simply dial this number from just any ordinary telephone. The voice-encryption technology required an identical secure communication system be used with the identical voice-encryption program code, which was changed daily. The program could not be broken in less than twenty-four hours, even with the fastest computers available. The CIA and FBI had once matched their best computer technicians with their fastest computers and it took nearly four days to get the first of twelve strings of the encryption code. The new randomizers, the latest digital technology, prevented any but an identical system, with the same daily code, to communicate.

Robert gestured toward the receiver and was stopped by the President, who answered it personally. The caller's voice was not recognizable even with the experience the President had with using the encryption device. Bill always referred to the telephone as the "squawk box", not just because of the sound of its ringing, but because it reminded him of what the voices sounded like when using the tin cans and string as a boy to talk to his friends. The only words spoken were the caller's, "Your family is dead, and you will be dead before the reelection for what you have done tonight." There was a short pause and a few more words before the link was severed, "Now you have time to think about how we will do it and who will be first."

Dead. Nothing. Who? How?

The caller's voice was cold, calculating, piercing and ruthlessly convincing. It caused him to shiver and visibly shake with cold fear. For the first time since being a prisoner in Afghanistan in that filthy cell, with dirty scraps of food, tortured by Taliban operatives, William Thurston Covey, President of the United States, the most powerful man in the world, was helplessly scared.

The air in the Rocky Mountain region of Colorado was frigid, dry and deadly still. The quietness in the remote camp was penetrated by the abrupt sound of a telephone receiver being slammed down on its cradle inside the portable briefcase-like box. Carlos Ortega was not a happy man. The President's declaration of Martial Law on drugs will certainly disrupt my business for a time, he thought, but in the end it will be business as usual. It always was. That is why he paid so dearly to those government pukes. They'd better come through or they'll be dead, along with their family, friends, even their pets.

Carlos did not like coming to the United States. He was a cautious man, and as a result had outmaneuvered and outlived all the drug lords. Still, he had to make an appearance to keep his national organization aware that he was watching their movements and absolutely no disloyalty would be tolerated. He, like any businessman, was also concerned about the quality of his product and monitored its production carefully. Most especially his new product.

Carlos left his tent and walked to the production tent. Before lifting the flap to enter, he stopped and looked at the moon just beginning to rise, barely visible through the tall evergreens, and felt its calming effect. With his head lifted slightly, his slight double chin was less visible and he gave the appearance that he was taller than his five-foot-eight muscular but trim frame actually was. Once inside, he nodded to the two well-armed guards who were keeping a close watch on the two women working at the table in the center of the tent. The poor light from the gas lanterns cast eerie shadows and gave the correct impression that something sinister was happening, with more to come.

The women were both in their twenties, white and petrified. Their hands were shaking so severely that they had difficulty funneling the small translucent sand-like crystals into the small plastic sacks. There were three large boxes of filled sacks and only a small pile of crystal left on the table. Soon the pile would be gone and the fun will begin, thought Carlos. As the General, I always go first and I deserve the privilege and need the stress relief.

"Jesús, cuando haya terminado de traerlos a mi tienda," Carlos ordered: Jesús, when they are finished bring them to my tent. Jesús, a large brawny Mexican with one missing front tooth and a face that hadn't seen a razor in months, nodded slowly and squinted slightly when a telling grin broke, drooling slightly from the corner of his mouth as he gave a short laugh and nodded in a fast and jerky motion.

It was the night's point of peak light, with the half moon directly overhead, when the two women were pushed into Carlos's tent. Both fell to their knees, partly due to the severe exhaustion of being forced to work nonstop for two days filling the small sacks, and partly due to Jesús's brute force. It was obvious he enjoyed overpowering women. Carlos just watched as they tried to get to their feet, and laughed as a few tears came to their eyes as Jesús removed their leg irons. Had the women only known that their car might not be able to handle the mountain altitudes, they would never have left the lodge for a bit of mountain sightseeing, much less accepted a ride from a helpful stranger. A regret they will not have much longer.

"Stand up and let me see how pretty you are," he said, in a sensitive and caring tone. His voice gave them a bit of hope as they slowly stood. "Very pretty, now I want to see more of you. You with the blond hair, take your friends clothes off. Now!" Carlos commanded, his tone becoming more forceful. She was too tired to fight, and tried to look away while she unbuttoned her friend's blouse with trembling fingers. Carlos commanded her to look directly into her friend's eyes while she disrobed her. Her friend was now naked. They were standing face to face, tears swelling in both of their eyes, never having felt so helpless.

Carlos opened one of the sacks. He filled the bowl of the pipe with the translucent sand-like crystals, soon to be known as White Ice on the street. This sack was triple the dosage, not cut like the product for sale, but not full strength either... that would surely be instantly lethal. He handed the pipe and a butane lighter to the closest woman and ordered them to smoke the contents. They were trembling so much that most of the first bowl of crystals went on the canvas tent floor. She lit the lighter off and began to smoke the drug. The rich sweet odor from the smoke filled the tent. As the women shared the pipe, they became very relaxed, and soon sexuality charged through them like a white-hot burning fever. They started to kiss and to comfort each other, and soon the kissing became heated and more passionate than they had ever experienced with a man before. The drug was taking effect.

Their tongues darted and fought with each other, moans coming from deep within grew louder and more frequent. Carlos looked on and began to pleasure himself. Slowly, he thought, there is still plenty of time. They were both tearing at their remaining clothing, they needed to be in each other's bodies, that was all that mattered now. Carlos had enjoyed this scene many times before and he would never tire of it. Women, so overwhelmed with sexuality, so in need of release, so needing that sexual climax that they would do anything for it. But the effects of White Ice terminate abruptly, and when it comes, the rapid icy plunge into cold reality is almost as frightening as was the rapid heat.

Slowly, they began to lose the drug-enhanced energy to go on. They lay back, exhausted and confused, but with a strange satisfied glow on their glistening faces. Carlos was just fastening his belt when Jesús and Julio knocked on the tent post.

Carlos, using the same tone that he would use when giving someone his car keys said, "They're all yours, but when you guys are done, bury them deeper this time. Clear? Don't screw up!" Before the women could scream, Jesús and Julio were gagging them to prevent the sound that travels so easily in the mountains from alarming any nearby hunters.

CHAPTER 2:
MISTAKES

"2015 was a very profitable year for AIEC, partly due to the economic expansion effecting our markets and partly because we can still price our services lower than our nearest domestic competitor while delivering superior quality," Mr. Bear said as he addressed the company's Board of Directors and employees. "Sales rose 21.2% to two hundred eighty-five million dollars and profits rose 27.8% to thirty-seven point three million dollars. We have continued to invest in the American Indian community by building more schools, housing, hospitals and have established specialized drug and alcohol abuse clinics."

Clint Bear, President and Founder of American Indian Electronics Corporation, was pleased with the company's progress and even more pleased with its civic and social activities. Clint beamed with pride during moments like this. He talked much like most Chief Executive Officers, only with more conviction, but looked more like an Indian with a thigh length buckskin jacket covering a white shirt and string tie, tastefully ornamented with tribal beads and his long coal-black hair parted in the middle and pulled back into a ponytail. His physical six-foot-three, nearly two hundred-pound frame dwarfed the podium and contrasted his peaceful crimson-toned face. He finished his address in a low resonant voice, "The best news is that we see no reason why AIEC's performance will not continue through 2016, and if President Covey is reelected, as I believe and hope he will be, the continuation of productive domestic economic policies could enhance our performance into the next five years. Thank You."

You would think that applause would be appropriate, but that is not the Indian way. They were more quiet and introspective. Their way of showing the deep respect that Clint had earned was to elect him as their leader. When Clint Bear formed AIEC, his motives were not self-serving, and they are not today. The electronics manufacturing and assembly corporation had assisted in putting the Indians back to work. He, almost single handedly, built the company, and with it, the self-esteem of all participating tribes of the American Indian people, but in a very unique way. He banded the various American Indian nations together, amalgamating them into a single powerful force, but segmented the company into divisions so that the nations could work on their own land, keep their own identity, reinvest most of their own profits on their reservation, and to a lesser extent, build autonomy. It was brilliant, a cultural-based decentralized civic for-profit corporation, as Clint had described it.

Clint was thinking of the other times he had walked off a stage, leaving a podium and proceeding to an assigned seat, while wearing a different uniform. They were not as pleasant as this memory. Today, he was walking in the American Indian Cultural Historical Civic Center building, that his company has financed and donated to help

American Indians stay in touch with their ancestry. The huge one hundred and twenty-acre plot was donated by the U.S. Government which cost President Covey dearly in political capital. But Bill Covey was deeply indebted to Clint, and would do more if he could to help Clint in such a worthy cause.

He sat down between his sister Cabris and his fiancée Brook. His half-brother Art was seated directly behind them, along with their father Old Bear. Everyone watched a video produced to promote the American Indian Electronics Corporation to prospective customers. It was a professionally done high-tech production and focused on the dedication to quality, their on-time shipment record, and the technological advances AIEC had made in the past year alone. The audience, primarily Indians representing the Cherokee, Navajo, Hopi, Ute, and Apache Nations, applauded respectfully and chanted, "San-Ja-Ka-Ko-Ka," — The Deceiving Wolf, Clint Bear's Indian name, in memory of a direct ancestor more than one hundred years ago.

Clint was Mandan by blood and heritage, but with the amalgamation of the tribes, he, by his father's choice, began living amongst the Apache Nation before he could walk. Old Bear had kept the Mandan heritage alive by telling Clint of their history every chance he had. Clint had also learned the Apache warrior way, their warriors cunning, bravery and tenaciousness by living it, their respect for the land and the "One God" by experiencing it.

No one had done more than Clint to help the Indian Nation come back from the subjugation of the depths of long-term government neglect, alcohol and drug abuse, poor education and directionless existence's caused by the United States Government when it stole their land and heritage some one hundred seventy five years ago. The American

Indian, once a proud and productive group of nations, had plummeted into poverty and despair. The Removal Act of 1830, sponsored by the newly elected President Andrew Jackson, allowed squatters and land speculators to overrun and take the Indian land and forced them to abandon their homes for a new land. The forced march west, through brutal territory, in harsh conditions and at a fierce pace claimed the lives of whole families. Thousands of Indians perished. The forced march west to the "new land", now the in state of Oklahoma and parts of Kansas and Nebraska, was immortalized in what the Cherokees called the Trail of Tears, with the story passed generation to generation, so their children's children would never forget.

AIEC was helping to restore the pride and vitality that lay beneath the surface of the reviving Indian nations. Clint was their leader, not their Chief, but a figurehead of vitality and hope, wise beyond his years, who had never forgotten the Trail of Tears.

A young Indian boy with Nike sneakers, dressed in blue jeans and a white shirt buttoned to the neck, walked quietly to where Clint was sitting. He whispered into Cabris's ear and Clint noticed a shocked expression envelop her face. She whispered to Clint, "The President of the United States is on the phone and needs to speak with you. It's urgent."

Barely sixty miles from where two women had just been savagely and sadistically raped and murdered, the body of a man was found by three hunters. The man had been shot three times, the coroner would discover, once in the heart, once in the head and once in the balls. Almost gang-land style. The balls would not have interested the pros, just death interested the professionals, so their third shot would have been to the stomach.

He had been dead for more than five days and the smell of blood-soaked frozen flesh had attracted the animals, and the animals' had attracted the hunters. The arms and legs had been abused first by the raccoons and coyotes, the neck and head just beginning their unrebuked torture. The call went to the Durango Colorado Sheriff's Office, about sixty miles southwest of where the man's body was found. The trip into this area of the distant western part of the Rocky Mountains, along the Continental Divide, not far from an area called Los Pinos Pass, had to be finished on foot and the rugged but aging sheriff wondered how the body got here in the first place. Why would someone be out here dressed in light clothing… no, the body must have been transported here, but how? the Sheriff wondered.

Red Peterson had been the sheriff for nearly twenty years and murder wasn't a frequent occurrence in these parts, but it did happen. He took his time with the area, partly using the time to become accustomed to the 5,000-foot altitude and partly looking for any clues, anything out of the ordinary, before he approached the body. The hunters said they hadn't touched anything because it was obvious that the guy was dead and frozen solid. A deputy lifted up the yellow police tape that surrounded the crime scene and let Red pass. Red brushed some snow away from the body and checked for a wallet or ID, name tags on clothing, initials on jewelry, anything that might tell him who this was. Nothing, absolutely nothing in any pocket; no jewelry, no labels, nothing. Strange, very strange. Not likely a robbery way out here, then what…?

The animals' footprints were all that surrounded the body, that and blood-covered teeth-ripped clothing and bone. Red, satisfied that he would find no clues here, except the total lack of clues, ordered the body bag for transport to the coroner's office. Maybe that report will shed some light on who this man is and how he was killed.

The request for dental and fingerprint records was what alerted Cole Cunningham, Field Director of Special Projects, DEA. He flew within the hour to Colorado Springs, met the local area field agent, Sam Forest, and together drove south on Route 25 until the intersection of Route 160 where they started the longest leg west toward Durango. Sheriff Red Peterson was sitting in a squeaky old oak swivel tilt office chair with his feet crossed and resting on a matching oak desk. His proper and well broken-in cowboy boots caught Cole's eye first. The introductions were made and IDs offered.

"Sheriff Peterson, you've found the body of Paul Cudson, Special Agent with the DEA. He was also my friend."

"Call me Red, please. I'm sorry about your friend. And, Agent Cunningham, something stinks."

"The name's Cole. Hardly a fitting end for a decorated officer with a distinguished record, but this is what this work all too frequently does to a man, or to a woman. I'll need your cooperation in keeping this completely quiet until we find the bastards who did it. And I will find them, you can bank on that, Red," Cole said, accenting his visceral connection with bared teeth, reminiscent of an angry Doberman Pincer. "Let's find out what stinks."

"Okay, Cole, how else can I help?"

The President would not respond to the repeated questions from Robert regarding what had been said during that brief, but life changing, encrypted telephone call.

"Robert, just drop it! It was nothing that you need to be concerned about," Bill snapped. But Robert was always included in the goings-on in government and being kept in the dark was both curious and made him feel resentful. After all, to be a good aid he needed to know what was happening — everything — it was how Bill and he had worked since the camp. The President's ashen face reminded him of the mask he had looked into many times before while rotting away in the Taliban cell. He knew it represented a mixture of controlled fear and rage, and he knew from experience to leave Bill alone with his thoughts.

Robert had been a spoiled kid when he made the first of many good decisions, to enlist into the Marine Corps. After Basic Training, he was sent into combat in Afghanistan, and that started his road to manhood. He found he had the stomach for combat, one of the biggest surprises of his life. He had always run from trouble, from the school days when the class bullies picked on him to the early days in Basic Training. Something began to happen to Robert in Basic — he saw that he was just as capable as the next guy, sometimes much more capable. With all their hair shaved off and in identical uniforms, there was little to differentiate one from another except performance. And for the first time in his life he was physically performing, which in turn gave him the confidence to exercise cerebral performance.

"Bill, how can I help if you shut me out? Tell me what happened," he asked gingerly, and regretting his intrusion instantly.

"There are some things I can't tell you. Just accept that and let's change the subject," Bill said in a tone of finality. "Now, what is happening with the DEA's Special Projects? I just made my biggest commitment to the American public ever, and I intend to deliver."

Robert did not want to give his President this news so close to the speech that could get him reelected, but, "The timing could not have been worse. I just received a call from Cole Cunningham's group; the infiltration is in its sixth day with no contact. They say that's not good, but they have their best man on the job. That's why they are worried, the deep-cover agent is their very best and he knows the need for routine contact..."

"Damn it, how can we stop these guys? They seem more powerful than the U.S. Government," the President interrupted.

The limo was now turning left off Second Avenue into the Midtown Tunnel where secure communication would be impossible until they got to the other side. Bill was remembering the radical faction who recently tried to blow up the tunnel to protest the embargo on Iran, and wondered if his security team had checked out the tunnel. He then decided that if there was truth to the call, "Your family, will be dead, and then you..." he would be the last one to go so he could witness the horror of his family's death. Not a comforting thought, as was the terrorist's design.

"Robert, when we exit the tunnel, please get Clint Bear on the phone."

"Is there any connection to the last call we received?" Robert asked.

"For the last time, just drop it!" Bill said angrily.

Bill sat quietly, looking through the limo's bulletproof glassed side window, watching the tunnel lights flash by, and with each light came a new page of his life and a new thought of his wife and daughter. He had married before the war, just before leaving for Basic Training. It was against his better judgment to marry so quickly, but Judith was very persuasive. He remembered that day like it was yesterday, not the twenty plus years that it was.

Judith was a graduate of Stonehill College, and had certain privileges since graduating first in her class, allowing her to be married on the school grounds. It was a proper Catholic wedding, as nothing short of proper would do for the Stonehill College. She was radiant. Her naturally straight, shoulder-length sandy blond hair, freckles on her nose and dimples blossoming on her cheeks, were testimony to her Irish heritage. The peace and happiness were in her eyes, smile and aura. Bill loved her then and was still completely devoted to her today.

Bill had left the very next day, reporting to Lackland Air Force Base for Basic Training, then to Officers' school and then on to flight training. He took to flying like a fish to water. His reflexes were second nature from the start and he was certain to be the best SOAR MH-47E Chinook helicopter pilot in his squadron, all the more reason for surprise when he was reported Missing in Action after seven months of flawless performance in fifty-two combat missions.

Their first and only child, Katherine, was raised in a loving home by caring and devoted parents. Bill was happy to write the checks to Georgetown University, even though the tuition was outrageous. Kathy was studying to be a doctor, a pediatric surgeon; helping people was a trait that both her mother and her father cultivated whenever they found the opportunity. They both believed that giving something back to society was every person's duty and frequently quote the old maxim, "What goes around comes around." Circles.

The abrupt darkness when the limo exited the tunnel jolted Bill from his pleasant thoughts and Robert was already dialing the phone.

"Bill, he has just finished addressing his Board of Directors. Someone has gone to get him," Robert said, while handing the phone to him.

After a few minutes, Bill recognized Clint's voice saying hello.

"How are you doing, you old desert rat?" Bill said, half-laughing and half-serious, remembering the first time he had seen Clint's face. He would never ever forget that instant, like the moment of your first child's birth. Bill had thought of himself as dead and given a living sentence in hell until he set eyes on Clint's face. The terror of surprise, seeing Clint's blackened face contrasted by the whites of his eyes, was soon replaced by his rational thought that this must be an American, and he must be here to rescue them. He remembered weeping at first and then crying unashamedly.

"I'm doing fine, but you didn't call me to find out how I was doing, you have all that technology to tell you that. What's up, Bill?" Clint could never bring himself to call him "Mr. President", it just didn't fit their unusual and unique relationship.

"I need to talk to you, privately, very privately. How soon can you get to Washington? I need your help."

"It sounds serious." Clint remembered that Bill was not an alarmist, which alarmed Clint. "I can be there tomorrow."

"Thanks. Call me on my private line as soon as you arrive."

"Goodbye, Clint… and Clint, thanks."

Clint hung up the phone in the center's main office and wondered what the problem could be. He had known Bill since Afghanistan and knew he was deeply concerned about something. It was obvious from his tone. He turned around and physically bumped into his fiancée, Brook.

"You didn't tell me that you knew the President," Brook screamed. She was obviously impressed.

"Oh, it was a long time ago. He and I saw some action in Afghanistan. He has asked for my advice on a Bill that could affect the way we do business. I told him I would go to Washington tomorrow to discuss it."

"Wow. That's great! Can I come along with you?"

"Hey, you and Cabris need to review the AIEC, Navajo Division, this weekend, don't you?"

"She doesn't need my help, and I want to be with the man I love," Brook said as she put her arms around his lower back and squeezed their bodies together tightly. "Come on, we can see some of the sights, have a candlelit dinner, maybe some dancing and definitely some hot sex," she said, as she began kissing his neck. Brook knew how to get her way, usually, and Clint knew it too. He loved it when she tried to persuade him to do what he had already decided to do in most cases, but wouldn't let on. It was a little game they played to add excitement to their already exciting relationship.

'You make a tempting offer, my love, but it will be an all-day and probably all-night meeting and I can't see you waiting back in a stuffy hotel room for me." Privately, he was wondering why Bill had called him in the first place. Intuition had always served him well, it had kept him alive and it told him to go to Washington alone.

He hated to leave Brook that morning. He could feel something wasn't right. Brook was fast asleep, her nakedness partially hidden by the sheets that were torn from their tuckings by the lovemaking the night before. She was beautiful, and the way her long brilliant hair lay on the pillow with the slit of melted orange sunlight coming through the mostly pulled drapes highlighted her head like an angel's halo. Clint had never seen her so radiant. He kissed her on the cheek, inhaling and savoring her scent for what seemed like hours while dreaming of the night before, and realized he would have to leave now or risk missing his plane. Clint quietly closed and locked the front door, leaving for the Albuquerque airport, but not feeling quite comfortable with something. But what?

***

Cole Cunningham had just delivered his report to the President and was eager to get out of his office. William Thurston Covey had not made it to the top by luck; it was hard work, intelligence and refusing to settle for less than the best performance possible. He was a ruthless taskmaster and Cole had just been the latest subject of his controlled rage. With his best agent and friend now dead, Cole was at an impasse. Many months of work would have to be painstakingly duplicated to break the nation's largest drug ring. But he didn't have a lot of time to do it. After the President's Martial Law Drug Plan commitment speech, he guessed he would have less than three to four months to close down America's most infamous drug ring, an almost if not an impossible task for any law enforcement agency. It would be a near impossible task for many law enforcement agencies trying to work collaboratively.

Worse, he had the unenviable task of telling Barbara Cudson that her husband and father of their three children, would not be coming home for dinner, ever.

The boxes, loaded with filled plastic sacks, were carefully loaded into an old sun-bleached light blue Ford pickup truck and hidden by bales of hay. The bales were placed around the inside perimeter of the truck's bed, leaving a cavity in the center, where the boxes containing sacks of White Ice would be hidden. With five more bales of hay placed on top of the boxes, the sun-bleached Ford pickup looked like every other farmer's utility vehicle going to, or coming from, the market. The truck would be driven west toward Los Angeles using mostly secondary roads, where an old pickup truck with bales of livestock feed hay is as common a sight as a taxi in Manhattan on a sunny day.

Chet, the driver, was a white male farmer who had been offered the opportunity to earn fifty thousand dollars by simply driving the truck to L.A. and meet, at a prearranged time, Leon Beecher, who would pay him to disappear. The money was desperately needed to keep the farm from foreclosure, and who knows, maybe there would be some money left over to buy presents for the wife and kids.

Carlos was well out of sight, leaving the instructions to be given by his lieutenant in the southwest, Jesús.

"You are to go directly to this fucking spot," he said, banging his right index finger on the map. "I marked the route you are to take. Follow it exactly, got it? Change the license plates every time you go into a new state, new ones under the seat, do you understand, gringo? Be there at 9:00 at night. Leon will be waiting. Give him the fucking keys to the truck, take your fucking money and haul your ass out of there. We never want to see you again." Chet was thinking he never wanted to see them again, either.

Just as he was about to close the pickup door and start his dangerous, but rewarding, trip, Jesús said, as he held up his 9mm semiautomatic, "Chet, we know where you live and your esposa is kind of bonito, we could have a lot of fun with her, so don't fuck up." Jesús's eerie grin, with that missing front tooth and greasy, sweaty skin, and especially those wild darting eyes, completed the horror for Chet. Jesús was insane, he was sure of it now, but he was committed. He couldn't back out now. He would be killed, of that he was sure. It was too late, and once again, just like coming to the Western part of the U.S., leaving his job on the General Motors assembly line to become a farmer, he had jumped in over his head.

The banging on the door sounded far away at first, and just before consciousness overcame sleep, Brook dreamed of a large midnight-black mountain cat with phosphorescent green penetrating eyes stalking her, causing her to awake with a start. She sat up quickly and recognizing that she had overslept and hearing the banging on the front door, jumped out of bed and ran to open the front door to greet a slightly angry Cabris.

"Brook, we should be already on our way if we are going to make the Navajo Reservation before nightfall, get your butt in gear. I'll pack the notebook computers and calculators while you shower and dress, now hurry!"

"Let's go Brook, no time for playing in there," Cabris snapped as she rapped on the steamy glass shower door a few minutes later.

Cabris and Brook were as opposite as opposites could be. Cabris, like her brother Clint, was as disciplined and organized as Brook was artistic and creative. Both recognized that the strengths of the other made them a pair to be reckoned with. Clint saw that as well, and had structured the finance department with both of them reporting to Roger Whitehouse, the Chief Financial Officer and Senior Vice President, the only non-Indian senior executive, primarily responsible for divisional auditing.

Cabris had looked up to her older brother for as long as she could walk. It was Clint that saved the tribe, paid for her university education and introduced her to her now-best friend, Brook. She was comfortable with Brook being more attractive, although she was pretty in her own right, and she was happy that Brook was to be part of the family soon. Cabris had graduated from Cornell, Graduate School of Business with an MBA. Since then, partly out of devotion to Clint and partly because she was devoted to the business, its mission and its principles, she hadn't had time to consider marriage. Her admirers, those that appreciated her efficient beauty, had gone unrewarded with the business being the first priority. Now with Brook getting married, she was concerned that she might have waited too long.

Brook was not full Indian, half Hopi and half white, which was frequently mentioned by Clint's half-brother Art, but she had all the deep beauty of Indian skin and eyes. She had long coal-black hair as straight as wheat. Her skin was golden and supple, smooth without a blemish to be seen, and she had long perfectly proportioned legs that Clint fell in love with before he fell in love with her. Brook would dazzle Clint with her knowledge of computers by writing clever little programs that would break into the supposed secure terminal in his office and make sexy suggestions on the screen. Brook was a whiz at finding ways to do things differently; it was the artist's mind of perspective.

Cabris was already in the company pickup truck, engine running and in gear, when Brook closed and locked the front door.

"You know I hate being late for an appointment, Brook."

"Sorry, Clint didn't wake me like usual and we had a rather, long night." Brook said with a slight giggle as she closed the passenger's side door and buckled her seatbelt.

Both were dressed in casual attire by comparison to typical corporate standards. With jeans and button-down front cotton shirts, they could have been farmhands as opposed to corporate executives. But that was the way Clint had set up the business; casual, blend in with the natural environment, don't expect the environment to blend with you, the first rule of jungle survival. People who dressed comfortably acted comfortably, and those who were comfortable worked more efficiently. It was a simple, but usually overlooked fact.

Cabris drove west on Route 64. From the northern tip of the Apache Reservation near a town called Dulce, it would take about four to five hours to get to Newcomb in the center of the Navajo Reservation. It was a long drive especially in an old pickup, but they had made the trip every month for the past four years since the division was opened, and were accustomed to it. They stayed off the highways because the truck shook severely at high speeds and going too slow meant the eighteen-wheeler truckers' harassment. The secondary roads were more scenic anyway. They turned on to Route 170 southwest, just past Kirkland, being careful not to make the wrong turn at this confusing intersection and end up going north toward Durango.

She wanted to be there by Saturday night, and unknown to her, it was just two days after agent Cudson was found dead just ninety miles north of the northern-most tip of the Navajo Reservation.

"I'm getting thirsty, are we near the Patch?" Brook asked Cabris after waking from a brief cat nap.

"Yeah, it's just a few miles more and I need a cold drink and some food, and so does the truck. The engine seems to be running a bit hot."

"I'll see to the truck while you go an order some food. That way we won't waste too much time."

"Okay, how about some BBQ chicken and a salad… sound good to you, Cabris?"

"Yeah, go for it, and two diet Pepsis for me."

The Patch got its name for what it was, a patch of well-nourished land in the middle of the tundra right off Route 170. The water came from an underground spring and the gas station and diner had grown up around it more than sixty years ago, replacing an old western stagecoach rest station. The old hand crank pumps still stood there as a reminder, although they had been functionally replaced by the newer electric ones about fifty years ago.

Cabris pulled in to the Patch, but the gas pumps were blocked momentarily by a sun-bleached light blue Ford pickup truck loaded with bales of hay. The driver pulled out cautiously and headed west, allowing Cabris to pull up to the pump.

Jesús, sitting in his green Plymouth Roadrunner at the south end of the Patch's parking lot, watched Chet drive out and, satisfied that he was just scared enough not to fuck up, was about to leave when Brook stepped out of the truck and headed into the diner. Julio noticed her as well, "What a chica, Jesús, look at those legs and ass."

Jesús said, "Are you thinking what I'm thinking?"

"Yeah, I'll take care of the truck if they both go in, while you keep an eye out."

Cabris filled the gas tank and checked the oil and water. Only the water needed to be topped off as was frequently the case with this old truck. She then pulled to the nearest parking spot around to the left side of the diner. It didn't occur to her that the truck would not be visible from inside the diner since nothing ever happens there. As she was walking in the diner, she could smell the grease from the burgers that were the Patch specialty.

Julio went around the side of the diner and his thin, wiry frame slipped under the truck without the slightest effort. He had done this many times before. He quickly took his knife and made a quarter-inch hole in the radiator hose connecting the engine coolant inlet to the bottom of the radiator. Water was already leaking out when he quietly got to his feet and casually walked away back to the car where Jesús was waiting. Had either of the two girls come out, Jesús would have beeped the horn twice quickly and waved to them, signaling Julio to roll under the adjacent vehicle. It wasn't necessary, as Cabris and Brook were enjoying the chicken and salad not knowing it might be their last meal.

***

Clint caught an American Airline flight to Dallas connecting on to the Ronald Reagan Washington National Airport. The trip took seven hours including the layover in Dallas and the taxi to the Marriott Hotel. He liked staying at the Marriott because it was near the places he was familiar with, and familiar ground was always the most comfortable and more importantly, more secure.

He didn't bother to unpack, rather went straight to the telephone and dialed the private number he'd memorized long ago. The President answered after two rings and invited Clint to his office as soon as he could get there.

The Oval Office is not an easy place to get in to, one does not just walk in to the White House and ask to see the President, unless you are already cleared by the President himself or his immediate staff. Clint chose the North gate, mostly for old times' sake, and was surprised to see Robert standing there waiting for him. There was still some sunlight, at 6:35 PM, and Robert obviously recognized Clint, as well.

"Hello Robert," Clint said. No one ever called him Bob. He looked like a Robert. A few inches shy of six feet, he was thin and unimposing. His big deep-set brown eyes were further enlarged by the thick lenses of his small round glasses that perched on his nose. His short stubby receding black hair reminded Clint of a cartoon character rat.

"Hello Clint, glad you could make it on such short notice. How was the flight?"

"Okay, uneventful, as every flight should be," Clint said as he was being scanned for weapons, explosives, and technology. The new scanning systems were capable of detecting metal objects as small as the head of a pin. Since everyone has metal objects on them like belt buckles, pens, coins, jewelry, tooth fillings, and zippers, it made the scanning task more time consuming than necessary. The White House's new scanning systems were twenty times as sensitive as the typical airport security system. Cost was not an issue. They could detect plastic explosives, metal weapons, communications devices and chemical weapons. The one thing they could not detect was intent, and a professional assassin, with intent, could kill within seconds, with their body or with any one of a dozen objects found in a typical office.

Clint had this skill, and the Secret Service agents knowing this were doubly cautious around him.

The Secret Service agent, satisfied that Clint possessed no physical threat to the President, issued a bright red badge with a metal chain to be worn around his neck stamped "Escort Required at All Times" and informed him that it was valid for the next two hours only. Clint knew that the badge was also a tracking device that would alert the Secret Service detail if Clint was where he was not supposed to be as well as log his exact location every five seconds for later analysis.

"Clint, I assume you already know what this is all about so I won't waste your time reviewing it now," Robert said as they walked the corridor into the White House. "What I want to know is, are you willing to help?"

"How can I help?" Clint asked, intuition telling him he was being played, which meant that Robert did not know much, if anything, about why Clint had been asked to the Oval Office.

Robert, being a political veteran, knew he was shadow boxing with a very clever man, so decided to take a less obvious tack saying, "I'm not really sure. He trusts you implicitly and will tell you more than even I know about this... affair. As you know, I am his right arm, but I can do more to help if I am kept totally current. So, I'll help when you request it and stay clear otherwise. Now, how can I help you help the President?"

"Well, first you can brief me in the time it takes to get to the office regarding the Press Conference Friday."

"The conference was a complete success. It had the required coverage and effect. It is well covered in the major papers. What specifically do you need to know?"

"I specifically need to know why Bill called me and so urgently needs my help. But, since you obviously don't know either, I will have to wait until he tells me and you will have to wait until, and if, he tells you. And Robert, one more thing, don't try to pump me again, you're not very good at it," Clint said in a matter of way as they walked to the Oval Office.

Robert recoiled and seethed with spite at being treated like a gofer by this man. He privately committed to getting even, in time. For this and all the other injustices befallen him by this Indian "has been". No one should call the President "Bill", except for me, Robert thought. No one should be closer than me. No one should have his ear, except me. And, no one will, in time.

Privately, Clint had never liked nor trusted Robert. He was a fidgety man, always sweating. The squeaky voice made him sound more like an accountant than a politician. Still, he had served the President well over the last three plus years and a dozen years as Senator before that. Intuition never failed him and intuition told Clint to keep his guard up when near Robert.

They were nearing the Oval Office now, having been cleared by three separate Marine guards and two Secret Service men, one obvious weapons screen and one not-so-obvious. Clint had taken note of how the security had changed over the last few years. The terrorist threats have made a realistic impact on how we run our country and keep its leaders safe, he thought with a certain degree of comfort.

His thoughts were interrupted when Sheila Turcott, the President's personal and private secretary said, "The President will see you now, Mr. Bear." Sheila was a D.C. professional, forty-seven and never married. She had plain, dirty blond hair, plain physical characteristics, and a plain personality. Sheila was simply plain and ordinary, but a damn good, no, she was the very best secretary. Even better than Phyllis, who served Senator Covey in Massachusetts but wasn't able to move to Washington after the election.

Clint was walking into the office with Robert closely on his heels when Ms. Turcott said delicately, "Robert, I'm sorry but the President said only Mr. Bear."

Robert stopped dead in his tracks, and the President meeting Clint at the door said, "Robert, it's just old times. We need to reminisce. You understand." He greeted Clint with a warm handshake and hug after the door had closed.

"Clint, it's so good to see you again. It's been far too long,"

"Yes it has, Bill, but we both have responsibilities that consume us, don't we?"

"Sometimes I wish we didn't, but not often. We are the same in that way, we need and love our professional demands." After a long pause the President continued, "Clint, I still wake up in cold sweat screaming, telling them to stop. Judy has become accustomed to the nights when she can tell it will happen by the degree of restlessness in my sleep. She has taken to sleeping in another room during those nights. I can't escape it, just like I couldn't escape the Taliban."

Clint remembered how the prisoners were systematically and inhumanely stripped of their dignity, totally disoriented, brutally beaten. The constant interrogations and torture, the lack of food and water, the filth and disease, the sight of your friends and countrymen dying of malnutrition and some being mercilessly beheaded, sent many over the psychological cliff, too steep to climb back up. He had these memories too and knew what the President was going through, and lifting himself out of these thoughts said softly, "Is this the reason you needed to talk with me, in private?"

"No, I just never get to talk about it with someone who truly understands, someone who was there," the President said in a quiet voice. "What I need to talk with you about is much more serious. You know about my Martial Law Drug Plan…"

"Yes, a very gutsy move."

"Some say a very suicidal move."

"Bill, I don't understand, why suicidal? The country is rife with drugs. It is eating away at the core of our heritage. I agree with your National Security link; drugs are financing the terrorist operations. If anything you may have understated that link. I think of America as a large Indian reservation, in a sense. Each of our reservations has had the alcohol and drug problems America faces today. As a result, I understand all too well. In fact, I agree with your entire concept, but since I don't know how it is to be implemented I have to stop there, for now."

"I could always count on you for straightforward and insightful commentary, Clint." Then the President's face turned bleak and he said, "They have given my lovely wife Judith and my daughter Kathy a death sentence for what I have done, and I feel as helpless as the POW you saved years ago. And after I witness their deaths I will be dead as well," the President murmured. "Whether they kill me or not."

Clint was stunned and took a few seconds to put it together. "What are you saying? You're the most powerful man in the world. You have the most advanced and powerful army, the largest and most effective intelligence teams in the field, the most advanced technology… stop them!"

The President approached Clint, with eyes intensely locked and said, "They have infiltrated us to the highest levels. I cannot use the power if I don't know who the power is loyal to. They called me yesterday on my secure line — maximum security, voice encrypted dual-phased locked closed-loop synchronization — and told me my family is dead sometime before the reelection. Only seven people have access to that number and fewer than four have the capability of using it because they don't have matching hardware and the daily crypto codes. Now, it is a matter of National Security. At this point, you are the only person I can trust. Will you help me Clint?"

Cabris watched the horizon and marveled at the optical illusion of the heat waves radiating off the pavement. It reminded her of water pouring upwards toward the sky. She did not notice, until it was much too late, the engine's temperature gauge rising to over 220 degrees. When the radiator hose blew, the popping noise stirred Brook as well.

Brook was the one who discovered the hole in the radiator hose, "This hose was replaced not long ago. I bet Billy replaced it with a used hose. Wait until I get my hands on him, the little shit. How far to the nearest… anything, Cabris?" Brook said after looking both ways on old Route 170.

"This couldn't have happened in a worse location. We're about sixty miles from any civilization with no cell service. Our best bet is to stay with the truck and wait for the Highway Patrol to happen by."

"Hey, wait a minute, we have the gallon jug of spring water, and I have some tape in my briefcase. It's worth a shot, if we take it slow maybe we can make it before the truck overheats again. You get the water while I find the tape." Brook went through her briefcase and found the tape, what was left of it and went to the front of the truck. She hit her head on the bumper, and cursed silently, while crawling under the engine. The hose was fairly new... curious. Maybe we hit some road debris that flew up and cut the hose? It was a wide cut, almost half of the underside of the hose was cut but only about a quarter inch was neatly severed. Maybe some road debris had flown up and made the starter hole and the hot radiator water pressure burst the rest of the hole, she thought.

As tightly as she could, she wrapped what little tape was left around the cut, encircling the hose only four times before the tape ran out. This type of tape was for paper, not for auto repair, but it was all she had, she just hoped it would hold. She was sweating more now from the heat radiating from the engine than last night after making love with Clint and thought about how good an air-conditioned room with a bath would feel when they got to the Navajo Division.

"Well, that should do it, let's pray it holds," Brook said. "Pour the water into the radiator carefully, we can't afford to waste a drop." There would still be some water in the engine block and with the gallon they just poured in, with any luck they had about a third of capacity, she thought, not good odds.

Cabris turned the ignition key and the old truck engine turned over slowly, but wouldn't start. She let the truck engine sit quietly for a full sixty seconds and tried it again. This time the engine roared to life and they were moving again.

There was no chance of finding water where they were. The late summer temperature averaged 105 and the earth had long since dried out to dust. They would have to make it with what they have, which was impossible. The truck engine would have been straining to stay under 200 degrees with the radiator filled to capacity; with less than a third full it was only a matter of time, and not much time.

The truck engine was now running over 230 degrees and about to seize when it started to make a loud noise, almost like the horn was blowing. The gallon of water had turned to steam and was escaping past the pressure relief valve on the radiator cap. Cabris looked with concern at Brook and said, "We have only gone another fifteen miles, which means we have a least forty-five miles to go. That's a long walk without water. Let's pull over and wait until the engine cools and then do another fifteen miles."

Okay, what choice do we have?" Brook agreed with equal concern. "It is almost 1:00 PM, so we have plenty of daylight left and maybe someone will stop to help."

Almost thirty minutes later, Cabris saw a car moving toward them in the truck's rearview mirror. Even though she had tied a white handkerchief to the AM radio antenna, she got out to wave the car down. They were in luck, the green Plymouth slowed down and the man in the passenger side seat asked, "What's the problem?"

"We blew a radiator hose and overheated. Do you have any water?"

"Sorry, ma'am but we don't. We should carry some for, you know, emergencies 'n' all. There is a house not far from here, if you like we can call a tow truck for ya," the young Hispanic said. "Hey, wait, maybe I should have a look, you know, make sure it really is a busted hose," he said, gesturing that a male is the only species qualified to analyze a mechanical malfunction as he got out of the car. After looking under the truck quickly he agreed that the hose was blown and there was no water left. Neither Cabris nor Brook noticed that the young Hispanic went directly to the busted hose without being told which hose had burst.

The driver offered a suggestion, "Look, why don't we just drive you to the house where you'll be safe until a tow truck can get here, it's only about eight or ten miles down the road, but a hell of a walk in this heat."

Cabris and Brook looked at each other and hesitated, not feeling comfortable about the idea of getting in the car with these two guys, when the driver said, "Look girls, I got work to do, if you don't want to go to the house or farm or whatever it is, okay, I was just trying to help, that's all. Get in Julio, and we'll call from the farm, if they will let us Mexicans use the phone."

Cabris and Brook were thirsty and a little scared to be out there alone and both said, at the same time, "Wait, we'll take you up on that offer of a ride. Let us get our briefcases and computer notebooks."

Julio carefully opened the rear door to let them in, both on one side. Cabris slid in first and moved all the way to the left to make room for Brook. As soon as Brook had her legs in the door was slammed shut. It was then that Cabris noticed that there were no inner door or window handles. Alarmed, she was about to protest when she looked up to see Julio holding a pistol, aimed directly at her chest and grinning.

The green Plymouth Roadrunner's rear wheels threw some rocks and dust when Jesús stepped forcefully on the accelerator, laughing out loud like a crazy man, spit drooling from his mouth where the missing tooth once was.

Cole Cunningham was at his desk, desperately trying to think of another way into the drug organization when his phone interrupted his as yet unsuccessful thought process. He took a deep breath and slapped his slightly pudgy five o'clock shadowed face a few times to bring some life to his tired body. Since quitting smoking eighteen months ago, Cole had gained some thirty pounds, taxing his already depleted energy.

"Cole, you need to see this, now!" Turner said in an unusually strong and excited tone.

"See what? I'm up to my ass in problems and don't have time for any bullshit," Cole said and then immediately wished he hadn't. The stress was getting the best of him.

"I know you are under a lot of pressure, and what I have to show you will only increase that pressure, but Paul didn't die for nothing," Dr. Turner, Chief of Laboratory Sciences for the DEA, said.

"You need me now?"

"Yesterday," Turner said.

"I'll be there in five," Cole said, replacing the receiver into its cradle.

On his way to the lab, Cole remembered how Turner had saved his ass on the Mahoney case. It was Turner who had taken his own time to reexamine the coroner office's data to find that Mahoney was murdered by the nose cartilage being forced into his brain, the work of an accomplished martial arts assassin. That bit of information had saved Cole's life as well as broken the case. Ken Tucker was a friend and a professional. He had obviously found something of significance or he wouldn't send up this flag, he thought as he walked into the lab.

Ken was in his office, which Cole thought was the first time he had ever seen him there. In fact, he wondered why he had an office, since he was always in the lab, by a body, microscope or test tube, or some other piece of technology. It was odd, he seemed like brown shoes at a formal affair in an office setting. Ken motioned for Cole to come in and he then closed the door silently and closed the blinds that covered the glass wall looking out into his well-equipped lab.

"Cole, no one here knows this except for me, and it must stay that way, you and me, or I'm not talking. Do you give me your word on that?" Ken asked in a nervous voice, his tone reflecting the seriousness of what he was about to share. "I've just had the office swept for bugs. It's clean."

"Ken, what's this all…"

Ken broke in and almost screamed, "Do you give me your word on that?"

"Yeah, okay, you've got my word. You and me, no one else. Now what the hell is going on, Ken?"

"You, the Durango Sheriff, and the coroner all said there was nothing in Paul's pockets, nothing at all. That didn't make sense to me. I mean, even if the killers had removed everything from the pockets, with a deep-cover agent all they should have found is nothing. Don't you see, Paul wouldn't have kept anything significant in his pockets to begin with."

"Okay, you've got a point, so what?" Cole said, throwing both hands in the air.

"So, I looked where he might have put something and found this," he said in a hushed tone as he held up a small plastic sack.

Cole took the package and fingered its contents. "Looks like rough or dirty cocaine, wait… no, more like crack cocaine but you're going to tell me differently, right?"

"Right. It has some cocaine in it, about twenty percent. But it's not what you think. My guess is it has the cocaine in it to give the slight numbing feeling, other than that it is pure synthetic," Tucker said, keeping his voice unusually low.

"Okay, so we've got a chemist out there, what's the point? Why would Paul get killed over that kind of information? What aren't you telling me, Ken?"

"If you would let me finish, damn it, the stuff is a powerful narcotic with a chemical structure like crack cocaine, but made with commonly available ordinary and fully legal chemicals. Cole, what I'm holding in my hand probably cost about fifty cents to make, can be made without breaking major laws, is undoubtedly the best high around, especially if you like to be sexually stimulated, is hyper-addictive and is seriously and absolutely lethal. The chemical base is arsenic and after a few highs, the stuff will begin to eat into your brain like acid until you become quite insane and eventually die. If the chemist removes the cocaine, which has a minor impact on the high because it is in such a low percentage by volume to the base, it is completely legal. Based on the high I calculated for the average one hundred and fiftypound person, between two and three times will trigger the absolute addiction and after using between five and eight times, you absolutely and positively die."

"Holy shit, Ken, what your saying is unbelievable. Think of the…" Cole could not finish. His mind was running much faster than his lips could speak, and he slumped over with the weight of the burden he was now carrying. "How does it work?"

"The substance is ingested through the lungs. You smoke it. It can be taken orally, but the high will be less intense, although much longer lasting. The production process must coat the crystalline structure with an inhalant, that I haven't broken down yet, but is probably like toluene, or a strong industrial cleaner or paint thinner. It's probably processed with ammonia and Freon. The toluene will coat the lungs, after the heavier base chemicals have been ingested, and reduce the amount of oxygen the lungs can process. This amplifies the effect of the accelerated heartbeat and resultant blood flow caused by the chemicals and gives the user a powerful rush, for a prolonged time, maybe twenty to thirty minutes. The over-the-counter muscle relaxants thrown into the blood stream at such a fast rate will immediately relax the body, which is being told to rush, and the mind misinterprets this as sexual pleasure. There you have it, super lethal Spanish Fly. And Cole, there won't be much after effect."

Cole finished Ken's sentence, "If it feels good, doesn't apparently hurt you, is legal and cheap, everyone will be using it. Everyone will be dying. But wait a minute, why haven't we heard anything about this? I haven't been told of any unusual deaths lately, have you?"

"No, and that is strange, I agree," Dr. Turner said as he pulled at his lab coat.

"Just maybe, it has not yet made it to market. The chemist who developed this is probably a pretty clever character or works for an equally clever organization. So, if this stuff is so good it will sell like bubble gum — and probably for the same price — and if they don't have enough supply, they could lose to a competitor who would reverse engineer it and bump them out of the market. Yeah, they got to know that we will find a way to stop them… so, wait a minute, they won't price it like bubble gum but will price it like real cocaine, maybe higher, make a quick killing and get out. Christ, they could conceivably make five hundred million to one billion in clear profit in just a few months' time if they have a solid national street operation already up and running… Jesus Christ…" Cole was thinking at the speed of light.

"Cole, listen. Research done at Johns Hopkins University has shown that cocaine over stimulates the brain cell molecules, you know, dopamine receptors. These receptors help regulate the parts of the brain which control emotion and feelings of pleasure and pain. By overstimulating these areas of the brain, the cocaine causes immense feelings of euphoria and pleasure, especially during normally intense pleasure, like during sex. My guess is that this synthetic was designed around the Johns Hopkins data by a very clever and capable chemist. It might be a place to start."

He knew where to start, again, and he didn't have much time. "One thing Ken, there is another person who will need to know about this."

"You gave me your word, no one but you and I," Dr. Turner countered.

"That's before I knew that there are hundreds of thousands, perhaps millions, of lives at stake, Ken. I won't tell him unless you are there and approve. Okay?"

Bill waited for a response to his question, and hoped Clint would help.

After what seemed an eternity, Clint said, "Bill, I have responsibilities to other people and organizations. I just can't stop what I'm doing and leave them hanging for a few weeks. My work is important, too. Isn't there someone you can trust? What about Robert?"

"He is loyal but does not have your insertion skills. I need someone who can infiltrate my organization and find the leak. After the leak is found, and neutralized, I can continue with the Martial Law Drug Program."

"Wait a minute. Do you mean you are considering stopping the MLDP program based on this one call?"

"Yes, that"s exactly what I mean. I won't put my family in jeopardy."

Clint pondered, "Didn't you say the caller said, 'Your family, and then you will be dead before the reelection for what you have done. Now you have time to think about how I will do it and who will be first.'?" Clint asked almost too clinically. "Bill, the caller didn't say that the situation was reversible. In fact, what you told me indicates it is most certainly not reversible."

The President looked shocked. He hadn't thought of it as a fait accompli, but in reevaluating it he knew that Clint was right. Now he needed Clint's help more than ever.

"Bill, I'll spend the weekend and see how I can help from a distance, if you like, but I can't devote any more time. Search through your files and locate one person who we can trust and get him up here now. We'll work out a plan together this weekend. Okay?"

"It's a start, thanks Clint." Then the President pushed his intercom button, and asked, "Sheila please send Robert in and clear my calendar for the remainder of the weekend. Also, please have Clint's pass extended for the weekend."

"It won't be easy to clear your calendar, Mr. President, but I'll get it done," Sheila responded enthusiastically.

"She is quite chipper," Clint said.

"Probably her new significant other," Bill replied.

The green Plymouth Roadrunner continued north toward the San Juan Mountain range and with the higher elevations came the lower temperatures. Cabris and Brook sat nervously in the back seat and had not uttered a sound in the last two hours. They were both mentally beating themselves to death for being so stupid to get into a car, in the middle of nowhere, with two strange men.

How many times had they lectured young children about the dangers of even getting too close to strangers, and here they were voluntarily getting into a car with two strange men? How stupid!

Cabris had already beaten herself unmercifully and decided that she needed to put that same energy into finding a way out of this mess, but how? The doors and windows had no handles so how could they be opened — she could break the window, maybe, and then open the door from the outside — but the gun was pointing directly at her. No, she would be shot and at that range the guy didn't have to be a marksman. Julio did have frequent laps in attention span, but not enough. And even if she did get out of the car, where could she run? They were nowhere close to civilization, and if she did get away they would still have Brook. She could try to signal a passing car, but how? No, she would wait until they left the car and hope for an opening.

Three hours later the car stopped, after traveling about fifteen miles on what appeared to be an old logging road. Julio had gotten out of the car for a moment to remove the brush cover from a smaller intersecting logging road, more like a path, and after the car had turned onto it he replaced the brush cover. They continued on for about another five miles, although it took about thirty minutes, and came to what appeared to be a camp with three canvas tents. This might be their chance to cut and run, and Cabris hoped she'd communicated her plan to Brook with her eyes as the car came to an abrupt stop. Brook gave a small nod.

Julio got out and unlocked the trunk, taking out two sets of large handcuffs, actually leg irons, throwing one set to Jesús. Cabris and Brook didn't have a chance. Jesús and Julio had practiced this six times before and not one had escaped, although most never tried.

Julio came around to the passenger's side door, holding the gun carefully. Jesús was on the right side and they opened both doors at the same time, which startled Cabris.

"Don't you bitches move a muscle, understand?" Jesús said.

"Get out on your knees and lay facedown on the ground, now!" Jesús yelled.

Jesús and Julio had abducted Cabris and Brook just for fun. They had no more crystals to package until the plane returned, although they did have enough for their hour of fun, before the work of digging the next hole.

Brook was thinking about Clint and how long ago it seemed that they last made love, even though it had only been the night before, and how she may never see Clint again. How quickly life can change. Just a few hours ago life was magnificent, she was going to get married, have a small family; business and friends were happy and now her life might end.

Mistakes.

CHAPTER 3:
TRAGEDIES

The massive black bear tentatively lumbered out of its cave and greeted the darkness. It stood motionless just outside the cave, as its eyes adjusted to the moon's illumination and, lifting her nose to the night, sought out any new scents that might lead to danger or food. Satisfied there was no danger, she sauntered away from her home, leaving her three newborn cubs, and started her night of foraging for food. She moved with considerable grace and agility for a beast of her size, confident in her strength and speed. The river's whispers were calling her, promising fresh fish for her dinner and some for the cubs. She began to pick up her pace, breaking into a slow run and for the first time waking the surrounding forest with her movements. Her own noise concealed the noise of her only natural enemy, a rifle bolt. She could smell the river's reeds and sand beds and her hunger encouraged her to break into a full run to the river. The cubs jumped when they heard the blast, they cuddled each other and hoped their mother would be extra careful. The great bear had just made it to the river's embankment when the bullet entered her chest near the shoulder and found her heart. She died almost instantly, with her two massive front paws in the river cradling her head as if she were sleeping. She would not feast on the river's bounty this evening, nor will she ever return home to care for her three helpless newborn cubs. The newborn cubs never ate again and didn't understand why their mother had never returned. They died slowly, of hunger and malnutrition, of loneliness and fear...

He sat on a plateau overlooking the barren rock and dust valley below. It was only three hours into the new day, and Clint's father Old Bear knew it promised to be the worst day of his ninety-four years of life. He was sweating heavily from his forehead and chest, seemingly unaffected by the cold motionless air surrounding him. His long black and gray hair hung to his shoulders, hiding his years, and seemed to give him a Samson-like strength and confidence. His once powerful frame was weakened by age and use. He directed his tired eyes into the black sky. It was devoid of anything except an angry yellow full moon and Old Bear wondered why. Why had his sleep been violated by this dream for four successive nights? Well, not why actually, he knew why because he knew its absolute meaning, but not its specific meaning. He must look to the heavens for more, he must ask the Great Spirit specifically.

Old Bear, Mah-to-he-hah as he was called, was a descendant of a family of Medicine Men; his father, his father's father and his father before that. The skills and Medicine Craft were not written but learned, internalized and enhanced, and passed on generation to generation. Old Bear was a descendant of the greatest Mandan Medicine Man, Wak-a-dah-ha-hee, or Rain Maker. Rain Maker became a Medicine Man as most do, by creating an unexplainable and much desired occurrence. In the year 1835, the Upper Missouri Mandan Village was suffering the worst drought in memory or legend, the corn fields were dried to dust, livestock were dying, and the hunting was fruitless partly because the animal's were gone searching for water and partly because of the difficulty in moving through the burnt forest without breaking a dry twig and scaring off the prey.

As the legend goes, Rain Maker had performed many ceremonial dances that cured some sick, called the Buffalo, and foretold of a fierce storm or winter. He had been able to curse a foe and was generally thought to actually be a Medicine Man, but lacked the full respect that truly powerful Medicine Men achieve. He set out to achieve this respect on the chosen day by setting up on top of his lodge, a fort-like structure made similarly to a log cabin but with an earthen flat roof, and started his most powerful dance precisely at sunrise. The chanting awakened the village, many of whom congregated and began to watch Rain Maker with amazement. No one knew the meaning of the dance, although this was not unusual as most dance meanings were known only to the Medicine Men themselves, but the family villagers who encircled his lodge knew that this dance was new. Throughout the day, through the night and into the next afternoon he danced, without a break for food or water. A dark cloud began to appear over the horizon and Rain Maker picked up his shield and bow. He drew an arrow and pulled the bowstring as far back as it could go, further than he had ever pulled. Aiming at the center of the cloud, he let his fingers straighten, heard the swish of the sinew bowstring, and watched the arrow disappear into the cloud. The villagers watched the flight of the arrow in total disbelief and wonderment, and began to cheer Wak-a-dah-ha-hee, Rain Maker, when the rain began to fall. The entire village now knew that his magic was very powerful and Rain Maker was to sit next to the Great Spirit, the Creator of all things.

Old Bear's magic was strong as well. He could foresee events, but could not interfere. He was only allowed to plead to the Great Spirit and offer sacrifice, as what will be done will be done. The dream of four nights was incapable of being misunderstood; it meant the certain death of four of his family, three of whom were unknown to him. He sat looking into the heavens, reliving every detail of the dream, the unfair killing of the mother bear and the unrighteous slow frigid death of the three cubs, the unknown and unseen hunter, the dark night, the river… they all had meaning. He knew that he would soon awaken in the beyond, it was just a matter of days, maybe less.

On that plateau, Old Bear began his last chant, that would last the day and into the next day, appealing to the Great Spirit for mercy, guidance and acceptance of his three unknown family members chosen to soon enter the beyond to change worlds

Robert entered the President's office with an air of smugness that Clint disdained and the President dismissed as childish.

"Robert, we have a serious problem that you need to be informed about and coordinate the efforts to help solve," the President said, and was interrupted by Robert, "It's the call you received on the secure phone in the limo, isn't it?"

"Yes. Yes, it is."

"Why are you waiting until now to bring me in? We may have lost time."

"Robert, that question will be answered by the knowledge you are about to receive. You must understand that you, Clint and I are the only people who know about this and it needs to stay that way. Is that clear, absolutely no one, even top secret and code access, can know this. Is that clear? No one, unless I personally authorize it. Period. No exceptions."

Clint spoke up, "Bill, that is not correct. There is at least one, probably two more people who know about the contents of that call, The Caller and the Leaker, if he is not the Caller. Let's not forget that."

"What the hell is happening? Are we going to war?" Robert screamed.

"The caller said that my family would be killed before the reelection, and after they are killed I would be killed. I am supposed to watch the death of my family as punishment for the Martial Law Drug Plan. It was a serious call. The people who have access to that phone are limited to my immediate staff, including you, and those who would have the day's codes and the same encryption system. The heads of the CIA, FBI, Secretary of State, Chief of Staff, and the Vice President. There is also the system at GenCom for the Joint Chiefs' use. Someone fucked up or purposely leaked the information. If we can isolate the leak, we might be able to save my family and the lives of thousands of Americans by implementing the Plan."

"Wait a minute, you are not suggesting that we delay the implementation of the Martial Law Drug Plan because of this call, are you? I mean, we can protect your family, and you... we'll get more Secret Service all over them. But the Plan must be implemented," Robert said with an unusual level of force. "At least think about it."

"Robert, what we need first is a single individual who we can trust," Clint added. "Someone who can move freely within Bill's organization, someone from the outside, maybe from state level or the CIA. We need to find the leak and fast, and we can't do that with a known entity... the cover will be easier if the person is an unknown. The first job will be to review the transmission records for every squawk box in the company and the whereabouts of each of the cleared code users."

"Hell, I can do that in a few hours and frequently do as a matter of record," Robert said, now with an air of superiority.

"Great, go to it quietly!" Clint said.

"Clint, I work for the President and therefore I take orders not from you but from the President."

"Robert, Clint will be here for the weekend, maybe longer, and will be in charge of this program until I say differently. I appreciate your support, but Clint has skills far beyond mine and yours in this area. Please work with him as you would me," the President said, stroking Robert's ego.

"Sorry, just a little on edge about this, Mr. President, it won't happen again. As for the man you need, I would suggest Douglas at the CIA as a starting point. I can tell you he is not the caller. He couldn't be, he was on the Hill testifying in front of ten Senators regarding that questionable appropriation for an arms shipment."

"Clint, what do you think?"

"Let's confirm he was there and then call him in," Clint said as Robert was dialing the phone.

Robert knew his way around the administrative jungle better than anyone Bill had ever known. More times than he could count, Robert had proven himself worthy by tracking down a stalled report, a key missing vote, or webbed lobbyist allegiances. He was now talking to the Department Manager for Official Stenography, who was quickly able to verify that C. Eric Douglas, Director of

Central Intelligence was indeed testifying before the Senate Appropriations Committee on the day and hour in question. His next call was to the director's house in Reston, Virginia before handing the receiver to the President.

Douglas, on his way home for the evening, took the president's call on his secure mobile phone. Few details were discussed, but the urgency that Douglas divert to the White House was clearly understood. He arrived twelve minutes later.

C. Eric Douglas was an intimidating man at six feet three and two hundred and thirty pounds. He had oppressive steel blue eyes that acted more like an X-ray than a visual device. Bill liked and respected Eric for his ethics and dedication to his country. Looking at Eric, it was clear to Bill that he was not the leaker or the caller and was unlikely to have let the code and communications hardware fall into unauthorized hands. He'd had a distinguished career in Navy Intelligence having been a front line operative and spent almost one year doing classified BEL, behind enemy lines, work. He is tough and proven, Bill thought, as he told Eric the situation.

Eric listened without interruption, waiting for his President to finish. Then, after a few minutes of silence he began asking questions of the President.

"How compartmentalized is this?"

"Just the people in this room and the caller, and if different, the leaker."

"How long was the telephone call?"

"Not more than one minute."

"Have you looked at the incoming call log?"

"I was not aware that there was a log of incoming calls."

"Mr. President, every call made within Washington D.C. is logged, no matter by land line or by wireless. Every call made on a code-access encrypted communication system owned by the United States Government anywhere in the world is logged. It is required by law and it makes practical sense for just this reason. Who besides me has both hardware and code access?"

"The Director of the FBI, Secretary of State, Vice President, Chief of Staff, and GenCom."

"Have you reviewed their usage reports?"

"We are in the process of acquiring that data as we speak."

"Have you begun to cross reference usage with opportunity?"

"Yes, we started with you. You were testifying on the Hill when the call came in, so you were cleared. The others have not been started."

"Thanks for the confidence, and you were correct in calling me but you were also foolish to do so based on the alibi. The caller had no interaction with you. It could have been taped and automatically called and played. You do keep a fairly rigid schedule, so knowing when you would have completed the speech and retreated to the limo would have been child's play."

Clint felt foolish for not making the same observation, and Bill's immediate sharp look at him indicated he knew it as well. He was rusty. It had been over twenty years since he was in the intelligence game. It will take more time to dust off the old skill set.

"Let's break down what we know so far," Douglas continued. "We know the caller had access to the daily communications access codes, had access or possesses identical communications hardware, had access to your schedule, was informed about the content of your highly classified Martial Law speech, and knows about your family."

C. Eric Douglas was in his element, thinking on his feet and captivating his audience. "We can assume that the speech was the trigger, and that the caller must have had access to its content three to five days prior to its delivery. Therefore, we can assume the caller is a controlled, calculating, terrorist-like man or organization. We can assume there are considerable financial resources at play, for without them the hardware and the codes could not be acquired. The most difficult part for me is the lead time to action. The caller's main purpose was, is, to create fear, possibly even panic. The reaction was calculated to be a delay in implementing the Martial Law Plan, certainly not to prevent its eventual implementation for the next president would pick up where you have left off, if you were to… pass on. Therefore, I cannot come to any conclusion, but, that it is a delay the caller seeks. And, since the trigger was the Martial Law Drug Plan, there is a strong possibility this is drug related. But, what motivates the caller to seek this delay, what does it mean to him, or them?"

The wheels were beginning to turn in Clint's mind; he was coming back, slowly, to the intelligence mind he once had. It is a method of thinking, not merely intelligence. "We need to concentrate on the most contained portion of the leak, the speech. Bill, Robert, and, I assume Sheila Turcott, were the only ones to see it, prior to delivery?"

"Can't be true, Clint," Douglas interjected. "Every speech has speech writers, plus it would have been seen by PR, the Secretary of State, and maybe the Chief of Staff and certainly the Attorney General."

Clint was both impressed with Eric and disgusted with himself for not thinking through the possibilities of the communication process himself. He had become rusty after years of thinking like a CEO and not thinking like an intelligence man. Clint took advantage of the silence and asked Eric for his help. "We need a cover man to infiltrate the President's organization and find the leak, can you suggest someone?"

"You have obviously asked CIA for help because we have no purview here — ours is outside the USA, therefore one of my agents would be unknown to the organization making insertion fairly quick and easy. Clint, I am aware of some of your talents from your Asia and Eastern tours, a highly decorated deep-cover agent working for Naval Intelligence. You see, I planned a number of your projects and most were successful because of your expertise. Why don't you do it?"

Stunned by the thought that the man before him, C. Eric Douglas, was his black control during his Middle-East tour, caused him to drift off to a rescue mission that had saved Captain William Covey and seven other POWs but had also caused the deaths of three experienced Navy SEALs. Regaining focus, Clint responded, "As I have explained to Bill, I have responsibilities that I can't walk away from, but will help set up the insertion strategy. Do you have someone we can use?"

"I have two that might fit the situation. They are both talented field agents," Douglas said.

Clint said while thinking out loud, "No, I don't think so. The type of person we need to insert here is the kind that will blend with the surroundings, the type that no one takes too much notice of, but yet has open access. I'm thinking of a secretary or administrative assistant. A woman who is capable of being feminine, alluring, even sexy one minute and plain and ordinary the next."

"Clint, you were always the master of camouflage. It saved your ass many times and it may save the President now. Yes, I agree, a woman, and her name is Anne-Marie Meceli. Would you please dial this number and hand me the phone?"

Trooper Bobbie Wade of the New Mexico State Police stationed at the Farmington Barracks about seventy miles south of Durango, Colorado, a four-year veteran and one of only five women on the force, found an abandoned pickup truck with the hood up and the occupants gone. A white handkerchief was tied to the truck's antenna to alert the passersby of their trouble.

Trooper Wade called it in, providing the make, model, license plate number, and location. While awaiting the dispatcher to check the truck's status she walked to the driver's side door and reached through the window to lower the sun visor. On the rear of the sun visor she saw the typical registration form, made out to American Indian Electronics Corporation. The dispatcher confirmed the information two minutes later.

"Better call for a tow truck and notify the owners, the driver is nowhere in sight but I'll continue down 170 to the border in case the driver is on foot." Trooper Wade put the gear lever in drive and felt the powerful V8 roar to life when the accelerator was depressed.

Ms. Turcott knocked gently on the thick antique mahogany door leading into the President's office. Robert got up from his chair immediately to let her in.

"Please forgive the intrusion," she said, while looking at the President. Then she changed her view to Clint and said, "Mr. Bear, you have an emergency telephone call, would you like to take it in private?"

"Thank you, but here would be fine," Clint said, thinking it could not be that important.

"I'll put it through to the phone on the corner table, Mr. Bear," Ms. Turcott said, pointing to the corner discretely.

Helena told Clint how sorry she was to interrupt his meeting, and it was probably nothing, but she just got a call from the New Mexico State Police telling her that the pickup truck Cabris and Brook were traveling in was found broken down on Route 170. They were not in the truck when it was found.

Intuition told him of danger in a way he had not felt since… twenty plus years ago. The President noticed the concern on Clint's face and asked if everything was all right.

"Helena, don't worry, Brook and Cabris are a pair to reckon with. They are probably in some air-conditioned motel room cleaning up before they call the office. Just the same, would you stay by the phone and call me when you hear from them?" Clint said, reassuring Helena but not himself.

Field Agent Sam Forest and Sheriff Red Peterson were debriefing the on-site forensics team. Sam was convinced that two dead women, found so close to where the body of Paul Cudson, DEA Agent, was found, must be related. He did not know how, but hoped that he was justified in sending it up the line.

Cole was called by Sam from the field site on a mobile Class Two secured cellular telephone. The new information was too coincidental to be unrelated, although he, too, could not think of how, and took the next available flight to Colorado Springs. He was met again by Sam and they started their trek south and then southwest toward the Durango area.

After following the identical route as the last trip, they went north on Route 149, about seventy miles east of Durango, heading toward Wagon Wheel Gap. Just after

Wagon Wheel Gap town center, a mere few buildings, Sam took a sharp left onto a poorly paved old mining road heading west toward Spar City. Cole wished he had used the toilet in the Colorado Springs airport, and every pothole reminded him what a foolish oversight that was.

"Sam, I don't want to burst your bubble, but I think we are going to drive into the fucking Pacific Ocean soon! Where the hell are we and when will we be wherever we are going?" Cole said in a more-than-a-little-aggravated tone.

Cole was thinking about the Cudson family, probably triggered by the newly reported dead bodies he was on the way to investigate. How would they make it? Paul was not well insured and a government pension would go only so far, the kids needed a father and Barbara needed her husband. Life is real shitty, most of the time. It's funny how those few perfect times, where everything comes together as planned or desired, can carry you through the hundreds of disappointments, tragedies and heart breaks, he thought privately while shaking his head slowly.

Paul had been going through a period of introspection and he had been almost certain that this was to be his last undercover or deep-cover assignment. He was going to surprise Barbara by taking a more passive, but no less important, job in the DEA, maybe in field management or a deep cover instructor's position, but certainly a position that would allow him to be home more regularly for her and the kids, and reduce his chances of never coming home. Paul did what he did for a variety of reasons, including the added money for the family and because he was very good at it, and had believed it needed be done in the most patriotic sense.

The next pothole was deeper than the past several hundred, and Cole had to ask Sam to pull over to he could relieve himself.

Sam said, "We're almost there, just over that hill is the field camp and there should be a portable latrine set up by now. Can you wait?"

"Yeah, as long as you lay off the mortar holes!" Cole winced out.

Cole was appalled at the sight. He had seen more than a few dead bodies in his military service and his tour with the company. Some were routine, a gunshot or two, a lethal knife wound, most were thugs or druggies and somehow he couldn't feel sad for the loss of their life because they had forsaken it themselves for doing what they were doing. But the death of clean and uninvolved people, especially young people, hit him hard. And these two women had been brutally raped and tortured for an extended period of time before their captors had shown them mercy, or the sick-minded boredom, to end their suffering.

The hole was no more than three feet deep, probably what called the animals, that again called the hunters who called the County Sheriff. There was very little disruption to the scene caused by the animals, since the hunters happened by too soon. Both women were naked, one lying on top of the other, strangely embracing one another with an expression even more distant than death on their faces. The leg irons were evident only by the marks on their ankles, now a deep purple, which contrasted with the nauseatingly sallow, pale white skin color. The dozens of cuts on their thighs, breasts and buttocks were superficial and of unknown origin, but were more noticeable by the earth that had stuck to the once-wet blood. The deep blue bruising around their wrists was noticeably different from the ankles, another question. Cole found his stomach weakening and had to turn away.

The field forensic team had completed their work and the bodies could be lifted from their shallow grave and transported to Durango for the more detailed work that would hopefully provide some insight as to who these women were and the identity of their murderer. The entire area had been painstakingly searched, inch by inch, by field agents on their hands and knees. They knew that there was probably a connection between this murder and Paul's, a fellow agent, and if there was a minuscule shred of evidence they were determined to find it.

Working cooperatively with Red Peterson's deputies they had closed off the area from the press and anyone else who might happen by, albeit unlikely in this remote area. The field forensic team had lifted tire prints, found a cigarette butt and found the saliva from someone's spit dripping from the needles of a blue spruce tree no more than six feet from the shallow grave. Not much to go on, but better than nothing at all.

Learning the identities of the women happened completely by accident, a very rare occurrence. The dispatcher for the Durango Sheriff's Office had been alerted to the overdue women by the Navajo AIEC Division President, hoping to encourage a patrol car to find and help the women with their broken-down pickup truck. The dispatcher, hearing of two women found at the site, and having met them at many Indian functions, asked to view the bodies personally. The positive ID was given before they were taken to forensics just after coming off the ambulance.

The brutal deaths of Cabris — the Deer — and Brook Fontaine would require only one notification call. Red, having met Clint Bear, and even though not knowing him very well, suggested he make the call. Red called information for the AIEC Corporate Headquarters telephone number and was connected immediately. As the phone rang, he wondered what it would be like to get this call himself, which helped temper his words.

"Hello, American Indian Electronics Corporation, how may I direct your call?"

"Please connect me to Mr. Clint Bear," Red said in a monotone voice.

"I'm sorry, Mr. Bear is away for a few days; may I connect you to his assistant?"

"Yes, please, this is an emergency."

"Mr. Bears office, Helena speaking, how may I help you," the voice echoed in a rehearsed, but professional tone.

"Helena, my name is Sheriff Red Peterson, Durango, and I need to reach Mr. Bear immediately. It is extremely urgent," Red said in a firm but non-alarmist tone.

"I'm sorry but Mr. Bear is not available at the moment, but I may be able to reach him. Can you please tell me the nature of this emergency?" Helena said sincerely.

"Helena, I'm surprised to find you in the office on Sunday afternoon."

"Mr. Peterson, all Mr. Bear's calls are transferred to my home on the weekends. Now, do you care to tell me what the emergency relates to?" Helena said with a growing concern in her tone.

"Helena, I am messenger of very bad news…"

Red was interrupted by Helena's alarmed voice, "This concerns Brook and Cabris, doesn't it? They are well overdue at the Navajo Division and I got a call from the New Mexico State Police that their truck had been found south of Farmington on Route 170. Have you found them? Are they all right?"

"Helena, I need to talk with Mr. Bear, now. Where can he be reached?" Red was an experienced officer and kept his tone low and as non-alarming as possible. He knew that he must keep Helena calm or she could go into temporary shock and he would lose his connection with Clint Bear.

"He is with the President this weekend," Helena said, barely holding back her tears resulting from the fear of the unknown, but obviously, serious happening to Cabris and Brook.

"The president of what, where?" Red snapped back.

"The President of the United States, and he is staying at the Marriott in Washington D.C., do you need the number," Helena said in curt response.

"Thank you Helena, and I'm sorry I can't tell you more at this time. You will understand later. For now, please keep our conversation confidential. But, just in case Mr. Bear and I don't connect, please have him call me at the Durango County Sheriff's Office immediately," Red said in as much of a consoling tone as he could muster after such a long day and a half.

Red asked Cole to come into his office and closed the door behind him slowly. He would normally offer coffee, but based on the new information he offered Cole a neat glass of Jack Daniels. Cole was beginning to protest when Red said he was going to need it for the latest news.

The President of the United States? What the hell is going on...?

"I can't even begin to know what the connection is, but it's there; it's got to be. But this is now your call to make," Red said handing the telephone to Cole. "And after you call the White House, you need to contact the New Mexico State Police, Farmington Barracks. They have found the pickup the women were traveling in abandoned about seventy miles south of the Barracks. I think you ought to blanket it and have your people go over it with a more experienced eye, so to speak," Red said, while picking at his teeth with a worn toothpick.

***

The roughly nine hundred and fifty-mile backroad trip was taking longer than Chet thought. The light blue Ford pickup truck couldn't do more than fifty miles an hour before it shook so badly it was about to come apart with the heavy load of hay in the back. It didn't matter much, since most of the backroads kept their passengers to less than forty-five miles an hour.

Chet was just south of the Fort Mojave Indian Reservation in a small town called Needles, California. He pulled the old truck behind an abandoned garage to change the license plates, as Jesús had told him. He was hoping to meet Leon Beecher by tomorrow night and be on his way home Monday morning, a richer man.

Robert had finished cross checking the DCIA, DNSA, COS, GenCom and VP for opportunity with access and had found everyone accounted for and all communication equipment secure. He was just finishing his report to the President, Douglas, and Clint when he was interrupted by Douglas.

"This leads us to the conclusion that it is a leak, am I correct, Robert?"

"Yes, there is no other way."

Douglas took a long deep breath and continued after Robert's intrusion, his question being rhetorical, "It does not rule out the possibility, or more likely the probability, that one of the senior staff has turned. Remember, someone who has access — who has the code knowledge — must have provided that information to the caller. In addition, the caller was told when and where the President was going to be when the call was made."

"More importantly, the caller knew what the President was going to say at that press conference before the speech was delivered. He had to know at least a few days in advance, probably a week or more, to properly plan," Clint added, trying to concentrate on the problems within this office and Brook at the same time, and not too successfully.

"I'm happy to see you are coming back among the thinking people of this world, Mr. Bear," Douglas said jokingly and then turned deadly serious, "Our access list has just been reduced by the overlay of access to the means — the secure communications equipment and code access — and the knowledge of what the President was to say during that speech: the Martial Law Drug Plan. It just got a whole lot more complicated."

"I don't understand; didn't you just say our access has just been reduced? How then is this more complicated?" asked the President.

Clint filled in the missing information, "Bill, if the knowledge of the content of your speech was as closely held as you indicated, and there didn't appear to be any press leaks prior to the speech, and the impact of the message clearly substantiates the security, then that would mean it is limited to you and Robert, and since we have already ruled Robert out, that means…"

"…more than one leak, holy shit!" the President finished Clint's sentence.

"More correctly stated, Mr. President, a mole. You see, to acquire the access takes considerable time. One must build a reputation of trust and competence, undergo the deep scrutiny of Top Secret security clearances, and have the need to know. This takes years of work and at great risk, because if caught they will certainly be imprisoned for life or worse," the DCI intoned.

Ms. Turcott knocked on the door again without interruption this time, as everyone was overwhelmed with thought and were taking a cerebral break.

"Mr. Douglas, your Field Agent Meceli is here, should I send her in?"

"Mr. President, with your permission… yes, send her in."

Douglas made the introductions and got right to the point. Clint was impressed with her immediately. She carried herself with extreme confidence, even amongst all the brass. She listened to the brief given by Douglas and interrupted for clarification or questions at will. She was neutral, beautiful in a way but somehow homely, which gave her the ability to dress up or down to blend in with the situation. The loose-fitting clothes could have hidden a sumptuous body or a twiggy figure. Clint guessed the former matched her personality more.

She paced during the brief, sizing up the room's occupants, looking directly into their eyes. Not cocky, nor disrespectful, simply gathering all the knowledge possible in as short a period of time as possible. She was in her late twenties, with chestnut brown shoulder-length hair and blue eyes accented by little premature crow's feet. Her face belonged in Boston Magazine along with the other proper elite, but her eyes told of a different person, someone who had seen the worst of life and was tiring of not seeing the best of life.

"Any more questions, Anne-Marie?" the DCI asked.

"Yes, this is not the purview of the CIA. I can understand the rationale of mobilizing limited CIA resources, but that may be picked up by FBI, DEA, or Secret Service, all of whom have some jurisdiction, the CIA has none. For me to be legal, I need to be empowered. I suggest making me an undercover loaner to Secret Service, with the proper paper work to back it up. Agreed?"

Everyone nodded affirmatively, their confidence in Agent Anne-Marie Meceli building.

"Next, I will need a job cover. I suggest that working for Robert doing tactical research for the Martial Law Drug Plan would provide fairly open access to most areas we need to bottom fish in. Agreed?"

Again, everyone nodded affirmatively and then Clint broke in.

"Problem. The tactical planning would certainly be the purview of the Chief of Staff. How better to clear him than to have Anne-Marie report directly to him. That will give her more access to his movements, as well as those around him. She could be required to debrief Robert regularly by your request, Bill."

"I like it," added Douglas, "It also gives us more use of Robert to look under some other rocks."

Anne-Marie was wondering who Clint was, and decided to do some research the first time she had the opportunity. He had the eyes and presence of an intelligence guy but the mind of a solid blend of strategy and tactics, and she was experienced enough to know they were rare combinations. And to be wrapped up in a well-built handsome package, she was definitely going to do some research.

The knock on the door was blanked out by the conversations in the Oval Office, but heard by Clint and Anne-Marie. Clint motioned to Robert that someone was at the door and Robert went to the door after he had given Clint a look meaning that he didn't intend to be Clint's flunky.

Ms. Turcott asked the President's forgiveness again and told Clint that Cole Cunningham, Field Director of Special Projects with the DEA was on the telephone, and it was an emergency. This startled Clint, the President, Douglas, and Field Agent Meceli. Robert either did not see the uncanny connection or was keeping it well hidden.

"Wait, Clint, don't pick up the phone yet. Cunningham is the guy in charge of the Martial Law Drug Plan's street operations, you know finding and putting the bad guys out of business. Why would he be calling you?" the President said quickly.

"I don't know. If you have a speakerphone, we will all know in a moment," Clint responded.

Ms. Turcott took that as the cue to put the call on the President's line, and with a single finger hastily pushed the speakerphone came to life. She waited in the Oval Office discretely by the door, listening to the call with everyone else.

The President said, "Cunningham, this is the President. I am here with Robert, the DCI and Mr. Bear." He left out Field Agent Anne-Marie Meceli appropriately. "Now, what is so urgent?"

Somewhat startled, Cole paused, collected his thoughts and responded, "Mr. President, I'm sorry to intrude, but this is extremely urgent. It may be better for Mr. Bear if he and I spoke privately."

Clint spoke up, wanting to hear why Agent Cunningham was calling. Intuition told him this was not good news. "Go ahead, Mr. Cunningham; we are among friends here. What is so urgent?"

Cole hated doing this, everyone did, but to be asked to tell a man that his fiancée and sister had been brutally raped and killed on a God damned speakerphone was too much. "Mr. Bear, this is of a personal nature and quite serious. Are you sure you wouldn't prefer to pick up the receiver?"

"No, go ahead please," Clint said, controlling his anxiety.

"Mr. Bear, we have had a positive identification on two female bodies found about one hundred miles north of Durango, Colorado. I'm sorry Mr. Bear, they are the bodies of your fiancée, Brook Fontaine, and your sister Cabris. I'm truly sorry to have such news and to tell you in this way." Cole Cunningham had never hated his job more than at this very moment.

All eyes were on Clint. Everyone was paralyzed. The shock of two women, the immediate family of Clint Bear, dead. The impact of losing his sister and future wife caused lightning bolts to fire off in his head, with thunderous explosions which rocketed him back to the jungles. His head was pounding, exploding. Then he could see, a Special Forces patrol was to pick up him and his rescued POWs at 0300. They were an hour overdue. The Taliban was getting close and he had to drop his weapon load to carry an injured POW on a full run. The explosions were all around him, mortar fire. The 35mm cannons started firing into the night at their noise with no target sighted. They kept running further up the trail and using the three for seven fall back, where three fresh legs covered the back door while the slower ran ahead, then switched. He was carrying the POW and couldn't help his team when they were flanked. He watched and ran as three of his unit, cut off, were literally torn apart by cannon fire. He remembered hoping they were dead, as the Taliban were master torturers, especially to elite Navy SEALs. They made it to the alternate pickup point and finally, with luck on their side, saw the Chinook. The helicopter support team laid down a blanket of fire while the remaining SEALs and POWs climbed into the Chinook. He felt the bullet enter his right shoulder as he dropped the POW he was carrying and the pain, so intense, caused him to open his eyes and reorient himself to the Oval Office.

His body was awash with pain and his anger was about to control him. He thought about the other morning, and how beautiful Brook looked as she lay entwined in the restless sheets. She was radiant in the morning, a rested innocent face, lean and muscular but with supple legs, skin silky smooth, gentle fingers. Knowing he would never touch her, be with her again, pushed him to the edge and then from a distant past his training came back and physically took over his bodily functions. He then thought of Cabris, his only sister and his training stopped him from weeping, stopped him from feeling the immense hurt.

The nightmare, his and theirs, was just beginning. More than intuition.

Agent Meceli watched Clint and was amazed to see he appeared more relaxed now than earlier in the evening. She had seen it before, years of conditioning to control one's emotions, physical or psychological pain, but she had never seen it so smoothly transitioned. She walked over to his chair, put her hands on his shoulders and softly asked if he would like to be alone.

Clint responded in monotone, "No, thank you for your concern, but I'll be fine. Cunningham, how were they killed and why is the DEA involved in a homicide?"

Anne-Marie was stunned with Clint's clear thinking at a time like this. She and Douglas should have had those questions already asked and answered. She was doubly determined to get to know this most unusual man.

"Mr. President, is the room clear?"

"Yes, Cunningham, speak freely," responded the President.

"Do not discuss classified information beyond the communications security levels, Agent Cunningham," Douglas interjected, his mind still trying to fit the pieces together.

"Mr. Bear, I head up a task force chartered to find drug importers and wholesalers — the big guys. We lost an agent in the same area where the bodies of your family were found. We have reason to believe that they are related by happenstance. We understand that your loved ones had nothing to do with drugs. We believe they were abducted by the ring we are trying to expose, and killed." Cole had to leave out the brutality and the rape details for now. That might push Clint over the edge.

"Thank you, Mr. Cunningham, I know this call was not easy for you. Where are the bodies now?" Clint was already getting up from his chair and moving while awaiting the answer. As he was leaving the Oval office he asked Ms. Turcott where there was a private telephone. He, like Cole Cunningham, had a few unpleasant telephone calls to make.

Cole broke off the secure communication and began thinking about why Clint Bear and the Director of the CIA would be in the President's office. It must be connected to events somehow, but the CIA has no jurisdiction in domestic affairs. It was technically illegal for the CIA to operate domestically, but he could think of no other explanation. What the hell? Maybe when Clint arrived he would share some information.

The Short Takeoff and Landing plane, known as a STOL aircraft, lifted quickly out of the canyon near Los Pinos Pass, being careful not to come into the Rangers station tower's line of sight. Carlos Ortega wished he could fly the aircraft himself and prevent yet another person from knowing his business.

Looking over the blanket of pines, he began thinking of what was left to do. L.A. would have their supply by tomorrow, maybe even today. San Francisco, Boston, New York, Chicago, Philadelphia, Toronto and Dallas already have theirs. D.C., Miami and Denver are all that is left. Maybe as soon as a week, certainly not more than two, and he would be ready to sell the product he had been staging for the last two months. They would hit the market hard, price it higher than cocaine, make a quick big time killing and exit within a few months. He just needs to keep up the cocaine supply to hold the street distribution system together until the White Ice started selling.

Then I will retire, he thought. I will have added four or five hundred million U.S. dollars to my accounts, scattered around in U.S., European and South American banks. Christ, I will live like a god! No more cartel orders, no more inner circle bullshit. Free at last.

He did not want to move the camp again, although he should for security reasons, rationalizing that he would be finished producing the product in a week or two. Jesús and Julio were to expand the perimeter's security while he was gone. Hopefully, they would complete the two-day job before they went into town for a few beers, a good meal and some relaxation. And hopefully they would keep their mouths shut when they went into town. The odds that the cartel would discover his private venture were remote. He was the only "inner circle" member who dared come to the U.S. to check on the cocaine organization. And he was the leading revenue source to the cartel and their Afghanistan cocaine suppliers.

The STOL aircraft had a range of nearly seven hundred miles as outfitted with extra wing tanks, so with luck they would only require one refueling stop. Still, he ordered the pilot to do a fly-by so he could survey the camp from above. He could see Jesús and Julio sitting at the mess table with the camp plans out reviewing the security arrangements. Less visible were Julio's off road Ford Bronco, even with those huge off-road tires, and Jesús's green Roadrunner. Good, he thought, things were progressing nicely and not moving the camp should not hurt this one time, although it would break his procedure. The added security the guys were installing should be all they'd need. They have been very careful so far, the only mistake made was not burying those women deep enough so that the hunters found them. Shit, I hope Jesús buried the last two deeper, like I told him to, he thought, feeling a little less comfortable now. He'd better not let Julio handle it. That guy could screw up a wet dream. I will remember to talk to Jesús about it when I return in a few days, he thought, feeling a little better now that he had addressed it in his mind.

Their destination was Chihuahua, Mexico, about three hundred miles south of El Paso, Texas. Carlos was to pick up additional chemicals there for his last batch of White Ice, without the slightest risk of curious police. The route was almost due south following the mountain ranges weaving within the Continental Divide's peaks for cover. They wouldn't break out of the mountains until they were due west of Chihuahua.

He was looking forward to spending a few days in Mexico relaxing while Jesús and Julio tended to the security arrangements. He fancied an Executive Secretary, working in the local Ford electronics assembly plant. She was wild and he couldn't wait.

Carlos answered the awful squawk by simply lifting the receiver and saying, "Yes?"

The voice from the other identical secure encrypted communications system responded without delay, "They are not delaying the Martial Law implementation. Plans will be complete and implementation started within ten days, fourteen at most. Covey has enlisted the help of a war-time friend, Clint Bear, to find a suspected leak in the house. They have planted a mole in the house, CIA agent Anne-Marie Meceli. Things are getting hot. Out."

The total transmission time, twenty-six seconds. Too short for trace, if anyone intercepted the transmission.

Carlos replaced the receiver gently in midst of deep concentration, and concluded two things. He will still have time to market White Ice, and the caller was now a dangerous weak link tied loosely to him.

This time the call was logged and recorded, unknown to both the caller and Carlos.

Clint arrived early Monday morning, thanks to a military jet arranged by the President that flew directly into Durango. Red and Cole were both there to meet him.

The sun had just graced Washington D.C. and was a full two hours or more from Durango. It seemed fitting to have such darkness, Clint thought as he walked out of the terminal toward the only car at arrivals; it matched his mood. He had more time to channel the emotions, and some of the time was used to reflect on and mourn the losses. Not to let the emotions out, not to feel the hurt, no crying, no weeping, but to channel the emotions, use them as fuel, fuel to find the bastards who did this and make them regret they were ever among the living. He knew a hundred ways to kill a man cleanly, but he wasn't thinking about a clean kill. These murders are going to feel the fear, taste the eventual death, and he wanted to look in their eyes when they were so very slowly and so very painfully dying, and spit in their faces before they were lucky enough to die.

Agent Cole Cunningham was leaning against the black Chevrolet Caprice, the stripped-down exterior giving away its Government ownership. He recognized Clint immediately from the picture he was emailed six hours ago. He would have recognized him even if he wasn't the only person exiting the terminal at such an ungodly early time. Cole began to walk toward Clint when Clint said, "Agent Cunningham? Thanks for meeting me, and I would appreciate it if you would take me directly to the morgue, or wherever the bodies are being kept."

"Clint, we should talk some before we do that... how about a cup of coffee?" Cole said with a mixture of light sincerity.

"Agent Cunningham..."

"Please call me Cole."

"All right Cole, my fiancée and sister have been murdered. How do you think that has affected me?" Clint said in a fierce tone, but without raising his voice.

"Well, I imagine you're hurt, angry and a little lost. That's to be expected. I understand..."

Clint stopped at the car door, stopped, paused for about ten seconds and then turned slowly and looked directly into Cole's eyes. He was a good three inches taller than Cole and at least that wider. Cole was noticeably intimidated, not from the size differential, but from the look in Clint's eyes that said, "Don't fuck with me. Period."

Clint, smiling, said, "Thanks for your psychology 101, and no, you don't understand. Now, are you going to take me to see the bodies or not? Frankly I don't give a shit."

"Hop in. We can be there in about thirty minutes, but Clint, we will need to talk on the way. That's my only condition. Okay?" Cole said, mustering all the authority he could.

"It's your ride. I'll accept your condition if you will accept mine."

"What's that?" Cole beginning to worry about this guy.

"If it takes thirty minutes to get there, I'll answer your questions for the first fifteen minutes and you answer mine for the last fifteen. Agreed?"

Cole, wishing he had slept at least a few hours last night instead of working the evidence replied, "Okay."

Cole sat in the driver's seat, rubbed his face and, still not feeling alert enough to face an obviously more than worthy advisory, decided to slap his face a half a dozen times. Clint noticing Cole's fatigue, broke the agreement as soon as he closed his door by asking Cole, "When did you sleep last?"

"This is my fifteen, if you don't mind, and it was two days ago. I have been working the evidence, trying to put these bizarre murders together."

"Murders? You say that as if there are other murders, I mean in addition to your agent and… Brook and Cabris," Clint said, showing a bit of fatigue himself.

"Security prevents me from answering that question. Do you understand me?" Cole looked over to his right to see Clint nod affirmatively, and continued. "There were two other women killed in the same way, which is what I need to talk with you about. That's why we think —no, we know — they are connected." Cole hoped he would not excite Clint, because he was convinced he could do him some real bodily injury.

"What was the condition of the bodies when you found them, Cole?"

Cole dodging the light traffic, typical for this time of the morning, and thought about how to respond, and in the end decided to be clinically honest. After all, Clint was about to see his sister and fiancée's bodies and would be able to make his own assessment. The more he talked with

Clint, the more he was aware of his physical and intellectual strength, and the more he hoped that Clint was in control of himself. If only Cole knew how much in control Clint was, he would not worry about himself as much as the druggies he was after.

"This is going to be tough. Are you ready?"

"I wouldn't have asked if I didn't want to know the answer. And watch out for that dump truck in front of us. The rear left tire is about to blow," Clint said casually, as if he was talking to a friend driving them to a ball game.

Cole was dumbfounded by this guy's control. It was unnatural. His mind ran in circles as he thought. What am I missing? Could he have had prior knowledge of the murders? Was he involved? Why was he so controlled? What the fuck was I missing?

Just then the left rear tire blew and the truck swerved and almost rolled over, causing Cole to swerve two lanes over and brake hard, coming to a complete stop to prevent being hit. He looked over at Clint, and Clint slowly turned to look at Cole. They locked eyes for the briefest of moments, seconds turning into minutes and finally Clint broke the moment and asked, "What was the condition of the bodies when you found them, Cole?"

Cole felt a chill, no a glacial cold come over his body as he answered, "They were both buried in a shallow grave outside of Spar City, Colorado. They had been dead for less than twenty-four hours; forensic will confirm more exactly. Both women were naked. Both had been sexually abused, repeatedly. Both bodies suffered physical torture while being bound at the ankles and wrists. The M.O. was exactly the same as the last two young women we found no more than sixty miles from this site. We believe it to be drug related but can't, yet, make the link. I'm sorry to be so blunt, but I sense it is what you want." Having answered, he thought himself a real ass for being so sterile, so damn cop-like, and expected Clint to lose it now and for his anger to be directed toward him. Well, he deserved it, but was too tired to defend himself.

Cole made the turn into the Coroner's Office parking lot, at the rear of the Sheriff's Office, and parked not-so-evenly between the marked lines. He turned to Clint, expecting to be punched in the mouth by a good-sized fist, but instead heard, "Cole, thank you, I know this is hard for you, and I know you are working your ass off to find the bad guys. Take a break, rest. I won't need you while I view the bodies." Then he was gone, and Cole was asleep, against his will, kind of like he was drugged, or hypnotized.

Clint went around to the Coroner's Office entrance and found the door locked. He went to the adjacent Sheriff's Office, entered and asked the officer at the desk where the coroner was. The commotion awoke Sheriff Red Peterson, who was in his squeaky oak chair with his feet upon the desk, dozing. Rubbing his eyes and next his legs, he walked unsteadily to the desk officer and Clint.

"Clint, I know we have met before but I can't put it together," Red said, extending his hand. "I'm really sorry for your loss. It's more than a bitch."

"Thanks Red, and you're right, we do know each other, but I can't place it either," Clint said, shaking Red's hand. "I'm here to… view the bodies, can you arrange it?"

"It isn't necessary, you know. Your brother, Art, was here a few hours ago and made a positive ID."

Clint was confused. How could Art have known? Helena, his personal assistant, loyal and dedicated for many years, was told not to tell anyone other than him. How could Art have found out? "I want to, no need to, please," Clint uttered, pushing his current thoughts out of his mind.

"Okay, I understand. Ya ready for this?"

"Yes."

"Okay, let's go this way," Red said pointing with his arm toward the hallway on the right.

The Sheriff's Office was like most police stations at this time of night. Drunks, druggies and weirdos. When will America get it together? Clint thought as he walked down the hall.

Entering the Coroner's Office caused Clint to flash back twenty plus years. How many times had he walked into the field morgue to ID someone in his or another's command? Knowing that you will find what you're looking for would appear to some to make it easier. An unqualified falsehood. He couldn't explain it, but he had been on both sides, hoping to find and not to find, and knowing what you're looking for is by far the worst.

His entire body began to tense, starting with the limbs inward, as he entered "the box" as he called it. How many times had he identified soldiers in Afghanistan? Probably hundreds. Red then asked if he was ready, politely, more sensitively than a man of his weathered exterior would be expected to.

Taking a deep breath Clint said, "My sister, Cabris, first."

The air in the box was cold and humid, and Red's voice echoed off the stainless steel drawers and sterile white ceramic tiled floor. Clint was thinking how remarkable it was that all morgues are similar. All have a place to keep the cadavers cold to prevent premature decay, all must be sterile clean, all have gloomy lighting, all have the sticky sweet smell, and all have corpses. In the deep of his conscience he was hoping the identification was wrong and his family were not here. It was normal, he understood it, but still prayed silently, covertly, that he would not find what he expected to find.

Red pulled at the drawer. It resisted for a moment and then opened abruptly. The body was covered with a clean white sheet that glistened in the cold damp air. Red placed his hand on the top of the sheet, near where the head must be, and before lifting the sheet looked at Clint and waited his acknowledgment. Clint nodded his readiness, and seconds later closed his eyes and nodded again.

The next one may be tougher, Red thought, so he offered Clint a moment to collect himself and was surprised when it was refused. He went to the adjoining drawer and opened it slowly. But when the drawer was opened Clint reached for the sheet, lifting it delicately and holding it up for an awkwardly long time. Red was even more surprised when Clint lifted the sheet off completely and began to visually examine the body. Clint scanned every limb carefully before moving to the torso and finally to the head. Red thought he saw Clint shaking, maybe vibrating is more the correct word, as his report would later indicate. And then tenderly, lovingly, he kissed her on the lips and slowly pulled the sheet back over her body. Red's report would indicate that Clint had said something, but it was murmured and partially undiscernible, something like "mandan range" or "rage". He wished to God he had heard, and then again, maybe it was best not to know.

In Clint's mind, the remembrance of their lovemaking three short days ago kept spinning around and around. Her golden supple skin was gone, replaced by a cold gray white shield on a body that was obviously raped and badly abused, just like his sister. Those animals! He shouldn't have kissed her; the touch of their lips was clinical, frigid, dead, sending the fireworks in his mind to triple the intensity. He suppressed them long enough to renew his promise to himself, this Mandan Indian will have revenge.

Clint walked quietly out of the morgue and Red closed the drawer, being sure to note on both drawer tags that another next-of-kin had made a firm ID, and that transport to a local mortuary would be arranged.

Red walked out of the morgue ready for the questions and emotions that were the norm from the surviving kin. To his amazement, and subsequent horror, Clint was nowhere to be found. Vanished. It was just then when he remembered where he had met Clint.

Red Peterson was not easily frightened; this was one of those rare exceptions. He knew he had not seen the last of Mr. Clint Bear.

"Mr. President," Douglas said at the start of their morning briefing, "We may want to expand the scope of the current DEA investigation. I see two reasons for considering this. One, you have made the largest commitment to the American people in history and your groundwork has fallen apart. Two, the scope of the drug network is obviously considerably broader than anyone of us would have guessed prior to these recent events."

"That's a good idea, but how can we expand? I mean, the resources normally associated with an operation such as this are, well, suspect at this point," the President said somberly.

Agent Meceli spoke up, stealing Douglas's thunder, "Why not establish a special group of law enforcement professionals, empowered to do the job? You can do such a thing with Martial Law in force, can't you?"

"Yes, yes he can," Douglas interjected, cutting off Anne-Marie and Robert, who obviously had an opinion on this, "Mr. President, your point is well taken. We can't use those resources normally associated with operations of this type, but we can use experienced Intelligence Operatives.

The CIA has an unusually light load now due to the Democratization of the former Soviet Union and the Eastern Blok. I can reassign a complete team of field and support people for this project. Further, it makes sense since the drugs are probably coming in from outside the U.S., which is the CIA's area of expertise. With the loyalty factor still an unknown, I suggest that this new department be a collaborative of new CIA personnel and those DEA agents already in the field working for Field Director Cunningham. Further, I would suggest that he report directly to you to keep this program compartmentalized." Douglas waited for the President to assimilate what had been said.

"Douglas, this all makes good sense, but I can't have Cunningham reporting to me. I am not qualified and I don't have the time to manage this effectively. Why not have him report to Robert?"

"Mr. President, and Robert please understand I mean this with no disrespect, but Robert does not have the experience to manage this either," Douglas offered in a calculating manner. The manipulations were lost on all but Agent Meceli, who did not let it be known what she suspected. C. Eric Douglas was a consummate statesman, and knew soon after he arrived in the Oval Office that there was a tremendous opportunity here. All he had to do is play it right. And he felt he had played it perfectly.

"Sure, and I suppose that you are the only one capable, right?" Robert blasted back, the fatigue of the long night showing.

"Well, in this room and in the current compartment, yes Robert, I am, and you know that as well as I do. I am not asking for this assignment, Christ I have enough to do in the world. But, if the President would like me to assist until a permanent boss can be appointed, I'll do my best to help," Douglas said humbly.

"Then you have a theory on who comprises the drug ring that took Agent Cudson's life?" Robert asked flippantly.

"Actually, no I don't. I have not reviewed all the evidence and field reports at hand since I have not been part of this investigation up until now. I suppose you do though, Robert?" Douglas said slyly.

"Yes, I think it is the Indians. Look, they are impoverished, they know the territory better than anyone else, the drug business brings in good money and, hell, as a people they have the worst drug problem going!" Robert blurted out, suddenly feeling a bit foolish.

Agent Meceli made a note that there might be something to this.

"Robert, this is why it would be wrong for me to offer an opinion yet. It is like arm chair psychology in that it can be dangerous, very dangerous. You have just incriminated a whole people with nothing more that circumstantial hearsay," Douglas lectured in exasperation, but made a mental note about what Robert had said. He may be a brash asshole, but he was bright.

"What would you suggest we call the new department, Douglas?" the President asked, rubbing his tired face and bringing the meeting back on track.

"Well, I hadn't given it any thought. Let me see… well it is a collaborative effort of the CIA and DEA. Why not call it the Collaborative, or 'Department C'," Douglas said, motioning with his hands.

"I like it, really like it. Robert, please initiate the appropriate paperwork and make sure the Attorney General blesses everything, but leave Agent Meceli's name out of this. She will be undercover and known only to the people in this office, plus Clint. One more thing before we adjourn for some sleep: Douglas, would you head this operation?" the President said with newfound energy.

"Yes, Mr. President, I will be please to help. I consider it an honor. I assume I will report directly to you, and you only," Douglas said, playing out his final hand.

"Yes, absolutely, me and me alone," offered the President as he stood, signaling to the rest in the room that the meeting was over.

Agent Anne-Marie Meceli was now reporting directly to C. Eric Douglas, Director of the Central Intelligence Agency. My, how things changed quickly around here, she thought. The few hours' sleep she had been fitful. She spent the morning tossing and turning in bed with the events of the last night buzzing in her head. This would be a tough job, finding one or more moles in the White House, moles who have been clever enough to avoid detection for many years, possible tens of years. That's a thought, each administration changed most of the staff to "their own" when they came in, maybe that's worth looking into first; tenure in the White House cross-indexed to access and then opportunity.

She decided she was just wasting time lying in bed so got up, showered, and headed into the Company to do the research on one Mr. Clint Bear. Having exchanged pleasantries with other Company people, she sat down at the desk and booted her secure terminal. From this terminal, she could peek into the lives of tens of millions of people, and with the network connections to Interpol, FBI, State, British Ministry, she had access to hundreds of millions of personal histories.

She was adept at search work. Every agent who was successful at their job was. The computers databases represented hundreds of thousands of man-years of investigatory work. The key in the investigation business was to get where you wanted to go quickly, and the data helped agents do that by not reinvestigating what was previously investigated. Every field report was digested by a mass of research agents and forwarded to computer operators for cross-referenced entry. The data was relational, meaning that obscure events could be related to others so that the inquirer would get the full picture even when they only knew to ask about one small element.

Agent Meceli typed in "Bear, Clint" then pressed the search function key. What she had in front of her, on the full high-resolution color screen, more than surprised her. But, thinking again, it didn't surprise her at all. She scrolled down through the data:

Search subject: Bear, Clint
Date of Birth: 18 November, 1969
Place of Birth: Deluce, New Mexico
Nationality: American (Indian), Mandan, raised Apache
Military Service: USN
Date of Enlistment: 4 July, 1991
Date of Discharge: 20 June, 2004
Rank at Discharge: Lt. Commander, Field Commission
Unit: Navy SEALs 1992 - 2004
War Time Assignment: Afghanistan, 1994 - 2003
Outstanding Decorations: Navy Cross, Purple Heart (3), Medal of Honor, Bronze Star, Medal of Valor, Silver Star
Specific Talents: Hand to Hand Combat, Karate, 9th degree Black belt, Intelligence, Espionage, Reconnaissance, BEL, Weapons, Explosives, IQ:151, Special Forces Instructor, Additional Talents: Classified.
Languages: English, Apache, Spanish, Arabic
Physical description (as of discharge):
    Height: 6'2"
    Weight: 198 lbs.
    Hair: Black
    Eyes: Black

Noticeable Marks: Bullet wound right rear shoulder; Bullet wound left leg; Knife wound mid abdomen, Small scars about the legs and abdomen from shrapnel. Additional Information: Classified.

Current location: Personal residence: Apache Indian Reservation, New Mexico

Current occupation: President, Founder, American Indian Electronics Corporation, New Mexico.

Last Record Update: December 12, 2009

FURTHER INFORMATION AVAILABLE, TOP SECRET CLASSIFICATION
THIS INQUIRY HAS BEEN LOGGED

Agent Meceli didn't need to dig deeper, for now. She knew the profile and it explained his presence and attitude in the Oval Office when he was told about his wife-to-be and sister. It helped her understand how Clint was able to control his emotions, his response to such appalling news. It also told her that she should get a message to Agent Cunningham, because Clint was no one to fool with, and those responsible for his family's death would most assuredly have the unfortunate occasion to meet Mr. Clint Bear in person, probably very soon. They had sealed their own fate and deserved what was in store for them, but Cunningham might not like the intrusion into his investigation.

Anne-Marie closed the data base file and logged out of the network. The Network Control Office noted that Agent Meceli was logged on for 17 minutes, start and stop times, and completed a search for Bear, Clint.

***

Three thousand miles away on the opposite coast, Chet, in his light blue Ford pickup truck, having negotiated the on-ramp from the 405 North onto the 7 South toward Long Beach, California, was on the final leg of his journey. He would meet Leon Beecher at 9:00 PM, as prearranged by Jesús. The hay, showing a little wear from the trip, was still in the truck's bed, hiding the… merchandise, whatever. Jesús hadn't told him what he was carrying and he didn't really want to know, but anyone paying him fifty thousand dollars for a three-day delivery and not doing it himself would indicate it's not legal.

Chet didn't care. He needed the money to save his farm. Drought had caused four bad crop years in a row and was more than a heavily-leveraged farm could manage. Chet would lose it all, farm, savings, equipment, furniture, truck… everything, including his self-respect. He had no choice unless he and his wife and two children wanted to be on the dole.

Okay, he said to himself, with the traffic so light he was at his next turn before he expected to, let's see, past Long Beach Boulevard. and straight on to the island. Somewhere there is supposed to be a boat tied up to a pier called the Queen Mary, supposed to be a hotel or something now. He was thinking it was not the best area for a hotel when he spotted it off to the left just past the Hyatt.

The note said to go to the far side of the parking lot. Chet felt a little squeamish, scared actually. Funny, he thought, after driving almost a thousand miles on back roads with whatever in the back, and he just now began to get scared. He hadn't been scared since he left Jesús, with his missing tooth. Fortunately, the parking lot was at least half-full, but there were very few people around, and then he spotted two well-dressed black guys standing near a White Cadillac, smoking. He drove over to them slowly, parked, got out and walked over to them slowly.

"Are you Leon Beecher?" Chet asked impishly.

"Who the fuck are you asshole?" the big guy snapped back, catching Chet a little off guard.

"My names Chet, sorry, I'm trying to find Leon, thought it might be you," he said while turning around and heading back to the pickup truck.

"Yo, hayseed! I'm the guy your looking for. Is that truck a gift for me?" Leon said while laughing.

"Yeah, Jesús said to just give you the keys," Chet said while throwing Leon the keys.

"You touch anything in the back, hayseed?" the other guy said, walking over to the truck and looking all around for unwanted guests.

"Nope, was told to just drive to this spot, that's all I did."

"Good boy, you got a ride out of here?" Leon asked.

"Well no, I didn't really think about it. You got my money?" Chet said.

"Yeah, I got it and as soon as the load is verified you'll get it. I didn't keep it here, you know, just in case." Leon, looking over to his partner who nodded that the load was there added, "Okay, hayseed, let's go get your money and we'll drop you off at the bus station after that, and I don't want to hear from you again. Got it?"

"Bernie, you and the hayseed get in the truck, you drive, give him a break. We'll go get his money," Leon barked.

Chet thought that everything had gone fine and then was concerned when Bernie slowed the truck and stopped on the bridge connecting the mainland to the island, Leon was right behind them in his Cadillac.

"Looks like I didn't put the hay back right when I checked the load. A bale is about fall off, give me a hand fixing it, hayseed," Bernie said as he opened the driver's side door.

Chet didn't see any loose bales and was about to protest when he felt the first of three bullets enter his chest. His eyes went wide, his mouth wider and in the few seconds before he died he realized that his farm would be saved anyway, but not in the way he'd planned. The life insurance would pay off the loans and hire more hands, but he wouldn't be there to manage it.

He died before he hit the swirling frigid water of the San Pedro Bay coursing under the bridge, carrying the lifeless body out to the Pacific Ocean.

Chet Whithers' body would be carried out to sea and never recovered, food for the circle of life. One of the many-cloaked tragedies in the world of illegal drugs.

Tragedies.

CHAPTER 4:
THE AWAKENING

The Indian sweat lodge hasn't changed much in five hundred years. It is still secluded from the main living areas, frequently well away from the Indian village, still made from sticks, mud and bark and still uses hot stones to create steam to heat the lodge. Clint's, actually his family's, sweat lodge was over five miles from the central part of the village, well into the barren hills. He had built it with his father and brother when he was a teen, selecting this site because it had a lazy creek running just outside. The creek provided the necessary water and also provided the only sounds, which helped Clint's meditation

He was taken back almost thirty years, when, at the age of fifteen, he, his brother Art, seven years his senior, and his father had built the lodge. Old Bear had used the opportunity to teach them of the old ways and hoped it would help build unity between Clint and Art. But Art didn't want unity between them, and Clint, not his father, knew why. Old Bear thought it related to his mother's death.

Art was born to Old Bear's first wife, Ko-Ka — The Antelope — in 1962. His mother, revered by all within the tribe, died during childbirth. She was a beautiful woman with the heart of a spirit, who always held the benefit of the tribe before herself. When she died, unexpectedly, it was thought by many to be a sign from the spirits that Art was a demon to be watched and given a wide path. Art found it impossible to accept the curse that had befallen him, and for which he was constantly blaming his shortcomings. Old Bear would frequently remind him that if he spent as much time blaming as curing, he, and his family, would be better for it.

Old Bear created ways for Art and Clint to build lasting memorials, like the sweat lodge, in hopes it would build the heart and mind in the process. It seemed to work with Clint, but he was not certain about Art.

Together they built the small round sweat lodge, cut into a hill, made of sticks and sod, and they had an ancient heavy bear hide for the door. The fire pit outside, was dug deep to hold a substantial amount of hot coals, and a circle of flat rectangular rocks fitted around the perimeter. He remembered Old Bear repeating the story of the circle… everything happens in circles, one of the many Indian principles of life. He taught them how to fabricate sod bricks out of red earth and straw, how to use the sod to fill between the logs like grout in tile and how to use the lodge for seeing and healing.

Clint thought that Art was always going through the motions, always taking the easy road, the way he seemed to approach his life. Maybe Art sensed that he did not respect him and that was the cause of his aloofness. Maybe that is the way father felt, as well.

A fire was built outside the lodge with stones piled closely around it to soak in the heat and usually a second person was charged with tending the fire and replenishing the hot stones and cold water from the creek. It could be done alone, however the disruption of tending to the lodge during the sweat hindered the experience for many, but usually not for Clint. He found that it enhanced a relaxed sweat, and therefore he preferred the privacy.

As a man, many years later, he had developed a routine that included a run to the sweat lodge with a backpack filled with food and clothes. He would collect enough firewood for two days, move the stones from the last sweat out to the fire area, and fill the buckets that are kept at the lodge. That night Clint would sleep outside and the communing with nature would start his experience. Some would call it a trance but Clint's Medicine Man heritage thought it more an intense period of concentration and introspection. On this night, after all that had happened over the past seven days, the deaths and the burials, he gathered more wood than usual because his period of self-examination and questioning would be the most intense ever.

Clint had just settled into his sleeping blanket when he became aware of a presence. He couldn't exactly hear or smell anything, but he knew someone was near. He could sense it; he'd always had the capability. Silently coming to his feet, he trained his ears to localize a sound or his eyes to detect a movement. There, about three hundred yards east of the camp on a ridge was a man, approximately six feet tall, walking directly toward the sweat lodge. His walk was that of a hunter, sure, silent. Clint smiled, his first smile in a week, when he recognized it was the walk of his father, Old Bear.

They talked for most of the evening, and oddly mostly of Old Bear's heritage, his medicine. Then he told of his dreams of the black bear.

Clint understood the significance to his father, but could it really be a vision? he thought privately. The death of Cabris and Brook.

"San-Ja-Ka-Ko-Ka," his father said in slow, sincere words. "I know most of the spirits' meaning, but not all, as it has not been decided, but it soon will be. What I know, my son, I need to share with you now. You are most skeptical about the spirits and the visions we Medicine Men, me, my father and my father's father, and now you, have and it is most unfortunate that the loss of four of our family will make you a believer. My son, the three cubs in my recurring dream, the dream of four nights, are Cabris, Brook and my son. I, the last surviving parent, represent the Mother Bear."

"Come on father, Brook was not your daughter."

"Yes, my son, she was in the Indian sense. She was adopted by me as your wife when you agreed to marry. It was part of our personal relationship. She was half Hopi and well aware of the Indian traditions. Your engagement marked the adoption into our clan. She and I had a ceremony, privately. I'm sorry we did not share that with you. It was to be our surprise to you on your wedding day."

"But you… you're healthy and alive. How can you represent the Mother bear in your dream?" Clint said as he looked in awe at his father. He seemed as though he had centuries of wisdom. The character, chiseled into his aged face, was accented by the fire's light and his eyes were brighter than ever before. He seemed more alive now than he remembered as a child. It was odd to see such an old man so young in spirit.

"No, my son, I am dying. I have but a few days, no more and possibly less, left. I have seen this. It is true."

It was as if Clint's world was getting sucked into an opening in the earth. He could see it clearly in his mind. The spinning was like a tornado sucking up everything in its circular path, and it was making him nauseous. The loss of his fiancée and sister, and now his father…

"Wait," Clint screamed, holding his hand up as if the pieces were beginning to come together. "You said Cabris, Brook, and… your son. If it is not me, then Art is dead, as well?" Clint was beginning to the show the emotional toll his overwhelming loss was taking.

"No, not yet, but soon," Old Bear breathed out wearily. The world seemed heavier, and Old Bear felt, finally, his age.

He was pulled back to the fire pit by his father, continuing his sentence, "My son, I have seen your purpose. It is bigger than amalgamating the tribes in a successful business enterprise. This was important and you should be proud of your accomplishments. I am. It is done. What I have seen tells me you need to move on to your Creator's purpose. This, I have not seen, specifically. But I do know that it will involve the lives of many people and the spirits say you will be remembered among the greatest of Medicine Men, maybe the greatest Medicine Man yet. My son, the spirits say that the lives of my daughters, my son and my own are a sacrifice for the greater purpose. The worthiest reason for parting this earth. You must stay to insure the sacrifice has not been desecrated. And now, my son, the sun approaches us and your sleep is important. I will wake you when the hot rocks are in the lodge and you can begin your meditation."

Old Bear stood and walked to the other side of the fire where Clint was sitting, and placing his hands on his shoulders, looking at him straight in the eyes, his face so close Clint could feel his energy, and said, "San-Ja-Ka-Ko-Ka, you are the great one. This I know, and you have always had, and will always have, my love and respect. Your new journey will be dangerous and difficult. More so than ever before, even Afghanistan. Rely on your instincts and remember your heritage as a Medicine Man, it will save your life. I have seen it. I will be with you. Always."

"Father, I don't understand. What have we done to deserve this?" Clint wept.

Old Bear, still looking in Clint's watery eyes, said, "The Creator has a reason. All that has been revealed to me in my dreams and chanting is, 'It is not man's time to perish.' The specific meaning has not been revealed. Perhaps it will be revealed to you."

"Father, I will miss you."

"San-Ja-Ka-Ko-Ka, I will always be with you. I will be in your intuition," Old Bear said as he embraced Clint for the last time.

The ninety-four-year-old Old Bear was fully awake before the sun, having been up many times during the night to keep the fire fed. He wanted plenty of hot coals in its bed to heat the rocks for the sweat lodge. No food was to be prepared this morning, not until Clint emerged from his inner quest, and that could be many hours or days.

Old Bear would awaken Clint after he had placed the first six hot rocks, making a tight circle in the pit at center of the lodge. The only light that would enter the lodge would be from the slit between the bear pelts covering its only door, and the small hole in the roof that encouraged the fire's convection process. The colder air from the lodge's earth floor would be drawn to the hot pit, be heated by the rocks and rise upward toward the small hole in the roof. The air would always be fresh, and the lodge temperature would get progressively hotter, frequently exceeding one hundred and twenty degrees.

It was not like the massive sweat lodges of the early 1800s, where dozens of Mandan Indians would experience the four-day long summer O-kee-pa ritual. The Mandan, like most of the Plains tribes, believed that animals, birds, rocks, trees and the earth all possessed xo'pini, spirit power. The power, xo'pini, could be transferred to the Indian, if they passed through certain rituals with bravery and honor. The most important ritual was O-kee-pa, where the creation of the earth was reenacted, along with its struggles, and those of its people. The struggles were the most torturous part of the ceremony, with the participants being suspended many feet in the air by splints piercing through the muscles in the chest or back, tied to rawhide ropes suspended over the lodge's beams. They were suspended for many minutes while the onlookers danced. Those who survived, with bravery and honor, would be revered by all the Plains tribesman for the rest of their natural lives. The ceremony enabled the participants to reawaken the power of xo'pini. Clint's ceremony would awaken a xo'pini as well, a spirit power of unprecedented dread.

There would be no talking, nothing to interfere with the introspection leading to the trance. Clint would sit, naked and cross-legged near the fire pit, and revert inwards. He would search his inner self, until his inner self led him out and his purpose made clear. He would allow himself no sustenance, only water to prevent severe dehydration that would surely befall him in the lodge's heat. He may wander out to the stream, to cool his body, he may not.

Old Bear will keep heated rocks in a tight circle in the fire pit and the water bucket full for steam. Having placed the first six, and the bucket full, he awakened Clint and escorted him to his place by the pit. The sweat had started. Old Bear's end had started as well.

Agent Meceli walked, more slowly than usual as she visually recorded her new surroundings in the White House. Her job was to find and confirm beyond doubt, and terminate the mole that has been leaking highly classified information and who has, or whose organization has, threatened the lives of the President and his immediate family. Just another day in the intelligence business, she thought privately, just another day that she will, hopefully, see to the end.

It was finally decided that she would report directly to Robert, as far as the White House staffers were concerned. In actuality, Agent Meceli would report directly to C. Eric Douglas.

Meceli was on her way to a meeting with Douglas in one of the many plush secure conference rooms in the White House's lower level. It was the basement, actually, but few diplomats would want to meet in the basement, so in 1955 Eisenhower mandated it be called 'the lower level', and it stuck.

Her report would be very brief, having only been undercover for part of the day yesterday. Still, there were a few odd goings-on which Douglas should be appraised. Meceli decided to dress slightly on the sultry side, just slightly, since most of the possible suspects were men, young men. Anne-Marie was not known to anyone here, or even to friends of friends. She was an experienced deep-cover agent, working internationally almost exclusively. Therefore, it was Douglas who decided not to needlessly invest the time to create a new name, as part of this cover, simply a new job and prior employment history. A reasonable prior job was assistant to the Ambassador of Great Britain, Reginald Walcott, III. In this position, a high-level security clearance would be required, which would explain, to the curious, why Anne-Marie Meceli's file had limited access, and why she would be entitled to this new position over those who had seniority at the White House.

The new position, MLDP Coordinator, was simple, and in cover operations simplicity is an absolute necessity. The cover agent must remember, cross-link remembers — for example, even though Anne-Marie was actually undercover in Turkey in April of 1990, her cross-linked memory tells her to say and act as if she were assisting Reginald Walcott in London — for dozens, if not hundreds of things. One of the many duties of a control is to structure the insertion, background and backup such that the agent has the fewest number of cross-linked remembrances necessary. There is a direct correlation of deep-cover success and limited cross-linked remembrances. Those agents, alive today, would agree, and C. Eric Douglas was one of those agents. As Martial Law Drug Plan Coordinator, Meceli would be involved with the President's MLDP installation, administration, and effectiveness monitoring. The newly-created position would require frequent contact with all President Covey's staff, as well as give her the mobility to accomplish her real job.

Meceli was surprised how much the office area of the White House looked like what would be found in an insurance company. Mostly young men, and some women, scurrying around with papers, files and tablets in their hands. All professionally dressed, all trying to make an impression, all trying to be noticed. There was a difference, however, she couldn't put her finger on it, but she could sense, no… feel it.

That's it, she thought. I am new to the office personnel group and no one had greeted her, looked at her or stopped her, asking for ID. After all, this was a secure area. Just before going down the stairs to the lower level, Anne-Marie stopped and looked around, blatantly. A typical fluorescent lighted office area, about thirty cookie cutter wood vaneer desks, tightly surrounded by pale blue sound-absorbing partitions, telephones beeping, keyboard keys clicking, mostly just the odd sight of moving heads of hair barely visible above the sound-proof partitions. The offices around the perimeter of the partitioned area had closed doors, portending the seriousness of their work, closing off the sunlight from the office pit. There were no Marine security guards, no windows, no eyes on her. Just drones doing what they thought would get them noticed. An ideal environment for a mole to move with unparalleled freedom. Shaking her head, she walked down the eighteen stairs, then turned left toward the Philadelphia Room for her debriefing with Douglas.

The room was known to her, before seeing the engraved nameplate, by the two Marine guards stationed outside.

"Good morning, ma'am," the tall Marine sergeant said while coming to attention.

"Good morning to you, Sergeant. Sergeant, I noticed there were no Marine guards in the office area. Is that customary?"

"Yes, ma'am. The guards were removed almost three years ago when the office workers complained of the 'Big Brother' syndrome. The rationale was that everyone had to be cleared to be there in the first place and were tripled-checked coming into the House," the Marine said, letting his disagreement with that action be known through his tone while the second Marine's eyes bored into the wall across the hallway. "Anything else you need to know, I suggest that you talk with the head of security."

"Thank you, Sergeant… Jacobsen, I may just do that," Meceli said as she looked at his nametag.

Sergeant Jacobsen then knocked twice, in military precision, and not waiting for confirmation, opened the door for Anne-Marie Meceli.

"Good morning, Mr. Douglas." And hearing the door quietly close behind her, she started her debriefing, not waiting for a return greeting or small talk. Meceli liked to be in control at all times.

"There are only a few issues to report, since my few hours 'in'. First, the insertion seems to be clean. No unusual inquiries or confrontations. Second, the cover also seems perfect. An expected level of disappointment from the want-to-bes. Third, the White House office security, isn't. I have never seen such a lax, open for compromise, 'secure' environment ever, anywhere. I am convinced it is where our mole operates. I need the office floor plans, names associated with locations, function, background and clearance. Yesterday, if possible, sir. Also, I need a task that brings me in contact with the most likely. I will narrow the possible suspects list within the next forty-eight hours."

C. Eric Douglas was impressed with Meceli. She was well beyond her twenty-nine years. Her grasp of a situation was more expansive than even his when he was ten years her senior. She was bright, quick, confident — but never over confident, that invites compromise and death. He took a long pull of his hot black coffee and studied Meceli. His mood matched the dark diminutive room. The overhead inset dimmed flood lights, positioned above each writing area of the conference table in front of each of the eight chairs, cast an ethereal shadow on each of them.

"Thank you Meceli. It appears that everything is working to plan. It is important that we narrow this list of possible suspects in twenty-four, not forty-eight hours. The President is counting on our success, as are the First Lady and her daughter. They have not been told, yet, and we can't keep it from them much longer. Twenty-hour hours, no longer. And one more thing, Meceli."

Anne-Marie was on guard. That phrase always meant more than it were positioned to mean, always.

"The Network Control Office notified me, as I have instructed, that there was a computer search inquiry made on

Anne-Marie Meceli, less than three hours ago. The source was modem linked, dual phase locked loop synchronized, code access. The physical location, unknown. The hardware, known. I want the list in twenty-four hours."

The steamed air hung like a cloud, twelve inches above the earth floor of the lodge. Clint's naked body motionless, his legs crossed and arms limp, resting on his bare thighs as he sat with his back erect and head well into the hot steam. The condensed water, mixed with his sweat, dripped down his body, the large puddle evidenced the hours of his sweat. Old Bear had refreshed the six large heated rocks seven times, each lasting about an hour and a half. The bucket just refilled for the third time and the rocks newly heated, the temperature slowly moving higher, pushed Clint deeper.

Clint didn't chant during his sweats like many others, including Old Bear. In his mind he was doing his form of chanting, a blend of his Indian heritage and his martial arts discipline. His mind drifting, he could feel his spirit being taken back. He would wander his experiences, his thoughts and his senses, let the sub-consciousness of his mind go where it needed to go, where the consciousness could not.

The hot, humid, dank, almost breathless atmosphere hurled him back to other lives lost. The underbrush thick with thorny vine, the sodden earth giving way to his elbows and knees as he silently crawled toward the camp. The constant rain his companion and his adversary. The white noise created by the millions of raindrops colliding with the leaves covered the unlikely accidental noise he might make, but also covered that of the enemy.

Eight experienced advanced unit Navy SEALs, assigned to JSOC, Joint Special Operations Command, were within ten feet of one another, but could not see or hear each other. All eight were masters of blending with their environment, Clint the best of the team that he commanded. They have worked as a team for nearly fourteen months, five in training, nine while on behind-enemy-lines black missions. Their specialty was twofold, to destroy prisoner of war camps and recover the POWs, and to find and compromise by any means, enemy remote intelligence posts. Maximum extreme personal risk, extreme importance to the Afghanistan war effort.

Clint signaled his team that they were nearing the destination, POW Camp 36, by imitating the sounds of crickets. Not even crickets could discern between imitation and reality. In unison, each of the remaining seven signaled back, crickets talking to crickets. They knew their job, having practiced it dozens of times in the mock Camp 36, now a hundred miles away. Neutralize the perimeter guards, then the sleeping quarters. Two would go to the communications room, neutralize the operator and his equipment, while retrieving any records and hard drives. Two would go the headquarters building, neutralize the guards and capture the Camp Commander. Two would wait for confirmation, and then neutralize the POW cell guards and retrieve the imprisoned Americans, Australians and Canadians. Best HUMIT, HUMan InTellegence, available estimated the seven Americans, three Canadians and two Australians had been in the camp for five to seven months. A long time to live a life of torture.

They would bring the imprisoned into the mountains more than seven miles, carrying those who had suffered more than their physical bodies could withstand. There would be four tactical assault teams waiting silently at the base of the mountain that would help the SEALs, the former prisoners, and the captured Camp Commander to four heavily armed Chinooks for transport back to base.

Clint had gone over the plan a hundred times in his mind, and could find no holes. He was experienced, and therefore knew there were always holes, and the enemy had the sickening habit of finding them with lightning speed. The holes meant probable death.

He could see the first of four guard towers silhouetted in the full moon's raincloud-muted light, placed at the corners of the abandoned town that was a walled fort-like camp. The rain continuing to mask their approach, the white noise louder, now, as it splashed on the surface of a pond, and the small stream feeding it, to the left of the main gate. Hole number one, the HUMIT didn't report a stream or pond, the crickets telling him that the others have seen the hole, as well.

The new observations did not change their basic strategy; it simply complicated the approach. Each has been trained to expect, and take maximum advantage of the unexpected.

Clint would supervise the mission, accompanied by the newest recruit, Willie, nicknamed Wonka for two obvious reasons. They would await confirmation, prior to taking out the prison cell guards, and provide cover for the other eight. Clint cricket-signaled for the team to await his visual recon on the camp, and began snaking to a higher vantage point. Soundlessly, he slid a pair of Nikon night vision light-enhancing binoculars in place, and began to survey the camp. It looked as if the moon had turned green, but the high-contrast image clearly showed what Clint didn't want to see. Hole number two, there were two additional buildings, both to the right of the communications shack, that appeared to be sleeping quarters, without any lights.

The camp was still, not unusual for 04:00, the time of deepest sleep. Reminiscent of an old west Army Fort, about three hundred linear feet of razor-sharp wire topped the wall, with one double-hinged door leading to the bridge over the stream, and six buildings, all but one with their doors facing the camp's center. That one was the most decrepit of all, and closest to the pond. The communications shack was as expected, the HQ and sleeping quarters as well. Clint studied the other two; one was identical to the sleeping quarters, while the other had opened sides with tables and benches, probably a canteen. This means that there were probably more Taliban than expected, estimate, six. His mind racing, taking everything in.

The guards were smoking, a very good sign of relaxed security. The glow of their cigarettes providing visual feedback of their positions. Two more guards, one sitting on a chair, propped up against the POW shack on two legs, and another foot patrolling the camps interior. Assessment: they are over secure, another good sign.

Clint cricket-coded the information to the team, his final message: GO.

The team began their move, snakes of the night, undulating noiselessly toward their assigned positions. Their equipment especially selected for its reliability and necessity: canvas camouflage bodysuit, bullet-resistant vest, black hood, Smith & Wesson .357 caliber Model 66 pistol, double magazine SHRIKE 5.56 submachine gun with silencer, two bricks of C-4, at least four grenades, dull finished survival knife, compass, eight-ounce plastic water pouch, thirty-foot length of quarter inch black nylon rope, two cyanide capsules and absolutely no personal identification. Their food and basic medical supplies were hidden to be picked up, only if needed, on the way back to the river.

The team knew this was the most dangerous part of the mission. Land mines, trip wires, booby traps and real snakes could not only kill the misfortunate team member, but alarm the camp, causing the mission to be scrubbed, permanently, the prisoners to be blamed for the attempt.

Clint felt the sharp sticks and thorns tearing at his camouflaged gear, penetrating to his skin all too regularly. Then he heard it, what the team always hoped not to hear, cricket-communication telling of a trip wire. That explained why the guards were so relaxed... Hole number three. The last three hundred feet would take much longer than expected as the team searched inch by inch for wires and mines. He was perspiring so much he couldn't tell the difference between his sweat, the rain and the water near the stream's edge. Each noiseless minute that passed made him more grateful for his training. He was nearing the main gate and could see that there was a simple door, made for people, as opposed to vehicles, that they could use for entry.

Clint knew he was not alone; there were seven team members out there, somewhere. He eased to the gate, aimed his SHRIKE 5.56 carefully at the closest guard, and waited. Soon, all team members had cricket-called their readiness, and he pulled the trigger, once. Thankfully, the guard fell quietly, not alerting the others. Within ten seconds, the other guards were neutralized, and Clint, after checking the door for alarms and wires, opened it slowly and peered in. Seeing the foot patrol and the seated guards clearly, he awaited the foot patrol to turn away from his mate. The minute the guard turned, he fell, and before he hit the ground, the seated guard took his last breath.

The team scaled the eight-foot cement walls with ease, despite the razor sharp wire and rusty barbed wire. They crept to their destinations, like stealth fighters on foot, covertly, confidently awaiting the cricket-communication, 'GO'.

Clint's heart was pounding, even though he had done this dozens of times before. He remained in the shadows, blending with the environment, now kneeling behind the breathless seated guard. He signaled for Wonka to stay, while he handled the second sleeping quarters. The walls were also cement. Clint could hear snoring, probably four to six, tough odds, even for a trained SEAL, if you need to work quietly. Clint heard the last cricket ready, and he signaled GO.

The communications shack was hit first, the one operator asleep in front of the radios, now permanently. The Commanders and two other sleeping quarters were hit simultaneously, with un-silenced gunfire erupting from one. Clint's estimate was accurate, five sleeping guards. By the time he aimed at the last living guard, he had his Chinese-made AK-47 in hand, but his finger never made it to the trigger.

The Camp Commander was not in his bed, but returning from a trip to the latrine, pistol in hand. He had fired two rounds while falling to the ground, neither bullet hitting its mark. He was better off dead than facing his previous prisoners.

The camp was neutralized, with only minor team injuries.

Unknown to Clint, the Camp Commander's two shots awakened an encamped Taliban patrol, less than a mile away.

Clint motioned for four to go to the guard stations, and three to accompany him to the cells. What he saw sickened him more. The first cell on the right had a single occupant laying on a cot. His gaunt stick-like figure was accentuated by his sallow, sunken eyes and long, stringy, filthy hair. He turned to the right to see another tiny cell, no more than four by five feet, its occupants' torsos half covered by the pond water, with one surprised prisoner frozen in shock with a river rat half eaten in his hands, its blood dripping from his chapped lips.

"Commander Clint Bear, sirs, US Navy SEAL Team Black, here to bring you home. Who is in charge?" No responses, everyone was in shock and physically and mentally beaten through months of physical and mental torture looking for secrets that were not within. Clint has seen this before, their minds, having been abused for months, disoriented, depressed, dismayed and hopeless. Then a camouflage-painted face appears out of nowhere in the darkness of night, telling them they are being rescued. It is beyond their reason. What lives, still, is the memory of their families and the patriotic duty to their country, and that is what Clint must tap into in a few short seconds. Clint removed his black hood and repeated the question.

"Sirs, the President of the United States has asked me to convey, to each of you, his heartiest congratulations on your rescue. Your wives and families are waiting for you back in America. Now, I have very little time, who is in charge?" Clint said in a more comforting tone.

"Lieutenant Covey, US Air Force," a man uttered, barely audible.

"Good. Lieutenant Covey, how many are you?"

"Six, no seven, counting me! Are you really here to rescue us?"

"Can you all walk, Lieutenant Covey?"

"Yes, I think so. I don't know," Covey said, seemingly using his last ounce of strength.

"Wonka, break these doors. Dobbs, you and Rollo help them outside. Let's take a capabilities audit and see how far these guys can make it. You've got three minutes. Move!"

Clint watched as they took the six malnourished, half figures of men out of the pond-filled cell. They were barely walking, their legs moving like stilts. He had to bend down and walked in a crouch to enter the small cell, his only hidden weakness beginning to surface. How could six men live, no, exist, in here, he was wondering when the anxiety caused by claustrophobia began to envelop him. Within seconds the sweats were beginning, a sign that his one weakness was not to be deprived. The smell was more than *foul, hair and shabby clothing rank with the months of food and human waste. Looking back and watching them walk out — Zombies, Clint thought, the poor bastards. The rage building within him for what he had seen too much of, and he very quickly shuffled out of the confined cage, before the anxiety claimed a position of authority within him.*

Once outside, he was startled out of his thoughts when he saw Covey jam his two fingers into the dead guard's eyes, and then spit in his lifeless face. It seemed to revive the other five with a new energy that they would need to survive the next three to four hours.

Why was one prisoner kept dry in the other cell...? No time for that now, cricket-communication told him of movement in the hills a half mile to the west. They needed to move out, now. He called the lookouts down, assigned one prisoner to each of his team members. The point and rear would have no one to look after, except the entire group. Clint would help where needed.

They moved over the bridge, making considerably more noise now. The former prisoners were ambulatory, but just, their movements mechanical, their eyes still in disbelief. Clint figured he could keep them moving for thirty to forty-five minutes before they would require rest. The once-fit solders were now skin and bones. He passed between them, handing each soldier a Snickers candy bar, hoping the sugar would give them another fifteen to thirty minutes, and telling them to stay in the path's shadows, to blend with the environment. Some tore at the wrapper as if the package contained a lifesaving medicine, others just bit through and ate, wrapper and all.

A half hour later, Dobbs came in from the rear and told Clint that company was no more than a third of a mile back, and closing. His estimate, a well-equipped patrol of eighteen to twenty, moving quickly, meaning they were experienced Taliban. Clint calculated that reaching the tactical team before they were hit by this patrol was remote. They had closed by a quarter mile in less than thirty minutes, at this rate they had ninety minutes tops, but needed double that to get to the support.

Dobbs didn't need the order — he volunteered, so did Wonka and Rollo. Clint took charge of Covey, who had been under Wonka's care. The team, less three, moved out, after leaving half their grenades and C-4 with the rear guard.

Dobbs, Wonka and Rollo went to work, having less than thirty minutes to engineer a welcoming committee for their hunters. The hunters would become the hunted. Eighteen men, single file, ten feet between them, would consume one hundred and eighty feet of path. They would wire two hundred feet, every five feet with the C-4 behind rocks that would become thousands of mini-missiles, tearing flesh from the bones and severing the bone itself, the triple trip wire at the lead. Two hundred feet further they would trip wire ten grenades and set three as land mines, to catch the few that survived the C-4. They would then double time it back, within an eighth mile from the team, dig in and wait for stragglers. They were exhausted when they heard the first explosion.

Clint was aware that Old Bear had replaced the six hot rocks in the lodge's tight circle and was now refilling the bucket, but his vision was not disturbed.

The former prisoners fell to their knees when the explosion's shock wave hit them. Clint sympathized, once fit and trained bodies that were accustomed to hardship and strain, but would now not respond. But they had to push on, or none of them would live to taste tomorrow.

Strangely, it was Covey who rallied the weak former POWs. His hands shaking, his voice scratchy and hoarse, commanded them to their feet.

"This is what we have prayed for! This is why we ate the rats and insects to stay alive. Our wives and children expect nothing less and we owe it to them. Now get up. Get up and live!" Covey cried. And after the last had risen, he turned to Clint, barely able to stand, and said with a smile, "We are ready when you are."

Everyone laughed a little. The tension was relieved, for the moment. Even Clint's. An interesting man, this Covey. I hope he makes it, Clint thought.

The second set of explosions happened about fifteen minutes after the first. A series of six explosions, which ones were the trip wire grenades or the land mines could not be determined. Best guesses at this point were that five to nine Taliban survived, and were continuing the chase, with a new fervor born out of seeing their countrymen, literally blown physically apart.

The hunters were moving much more slowly, now, but so were the hunted. The former POWs were so malnourished and in such poor physical condition they could not stand the pace much longer. Sixty minutes to the alternate destination near the mountain, the Chinooks better be there, Clint was thinking.

The gunfire erupted behind them, less than a quarter mile. Hole number four, there was a lot of gunfire for five to nine Taliban. Unknown to Clint, or the rear guard, another patrol heard the explosions and intercepted to help. There was actually now twenty-six fully armed, mad as hell Taliban. The gunfire and sporadic explosions lasted for almost twenty minutes, then silence. The team knew from the amount of fire what had happened, what they didn't know was how many Taliban were left and now on their trail.

Clint was thinking faster than words could be summoned to describe his thoughts. "Covey, can you walk without my help for about fifteen minutes?"

"Yes, do you want some help?"

Clint was momentarily stunned that Covey would ask him if help was needed, but replied, "Yes. Keep your men moving as fast as possible, faster than that, if you can! We will get out of this. Your wife Katherine loves you very much."

Covey, hearing her name, Katherine, was instilled with energy and determination where it was failing just seconds before. He could, no he would make it, now.

Clint then collected the last grenades and C-4 and ran toward the rear, alone. He made good time, but, with the sun beginning to rise, the heat and the extra weight was taking its toll. No more than an eighth mile later he stopped, calmed his breathing, and listened. They were close; he had ten minutes, no more. Setting plastic explosives came easy to Clint, he could see where and how to place them, intuitively. The grenades were just as easy. He calculated a fifty percent yield, cutting the hunters by half. While running back to the team he heard and felt the first of the three explosions, thinking that would slow them down, again.

Clint reasoned the low trip wire explosions would cause the hunters to be looking down, and therefore he set the next trip wire at five feet. Boom! He was right. The final trip was concealed in a sapling branch that partially protruded into the path. Five seconds after the first soldier passed, the four grenades exploded killing or severely injuring everyone within sixty feet. That's all he could do, the plan now being to make it to the tactical team before the remaining hunters made it to them.

Clint caught up to the team and saw Covey lagging behind, devoid of energy.

"Covey, put your arm around me."

"Hi, glad you made it."

They were close, maybe five more minutes. The first bullet hit the tree to Clint's left and sent bark and wood chips into Covey's face. Clint screamed, "Rear attack! Run to the mountain!"

Covey couldn't make it, with zero energy left he fell to his knees. Clint picked him up, throwing him over his left shoulder and continued to run. The gunfire increased, and they were getting close enough for a clear shot.

Clint heard the Chinook's engines roar to life. They were close. The team helped their rescues into the Chinook. The Chinook was beginning to lift when Clint shouted. The pilot hadn't seen Clint carrying Covey and assumed no more had made it. Hearing Clint yell, he turned the helicopter on a dime, heading closer to the path.

Clint was running toward the helicopter with Covey over his shoulder when the first bullet hit him. Undaunted, he made it to the helicopter, throwing Covey in, when the second bullet found its mark. The team pulled him in with one arm, while turning and gunning the engine with the other.

It was forty-five minutes later when they made it back to base. The pounding, caused by the rough air, constantly bounced Clint on the deck, keeping his wounds bleeding and the pain increasing.

The sweat was pouring off his head, his ponytail more like a hose for the sweat protruding from his scalp than hair. Clint was sitting in a puddle of water that had turned the sitting area into mud, having been in the sweat lodge for twenty-seven hours. Old Bear had carried nine sets of six hot stones in the leather satchel, refilled the bucket five times and slept zero times. The ninety-four-year-old man was exhausted, but proud of his most important vigil.

Clint awoke from his inner trip, squinting his eyes from the little light that shown through the small slit in the bear hide door of the lodge. His body was fatigued, but his mind was rejuvenated. He knew what his greater purpose was; his father was right, as he always was. The subconscious could bring clarity where conscious-muted disjointed thoughts brought confusion and frustration. The subconscious had taken him to where he had met, and once conquered the apocalyptic forces, the ultimate evil of man. The subconscious delineating what must be done, in perfect order for the more limited conscious mind to comprehend.

Momentarily, he thought of Brook, but it was a different, more evolved emotional and spiritual level of thought. She had touched him like no other. She had been sacrificed, as had Cabris, to save the lives of many, the worthiest purpose of a human life. The once-controlled emotions were now ready to be heard. Clint's heart filled with pride, his eyes swelling with tears, his body bending and his head nearly resting on his lap as he cried, uncontrollably.

Old Bear, much older today than twenty-seven hours ago, sat across the circle of six cooling rocks inside the lodge and waited for Clint to fully come back. He used the time efficiently, allowing his body to deeply relax, a poor substitute for his much-needed sleep. As Clint's crying slowed to weeping, Old Bear eased him into full reality, "Son, do you now know your purpose? What have you learned, my son?"

After a minute or so, lifting his head slowly, but purposely, Clint looked at his beloved old father, just boring into his rich black eyes. After a few more minutes, he said, "It has been a long time since I became the firsthand witness of the inhumanity of man. It has awakened the fire within me that I hoped would rest for eternity. Yes, I know my purpose, father, specifically in most part, generally in some."

"Tell me, my son. I need to know the purpose before I begin my own journey, to be your guide from the beyond."

"The vision of my purpose has always been with me, father. I chose not to see it. When in Afghanistan, I had the misfortune of seeing both the worst and the best of men, and when we abandoned the war I buried the worst memories out of the embarrassment and humiliation of association with a war our country didn't want. I was wrong, as the U.S. Government was wrong not to have finished what the others started, but could not complete alone. I must find the people who abused and took the lives of Brook and Cabris, and prevent them from doing it again. Ever! Not because they took my family —although I will enjoy funneling my rage to inflict slow and very painful death — but because of who they are and what they represent. The vision made this clear by focusing on the Camp 36 raid, killing of the guards, and the rescue of seven soldiers, one of whom is now President of the United States."

"San-Ja-Ka-Ko-Ka, why have you never told me of this?" Old Bear asked in astonishment.

"I had buried it, buried it too deeply. I did not want to remember, it caused a lot of pain."

"Yes. This is as it must be. The greatest Medicine Men went through a long period of pain and humiliation before those causing the pain could see. This is as it must be. You have told me specifically, but not generally. The killing of the camp guards would not stop the war, yet it had to be done. Saving the few who could be saved had to be done, but many were lost in the effort and many were not saved. The killing of the men who took our family will not stop the human sickness, yet, it to, must be done. Finding, and choking out the ultimate source, its motivation unknown, must, also, be done. But what has been told of the full purpose, generally?" Old Bear asked.

"I know that there is a sequence of events that starts with those men. Just as the camp was a single bee of a hive, these men are bees of a hive I know nothing about. That is my purpose, not just the bees but the hive and most probably well beyond. I hope the Creator guides me well."

"Come, bathe in the stream while I prepare some food. The fire still burns and we have a few hours before the full sun. We will talk more," Old Bear said as he struggled to his wearied feet.

CHAPTER 5:
MANDAN

C. Eric Douglas had taken the Philadelphia Room as his temporary office of Director of the Collaborative, using the Andrews Room for support staff until more appropriate facilities could be arranged. The location gave him easier access to the President, as well as the Secretary of State and Chief of Staff. He had an impressive array of capabilities and assets in place and functional for a short few days in office.

He relied mostly on CIA assets, those that he could commandeer with a telephone call as DCI. Eric has set up a mobile International Inter-Country Crisis Communications and Countermeasures Center in a newly leased old mill building. With the President's authorization, he had linked the II4C's impressive computers into both NSA and CIA to monitor the secure message traffic worldwide. The only unusual interception was a twenty-six second, dual phase locked loop, synchronized encrypted voice-to-voice transmission, recorded just seven hours earlier.

Also, with the President's authorization, II4C was included in the daily code change which enabled it to listen in, just like tapping a telephone, to all communications' traffic. The decoding was unnecessary; every word was recorded as spoken.

"Paul, what have you got for me?" Douglas said with a mixture of authority and helplessness.

"Sir, as you know we can't trace the call to a fixed geographic location. There were no discernible background noises but the receiver spoke with a Latin accent," Martin said quickly.

Martin was the best of the best. Douglas had asked, not ordered, him to this assignment. He was the best CIA communications junkie the agency had, or ever had. Martin was the one who broke the Soviet ultra-low frequency transmission codes after eleven months of nonstop deciphering.

"Sir, something bugs me about this transmission," Martin added. "There's no dialog. Just a core dump of info. I don't buy it. Stuff this important would incite some emotion, a few questions. You know, like, 'Are you sure, when, how long, what about', but nothing."

"I trust your instincts Martin, you know that. We are in a real time crunch here, and we only have time for instincts. What is your analysis?" Douglas said as he put his left hand on Martin's right shoulder.

"My bet is that the transmission was prerecorded. Based on the written transcript of the one the Pres' received, I'll bet that one was prerecorded as well. Now, why go through the bother of pre-recording, why take the added risk of having the equipment and evidence found? My money is on the diversion factor. The guy, the leaker, wants to be with someone else when the transmission is made to keep him clean in the eye of his friends. Kind of a Brutus with technology."

"You're going places, Martin. I'll be working for you some day. That is as accurate and concise an analysis as

I've ever been given." Douglas turned slightly as he walked out of the mobile II4C and added, "And I think you're right on target. We find the com system and we find our leaker."

The guitar music blared out of the cantina, along with the laughter and screams of the drunken customers. Inside the decrepit freestanding building, Carlos had his arms around his sexy 'executive secretary' lover's trim lower waist, with both hands kneading her ample ass. His remote lover, Catrina, loved the attention, from both Carlos and the drunk men sitting with their elbows on, and their back to, the bar.

Catrina not only loved the attention, but the pesos Carlos left behind, supplementing her income as a secretary at the Ford plant. She used a portion of the money to keep a fresh supply of skimpy fashionable dresses, the kind Carlos liked and kept coming back for. Tonight she was wearing a white knit body-hugging dress with a plunging neckline, selected to show her sizable unrestrained breasts. White was Carlos's favorite color, both because it contrasted with her golden skin and shoulder-length chestnut brown hair, and because it matched his typical white linen suit. The mid-thigh hem was also selected to show her black silk stockings, supported by the matching garter belt. To top off her visual seduction, she was as unrestrained in the crotch as she was in the chest.

Catrina was not a whore, but she enjoyed her time with Carlos. It was safe, very safe. Everyone knew who he was and their interference would risk their lives as well as their families' lives. She knew what Carlos did, and never pried, never wanted anything but safe raunchy, exhibitionistic sex, and the expensive gifts and added income.

Carlos needed this escape. The next batch of White Ice supplies would be ready for processing upon his return. He was high on his success, higher than ever before knowing he was so close to being finished with this business, the cartel and inner circle, forever. He wanted release, not by satisfying himself, but to be with his woman.

While they danced, he was thinking about her inner moist warmth and began to become erect. His hands squeezing Catrina's buttocks, fingers pulling the dress higher as they kneaded her buns. Several men at the bar were whistling and encouraging them to keep going. "Amarrar! Amarrar! Ramera!"

Catrina heard the yelling "More! More! Whore!", and knowing she was no whore, but, also knowing she was exciting dozens of men in a safe environment, kept it going. She protested to Carlos, just enough to let him know that she, to, was enjoying herself, an act they had played out many times before.

They were alone on the dance floor, with only a few couples left at tables at this time of the evening, who were all intently watching them, their passion being ignited. The jukebox stopped, but they continued the mock dance and, finally, someone invested in more music. The bartender dimmed the lights around the bar, and watched expectantly.

She felt the dress hem rise above her butt, knowing her ass was fully exposed, except that covered by Carlos's hands. His head buried in her chest, her hands fondling his crotch, passion getting out of control. They decided to go back to his hotel and continue in private, much to the disappointment of the men at the bar.

Carlos would depart in the morning, for his meeting with the cartel, without waking Catrina, leaving double the normal amount of pesos, for what he hoped would be his last low-flying airplane trip through the mountains.

***

Helena had sent notice of the emergency Board of Directors Meeting for 9:00 AM the next day. As Corporate Secretary, she was the responsible party, but Clint had not told her the basis of the emergency. Everyone had been expected to attend, and was there. The meeting was about to be called to order by the Chairman and Chief Executive Officer.

The gavel hitting the wooded stop opens most major Board Meetings, not AIEC. Clint's bare knuckles rapping on the table, while asking for silence, opened this and all Board Meetings before it.

"Can we come to order, please?" Clint said in monotone. "Thank you all for coming with short notice. Helena, please verify a quorum and confirm to me."

"We have a quorum, full Board attendance," She replied knowing that a simple majority was all that was required.

Clint had personally selected each individual on the Board. He did so not build a "rubber stamp" Board, but to build wisdom in all vital areas of business within each decision taken. Of the five members in addition to Art and Clint, there was Stephen Weisman, Senior Partner of the Price Waterhouse LLP accounting firm; Addison Brinkston, Partner and Founder of Brinkston, Tate, and Hannah, the elite Wall Street investment banking firm; Senator Lloyd Phillips, Republican, Colorado; Eleanor Wallace Esquire, Senior Partner of Hale, Hinglesly, and Wallace; and Dr. Bernard Thurston, Founder of Thurston Industries, a billion dollar international electronics manufacturing company.

"Good. Please note that in the minutes, Helena," Clint requested and then went on. "This meeting has but one purpose, to ask your support and forgiveness. I need a leave of absence to tend to personal business. I expect to be gone anywhere from three to nine months. In my absence, I want the company under the capable supervision of Roger Whitehouse, our Chief Financial Officer."

All eyes immediately shifted from Clint to Art, his half-brother and Senior Vice President. Art was visibly stunned, his eyes bulging and his body lurching toward the conference table. His lips were drawn thin, breathing heavier and the anger finally escaped, "You son-of-a-bitch! I have slaved for this company. You owe me! And this is how I am treated, humiliated in front of my friends! Well fuck you Clint! You'll get no support from me, now or ever!" he screamed as he slammed his fists on the table. "We will see who wins in the end, loser! We will see who really helps the tribes," he spat out as he stormed out of the conference room, slamming the door shut behind him.

The rest of the Board were shaken by the visceral threats, but not surprised. Clint, not surprised either, continued, "I have executed a Power of Attorney, giving Roger full voting control of my stock, and your support will give him control of the company."

Roger was completely surprised, but stereotypical to his financial profession, he remained silent. He respected Clint. Beyond respect, he loved Clint, and although he was not of Indian blood, he respected the Indian way. The Board, knowing the importance of Indian leadership, would be taking a leap of faith for both him and Clint to vote with Clint's wishes.

"All in favor of my request, please indicate by raising your hand."

Slowly, with heads darting from one another, to insure they were not the only one to take this unprecedented action, placing the American Indian Electronics Corporation in the hands of a white eye... all hands went up. All hands, amongst whisperings.

"Clint, I'll accept this responsibility only if it is given temporarily. You must agree to assume your rightful place as CEO upon your return. Therefore, let the minutes show that this is a temporary assignment as 'Acting CEO', only. Agreed?" Roger stated clearly to a very receptive Board.

"Agreed. And thank you Roger," Clint said and then added, "Meeting adjourned." With another wrap of knuckles on the table the meeting was officially over, and with the sound still reverberating off the walls, Clint turned and left the boardroom.

Clint had packed what he thought would be needed: food, clothes, money and weapons. He threw the black nylon duffel bags and the stuffed camouflaged backpack in the truck and headed off to Art and Old Bear.

Art's house was in shambles, the result of his very recent lost temper. He was gone, with nothing to indicate where. Maybe his father would know, unlikely, but possible.

Old Bear was home, his house packed for gifting. He wanted his friends and distant family to have many of the gifts his father had given him, and whose father had given him. Old Bear tried to pass the Indian heritage on, to keep the memories alive. He had presented his most personal treasures to Clint and Art a few days earlier.

The pungent odor from the lit Nic Nic, Old Bear's special mixture of tobacco and various aromatic herbs, did not surprise to Clint as he entered the small ranch-style cabin. For the American Indian, pipe smoking was the introductory step to all-important affairs and no business could be entertained before the ceremony of smoking is over. Old Bear was sitting cross-legged on the family room floor, chanting softly while he smoked his double bowl ceremonial pipe. It was time.

Clint sat directly in front of Old Bear, cross-legged, knees to knees, his eyes watering, but not from the smoke. The ancient pipe was the last artifact from their Mandan forefathers. Its painted markings had long since flaked off, but the story of the great Mandan sickness, the smallpox epidemic started in the 1830s by white traders that virtually eliminated the race, was told by the elaborate gold inlaid engravings on the pipe's body and bowl.

Old Bear took a long pull, lifted the pipe to the heavens using his free hand to gracefully fan the escaped smoke to his face and hair, and then offered the pipe to Clint, holding it parallel to his chest. Old Bear continued his chant. Clint, using both hands slowly, accepted the pipe, raised it to the heavens, the earth, and then brought it to his lips taking an equally long pull.

He was now appointed, the authority passed by the presentation of the ancestral medicine pipe. All the power of the Mandan people, now, and forever, would be with Clint until he passed the power to another of his choosing.

Clint saw his father's ancient and weathered buffalo hide medicine bag leaning on his right leg. Clint faded back to his childhood when Old Bear told him of the medicine bag. He could see the power and sincerity in Old Bear's night-black eyes as he passed a piece of Mandan history to his son. "The medicine bag is the key to Indian life. It will be your life's guardian, it will keep you safe in battle, warm during winter and provide company when alone. You will construct your own medicine bag on your fourteenth season and place within it your person. It will be sealed and never opened."

Rising unsteadily, he embraced Clint lovingly and handed him his most precious possession, his medicine bag. Clint held the embrace and looked a long, last look at Old Bear's face. His sun-darkened face didn't show the ninety-four years, with just a few wrinkles sloping down from the eyebrows. The once free-falling gray and black hair was now loosely braided on both sides, draping down hiding his ears with his mouth slightly opened, hinting to his real age.

Clint then watched his father walk silently from the house toward the baron hills, his last sight of Old Bear being blurred by his tears. Old Bear would go to his place, ending his circle of life, back to dust. Circles. Clint watched until Old Bear was well out of sight, and then watched hours more. He felt more alone than he could imagine… Cabris, Brook and now Old Bear, gone, but in his heart and memories.

The place to start his hunt was where the bodies of his sister and fiancée were found. He would triangulate that position with that of the place where the two other women were found. The third position of the triangulation would be a series of the most likely remote positions, calculated by a four hour, or less, one-way trip and access to fresh water. His logic being influenced by paved and unpaved roads. They would be prioritized and sequenced by "on-foot access", to maximize his use of time, just like he was searching for an outpost of camp. It was all coming back.

The hunters have unknowingly become the hunted.

Clint parked his truck in the parking lot of the Creede entrance to the Rio Grande National Forest, and proceeded on foot due east to Pool Table Mountain, the first of his sequenced possible locations. It would take half the day to reach the plateau by foot, assuming he could average five miles per hour in the mountainous terrain.

He would avoid the rangers station and the hiking paths, to avoid all people, except his prey. Silent movement came natural to him, stepping on the embedded rocks, moss and pine needles, never on dry leaves, sticks and loose rocks. He stayed in the shadows as much as possible for camouflage as well as to reduce the increased dehydration resulting from direct sunlight. Dehydration would become more prevalent at the higher altitudes.

His appearance would raise suspicions here, not in Afghanistan. Clint wanted to blend with his environment, selecting his canvas camouflage bodysuit in dark greens and browns. The cover story would be a single hunter, looking for bear. He would change if he entered the snowcapped mountain peaks. Clint could survive for an indefinite length of time with the contents of his backpack and his many nylon zippered pockets. He was determined not to become a CEO again, at least not until this mission was successfully completed, the hive terminated.

The crisp mountain air was getting progressively colder as he neared the plateau near Pool Table Mountain, elevation 12,142 feet. Clint noted this as a key difference from the hot and humid lands of Afghanistan in the summer, and compensated for it with warmer clothing. The map indicated a rise, overlooking the plateau, that he would use as an observation area. Only another thirty minutes, with the sun almost directly overhead, his breathing accelerated only slightly due to thin air and physical exertion.

Clint left his pack at the foot of the rise which helped make the last two hundred feet come faster. He eased up to its pinnacle, slowly inching his head over the top so rapid movements, which the human eye is most adept at detecting, would not attract attention. Once his eyes crested the rocky ridge, he viewed the location.

The plateau was breathtakingly beautiful, lush green fields protected by tall evergreen trees and fed by a small mountain stream. It looked like a pool table. There was no sign of human life, now or before. Possibility number one was ruled out, on to number two after a brief rest and nourishment.

Possibility number two was due north, over approximately six miles of extreme mountainous terrain. It was called Mesa Peak, elevation 12,958, because of its flat rocky mesa. Clint would be there within two to three hours.

Mesa Peak was also uninhabited. Possibility number three was Los Pinos Pass. He would sleep here and move at first light. Rest was a necessity, especially when scaling the mountain ranges of the Continental Divide. Los Pinos Pass is no more than twenty miles, as the eagle flies, but it will take Clint at least six hours to reach the area.

He camped for the night, making a small, contained fire to cook the rabbits he'd snared earlier. Using very dry hardwood from fallen trees insured a smokeless fire and continued privacy. It is unlikely that anyone would be near, except the possible experienced hunter. He nestled into a rocky crevasse, his belly warm with freshly cooked rabbit, and pulled his thin insulated blanket over his body. Sleep came quickly under the partially smiling moon.

Having finished the leftover rabbit for breakfast, Clint took care to leave the ground as he had found it, with no trace of his being there. Covet mother earth. The sun would rise in less than an hour. He wanted to be at Los Pinos Pass before the sun was fully overhead. The sun would be his friend, then, with no long shadows to alert the rangers sitting in their tall watchtowers.

The trip took less time than he had expected after finding an infrequently traveled old game trail that was well off the main dirt road. Clint was on guard. He could see that many branches of young saplings along the road had been bent back, some broken and stripped of leaves recently. Probably a vehicle, Clint was thinking while he walked and waited for a soft earth portion of road where the indentations would confirm his thinking. Not more than two hundred and fifty feet further, he had his confirmation, a puddle that would freeze tonight, but now was liquid enough to leave the markings of two different tires. One a regular tire print, that no doubt the police could match to the make, model and year of a car. The second was a wide deep-treaded off-road tire, and by the direction of the tire bite, it appeared to be headed away from Los Pinos Pass. Could be hunters, could be the hunted.

Clint moved more cautiously, now. If they were his hunted, then he did not want to alert them. He has been aware from the start that he knew nothing about these men, who they were, where they had come from, how many there were, were they armed, trained... In Afghanistan, he had always had the benefit of HUMINT or other form of intelligence, even if in the end it turned out mostly wrong. It was something to build plans around, knowing that his training would anticipate the unexpected and use it to maximum advantage.

The small rise was well positioned, and Clint could see three tents, a mess table and a five-hundred-foot straight-grassed plateau with tire indentations. They must have a plane, probably a STOL aircraft or a helicopter. Nothing else could land on such a short runway. Probably a plane, as the helicopter would not have the range. The camp looked deserted, but not permanently... they would have taken the gear, not wanting to leave any traces back to them. Clint studied the camp for another twenty minutes, taking in every detail, especially the partially hidden antennas, before he began to work his way down the rise and into the camp.

Trees and foliage have a natural lay, symmetrical and uniform to the trained eye, disorganized and random to the untrained. Clint's trained eye told him the trees and foliage had been disturbed, but why? Then he saw it, a red diode laser pointing at a photo-diode receiver. If Clint had broken the beam, an intrusion alarm would have been activated, probably a silent alarm. The entire camp perimeter was alarmed, obviously a well-financed but foolish amateur, he was thinking. The alarm system must have cost fifty to seventy-five thousand dollars, and it was the incorrect type of system for a wilderness camp perimeter. The beam from a photo-diode laser diode system would be broken by animals and falling branches, even windblown branches. It also required a great deal of power, and since there is no generator running, it must be a battery system, one hell of a lot of batteries.

This one thing told Clint more than he knew before most insertions in Afghanistan. They were well financed. They were out of their element. They were not knowledgeable about security, which usually extended to all aspects of warfare and intelligence. These were his hunted.

Clint stepped over the laser beam, silently and cautiously. The enemy could be sleeping in the tents. He stayed in the shadows, unseen and unheard. The hunter.

Clint removed the knife from his boot and made a small incision in the tent, the shadows covering his shadow. Enough for him to see the two sleeping bags, on cots, were unoccupied. He moved on to the second of the three tents and found the sleeping bag rolled up on the cot, the tent unoccupied. The third and largest tent had one front flap open, exposing the large table and boxes, but no sign of life. The camp was unoccupied, temporarily.

The search was quick, starting with the large tent. The boxes were empty. The spoons, bowls, funnels and plastic sacks on the table were the only sign of something abnormal. The single cot tent was totally empty, except for the Braun battery operated world-band clock radio on the small table next to the bed. The L.L. Bean sleeping bag was virtually untraceable, as was the cot and chair. The Coleman gas lantern was cold. Moving quickly now, Clint went to the third and last tent to find the same cots and sleeping bags. The table between the cots had one drawer just below the tabletop where the cold Coleman lantern was placed. Clint opened it carefully, looking for the booby traps that were not there. Inside the drawer was a brown paper bag, a Colt Series 80 Semiautomatic 45 caliber pistol and three boxes of hollow-point bullets. He took the pistol first, and with the speed and precision of a factory assembler, disassembled the action and broke the firing pin with his larger boot knife. The weapon was reassembled within 30 seconds, the owner none the wiser. He opened the brown paper bag and froze in horror.

Less than eighteen miles due west, Jesús and Julio were about to enjoy a late lunch at Lake City's most remote bar, The Flats. They ordered cold Coors beer, in long necks, and menus, unaware that their camp had been penetrated. Neither could cook worth a damn, so their diet consisted of canned spaghetti, beans, eggs and bacon. Carlos wouldn't allow beer at the camp, fearing, correctly, that alcohol would cause mistakes.

A sweaty fat woman, about fifty, with her gray hair piled in a bun on top of her head and wearing well broken-in jeans, hammered two beers down on the table. The action caused the beer to foam out the top of the long neck bottles and drip down on the stained and cigarette-burned wooden table.

"You guys got money? I don't run tabs here. Ya pay as ya drink," she said with her hands on her hips, like a prison warden.

Laughing, Jesús slapped a fifty on the table saying, "Keep them beers coming, honey. There's more where that comes from."

"We don't want no trouble. You boys drink quietly like. Hear?"

"Momma, we's thirsty and hungry. That's all."

"Good boys," she said as she spun around to the next table.

The bag of jewelry and credit cards told the story of how many young women were taken, abused, savagely raped, killed and buried in shallow graves. He didn't take the time to count the rings and bracelets, but there were dozens of them. As he was closing the bag, ready to stuff it into one of his deep zippered pockets, he saw Brook's engagement ring.

"Those bastards will die, slowly, very slowly and very painfully," Clint whispered out loud, partially to himself and partially as a warning. "They will never do this again. Never."

The second round of long neck Coors had arrived when they opened the menus. And, not wanting to show their ignorance, they called the fat waitress and ordered.

"Ya got just steak and potatoes?"

"Sure. You boys real hungry?"

"We could eat the damn cow!"

:I got somthin' for ya then. How's about two-inch T-Bones smothered with onions and home fried potatoes?"

"Ciertamente! Perfecto! Dos. And beer," Jesús said as he pointed to the two long neck bottless of Coors.

Clint reasoned that two were still here, one gone — two sleeping bags rolled out, one rolled up. Based on the lack of food supply, they have probably gone to the closest town, Lake City, eighteen miles due west. He would be there by 18:00.

The hunted unaware of the hunter.

***

Jesús finished his steak first and set out to the general store to load up with supplies. Julio stayed behind, taking his time with the enormous steak. The fat waitress was angry that the table has remained occupied for three hours and the bar restaurant was beginning to fill up with workers, thirsty and hungry after a long hot workday. She finally went over to Julio, took the fifty and rudely asked, "Ya need anything else? I need the table. You can finish your beer at the bar."

Jesús had filled the green Roadrunner's trunk with bottled water, eggs, bacon, canned spaghetti, beans and bread. He was on his way back to the camp, driving past The Flats and noticed through the window of the bar that Julio was getting up from the table, and should, soon, be right behind him in the off-road vehicle.

Julio had other plans, and ordered another long neck Coors from the bartender. After all, what was waiting for him at the camp? Ugly fat Jesús, no beer and no women, and this place was beginning to come alive. To hell with him, Julio was thinking, the señoritas are just coming in and I'm staying. Who knows, I could get lucky.

Clint had reached the very outskirts of the town called Lake City by 18:50 and the sun was beginning to set. He headed toward the town walking in the lightly forested area about one hundred feet away from the double lanes of Route 149. He was heading north when a green Roadrunner came barrel-assing past. It was too dark and the Roadrunner going too fast for Clint to see who the driver was. He could, however, make out the stationary sign that said Lake City Town Center, five miles. Clint picked up his pace.

The town, proper, could be seen for miles. The area was flat and the closer to the town he came the more barren it became. There appeared to be a roadhouse a few miles or so outside the town, and only a mile from Clint. He decided to make that his first recon.

The back of the roadhouse, called The Flats, provided plenty of shelter due to the beer boxes, spent kegs and other boxes piled up awaiting removal and replenishment. Clint stashed his backpack and put on an old shirt and jeans before venturing into the roadhouse. He had become a patron-to-be, as if he had parked his pickup around the side and walked toward the front entrance. He noticed the large off-road vehicle, a Bronco, close to the front door, and veered to look at the tires. Bingo! The tires had the same unusual "V" type bite. The hunted were in the roadhouse.

Clint wasn't sure what he would do if he, when he, encountered those scum. His immediate problem was identifying them amongst fifty or sixty people. He would rule out the women first. Then those that were in large groups, say more than four. That would reduce the possible suspects to a manageable number. But, what would he do when he identified those scum? *I want to kill them painfully,* he thought, *but something is telling me different. Intuition? Was Old Bear trying to guide him?* He could not discern, yet.

Clint walked into The Flats speedily, like he had been there many times before. He took careful note as to who was taking careful note of him. No one was aroused by his presence, a good sign.

He noticed that the beer of choice was Bud. "G'me a Bud," Clint said to the bartender.

"You got it," the bartender said grabbing one out of the chest just behind where Clint took a seat.

"Thanks. Always get this busy at this time of day?" Clint said while accepting his Bud.

"Yeah. The hands, they get off work at about six, come here to wash the dust down. Don't remember seeing you before."

"Just passing through, on my way to Durango."

"Kind of out of the way, ain't ya?" the bartender asked with a quizzical look.

"Yeah, safely out of the way. I ran a Statee's speed trap up on Route 50, goin' at least 110, and lost him on the back roads. Thought I would take the scenic route in case he's still out looking. Know what I mean?" Clint said with a big smile on his face.

"I love to hear those guys g'tting' beat. Here's another Bud, on me, motor man!" the bartender said as he handed Clint another beer.

"Say, whose the big off-road Bronko belong to? Hell of a rig!" Clint said in passing.

"I think it belongs to that Mexican at the other end of the bar. Why, think he stole it?"

"Who knows, I don't give a shit. You?"

"Nope. I gotta move, thirsty people," the bartender said as he went off to earn more tips.

Clint eyed the Mexican at the end of the bar. Tall, lanky, kind of greasy and a little drunk. He was hitting on a tough-looking weathered woman fieldhand, his interests clearly in feeling her breasts. She was just barely playing along, no doubt to get free drinks until someone better came along. Clint decided that he was that someone, and eased on over to talk.

"Hello darlin', this seat taken?" Clint said as he sat down on the opposite side of the Mexican.

"Free country, honey," she said with an experienced smile. "The name's Elizabeth, people call me Liz."

"Jake. People call me Jake," Clint said equaling her smile.

"Hey, you don't know who owns that off-roader out there. Hell of a piece of machinery!"

"Sorry, not mine, don't know," Liz said, a little disappointed that the topic of conversation was a damned truck and not her. But, Julio took notice of the question and began to wonder what to do. He wanted Liz for the night, but now this guy moves in on Liz and asks about his truck. What the hell?

"Hey Liz, who's your friend?" Clint said, pointing to the Mexican, "Why don't you introduce me?"

"Jake, he's not my friend, and I don't know his name. He's just buying me beers and stealing quick feels. I think I'm getting the best of the bargain," Liz said loud enough for Julio, the Mexican, to hear, while looking at Clint, obviously checking him out, head to crotch.

Julio, half-drunk and a lot stupid, yelled, "Perra, bitch!"

Clint walking around Liz toward Julio said, "Hey, calm down! That's no way to talk to a lady. She is politely saying she prefers me to you, so get lost, scumbag!"

Julio's move was clumsy and obvious. He reached under his shirt, pulling out a WWII jungle knife and started at Clint, slowly, cautiously. The Flats bar, once noisy and active, became quiet and still.

Clint in a chillingly icy tone, "Son, put that knife down before you get seriously hurt. It took a lot of will power to say this and this warning will not be repeated. Period."

"Gringo. Why are you interested in my truck? Why did you hit on my woman?"

"I'm not your woman! I don't even know you, asshole!" Liz screamed as she moved further away, giving them plenty of room.

Julio began to inch closer to Clint, the knife in his right hand, his back hunched and feet spread apart for balance. Liz motioned for the others to move way out of his way.

"I know who you are, and your two friends. I know about the other women who couldn't defend themselves," Clint said while standing perfectly still, totally non-threatening.

"Who the fuck are you, Indian? I don't care, you're dead, asshole," Julio said as he lunged toward Clint's chest.

Clint countered, easily, grabbing Julio's right wrist, and while looking straight into his eyes, very slowly forced the knife, still in Julio's hand into his own chest, almost like a movie in slow motion and then an upward thrust severing the sternum and the heart. Julio was dead in seconds; Clint had not moved from where he was standing. Liz ran in horror, thinking that minutes before, she was hoping to wake up next to this murderer tomorrow morning.

The blood was flowing out and around Julio's lifeless body, the smell sticky sweet. Clint was abruptly snapped out of remembering the many times the smell had reached his nose, when Cole Cunningham flashed his badge and ordered two plainclothes detectives to take Clint into custody and two others to take the Mexican's body.

Not a word was exchanged as Clint was whisked off to the field op's area, a stall in an old barn on the east side of town. "Just who the hell do you think you are? We have been trailing this guy for days, our only solid lead. Now he's a damn corpse! What the fuck do you think you are doing, Clint?" Cole tried to regain some composure. "I know you've lost your sister and fiancée to these scum bags, but this is a police matter. You take it personal and look what happens, you commit murder!"

"Wait a minute. The entire bar watched that guy come at me. Hey, you had the place staked out, you must have seen it too. I warned him. He attacked me. It was self-defense, one hundred percent, and you know it. That bastard killed, no raped, repeatedly, and then killed my sister and fiancée. What would you do?" Clint countered.

"I saw it differently, not self-defense. With your skills, you could have incapacitated him in the flash of an eye. No. You chose to incapacitate him, permanently! No, unless you give me a good reason, it was not self-defense, it was premeditated, cold-blooded murder," Cole said as he left the cramped barn stall.

Once outside the barn he whispered to Agent Forest, "Let's let him stew on that for a few minutes. Got any coffee? I just can't believe our luck, finally things are going our way."

There was not much on the President's mind, more important than the Martial Law Drug Plan, or more to the point, its impact on the lives of his family.

""Eric, I am aware that these things always take longer than planned and twice longer than one would desire, but I'm still growing impatient," President Covey said, somewhat exasperated.

"Mr. President, let me recount the latest events and provide a status report in the process," Douglas suggested. "Six days ago, you delivered the most important speech of your career and within minutes of leaving the Plaza Hotel, you were contacted on a totally secure communications medium. The message clear, with no counter dialog, was that your family will be dead and you will live only long enough to see them dead. Forgive me for being so sterile, Mr. President. Unknown to you or us at the time, our only deep-cover agent, who had infiltrated the organization, was dead. We, through process of elimination, have concluded that there is a mole within the White House, at the highest levels, leaking very sensitive information, amongst the information was the content of your speech and the codes to your squawk box. We don't, however, know the extent of the information leaked and therefore cannot ascertain the total damage done as of this date. Separately, although the possibility of the events being intrinsically related, or specifically related, seem possible if not probable, Clint Bear's wife to be and sister are found dead, presumably by the same organization's hand. We insert our own mole — Agent Meceli — into the White House organization, known only to us, Robert, and Clint, and we find a deplorable absence of security within the administration's core. This is where we believe the mole to be operating and a short list is due tomorrow morning. One more thing, Mr. President, Clint Bear has been arrested for the murder of the only suspect we have, or had, under surveillance less than an hour ago."

"Oh my God! How did he get to the druggie… I mean, so fast? Haven't we been working this for weeks, even years, and he gets there in a few days? He's good, I know that from firsthand experience, but this good?" Bill said, wondering. "No, I can't believe he would murder anyone. Self-defense, yes, not murder!"

"Mr. President, we are at an impasse. Our only lead is dead, but there is an option, if Clint goes along with it."

"What is it?" Bill asked.

"We could position Clint as our new deep-cover agent. He's indigenous. He's got better skills than most agents, maybe all of our agents. But most importantly, he's got motivation," Douglas said logically.

"It has some merit, if Clint will agree. How do you mean to convince him?" Bill queried.

"That's the delicate part. We can encourage him if he thinks that he will be charged with murdering the Mexican," Douglas eased out carefully.

"No way. That's dishonest and I won't stand for it. He will not be charged with murder, and you know it. It was self-defense, wasn't it? Wasn't it?" the President yelled.

"I was not there, but I believe it was self-defense, yes. I also believe, with his talents, he could have disarmed the Mexican and prevented his death, but emotion overcame him."

"There's not a court in America that would convict based on that, and you know it. No. I will not allow this to be used as leverage. Clint must make the decision voluntarily. If he agrees to help, he is to be cleared all the way. He's to know everything. Is that perfectly clear, Douglas?" the President demanded.

"Yes, that is perfectly clear," Douglas said, nodding his head but not at all happy about losing control of his decision.

Cunningham replaced the receiver in the secure field radio set and, shaking his head, walked toward the barn.

"Okay, Clint, what's it going to be? You going to help or are you going to fry?" Cole said wearily, ignoring the discussion he just finished with Director Douglas.

"It appears that I have few options, right?"

"No, not right. It was self-defense, emotionally charged, unnecessary, but self-defense. Make the decision to help based on your wanting to help put these bastards away, and only that." Cole couldn't manipulate Clint. Clint had been through too much already. His decision had to be clean and from his heart.

"My answer is the same. But thanks for making it voluntary, Cole. I'm in. It is my destiny, my greater purpose in life." Cole frowned in confusion "You wouldn't understand, but the Indians believe the Creator has a purpose for everything and every person. Our life's work is to determine what that purpose is and then to complete the circle. My father, Old Bear, has seen this just before his passing. I have seen it as well. What do you want me to do?" Clint's intuition was guiding him.

"You're right, I don't fully understand, but I'm personally grateful for your help. And, your country, even though they don't know it, is in your debt," Cole said as he sat down beside Clint.

"Now, hold on to your butt and let me bring you all the way in and you will fully understand why I'm so grateful," Cole said as he cut the restraints from Clint's arms. "Remember, this is fully classified and I am your control. There are only six people who know about you, and it is mandatory that it stay that way. Understood and agreed?"

"Understood and agreed," Clint responded. "But there are seven people, not six, who know about me. Everyone forgets about Sheila Turcott, the President's personal secretary."

"You're right, sorry. Now, let me brief you," Cole said. "Agent Paul Cudson was a deep-cover specialist. He and I were agency cadets together and became close friends, best friends. As you know he was killed about ninety miles from here. On his body was a small sack containing a substance that looked like crack cocaine. The labs broke it down to everyday chemicals and solvents. There was a trace of real cocaine, but unnecessary for the drug's effect. The drug, chemical really, is smoked or ingested orally. Let me tell you what the lab told me — the stuff is a powerful narcotic with a chemical structure like crack cocaine, but made with ordinary and fully legal chemicals. Enough for a single high probably costs about fifty cents to make, can be made without breaking the law, is undoubtedly the best high around, especially if you like to be sexually stimulated, is hyper-addictive and is seriously and absolutely lethal. The chemical base is arsenic and after a few highs the stuff will begin to eat into your brain until you become quite insane and eventually die. If the chemist removes the cocaine, which has only a minor instantaneous impact on the high because it is in such a low percentage by volume to the base, it is completely legal. Based on the high the lab calculated for the average one hundred fifty-pound person, using between two and three times will trigger the absolute addiction and between five and eight times you absolutely and positively die. Clint, this stuff will hit the streets and millions of unsuspecting hedonistic people will die."

"God help us Cole," Clint whispered. "The President's Martial Law Drug Plan couldn't have come at a more appropriate time."

"Yeah, the problem is that with Paul Cudson and Julio dead, we have few leads into the drug ring producing and distributing the drug. That's where you come in."

"How?" Clint asked with a little frustration.

"In just a few short days you were able to track the druggies to their outpost. I'm ashamed to say it took us months. You know about the new Department C and its charter, now called the Collaborative. Douglas is heading it up with the full support of the President. The President is aware of our conversation and supports your recruitment into the Collaborative. We want you to infiltrate the drug operation, undercover, and learn who makes up the organization, their plans for the new chemical drug, their distribution system and the identity of the chemist," Cole spat out in military precision.

"Clint, this operation has killed at least sixteen women that we know of, including your sister and fiancée. We believe they are working this geographic area because it is easy to divert the drug attention to the Indian tribes. You know, build on the stereotype Indian reservation drug problem."

Clint was in deep thought, recalling his sweat and his purpose, specifically. Then he remembered the brown paper bag of "personal effects" he had taken from the druggies' camp. He looked around for his duffel bags the agents had recovered from the rear of The Flats. Reaching in the front zippered pocket, he retrieved the bag and after removing Brook's engagement ring, tossed it to Cole.

"Their camp is in Los Pinos Pass, eighteen miles west of Lake City. There appear to be three regular inhabitants, two road vehicles and one STOL aircraft. The families may want the personal effects of their loved ones. I think you have underestimated the number of women," Clint said while caressing Brook's gold band with his fingers. "Promise me you will attempt to find the families of all these women."

Cole caught the bag and gently emptied its contents onto a table near his chair. He was horrified at the sight of the watches, wedding bands, necklaces, earrings, bracelets and credit cards. A quick count indicated the Cole may have underestimated by one hundred percent, that upwards of thirty-two women had been victimized. He was horrified, but it was helpful information about the enemy. Only those things that had easy street value were in this bag. That indicates the druggies are not pros, but well-financed street thugs.

"One more thing Clint, you must agree to follow orders, be re-trained in the latest weapons and tactics and most important, put the interests of the U.S. Government first," Cole added with perfect timing, hiding his horrified reaction to the contents of the bag. "And, I will have the labs work the evidence and... Oh, damn it, it sounds so DEA-like," Cole spat out with both hands rubbing his face. "Clint, I want these bastards, maybe not as much as you, but I want them. They'll bury me before I'll let this close unsolved, and I won't sleep a sound night until they are out of business. Permanently," Cole breathed out with tears building in the deep corners of his eyes.

Clint simply nodded gently, closing his eyes and breathing deeply, knowing his purpose had started. The tranquility of his awakening was interrupted by Cole, "Your code name is Mandan."

CHAPTER 6:
THE BEGINNING

"Sir, this transmission lasted only twenty-one seconds; would you like to hear it now?" Paul Martin, geek communications expert extraordinaire, asked.

"Play away," Douglas responded.

Paul switched on the digital playback and adjusted the volume of the sound fanatic's dream system:

"Clint Bear recruited into operative role. Deep cover to infiltrate our organization. Be extremely careful with recruits. Photos and biography to follow."

Douglas pondered the message. No names, no hint of location. Some hint of concern. Knowledge of the cover operation. The caller said "our organization", clearly traitorous, if from anyone at the highest levels. What was more interesting, he thought, was what the caller did not say, and therefore, what the caller was not aware of.

"Thanks Paul. Keep listening," Douglas said as he turned on a dime and quickly stepped out of the Il4C's compartment door.

Paul assumed, correctly, that Douglas had an idea of the caller's identity and was on his way to confirm it.

***

"Mr. President, it is time to fish or cut bait. I believe the leaker or mole is one of two people close to you and we need to confirm, as quickly as possible and beyond doubt, which one is the traitor."

"Who do you suspect, Eric?" the Bill said with a blend of excitement and concern.

"Mr. President, I should not respond. Hear me out on this please, sir. If I do respond you will treat them quite differently and they will, as a result, go dormant on us. Then we'll lose our chance for confirmation. I respectfully suggest that you allow me the time to confirm before I reply to your very legitimate question," Douglas carefully responded.

"I see, and it does make sense, but mine is a concern for national security. If these suspects are within my confidence, as they surely must be, then we have the opportunity to prevent another breach of security. Christ, just the ability for them, I mean him or her, to view new confidential information every day is a frightening thought. Are you sure this is the best way?" the President countered.

"Yes, that is very true, and yes I am sure, Mr. President. We more than likely have a mole who has had access to the most secret of information in this office, for many years. The leaker could have come with your administration or have existed for countless administrations. We simply don't know. If we risk alerting the mole to our suspicions, and the mole goes dormant, it is unlikely we will ever know who it is. Therefore, we risk the mole staying within the secret information circle for years to come. Mr. President, I suggest that the decision is one of taking the lesser of two evils," Douglas postured.

Sighing deeply while rubbing the rough stubble on his chin, eyes closed and in deep thought, the President finally responded, "How long will it take to smoke out the son of a bitch?"

"No more than a few days, Mr. President. And hopefully, with a break we are overdue for, in less time than that."

"Do it, and do it more quickly if possible. I'll maintain the business-as-usual attitude in this office. But I don't mind telling you I am mad as hell, and the wrath that will come down on the confirmed bastard will be such that you have never seen. That I promise you, Eric. Bank on it," the President seethed out.

Jesús didn't trust Julio's replacement. He was a good worker; he just didn't like Indians. That, and it was possible that the knife fight was staged and Julio had been taken hostage or arrested. Either way, Jesús was not going to turn his back on the Indian.

"Hey, Indian, you finished with that wire yet?" Jesús yelled.

"Yeah, I did that a half hour ago. I'm just connecting it now. Why do we need the second alarm system anyway? I mean, who the hell would come all the way out here?" Tommy asked.

Carlos had ordered the extra alarm system as a security measure after Julio's death. He was not going to risk the operation and his retirement to save a measly fifty grand. This system was like the other, but laid out one hundred feet further into the trees to provide an early warning silent alarm. The extra men Jesús hired would be heavily armed with silenced AK47s and prepared for any intruder. The silencers were an absolute necessity with sound traveling for thirty to fifty miles, bouncing off the hard rock face in the thin air of the Rocky Mountains.

"You ask too many questions and I don't like you," Jesús said, spit coming through the gap in his teeth. "We moved the camp just to be safe, and we're staying here for the next week or two, so just make sure everything is secure and shut up!"

"When do I get paid? I'm doin' this only for the money, ya know. I've got plans. I'm going to help my people," Tommy said.

"I said you ask too many questions, now shut the fuck up and finish your work before Carlos comes back from Washington. You better pray he had a good time with his cheketa there or he'll be in a bad mood. And you don't want to be around him when he is in a bad mood," Jesús said finishing with a sinister throat laugh.

"Meceli, the two suspects will be leaked distinctly separate disinformation by me personally. We have our II4C ears tuned and will have confirmation within a day or two, with the next transmission. Only you and I know of the disinformation plan, and it must remain in this compartment. Is that understood?" Douglas asked.

"May I ask what led you to these two suspects?" Agent Meceli asked.

"An appropriate and logical question. It was what was not reported by the caller. The knife fight between Julio and Clint Bear was known to only a few, including the President after my personal briefing. Robert and Sheila were not aware of this detail. However, everyone else in the compartment was. This would be critical information for the caller to report to the listener, and therefore, when it was not reported, the logical suspects were narrowed," Douglas pontificated.

Meceli was impressed with Douglas's reasoning. It was insightful and sound, and she agreed with the analysis and conclusion. She just disdained his egocentric method of communication.

"How will you plant the disinformation, and what specifically will differentiate each plant?" Agent Meceli asked as she paced around the conference table, hands crossed on her chest.

"I would like your opinion, Meceli; I'm happy you asked. Robert will be told that Clint is ready to begin the infiltration. Since Robert and Sheila both know of Clint, and the caller has already passed this on to the listener, there is no worry here. I will add that we have located the camp and will be initiating satellite surveillance by tomorrow. Sheila will be told the same thing except that satellite surveillance will take forty-eight hours to program and initiate. Subtle, but different enough to discern beyond doubt with an II4C intercepted communication. What is your analysis, Meceli?" Douglas sincerely asked.

Meceli was not prone to a quick, shoot from the hip, analysis, especially when it was possible to give it consideration. She reasoned that given the seriousness of the leak, there was no time for detailed consideration, and therefore she shot from the hip with her response.

"It seems logical both in content and in deviation. Assuming there is little contact between Robert and Sheila, and with the security blanket and compartmentalization, there should be no contact with relevant discussion, it should work. However, the mole has been undetected for years. My conclusion is the person is smart and cautious. Therefore, the disinformation planting has to be exceptionally skillfully executed to prevent the mole from sensing the plant and going dormant. How do you intend to do it?" Meceli asked respectfully.

"Your points are well taken, and I agree on the planting. However, I'm afraid speaking honestly, that I'm planning on winging it," Douglas said, somewhat embarrassed. "There is just no time to set the proper stage, and hopefully the spontaneity will add to the planting credibility."

***

The sweat was pouring down Clint's back as he ran the ten-mile obstacle course in the day's peak heat, by choice, not by necessity. Clint was already in good physical condition so his training focused on the newest weapons and communications, with a refresher course in Spanish. Spanish was the only language spoken during his week of intensive retraining at a NSA camp in central Virginia. The weather was mild during the day and chilly during the early fall evenings, perfect for a relaxing vacation, the furthest thought from his mind.

Each of the five days was like the other, up at 05:00, a five-mile run, then a breakfast of grains, eggs and fruit, off to weapons, hand-to-hand combat and communications school, then the ten-mile obstacle course followed by lunch. The afternoon was a rerun of the morning. After dinner, there was always something special. One evening it was an ambush on the way to the barracks, another time it was a series of coded messages that he had to decode and follow within a set time limit. All the exercises were designed to realistically surprise and challenge Clint, emphasizing the skills he would need to rely on during his assignment. He was always ready and responded with almost textbook precision. Unknown to his instructors, the mental image driving him was seeing the killers dying, painfully and slowly, by his own hand. The relentless image burned in his veins, along with the images created by the stories about the Indians' mistreatment, passed by telling.

The only break came over dinner, usually taken in the officers' mess. Clint looked forward to this time when he could continue to compartmentalize the newly acquired knowledge for future instant retrieval. On this, his last evening, while sitting alone at a corner table, a Navy captain asked if he could join him. Clint was not in uniform, and therefore his rank unknown to the captain, who said, "Sir, I am here for my last physical before setting to out sea for the last time. It's a bit like knowing in advance you are going to lose a loved one."

"Sorry to hear that. The Navy can't afford to lose experienced officers. What ship, if you don't mind me asking?" Clint asked.

"The Aquarius," the captain responded.

"Oh, a submariner. Then the Navy should do all it can to keep you," Clint said somewhat gratuitously. "Pardon me, my name is Commander Clint Bear."

"Yes, I know. And I'm afraid I didn't just happen by your table. Captain Preston Cornwell," the captain said as they shook hands. "I have watched you over the last three days, in between my psychological and physical exams. My assessment is that you're a Navy SEAL, CIA, or DEA. But the kind of training you are undergoing suggests to me that you will be involved in the war against drugs. Now, I know you can't comment. I've been in the Navy for nearly forty years, and hold the highest security clearance, so all I'm asking of you is to indulge an old man for a few more minutes"

Clint saw pain and loneliness in Captain Cornwell's eyes. His white thinning hair didn't match the broad shoulders, strong arms and muscular chest. Clint could sense his will to live waning, even as they sat in the officer's mess. This was a man struggling, but why and for what? "Certainly, sir," Clint responded softly, looking at his ribbons and noticing the Bronze Star, Medal of Valor and the Navy SEAL UDT — Underwater Demolition Team — crest.

"As a Navy man you are aware of the sporadic and unpredictable traveling duty assignments. Sixteen years ago, while on assignment, my sons — identical twins —

with new driving licenses, took the family car for a practice drive. They were to pick up some groceries for my wife. They must have taken a wrong turn and became lost, and eventually found their way into the worst part of Chicago. The undercover officer staking the street out said it appeared that they were simply stopped to ask questions when the guy pulled his gun and fired. They were both pronounced dead at a south-side Chicago hospital. I was… away and unreachable, so my wife managed the wake and funeral, alone." A tear was forming in the Captain's left eye and Clint now knew what his inner struggle was about.

"Abby, my wife, met me at the base as I completed tour debriefing. She had talked with my CO and requested that she be the one to tell me. The moment I saw her, I knew. The moment I knew, she broke down and never recovered. She couldn't live with it; she tried to take her life by overdosing on sleeping pills. It didn't kill her, immediately. Abby lay in a vegetative state for nearly seven months before God had the compassion to end our suffering. My family is gone for the sake of a wrong turn into a drug bust gone wrong," Captain Preston Cornwell said in an ever-lowering tone as both eyes began flowing unabashedly. "Commander, I'm sorry to unload on you like this, but my instincts and observations tell me you can make a difference and I thought my personal tragedy may add to your motivation."

"Captain," Clint said very quietly, knowing the Captain needed something to believe in. "I am going to tell you a story, at great personal risk, as well as at the risk of national security. You have never seen my face, repeat, *never seen my face*, nor have you and I ever talked. Agreed? Let's take an evening's walk, shall we?"

***

The instructors were severely outmatched by Clint in hand-to-hand combat, endurance and camouflage. Clint was in equal physical condition, but had inner personal drive and desire that made the clear difference in speed and precision. He was efficient; zero wasted movement meant zero wasted energy. Clint was simply not going to fail this assignment, his purpose. Every reaction, every jab during hand-to-hand combat training, every step on the obstacle course, was first preceded by the cold, gray, lifeless image of Brook and Cabris and the burning image of what he had planned for Julio's buddies. Yes, he had agreed to put the interests of the United States before his, but maybe they were one and the same.

Revenge is a powerful motivator, a most dangerous motivator. The Chinese say, "Before setting out for revenge, first dig two graves."

In one exercise, Clint was ordered to take out three of the four targets in a jeep parked in the center of a three hundred-yard circular tall grass field, and to capture the fourth, and then drive the jeep to the other end of the field. There were no trees and only a few shrubs and bushes, no large rocks or terrain aberrations. It was a mostly flat and open field, selected to be nearly impossible for an agent to navigate in stealth mode.

This was a graduation exercise for Advanced Navy SEALs and the best outcome to date was for the SEAL to be sighted and neutralized by the jeep's paint-ball shooter seventy-eight feet from the jeep one hundred and eleven minutes after the exercise began.

Clint completed the exercise in under sixty minutes, using no mock weapons at any time during the exercise, to the amazement and horror of the jeep's occupants as well as the NSA and CIA onlookers. Even the instructors in the watchtower, one hundred feet above the field, did not see Clint enter the field or approach the jeep. They thought something had gone wrong with the exercise. He was a master of blending with his environment, not asking his environment to blend with him. Camouflage was second-nature to Clint, taught as a boy by the Apache and Old Bear. The first sighting of Clint was when he jumped over the jeep's rear gate, looking like a grass monster with all the high grass fastened to his camouflage clothes and his blackened face, tagging the two seated in the front and then one seated in the rear with surgical precision.

Cole flew in for the last day's exercise and briefing. He wanted to handle it personally.

"Clint, there is no doubt about your readiness. Each section head of your re-training program has admitted to being taught more by you than the other way around, except of course for your Spanish instructor. She thinks you will be okay if you're careful with numbers," Cole said as he paced in the subterranean-level briefing room. It was lit with incandescent light bulbs so the light could be dimmed to use the projector screen, and therefore looked more like a WWII bomb shelter than a contemporary briefing room.

"Clint, now is the last time you will be able to back out. Once you have gone undercover, we won't be able to stop the mission without scrubbing it. I can't scrub it… the loss of time would risk the lives of hundreds of thousands, if not millions of people, including the lives of the President and his family. It's now or never," Cole said, knowing that Clint was not about to back out.

Cole knew what was motivating Clint to extraordinary performance, and it worried him, deeply. Cole wondered what Clint would do when the time came, and after watching the exercise, he knew the time would come.

"Cole, you know better than to waste precious time asking me that. But for the record, no I don't want out. Let's get on with it," Clint said abruptly. Clint, privately, was reassured by the question. It told him that Cole was not only looking out for the interests of the government, he was thinking of Clint as well. He was beginning to like Cole and respect his ethics as well.

Cole Cunningham was the consummate DEA agent, but looked more like an accountant. His tie was usually loose around his neck with the top collar button undone, sleeves typically rolled up. His hairline, well, what there was of a line, had receded to the back of his head with just a small crop of thin hair where a widow's peak would be. The thick black graying eyebrows hid some of the worry and stress lines, but not the fatigue shadows beneath the determined brown eyes. At five foot ten and forty-eight years, a small paunch was beginning to show. The only thing missing was the coffee and doughnut stains. Cole looked a little like that TV detective Colombo, and was equally dogged and talented. Cole was a policeman's policeman.

"I know, I had to do it for me. You know, after Paul Cudson. Thanks, Clint," Cole said warmly. "Now, we've been over this a hundred times, but one more summarized briefing while we go to the WET Room," Cole said as he motioned for Clint to walk with him as they talked.

"Your new name is Ricardo Marcus, born December 3, 1968, southeast of Mexico City in a town called Puebla. You are Mexican, not Indian. Your parents are Cristo and Sylvia Marcus. Your mother died during childbirth and your father, overcome with the loss, has been a drunk ever since. You have no brothers or sisters. Remember Clint, everything is verifiable, because it is true, one hundred percent true. Turn right here; the WET Room is at the end on the hall past those two Marine Guards. The last time Cristo saw his son, you, was over five years ago. He was being chased by the Mexican City police suspected of being involved with drug trafficking. It remains a closely-guarded secret that the real Ricardo was killed by FBI agents during a drug bust seven months ago in Los Angeles, close to where you are going."

"Yes, I know it like it was my own life, Cole," Clint sighed.

Cole took out his ID and gave it to the Marine on the right. The Marine on the left kept his 45 caliber hand gun pointed at Clint until the ID was checked and authorization to enter confirmed by inside. A voice from a static-free intercom provided the authorization and they were allowed to walk past the Marine Guards, now with pistols holstered, to a gleaming stainless steel door that reminded Clint of a bank vault door. He watched as the eighteen-inch round handle in the door's center began to turn counter-clockwise without sound. The door then abruptly opened and Clint had to step back to prevent being hit by it, the eighteen-inch wall's thickness now in full view.

A rotund balding man, a full eight inches shorter than Clint with a jolly face, greeted Cole as if he were a brother. He was dressed in a white lab coat with a pocket protector in the left front pocket filled with pens, pencils and a metal scale. Above his glasses, that were crooked on his nose, his eyebrows were both pointed up at 45-degree angles toward his forehead. The gray stringy hair looked as if it had been through a wind tunnel before opening the door. But, his energy and intellect were overpowering. Clint whispered to himself, "The crazy professor."

"Clint, meet Dr. Charles Bommister. If he likes you, he'll tell you to call him Bom Bom," Cole said as they both shook hands. Clint noticed the CIA photo ID Dr. Bommister had clipped to his right breast pocket. "Dr. Bommister is the WET Room department head and founder."

Bommister was motionless for several minutes after they shook hands, motionless except for his eyes as they roamed over every inch of Clint's body. He was surveying a new mechanical device, a new machine that he would have to understand in order to work with. Then he began nodding his head slowly, up and down, and turning to Cole said with his heavy German accent, "Good, very good. I like this Clint. He has strength, in the body and in the mind. His eyes are clear and have purpose. Please come into my play pen."

Clint was surprised to see how large the area was, not just a room but a series of rooms with a central center walk way. It was a buzz with activity, maybe eighteen to twenty people, male and female, working on weapons, weapon subassemblies, munitions and various devices. The atmosphere was sterile clean, with white vinyl flooring, white work tops on stainless steel legged benches securing microscopes, hand loaders, electronic balance scales, instrumentation, hand tools and more. The smell of black powder and gun oil was faint, but discernible. There were secure cages with what could be the world's most complete array of handguns, semi and fully automatic weapons, knives, garrotes, antipersonnel mines. You name it and it was probably in this cage.

Off to the right was a glassed-in firing range with three shooters, two with hand guns and one with a Chinese AK47. Odd, he could see muzzle fire but could hear nothing. The perplexed look on Clint's face drew a comment from Dr. Bommister.

"The glass is pure synthetic, an upscale version of Lexan. Not only does it stop a 44 magnum at point-blank range with less than 0.016-inch penetration, it is a remarkably effective acoustic shield as well. Come, let me give you a tour," Dr. Bommister said to Clint with pride.

"Tell me, do you know why this is called the WET Room?" Dr. Bommister asked Clint while gesturing to Cole to remain silent.

"Let me guess, Dr. Bommister, we are on the subterranean level, so the floors get wet when it rains?" Clint humorously responded.

"I like this man Cole. He has a sense of humor while facing a most dangerous mission. Clint, please call me Bom Bom and no, the floor never gets wet. Like everything in the government, WET Room is an acronym for Weapons, Explosives, Terrorism, and Counter Terrorism Systems. It is where the CIA Operatives come to be outfitted for their current special mission," Bom Bom lectured as we walked down the center isle on the guided tour.

"Dr. Bommister, sorry, I mean Bom Bom, where did the nickname come from?" Clint asked sincerely.

"Well, I make bombs and my last name begins with Bom. It was given me over thirty years ago when I graduated the Naval Academy, because I almost didn't graduate. I have always had a fascination with explosives and was experimenting in my dormitory room when there was just this little small explosion. Hardly noticeable, really. I was not hurt, much, but the windows blew out, causing quite a ruckus. My German accent didn't help when I was in front of the 'old man'. But, I explained that my family defected during WWII and played a vital part in the war effort for the Allies, and he let it go with minor discipline. The guys started calling me Bom Bom after that and it stuck," Dr. Bommister said.

"Now, while you were BEL, your favorite hand gun was the Smith and Wesson .357 caliber Model 66 and your weapon of choice was the SHRIKE 5.56 submachine gun with silencer. This mission will require quite different armaments. For security reasons, I am not within the compartment. However, I have been told that you will be undercover, in both potentially warm and cold climates, and must appear as a civilian. Based on that, I will make a few suggestions. Acceptable?" Bom Bom asked.

"Very much so," Clint quickly responded.

"Good. I'd hoped you would respond that way and took the liberty to lay out the probable choices. They are on the table in the Colt Room," Bom Bom said, pointing further down the hall.

"You guessed it Clint. Bom Bom named all the rooms after firearm manufacturers. The one I like the best is Daisy," Cole said while laughing.

"Funny man, this Cole Cunningham," Bom Bom replied.

As Clint entered the Colt room, he noticed in smaller letters under the larger Colt name was M1991 A1, which he remembered was the sidearm issued to WWII officers. On the table directly in front of him, in the clinical room's center, was placed a dozen weapons. Bom Bom and Cole stood to the side watching Clint appraise the equipment. There was a S&W Model 1066 10mm stainless steel semiautomatic, another Smith & Wesson model 629 .44 magnum six shot revolver, a Beretta model 89 long rifle 22 semiautomatic, a Colt MKIV Series 80 4.25" barrel 45 semiautomatic, Desert Eagle Mark VII 357 magnum, a Tokarev 9mm Luger, American Derringer Model 1 two shot 45 derringer, an Alcas 7" survival knife, what appeared to be a custom survival knife, a Daewoo Tri Action Compact 9mm Luger, a rubberized ringed garrote with stainless steel retractable wire, a Kostas boot harnessed black matte throwing knife, and more.

Clint hefted the S&W 1066; it felt right, a good fit for his hand. It brought back memories of a long time ago. He placed it down gently while thinking about what was not on the table. There were no laser-sighted pistols, no plastic weapons with plastic bullets, no advanced technology at all. Bom Bom was good, he thought to himself. Where he was going he must appear to be a druggie, not a sophisticated technologist, that would subvert his purpose.

Clint then chose the rubberized ringed garrote and placed it around his neck like jewelry. Next, the Kostas boot knife was inserted into his right boot and clipped to prevent it falling down to his foot or out of the boot. The American Derringer was then selected and its small slim frame easily placed in the left boot. Finally, Clint picked up the Daewoo Tri Action 9mm, hefted it a bit, slid the action, popped the clip, and said, "The action has been reworked. Excellent job. No chance for jams now. This will do just fine."

"Excellent. Clint, you have chosen well, not to be distracted by the glitz and technology. You remained focused on you mission. Blend in with the environment. Your choices will fit with a common street hood," Bom Bom said enthusiastically. "I would like to suggest a few more items, for your safety of course."

Bom Bom led them to his private lab and, after closing the door, suggested Clint and Cole be seated. Reaching into a cabinet above his many work areas, Bom Bom retrieved what looked like a small transistor radio, about the size of a credit card.

"This looks and functions like an AM/FM radio. However, if you press these two spots twice, in rapid succession, it becomes a broadband encrypted automatic transmitter. It's a beacon, that will send the encrypted signal for twenty-four hours. Only encrypted radar will pick it up the blip. In case we need to locate you or something you want us to locate. Douglas will have the II4C monitoring this frequency for the length of the mission. Neat, isn't it?" Dr. Bommister exclaimed in excitement as he handed it to Clint.

"Now, this looks like an ordinary diving watch, a cheap one at that. We call it a 'Half Moon' because of the half-moon depicted on the face. When you depress these two buttons, again twice in rapid succession, the watch becomes armed. It starts dual vibrators that move small magnets within a coil to high voltage charge a unique capacitor, like a high voltage battery. Precisely thirty seconds after arming, the capacitor will discharge through a piezo electric cell producing a massive sonic blast. The sonic resonator is tuned for the human audible frequency spectrum. The blast will stun into unconsciousness anyone within twenty feet for about sixty to one hundred and twenty seconds. Anyone who isn't deaf, that is. Hands over your ears tightly will protect you," Bom Bom said while demonstrating on himself.

"My last gift to you, Clint, are these three little marbles, just in case you are bored and want to play. Come, I'll show you what they do," Bom Bom said giddy as a schoolboy.

Clint and Cole followed Bom Bom to the firing range. Bom Bom asked the three shooters to leave for a moment and he then threw the marble against the back wall. A thunderous explosion was created, with the wooden target wall ripped to shreds.

Bom Bom laughing said, "This is actually an evolved explosive from that experiment in my dorm room. Each little marble has the explosive power of a grenade. However, since it is not encased in a metal jacket, it produces little shrapnel on its own. It is designed to take out a door, automobile, person, you get the point. It's designed to blow into something, not like a grenade that blows out. You must throw the marble hard for the explosion is triggered by impact shock."

"Bom Bom, you love your new technology. I'm sure Clint will feel more comfortable with it. Time is getting away… is there a room with a secure phone we could use before leaving?" Cole asked.

"Yes, I understand; please feel free to use my office or the Beretta Room. Both have privacy and a secure telephone that is swept daily by the CIA," Bom Bom offered.

"Thanks. You have been so cooperative, we would hate to inconvenience you more. We'll use the Berretta Room," Cole responded with a mixture of respect and admiration.

"As you wish. You know where it is Cole. And if I can be of any more help, I will be here working on the newest marble," Bom Bom said, "It's not quite right yet."

As Cole and Clint were walking out of Dr. Bommister's personal lab, Clint turned and said, "Dr. Bommister, thank you for your help. It will make the difference. Intuition."

"I don't say this often, if at all. I'll see you again Clint, intuition as well. May God be with you," Dr. Bommister said tenderly, arms extended with his hands holding Clint's arms.

Clint wondered about Dr. Bommister, the paradox. He was obviously a well-educated and caring man. One who cared about his people, probably all people. How could such a man make his life designing weapons and munitions that kill? Clint made a commitment to get to know Bom Bom and confirm his own gut instinct, that he was on the side of right and the broader good, and made the use of those weapons in the best interests of mankind. The better of two evils.

Once inside the Berretta Room, Cole, closing the door behind Clint, motioned for Clint to sit near the conference tables speakerphone and said, "Clint, Director Department C wants to have a few words before you start." And then dialed the Washington D.C. number.

The female voice on the other end came through as if she were sitting across the table, "Director's Office, may I help you?"

"Yes, this is Cole Cunningham, I believe the Director is expecting our call," Cole responded.

"Yes, I'll put you through Mr. Cunningham."

"Cole, is Mr. Bear with you, and are you alone and secure, with that exception?" Douglas questioned.

"Yes sir, exactly as you had requested. We have completed the WET Room and Bom Bom offered us the Berretta Room for this call," Cole said.

"Good. Clint, I trust you have the material you need?" Douglas directed at Clint.

"I have been well taken care of, sir," Clint said.

"Yes, Bom Bom is quite an asset to our organization. Clint, a great deal is placed on your shoulders. I'm sorry you have been brought into this and especially saddened by the loss of your family. I'm also sorry that what I am about to tell you will not make this any easier on you, Clint. We have intercepted a secure transmission from the leaker. The content was a report of Agent Meceli and your insertions. Clint, they know about you and may have photos faxed before we find the leaker," Douglas confessed somberly. The Director is not one who takes well to situations out of his control.

Clint was deep in thought, his mind whirling through the possibilities. Who was this leaker? It could be Cole, Douglas, even the President. No, he could not believe it would be Bill. What was he missing? There must be a pattern, but where was is it?

How was he to infiltrate the druggies if he had already been identified? The plan was an undercover infiltration, confidence building and detail gathering to a point adequate to destroy the druggies' organization up to and including the generals. Then it became clear, very clear. During his sweat, reliving the BEL work, saving the POWs...

"Mr. Director, we need a contingency plan. We will need to make one small change in our deployment strategy. Instead of infiltrating and becoming one of them, we should establish close field reconnaissance and take them at the appropriate time. When is it possible to have confirmation on who the leaker is?" Clint asked with a tone of confidence.

"Possibly within twenty-four to forty-eight hours, but we can't be certain," Douglas said, not wanting to add that he had already planted the disinformation and was waiting for it to work. "You are all too familiar with this type of work Clint, you hope for the best, but plan for the worst."

"Then, I suggest that we go forward with the original infiltration strategy. If at the time of separation and insertion, my photos are not and will not be disclosed, meaning you have the leaker, then we will go forward as planned. If the leaker has not been found, we will revert to our contingency recon plan. Agreed?" Clint asked.

"Cole, what is your assessment?" Douglas asked.

"I am hopeful we don't need a contingency plan. Clint's suggestion is more passive than I would like at this stage of development. But, clearly Clint cannot infiltrate, being physically identified before we start. Even with fast physical alterations, we can't be sure. If identified, he and the mission, and most likely hundreds of thousands of Americans, will be lost. It is simply too risky to implement. I would suggest we move forward with Clint's contingency plan, but only if absolutely necessary," Cole admitted.

"Then it's a go, as is, unless Clint is identified. No other changes are required to the strategy. Gentlemen, God speed," Douglas said as he terminated the call.

"Clint, there is a military jet waiting for us at Andrews. It will fly us to a private airstrip west of Anza, California, near the Cahuilla Indian Reservation. We will split there. You have a Jeep Cherokee awaiting you registered in California under the name of Ricardo Marcus with a full tank of gas and all the equipment you requested. This will be the point of insertion. Regardless of whether we infiltrate or recon, it will start here. Anything else?" Cole asked.

"Yes, with the possibility of our contingency plan, I'll need a pair of Nikon night vision glasses, 8x wide view, and full camouflage gear. In case I'm now hiding from, not within," Clint said as they left the room. "Also, I'd like to change these weapons for more familiar and trustworthy ones. We may not need to worry about what people will say or think any more. We will also need to review our communications protocol and provide me with additional equipment."

Clint was ready.

Paul Martin almost jumped out of his seat when the digital triple redundant recorders bleeped on, even though the chair was specially molded to his body to help relieve the strain of those twenty-four-hour communications surveillance marathons. They were set to the frequency of the day, with the randomizers synchronized to the President's, and the caller's, equipment. Paul was not a patient man, although he had to display patience in his profession. His heart was pounding while he double-checked his equipment — the government may own it but he considered it his — to ensure the transmission was recorded for immediate analysis.

Precisely sixteen seconds after the recorders bleeped on, they bleeped off. Paul marveled at their ability to do what they were programmed to do, unemotionally, no sick days, no back talk. Technology, it was the savior of the world, he thought.

He wanted to play it back, but the Director had said, "Immediately after the recording, bring him the playback." So, that's precisely what he was going to do, immediately. On his way out of the II4C, he asked his assistant to notify the Director's office that he was in route, ETA eleven minutes.

Paul Martin had been expected, the clearance given personally by Director Douglas, who had set up a temporary office in the White House ground level's Jefferson Room. The security procedure was just as complete, however, with a thorough weapons check by advanced X-ray. A pass was provided, indicating "Escort Required", and the big man himself awaited Paul just beyond the west wing security station.

There were a few questions asked and answered about the piece of equipment Paul was carrying, coddling actually. "It's a digital playback unit, that's all," Paul told Secret Service Agent Steven Mosler. "Please handle it with care. It's a delicate instrument."

"Yes, I'm sure it is. However, I need to ensure it is what it looks like and it is what you say it is. Please remove the top cover and allow me to see the guts, Mr. Martin," the Agent Mosler said respectfully. He was not about to let a concealed bomb get into the White House, no matter how unlikely it is that a CIA Agent, cleared by the Director personally, would be carrying it. The Secret Service were always thorough; it keeps the President, his family and staff alive.

"I'll need a Phillips head screwdriver," Paul replied, appearing patient, but containing his growing impatience.

"Just happen to have a complete assortment of tools in the 'Review Room' where we will have more privacy. Please follow me, Mr. Martin. I'll bring the instrument," Mosler said. Six minutes later Paul walked out of the Review Room carrying the playback instrument heading for Director Douglas.

"It was nice to get your call, Paul," Douglas said. "We will go directly to my office where another interested party is waiting."

The walk to the ground level conference room was longer than he would have expected, not being one who frequented the White House. Paul was wowed by the surveillance techniques within the building. He knew he was being tracked by the digital encoder within the 'Escort Required' badge. He also knew that there were three weapons screens, two obvious and one not obvious at all. Technology keeps the government safe, Paul thought.

The two Marine guards opened the door as Douglas and Martin approached the Philadelphia Room. Once inside the conference room, now office, Paul Martin was introduced to Agent Meceli.

"Paul, let's hear it please," Douglas stated as he and Meceli sat at the conference table, Douglas at the head and Meceli, right of the head.

"Yes, sir," Paul replied as he placed the playback instrument on the table and in one smooth motion depressed the play button and adjusted the volume. The recorded message was in digital memory and played as clearly as the original. He hoped that his equipment stored the message properly. It would be extremely embarrassing if it, he, screwed up.

Anticipation. C. Eric Douglas had been through the Korean Conflict, the Vietnam War, Grenada, The Persian Gulf, Afghanistan and more. He had been an agent as well as a black control, planned and implemented espionage all over the world. Still, he was beginning to perspire around the lips and forehead, anticipating the content of the recorded message.

Agent Meceli noticed Douglas's perspiration with surprise. He's not as stone cold as he would prefer everyone to believe, she thought. That's good. He's human like the rest of us. The recorded message interrupted her thoughts:

"The camp has been located and compromised. Satellite surveillance will begin in twenty-four hours. Still have not located recent photos of Clint Bear. Be careful."

Sixteen seconds later the player went off automatically. The squeaky voice gone. The leaker confirmed.

Douglas pondered why Robert would do it. What made a man compromise his country and friends? Could he be compromised himself? His family held captive or threatened? Was he blackmailed? The reason wouldn't make a difference. Robert would never see the light of day again without looking through bars, and that's on his best day.

"Sir, why have we not intercepted a return communication? It appears that all the communication is going out, nothing coming in," Meceli questioned.

"Maybe we will learn more when we have a chat with the little rat bastard," Douglas said as he reached for the telephone. But Meceli was right, he thought, all communication interceptions had been those originating from Robert to the receiver. Since Robert could not safely call or write the leaker, they must have met, set up a communications protocol which presumably included preset transmission times. There must be a pattern. And when, not if, we determine the pattern we can use it to our advantage.

"Ms. Turcott, this is Director Douglas. Agent Meceli, Robert and I need to brief the President on a change to our field operations for the MLDP. It is a matter of some urgency. How quickly can you fit us in?" Douglas asked without alarming Sheila.

"He will be finishing up the MLDP budget meeting in eleven minutes. I can squeeze you in for about fifteen minutes then. Is that acceptable, Director?" Sheila asked.

"That will be fine. Will you advise Robert, please? Agent Meceli is here with me," Douglas said as he hung up the telephone and picked it up again to talk briefly with the Attorney General.

"Good work Paul. I'll need to keep the player for a while. Would you please make a master copy and deliver it personally to the Attorney General? And, Paul, I mean you are to place it in his hands, and only his hands, personally," Douglas commanded.

"Yes, sir," Paul said as he left the conference room office asking one of the Marine guards to escort him to the west wing exit.

Robert was already in the Oval Office when Agent Meceli followed Douglas into the room. She wondered how he was going to handle the situation when he started speaking directly to the President, even before sitting down.

"Mr. President, thank you for squeezing us in. There has been an important development that we need to address. Less than twenty-four hours ago I, personally, advised members of this compartment that we had found the druggies' camp and had it under surveillance. Isn't that correct, Robert?" Douglas said as he looked from the President directly to Robert.

"Yes, and I hope we close in on them soon," Robert replied nervously. Something is going on here, he thought, and it is making me more than a little bit uncomfortable.

"Thank you, Robert. I briefed your staff that the camp would be under satellite surveillance within forty-eight hours…"

"No, that is not what you told me, Douglas, you said twenty-four hours," Robert shot back.

"Thank you for correcting me, Robert," Douglas said, and added, "Mr. President, this was recorded less than one hour ago. Agent Meceli, would you play the recording?"

"The camp has been located and compromised. Satellite surveillance will begin in twenty-four hours. Still have not located recent photos of Clint Bear. Be careful."

"That is the point, Robert. You are the only individual that was told twenty-four hours. Mr. President, I am sorry to tell you that Robert is the leak. Robert has compromised national security. Robert has subverted your Martial Law Drug Plan. Robert is part of the conspiracy to murder your family and the President of the United States. I have asked the Attorney General to join us in a few minutes to take this scum and debrief him. If I do it, he might have a well-deserved serious accident," Douglas said viscerally.

The President sat motionless, almost faceless, almost expressionless, his skin colorless. A tear fell from his right eye as he asked, "Is this true, Robert?"

Robert, still sitting, more slumping in the winged-back chair didn't know how to respond. He was thinking of running, but that was futile, he was inside the fucking White House and would never get away. He thought of denial, but Douglas had outplayed him. It was over, for him. But, maybe Carlos would take care of him when…. No, it was over.

"Yes, it's true," Robert whispered.

"Why, after all we have been through, why?" the President asked with compassion.

Robert snorted, and laughed through his nose, "It's just like you not to know. I've been living in your shadow for almost fifteen years, ever since your success in Massachusetts. Who the hell do you think masterminded the success, drove the grassroots efforts, kept the lobbies contributing? Christ, I ran the government for you. And what did you give me? Nothing. Table scraps."

The President, his glasses off, put his face in his hands, elbows on his massive desk, and said just loud enough to be heard, "I always wondered why you were in the dry cage in the POW camp. Why the rest of us were cramped into one cell. Why all our escape plans ended in failure. You were an informant. You told the Taliban what we were up to and when the break would happen, they gave you food and a dry cell. You worthless piece of shit. Agent Meceli, get him out of my sight."

"Agent Meceli, the Attorney General has made arrangements for a debriefing. There will be two Secret Service Agents waiting outside the door to take Robert to a containment area. After you are comfortable with the transfer, with your permission, sir, please rejoin the President and I," Douglas added. The President just nodded and was collecting his thoughts as the door closed behind Meceli and Robert, when his secure telephone rang.

"Mr. President, Watch Commander Scudder, sir. I understand that Director Douglas is with you. I recommend that you put this call on your speaker phone, sir," the Secret Service Watch Commander said.

"Done, Scudder. I assume this is important," the President said showing his lack of patience.

"Yes sir, it is. Agent Mosler, making his routine random physical inspection, found a transmitting device in the backup presidential limo. It appears to be a custom-designed transmitter that works off the limo's battery, turns on the limo's secure communications system, and transmits a prerecorded message. It appears to be on a timer, sir," Scudder reported, adding, "We have blanketed the limo and thought Director Department C Douglas would want to be notified as well."

"Mr. President, may I? Good work, Commander Scudder. You have executed well. Please have Agent Paul Martin, in the remote II4C unit, involved with the transmitter evaluation. I'm sure you have been careful for fingerprints, but I would like to know if you find those of Robert Dunkin. And Scudder, keep this in an extra-tight compartment. I'll be down shortly," Douglas said.

Both men sat speechless for what seemed an eternity. The events of the past fifteen minutes being put in their minds' proper places. The knock on the door broke their concentration.

"Mr. President, Agent Meceli has returned, Shall I send her in?" Sheila asked.

"Yes," the President replied.

"Sir, I don't want to seem insensitive to what you have just experienced. But we have an opportunity now, finally a break for us, not against us," Douglas said excitedly, having put most of the pieces in their proper places.

"Douglas, what the hell are you talking about? Sorry, Eric. What about the transmitter?" President Covey said, having regained his composure?

"We now have the transmitter that Robert used, that he did not pick up before he was caught. The voice encryption makes identification impossible. The caller is identified, it's Robert, the receiver not yet identified. The receiver is our main target now. We can use the same disinformation strategy using the transmitter. We have three intercepted transmissions; there is a transmission time pattern; we can sort it out and pretend to be Robert, but transmitting disinformation," the new Director of Department C exclaimed.

"We could craft and lead the receiver into a trap. This is indeed a break, Mr. Director," Agent Meceli added.

The knock on the door interrupted the flow of conversation, yet again. "Mr. President, I have an appointment this evening, if I'm no longer needed," Sheila said with an uncharacteristic smile.

"That will be fine, enjoy your evening, Ms. Turcott," the President replied to Sheila as she was already scampering out of the office. At least some one was in a good mood, he thought.

"Meceli, please go through Robert's office, car and home. Take a detail from Department C," the Director said.

Sheila arrived home an hour and fifteen minutes after leaving the White House. Not a home exactly, an apartment in downtown D.C. It was spacious with three bedrooms, a dining room, family room and a living room. She had set up one of the bedrooms as a library and one as a guest room. Her bedroom was the master with the private bathroom. She was excited about her friend coming... no, her lover, a successful leather manufacturer from Argentina, and she'd redecorated her bedroom for the occasion.

German Aldamado lived in Cordoba, about two hundred miles northwest of Buenos Aires, and came to the U.S. every month to negotiate new import contracts with leather distributors and retailers. Although the flight was long, over twelve hours, he would only have been through one time zone and would be looking forward to a late dinner and unwinding in his crazy way, that Sheila found so unusual and exciting.

She was always on guard to pronounce his name correctly, not like the country, but like Herman, with the emphasis on "man", pronouncing it "mon". He spoke perfect English, and Sheila was working diligently on her broken Spanish. German was so appreciative and attentive to her, calling regularly, sending flowers for no special reason, even a card for a special remembrance. He was tender, sensitive, handsome, rich, very hot and intelligent. Maybe he is the one, Sheila thought.

While the lasagna baked and the rich red tomato sauce with hot Italian sausage and meatballs simmered on the stove, Sheila went to her bedroom to prepare herself. German would be arriving in an hour or so and she wanted everything to be perfect, especially herself. Sheila knew she was no raving beauty, but she did have a sumptuous ample body that she dressed to hide while in the office.

German was the only man in over twelve years that had seen the real her and been with her sexually. She intended to keep German coming back until he fell as much in love with her as she had with him. And one of the ways to German's heart was through his Latin passion for rich, animal-like sex. Sheila loved his likes. It gave her the womanly attention she had craved and was denied for the last twelve years. Sheila had a lot of time to make up for, she was thinking… wouldn't the people in the office be shocked that the spinster secretary was her lover's hot sex machine? She began to tremble with the excitement, no the need, to have German.

They had met by chance at a Ministry of Trade social function four months ago. It was physical attraction at first sight for Sheila. He was suave, well-mannered and spoken, his dark complexion contrasting his white linen suit. His five-foot-eight-frame was a perfect match for her five-foot-two, her dirty blonde hair contrasting his dark complexion. His friendly broad smile displayed bright white teeth that seemed to trigger a sparkle in his clear, deep brown eyes. They left the social affair together and had two expressos at a nearby restaurant. They had danced in the restaurant's lounge to slow fifties and sixties music and held each other closely, his hands gently messaging her ample ass, without protest. German escorted her home, and turned down the invitation to come in for a nightcap. The kissed deeply, passionately, both wanting to have each other, their lust being communicated by tongues and hands, but both knowing it was too quick.

He called her the next day, at six in the morning before Sheila's six thirty alarm called out. He had had no sleep thinking of her, and asked to have dinner with her that evening. The relationship had started. That night after dinner, he did come in for a nightcap and enjoyed breakfast in bed the next morning. Sheila bathed herself in the memory of that first night....

He had made reservations in a little known, out-of-the-way Italian Bistro in Alexandria, Virginia. There were only eight tables in the dining area and a few more in the lounge area, the small music ensemble perched on a stage in the corner. They ordered cocktails, he having Pinch, she a vodka and tonic, while deciding what to enjoy for dinner and talking fluidly. He was a passionate man, who liked to touch the person while talking. He sat on the same side of the cozy private corner booth as Sheila so they could be near to each other. Sheila liked the affection and attention more because it was so publicly and uninhibitedly offered and reinforced that her spinsterish life was coming to an end. She had responded in kind, caressing the back of his neck, lightly touching his thigh and sneaking a kiss now and then.

All through dinner they talked and touched. Sheila was becoming overcome with passion, her wetness surely seeping through her new bikini panties by now, but she didn't care, she was in heaven, never having felt so stimulated. They moved to the lounge for a nightcap before returning home. The band playing unrecognizable soft, slow dancing music, with few patrons left and only two couples swaying to the music. German and Sheila swayed as well, arms tightly around each other moving in a small circle, their lips finding each other's, their tongues twisting and darting at each other like fighting snakes. German's hands moved to massage her ass, then her back and slowly moving to her breasts. Sheila remembered the powerful orgasm at that precise moment, her body shaking and German's mouth muffling her moans. Her wetness clearly becoming more visible as the glistening stream flowed down her inner thighs.

Taxis were waiting for late night dinner patrons who may have had too much to drink, and wanted a safe transport home. German, with his right hand tightly around Sheila's waist, flagged a taxi with his left. As Sheila slid into the cab's back seat, German caressed her thigh, moving her dress hem near her womanhood, the wetness plainly visible, covering her bikini panties and nylons. The cab driver, a middle-aged scruffy looking man, turned completely around looking directly into Sheila's soaked crotch, then slowly to her flushed face, and smiling, moved to German's smiling face. German gave him the address and added "Take it slow, please."

German had reached down past Sheila's waist, tucking his strong hands under her soaked aromatic pink panties, and slowly pulled them down to her knees, with Sheila lifting her feet off the cab's floor and out of her shoes voluntarily, off entirely. Boldly, German placed the panties on the top of the front seat, near the cab driver's right shoulder, meeting an approving glance by both the cab driver and Sheila. German kissed Sheila deeply before moving his head down to her wetness. She orgasmed again at his first lick. German was unbuttoning her blouse slowly, too slowly, she was helping him from the top down and unclasped her bra, her large firm breasts falling free.

The cab driver had pulled to the side of a quiet road and was holding her panties to his nose looking intently into her eyes while German was feasting on her wetness…

She had to stop thinking about this and get ready. He would be there in less than an hour. Sheila selected a black knit dress, black hose, black garter belt and black stiletto heels. Nothing else. Her body continued to tremble with expectation. She couldn't think about anything else. He was like a drug, and Sheila was happily hooked.

Sheila ran to the door and arrived before the knocking had stopped. Without looking through the peephole, she flung open the door and jumped into his arms, almost causing German to drop the Argentinean wine he had brought as a gift. It was as though Sheila had a death lock on German, hands locked around her arms which were around German's head, lips locked and passion building once again.

"Wo, wo, wo," German uttered through their lips, "We have all evening, my darling Sheila. God, it's nice to see you!"

"Oh God, I couldn't wait, German, I think I'm falling in love with you," Sheila blurted out, wishing she hadn't.

"Then this surprise may please you," German said as he moved his bags out of the hallway into Sheila's apartment.

"What is it, German," Sheila asked with excitement, still holding his arm, as if she let go he would get away.

"I have decided to move my Headquarters from Cordoba to Washington D.C. I simply can't live without you at my side. I think I'm falling in love with you, too," German said softly as he embraced Sheila, now behind closed doors.

"Does this mean what I think it means?" Sheila said.

"Will you say yes if it means what you think it means?" German replied excitedly.

"Yes, yes, yes!" Sheila yelled.

"Then it means what you think it means, yes, yes, yes!" German yelled back, "Let's celebrate! I have the weekend free. Let's go to the coast where we can be alone, if you know what I mean. I have rented a car and we can leave right away. There is a quaint little bed and breakfast I know on the Chesapeake Bay, down near Cove Point, called the Timbers. I've made reservations and we can be there in an hour and a half."

"Let's eat first as I've made your favorite, and get there for a nightcap," Sheila said with a devilish grin.

During the drive south on Route 4 toward Cove Point, they connected to Route 24 and then Rural Route 497 into Cove Point, talking of where they would live, where the offices should be and when they should marry. She had not told anyone about her new relationship, as German had suggested. There was no use causing rumors and alerting the required Secret Service security check in her sensitive position. But now she could brag a bit, but German suggested they wait until the next visit when he could meet some of her family and friends.

Sheila was surprised that the Bed and Breakfast was so upscale, in this neighborhood. The Timbers was an old English style B&B, that had seen its surroundings grow up and apart during its one hundred and thirty-year life. Not far from there was a little truck stop, near a truckers' bargain diesel fueling depot and an all-night topless bar at the end of a dead-end street. Then she began to understand just how German wanted to celebrate.

Sheila waited in the rented Cadillac while German checked in, noticing a little cash being offered for a better room, she guessed. She hoped her black dress didn't wrinkle during the long drive.

German got back into the car and said, "We have the best room in the house - you will love it - it's charming I'm told. Don't let the neighborhood deceive you. This B&B is one of the best in the world. I have entertained customers here before; a four-star restaurant and a quiet little bar. Just down the street there is a bar that's not so quiet, if we so desire."

They opened the old oak timber reinforced door labeled the "Kings Room", turned on the lights and Sheila sighed with contentment, "It is beautiful, just as you said, darling."

"Let's unpack later. There is a bottle of cold vintage Mumm Champagne on its way," German was interrupted as a knock on the door and voice saying, "Room Service."

Sheila, taking a cue, sat in the love seat in front of the glass coffee table and lifted her skirt and legs to tempt the room service waiter. German smiling, took the cue as well and let the waiter in saying, "Please put the tray on the coffee table and be careful when opening the bottle."

The waiter, in his early twenties and probably a college student freelancing for more spending money, sat the tray down in front of Sheila and looked up seeing her partially-exposed womanhood. Looking down quickly, so as not to be caught, he began to open the champagne, but snuck a look at her womanhood when he thought no one would notice.

Brazenly, Sheila got up and said, "I am going to take a quick shower before the champagne." Directly in front of the boy waiter, she stood up, reached down under the waiter's chin and raised his head with her index finger, then lifted her dress over her head, shaking her blonde hair back in place, exposing her naked body framed in black nylons, garter belt and stiletto heels. With a devilish grin she brushed her firm breasts on the waiter's arms as she sexily walked to the bathroom. The waiter was thinking about the story he will have to tell the guys tonight, if anyone would believe him, as he declined the tip from German.

A perfect time to add the White Ice to her drink, German thought.

"Honey, you are wonderful, how sexy and creative you are." German said, turning around from the coffee table as Sheila came out of the bathroom.

"Here, let's toast," German said handing her the right glass.

"To our long, happy and exciting life together," German toasted as he clinked her glass.

"To our lust and our love," Sheila toasted back, still nude.

"Let's go out for a nightcap, shall we?" German said as they finished their first glass of Mumm.

"Do you like what I'm wearing tonight, my love, or would you like me to change?" Sheila asked as she cupped her left breast and pinched the nipple. His smile was her answer.

It was no surprise that they would go directly to the trucker's topless bar. It was a seedy place, and the dirty squeaky door fit the building. Smoke spewed out of the building as German opened the door seemingly forced out by the loud brass music. The single stage, with a fully naked brunette grinding her ass close to the faces of the mostly drunk men, was in the center of the bar, with booths surrounding the perimeter. German paid three almost drunk truckers fifty dollars each for the booth near the stage's center.

The waitress came right over, thrusting her bare breasts close to German's face while asking what they would like. The air felt sexually charged, Sheila thought, but her thoughts were interrupted when the waitress turned to ask what she wanted, and giving her equal time thrust her left breast close to her right cheek. As Sheila turned to say vodka tonic, her open mouth almost caught the waitress's perky tit.

"That will cost ya a little extra, missy - you have five minutes to stop," the waitress said laughing while Sheila turned away quickly.

Sheila's head was beginning to feel that familiar sensation of animalistic need, but she was uncomfortable in this environment and turned to German and asked, "Let's leave this place. It gives me the creeps and I need you now!"

"Okay, honey. Let's go back of our room," German said throwing a ten-dollar bill on the table.

Sheila got some whistles and crude comments while walking out of the bar. One guy was gutsy enough to steal a feel, unprotested, German noticed, as he followed behind her. He decided to help the high along for Sheila by lifting her black dress over her garter belt while they walked through the crowd, eventually easing it up exposing her ass entirely before they reached the door. Now, many of the guys were stealing a feel, slapping her bare ass, openly encouraged by Sheila's slowing pace to the door. Surprisingly, Sheila lifted her breasts out of the top of the dress for the guys standing by the door to admire, one guy kneading the left while another, encouraged by his female friend, was sucking the other. It was beginning to get out of control, so German pulled the dress down and forced Sheila out of the bar toward the car, with some of the guys following. They reached the car, entered and locked the doors, just as Sheila was beginning to the high's peak.

"Honey, slow down," German said as she reached for his pants. He knew she was his, and he needed the information before he had some fun.

"Sheila, what did you say happened to Robert?" German asked softly while twisting her nipples hard.

"Christ, he was caught leaking information to a druggie," Sheila whispered out unknowingly while trying to unzip his pants.

"What druggies are you talking about and where are they?" German asked as he lifted her black dress off completely.

"They don't know," Sheila whispered again unknowingly, she was in the zone, real high.

"Honey we are being watched; three of the guys from the bar are standing beside the car drinking their beers.

Let's give them a show they won't forget," German said passionately while he finished unzipping his pants.

Sheila reached for the electric seat controls, lowering the white leather bench seat and moving it back, displaying her body for all three men outside to see, the parking lot spotlights putting her on stage. German was pleasuring himself as he lowered the passenger side window. He waved a pistol and then motioned for the guys to help themselves. As they began to open the car door, he waved the pistol again, and they realized they would be able to touch, and be touched, only through the open window, there in the far corner of the topless bar parking lot. German watched as Sheila reached new highs and, with four hands all over her body, she began to orally pleasure them one at a time.

Sheila would not remember this in the morning. She had had enough White Ice for it to start to damage her brain. Even with the smaller dosages he mixed in her drinks, her short-term memory would be affected. She was hooked on him, thinking it was he that gave her the lust and love high, unknown that it was the White Ice she was actually hooked on, and would eventually result in her death.

So, they don't know where the camp is, so there can't be any satellite surveillance, Carlos was thinking. My mole Robert has been taken. He was finished with him anyway. Too bad about Sheila. She was the best surprise I've had in a long time, Carlos muttered to himself as the last guy walked away. Sheila rolled flatly on to the Cadillac's seat, the high rapidly wearing off and exhaustion settling in, as Carlos depressed the passenger's side window closed, started the car and drove to their B&B for a good night's rest. He would tell Sheila in the morning, before leaving for Colorado, that the three men were watchers, not touchers, and she would think it was all a passion-induced fantasy while she and her German were making love.

The military transport was not what Clint had expected. He was thinking a USAF Spartan noisy transport plane, not the plush twin turbofan Gulfstream jet.

"Cole, is this where our taxpayers' money goes?" Clint asked only half-jokingly.

"Not what it looks like Clint. The Gulfstream is on the way to pick up Interior Minister Miro Hoto of Japan, along with our Ambassador at LAX. We were lucky enough to save the taxpayers' money by deadheading with the aircraft. See, we're not all wasteful bureaucrats," Cole responded adding, "We are nearing the airstrip in Anza. Let's make our last check with Douglas at C."

Cole flipped open what would appear to be a simple cellular telephone, and in a way it was, except that it communicated in the ultra-high frequency band and was voice-to-voice encrypted, level two. The call was patched through to wherever Douglas was, to an identical portable telephone system. The system was able to deliver sixty hours of talk time and be used as a standard cellular telephone to order a pizza delivered.

"Cole here, sir. We are ten minutes to landing, any update?"

Clint could hear a burst of what was Douglas talking, but sitting in the next seat sounded like a nagging horse fly buzzing around.

"I see, good news and bad news. Thanks. Out."

Cole flipped the phone shut and turned to Clint, "It's a go, no contingency plan needed; we will infiltrate as planned. The leaker was confirmed and taken before faxing photos. It was Robert." Cole was somewhat relieved for Clint, but not for the country. What was the extent of the damage Robert had caused, he wondered? Potentially extensive.

For Robert and Clint, it was the beginning.

For Robert, the beginning of months of physically and mentally challenging debriefing.

For Clint, the beginning of his quest to fulfill his purpose and avenge Brook and Cabris.

CHAPTER 7:
THE POINT OF NO RETURN

It was nightfall by the time the STOL aircraft had landed, the short landing strip marked by six battery-operated lights on each side. A light snow, common at this altitude, had coated the grass making the aircraft slip side to side, and its single passenger with it. The sky bright with stars and a near full moon created a majestic scene with the STOL aircraft and lights noticeably out of place.

Carlos used the time from El Paso, where the commercial American Airlines flight from Washington had left him, to think about the information Sheila had given up unknowingly in a White Ice-induced high. The FBI did not know where the camp was, who he was and what his plans were. The undercover agent, Meceli, tripped up Robert, but would Robert tell the little he knew during debriefing? Who was this Clint Bear and how did he fit in? Where was he going to infiltrate if they didn't know who or where he was, and didn't know anything about his operation?

He reasoned, that without knowing where to start, they would push Robert for more information and get the one additional piece of information he actually knew. Robert was spineless. That was why he had chosen and recruited him. He was weak and wanted responsibility without capability. He wanted recognition and praise where none was earned. Yes, Robert would talk, give him up, and he began preparations for it once on the ground.

"Jesús, I have the last batch of chemicals coming in on the STOL the day after tomorrow. You should be ready to break the camp in five, no more than six days. That will give you just enough time, no excess time. Comprende?" Carlos asked.

"We'll need to get some help to make the last batch. Is it the same size as the others?" said Jesús, asking more for the number of playmates he would ultimately have than for the need to plan.

"A little larger, but should be done with only two, no more than four, helpers. I don't want to change a system that works now that we are so close to the end," Carlos commanded. He continued, "Are all the extra security measures I asked for in place and functioning?"

"Yeah. We installed an identical laser sensing system but one hundred feet further into the woods. I set the alarm for silent, so an intruder would not know they had been detected," Jesús said, trying to appear more intelligent than he was.

"Have you tested the alarm systems, individually, every day?" Carlos spat out in military precision.

"Shit! No we haven't. Sorry," Jesús responded, lowering his head a little in shame.

"How are you silently notified if the alarm is activated?" Carlos asked curiously.

"I have the only vibrating beeper and I have clipped it into my underwear, here," Jesús said, showing Carlos a little more than he wanted to see.

"What about the added men; were they screened before you hired them?"

"Yup, the same contact we used last time. All came up clean or wanted for petty crimes," Jesús said, proud that most of Carlos's orders had been carried out.

"Good. Tomorrow you will need to recruit two more helpers. Who have you selected to replace Julio?" Carlos asked to insure all the details were covered. He was double-checking everything now, to prevent getting lax so close to the end.

"José. His name is José Ramos. He is wanted for murdering a guy in his Texas street ring who was stealing from him. He even looks a little like Julio, short and skinny," Jesús said.

"Bring him to my tent first, then I want to talk to the others you have recruited. Jesús, we are close to the end. You will have more money than even you can spend when it's over. There is no room for mistakes now. None! Comprende?" Carlos said, pointing his right thumb at him.

"Yeah, I hear ya, Boss. No screw-ups. Double-check everything."

"No, triple-check everything. And Jesús, you'll get Julio's share if it all goes according to my plan. Now, send Ramos to me first and check to see if each alarm system is working," Carlos said, turning to enter his tent.

Carlos was focused, only a few more weeks. I've got to keep the street operation working, he was thinking. Not just to insure the quick killing in White Ice, but to keep the cartel happy and unaware of his private operation. By cartel law, he was to share everything with the cartel. Holding out was seen as treason as was thinking for yourself and putting your personal wellbeing before the cartel. But White Ice was his idea, his brainchild. Ever since reading about the Johns Hopkins University cocaine research, and connecting it to a synthetic legal substance without telling the cartel, he had been one step to the right of his own death and one step to the left of wealth beyond imagination. The knock on the tent pole shattered his thoughts.

"José?" Carlos asked.

"Yes, sir".

"Come in and sit down. Tell me, Jesús says you killed a man in your street operation in Texas. Is that true?" Carlos baited José.

"Yeah, he was stealing from me. Selling a light nickel bag, making a few extra bags and keeping the coin. Comprende?" José responded. "Once someone starts stealing they don't stop. I can't afford no loyalty in my guys, so I shot him in front of the rest as a lesson, kind of, ya know?"

"Where did you shoot him?" Carlos asked, believing the story.

"In an alley in south Houston."

"No, where on the body did you shoot him?" Carlos pressed.

"Oh, sorry. Clean through the head. A little messy but if you're going to set an example, ya know," José responded.

"Yes, I know. José, we have had your story checked out. You're in. Just remember, I like to set examples too. We've got about two weeks to go, and I'll cut you in for a full share if you and no one else screws up. No one gets in or out of this camp without me or Jesús knowing. You are to shoot to kill, no questions asked, anyone who tries. We'll have a little female companionship in a few days, Jesús will fill you in, we've got plenty of supplies so there is no reason for anyone to leave. Any questions?" Carlos asked.

"You need to see Chico?" José asked.

"You vouch for him?"

"With my life, man!" José shot back.

"That's exactly what you have done," Carlos said, "Exactly."

"Yeah, what are we doing here?" José asked cautiously.

"You'll find out that in two days, until then stick to the plan," Carlos snapped.

"Okay Boss, sorry to pry," José countered to ease the discomfort.

"Send in Tommy," Carlos said to conclude the interview.

Carlos was back in thought. José had low-level connections into the cartel's street operations that reported to him. He will need to be careful not to let José near any form of communication device, just to make sure. I'll have Jesús keep an eye on him until he proves himself, he decided. The knock on the tent pole again interrupting his thought.

"Come in Tommy, and sit down over here," Carlos said.

Tommy was obviously nervous. His tension was obvious in his walk and posture, his hands fidgeting, left knee bobbing and eyes darting all around the tent. Carlos sensed he needed to determine what Tommy's problem was.

"Tommy, you're Indian. What tribe are you?" Carlos started.

"I am Apache, and proud of my people," Tommy spat out defensively.

"Hey, settle down Tommy. I've got nothing against the Apache or any Indians. Just want to get to know my employees better," Carlos said calmly, trying a new tact. "Tell me, why are you here Tommy?"

"For the money, nothing else. I assume we are in the drug business. How else could you pay so well? I don't do drugs and don't give a shit about people who do. It's their business. I need the money to help my tribe. They'll see!" Tommy machine-gunned out.

"Got something to prove, Tommy… if that's your real name?" Carlos inquired.

"Yeah, a lot, but that's my business," Tommy recounted. "And Tommy is my real name."

"You were difficult to check out. We're going to keep a close eye on you. Nothing personal, just business. Any questions?" Carlos asked.

"When do we get paid?"

"Pushy, aren't you. Really need the cash? You get paid when the job is done. Within the next two weeks. Not before. You screw up and you won't need to worry about being paid. You can't spend money when you're dead. Clear?" Carlos said in frigid clarity.

The military Gulfstream landed quietly on the abandoned airstrip in Anza, California near the Cahuilla Indian reservation. Clint could see for miles, and only one person was in sight. He was leaning on the front grill of a white Jeep Cherokee, his dark suit and aviator sunglasses giving him up as a FBI field agent now on loan to Department C.

Cole, sitting opposite Clint, and looking directly into his eyes, said, "Clint, remember, you are to infiltrate, learn as much as possible about how the drug is produced, who has the production formula, how it is to be distributed. Trace the money and deliver the generals — the guys who pull the strings — as well as anyone who knows the formula. Immediately, we have only days at best. By any means."

Clint knew what "By any means" meant.

"Clint, we've introduced you as Ricardo Marcus to the organization. The infiltration will start with a mid-level street manager. We've set you up for two to three cocaine buys. Each will be progressively larger. You have ten million in cash in your new home. Use it as needed. The first one will be a quarter of a million, the second a full million. The third will be your call. Your capacity to buy will push you higher in the organization. Hopefully high enough. But, be careful not to push too hard too quickly. They may smell something and shut you down. Permanently." Cole was cautioned.

"Cole, how can I not push hard? I've only got days to complete the assignment!" Clint countered.

"I know. I'm just normally a little concerned with projects that have not been thoroughly planned. Time has not allowed us to think of logical contingency plans to counter the likely holes. Christ, I sound so clinical! Sorry, Clint."

"I've grown to like you as well Cole. We'll get through this," Clint said reassuringly.

"Thanks, I hope so, for America's sake. Clint, the car is parked at LAX long term, space B184. Repeat, B184. Drive and park the Jeep anywhere, we'll pick it up later. Here is a twenty-four hour seven day a week telephone number to use with your special cell phone. Memorize it. You can use the number anywhere within North America and the Caribbean. It's a real-time reverse encrypted line. Wait ten seconds after connect before talking, then the line will be secure. Anyone who taps in will hear nothing but static and think they've screwed up. Good luck." Cole said while putting a hand tenderly on Clint's shoulder.

"We have the One God and the right purpose on our side, but a little luck won't hurt," Clint said as he closed the Jeep door.

Cole watched the dry earth flair up off the trail of the Jeep as Clint Bear, son of Native America, now America's last hope, started the quest. He wondered which quest would, in the end, win the inner battle, America's or Clint's. Then, as he climbed the Gulfsteam's retractable stairway he reasoned that America would win either way, but Clint would win only if America wins.

Clint took the direct route, heading west to the 5 and north to 405 and into LAX. He parked near B184 and placed the infiltration supplies, neatly hidden within expensive leather Hartman luggage, into the small trunk of the new Porsche 911, white with chrome alloy rims and Pirelli tires. Exiting the long term parking, Clint — now Ricardo Marcus — headed south on Route 1 to his home in Laguna Beach, where the San Pedro Channel meets the Gulf of Santa Catalina.

While Clint drove, he reviewed the insertion strategy and his new identity, memorizing and internalizing once again the details. The cross-links, Spanish, the need for speed, the gray abused bodies of Cabris and Brook. "Keep the focus," he whispered.

The first buy would be made through a mid-level street wholesaler named Leon Beecher. He had worked his way up through the organization from a street pusher. He had been selected because he is aggressive and a buy this size was not very common. The combination of his climb within the organization suggesting aggressiveness and the size of this buy work compatibly. Leon lives north of Los Angeles in an exclusive area called Venice. My first tactic, Clint was thinking, is to contact Leon Beecher.

It was a good omen to have remembered the directions to his new house. Turning into the driveway, Clint was impressed with the choice. A long single-story white stucco ranch, directly overlooking the gulf, with a long steep drop to the rocky surf below. The landscaping was meticulously maintained and designed to provide the maximum privacy from the typical close California neighbors.

Clint noticed movement near the rear shrubs as what appeared to be the gardener stepped out carrying a few dead shrub branches.

"Hello, nice to see again, Mr. Marcus," Louis Maldonado, the gardener said in Spanish. "Mr. Cunningham said to expect you and I wanted the garden to be just the way you like it."

"Nice to see you as well, Louis," Clint responded to the Department C, former FBI Agent. "The garden looks beautiful."

"Would you like help with your luggage?"

"Thanks, but no, I've only a few pieces," Clint responded as he walked around the Porsche to the trunk.

Taking the luggage in hand, Clint walked toward the house, taking in all the details. The double door unlocked, Clint walked in and stopped, taking his time surveying the home's interior, tastefully decorated in a Spanish motif. White walls, subtle green upholstery-covering twin sofas, a mahogany bar with leaded glass mirrors, massive sculptured and glassed windows providing a beautiful view of the water. Very elegant, very expensive, just perfect for Ricardo Marcus.

Clint dropped the luggage and went directly to the telephone resting on the bar. He dialed the number memorized and waited for Leon's voice. The voice came mechanically and Clint left a message to call him on a matter of large importance. No one uses the phrase "large importance", so Leon should correctly interpret it to mean big bucks.

Having planted the hook with Leon, Clint unpacked, changed into a pair of shorts and sneakers and went for a long run. He was hoping for at least a five miler, get the heart pumping and clear his head and get to know his surroundings.

The abrupt foreign tone of a new telephone ringing didn't faze Clint's meditation. It was 10:05 AM and he had been up for five hours preparing himself. Calmly he lifted the receiver from its cradle on the bar.

"Hello?" Ricardo said.

"You called me. What do you want?" Leon said, almost rapping to music.

"I want to do some business," Ricardo responded.

"Don't we all, don't we all. I only do business with people I know, and you ain't even an acquaintance," Leon countered.

"I was doing business with Joey, but as you know he's retired. He always told me that if we were cut off for any reason I should contact you. So I called. Listen, I was a loyal customer, probably his most loyal, but definitely his largest," Ricardo planted carefully. Joey was on the same level as Leon within the organization and was busted by the DEA two weeks earlier. "But hey, you don't need any more business, I understand. Goodbye." Ricardo said as he calmly replaced the received in the cradle on the bar.

The hook was set more deeply. Hopefully the fish will run, Clint thought.

Meceli was frustrated with the dead ends at Johns Hopkins and her gait showed it. The cocaine research was conducted by a small group of research scientists and graduate students. The few PhDs that had access to the research, in its entirety, were all accounted for and cleared. It was beginning to look like there were no links between the "chemist" and Johns Hopkins University.

But there must be a link, there must. Johns Hopkins was the only place that has the completed cocaine research and the synthetic drug mimics the symptomatic effects of cocaine. Okay, she said to herself, what do we know? The drug ring has produced the synthetic drug. There are multiple raped and murdered women, and it's related in some way. They have threatened the lives of the President and his family. Robert has been compromised, but as yet, remains silent.

Wait a minute, Anne-Marie Meceli said to herself, most of the grad students were women. Is it possible that one of them was compromised? I'll work that angle, but after the briefing with Douglas, she said as she entered the White House and cleared security.

"Good morning, Agent Meceli," Douglas said.

"Good morning, Director," Anne-Marie responded. "Any change with Robert?"

"Surprisingly, no. Robert either doesn't know much, or anything more, or he has developed a spine. My bet is he doesn't know much. In fact, I think he doesn't know that he knows something of value to us. Our challenge is to sort out what he could know and push the right buttons to make him let it out. Unfortunately, we have not yet succeeded in that endeavor." Douglas reported.

"I have a similar report. Everyone within the Johns Hopkins' research project is cleared. I'll begin to work on a sexual exploitation angle next since most of the grad students were female. Frankly, I'm a bit frustrated," exclaimed Anne-Marie.

"Clint Bear has made the initial contact with Leon Beecher. They are checking him out now. With any luck, and we are due for some luck, Clint will make the first buy tomorrow," Douglas said. "Not surprisingly, there have been no secure transmissions since we have taken Robert. We must conclude that either we have not determined the contact time and date, or they know that Robert has been compromised. Any comments?"

Agent Meceli pondered Robert's situation. "I'm inclined to agree that Robert does not know what he knows. Logically, he must have met the guy who compromised him at least once so he must have a physical description. Is it possible he doesn't know who it was?"

"I can create a scenario where a mark, Robert, has been made without the marker being compromised. This guy we call the 'caller' is crafty enough to create a legal synthetic drug and stockpile it for rapid distribution, then the caller is capable of not being physically compromised by Robert. Further, he chose his mark well. A man very close to the

President, loaded with information and access to more, and of such weak character to be capable of compromise." Douglas concluded, "Robert does not know what he knows, and that changes our debriefing methodology."

"Sir?" Meceli said, indicating that she was not finished. "How is Clint Bear emotionally?"

Douglas looked at Meceli for a moment and then started to look through her when he responded, "Agent Meceli, I assume that this query is purely in context with this mission?" his eyes telling her that he has deduced there was more to it.

"Yes, of course. Clint Bear is the only person standing between the deaths of hundreds of thousands of people. His emotional state is a vital factor; don't you agree Director?" Meceli said, overplaying her response.

"I see," Douglas said, having confirmation that indeed there was something more. "He was in control and highly motivated. The instructors in Virginia learned more from him than vice versa, no surprise. There was universal agreement that he was the best, by a wide margin mind you, that has ever undergone such advanced training. Our only concern is the source of the motivation. One more thing…"

There it is again, the 'one more thing', Meceli thought.

"Clint Bear's father has died. He was found by the tribe's elders and laid to rest in proper Indian custom. He died from natural causes and Clint knew before the body was found," Douglas added.

The room was becoming claustrophobic, a new experience for Meceli. She had genuine feelings for Clint. How could that be; I don't even know the man, she was thinking. What tragedy he has had to endure over the last two weeks and the last twenty plus years. My heart aches to comfort him. "God help him," Meceli whispered to herself.

"Mr. Director? Please don't misunderstand this. Don't take this for anything other than what it is. But there will be a time when Clint Bear will need an operative's assistance. Someone who has sound field experience in tactical undercover work. Someone who has killed and will kill again. I want to be the first person considered for that assignment," Meceli said with a strange calm and absolute determination.

Douglas pondered a few moments, remembering the last time he felt so in need. Meceli was one of his best field agents. She was like a daughter to him, and agreeing to her request could be sending her to her death. Not agreeing to her request could endanger the operation where quick response is needed, and she would probably just resign her commission and go to him without backup.

"Anne-Marie, you may not know that I frequently think of you as a daughter. Agreeing to your request may well send you to your death, something I could not live with. Are you sure you want me to consider this request?" Douglas asked in a fatherly sensitive tone.

Meceli was stunned to learn that the Director cared for her so, but still she responded, "Yes, I do. Sir, I don't fully understand this myself. It seems within me, something directing me to what I simply must do. I can't explain it, but yes, yes I do want you to consider it," Meceli said.

"Then if the tactical need comes upon us, a need that warrants your skills, you will be the first considered. And, Anne-Marie, it is love that you are beginning to feel. I saw it in your eyes when you first met Clint in the Oval Office. In our business love is a rare occurrence. We are always so busy being someone else, concentrating on the cross-links and covering our backs, there are just no opportunities for love to grow. If he makes it through this ordeal, take the time to find out if this is the real thing, and if it is go for it and get the hell out of this business. Anne-Marie, I know

Clint very well, and he is a man a father would be proud to have as a son-in-law," Douglas said while holding Meceli's hands. The sensitivity and caring would have seemed out of character if it were not so real.

"Now, Meceli, we have work to do. Dig into the Johns Hopkins' women's angle and see if you can get a physical description," Douglas said returning to the Director from the father-like figure.

"Hello?" Ricardo said into the mouthpiece.

"You checked out. I'll meet you for a drink at Captains, near the Marina del Rey, at 7:00 tonight."

The dial tone was the next sound heard. Leon was short on manners, but right on time, Clint was thinking as he pulled his cellular out and dialed the memorized number. Two rings, then a ten second void, encryption was activating and then, "Yes?"

"Cole please."

"Speaking."

"The meeting is set for tonight. Captains bar at 7:00 PM. It is near Marina del Rey. I like it. It's a public forum probably to see if I've got two heads. It's Leon's turf, so he'll know something's up if there are any strangers or anything out of the ordinary. Cole, stay back, way back and let me handle this meeting," Clint said.

"They'll go through your car, check the registration and your address. All that's covered and clean. Don't give them anything else to go on. Remember, up the buy, make the first buy one million dollars. And I've come up with a better distribution strategy for your drugs. Japan. You know Japan very well. There's a lot of money there to buy drugs. Let it out that you have a street operation and an upper-class network in Japan and can move all the cocaine he can provide. You just finished getting the organization set up when Joey retired. It's out of his area, so he will reason it won't impact his sales. It's pure profit for him. It should make him a little less inquisitive. Next contact, when you arrive home and are out of sight. Out," Cole said as he terminated the connection.

Clint was not going to let the murderous California traffic delay him, and set out three hours early for Marina del Rey. Driving the 405 north, he understood why it has the reputation of being America's largest parking lot. He overshot the logical exit and went on to the 10, going west a few miles to Route 1 south, figuring whoever may be watching for him would be more apt to be expecting him from the south, not from the north.

Captains was positioned at the end of Pacific Avenue, a dead end street ending at the marina. Anyone coming down the street was either going to the marina, to Captains or shouldn't be on the street. Good choice, Leon, Clint thought. Anyone or any vehicle would be easily trapped. It was 6:38, he would be early. Better than being late.

As Clint walked to the front entrance, he took in the building and its surroundings. A front and rear door, two emergency doors, large parking lot, weathered cedar shingled exterior and single story. Looked more like it belonged in Cape Cod, Massachusetts. Simple pine tables and chairs with pleated cushions to match the checkerboard vinyl tablecloths completed the ambiance.

He pulled the door handle, the rusted hinges announcing another visitor. His eyes were adjusting to the dark interior when he heard, "You're early. A little anxious, Ricardo?"

The voice came from a tall black man dressed in black trousers and a white silk shirt. His sunglasses completed the picture of coolness but looked out of place in such a dark room.

"You know the 405, could take two hours, could take twenty. Who knows!" Ricardo shot back.

"Just have a seat. He'll be here soon," the tall black man said as he walked out the front door.

Clint sat at the table by the window in the restaurant section so he could see Leon when he approached. About fifteen minutes later, a white Cadillac moved slowly down Pacific Avenue, pulling up to the front door and stopping. Welcome home, Leon, Clint thought to himself.

Leon Beecher exited the Cadillac gracefully, with a confident style, and walked to Captains' front entrance. He was a large, almost fat man, but he carried his weight fluidly. His black skin was more Hispanic in color than black, and his black hair was slick and shiny with gel. Leon always wore his trademark tailored white linen suit, powder blue silk shirt, open at the collar, and a matching pocket handkerchief. Leon had style.

"I said we would have a drink, not dinner," Leon said to Ricardo.

"I liked the view here better," Ricardo responded.

"Ya know, in my line of work we don't like it when people do what they want, not what they're told to do," Leon said calmly.

"Well, it's your show. Now that you're here," Ricardo said, giving Leon just a hint of back talk.

Leon walked in the bar a little further and said, "Let's go for that drink." Gesturing with his left hand toward the back of the bar, he added, "After you."

They sat in the rear windowless corner of the bar. A real built-in corner table that enabled both to look at each other as well as watch the bar.

"Are you a cop?" Leon asked starting his questions.

"You checked me out so you know the answer to that question. Now, let's not play games, okay?" Ricardo shot back.

"Yeah, we did check you out, but there is still more to do. Are you wired?" Leon said as he patted down Ricardo's chest and legs.

"Are you a cop?" Ricardo asked forcefully.

"What! What the hell is this? This a game?" Leon yelled out, turning the few heads in the bar.

"No, it's no game. Just that there's too many strange things happening in this business," Ricardo said, skillfully positioning them as allies in the same business.

They stared at each other for several moments. This is the toughest part. One's eyes always tell the story of the heart, like a transmitter of truth. The agency tells you the trick is to mimic the eyes observing yours. Your mind concentrates on this and the transmitter is working for you, not against you. Your observer sees what he wants to see, he sees himself. While that can work, Clint relied on a blend of his ancient Indian and Far Eastern teachings to enter "emptiness".

Emptiness is from the teachings of Miyamoto Musashi, Japan's most legendary martial artist, who in the late 16th century founded the Individual School of Two Skies. He believed he was never beaten in battle or in contest because he had mastered his craft so well he had entered the realm where nothing exists or cannot be known. Emptiness.

"No, I'm not a cop and I'm not wired either. Want to pat me down?" Leon said finally.

"No, that's not the best way to start what I hope is a long-term wealth-building relationship," Ricardo said, knowing he had won the battle between minds.

"What do you want, and when?" Leon asked quietly.

"I have my operation in place and they're hungry, I need a lot of coke, one million. Can you handle it?" Ricardo said equally as quietly.

"What you goin' to do with that much stuff?" Leon asked cautiously, hiding his instant excitement for potential new business.

"Look I went over this with Joey, but one more time. My operation is in Japan. I've got the street and the yuppie network. It took months of work to develop a foolproof way of getting the stuff from here onto the streets of Tokyo and without the stuff I can't afford to keep the organization together. One million is an appetizer. I can move all the stuff you can supply. No credit needed, this is all cash, if you can supply," Ricardo explained with just the right tone to imply, "I'm tired of this, sell me the stuff or I'm out of here."

"You're an interesting guy, Ricardo. You'll hear from me within twelve hours, or not. We'll see," Leon said as he stood up, straightened his suit jacket and walked out of the bar.

The smile on his face told Clint that he would be hearing from him, and probably sooner than twelve hours.

Luck had finally graced Meceli. The senior research grad student had had a brief affair with a wealthy South American businessman.

"Mr. Director, she had seen him at a foreign exchange function, and having a thing for older men, introduced herself. After all, in her words, he was admiring her frequently over the course of the evening, why not? They slept with each other that night and he met her in the lab the following day. That's where he must have copied the research. Nothing was or is missing." Meceli reported by telephone. "She has not been in contact since that day. I believe her."

"Good work. Get his physical description to the CIA and FBI. Let's see if we can find out who we are hunting," Douglas said as he replaced the secure receiver in its cradle.

***

Clint sat in the center of the living room floor, legs crossed with his wrists laying face-up on his thighs. His closed eyes opened slowly as he came out of the meditative state when the telephone call came, the one he was expecting, at a little after 9 in the morning. He answered the telephone pretending to be awakened by the call.

"Yes?" Clint said sheepishly.

"Cash deal, we'll meet at the same place, same time. You and me, any strangers and someone is goin' to get hurt. This time, do exactly as you are told."

It was Leon himself, and was unusual for the head of an organization to handle a deal personally. You paid people to take those risks for you. Yet, Leon was doing this personally. Clint wondered to himself, Why? Is he afraid of moving in on someone else's turf? Is he intending to keep the proceeds personally by hiding the transaction from the cartel? Or is intending to kill me and take the cash?

Clint reasoned that Leon was both power hungry and money hungry. The power came from the cartel and the money came from the drugs, which came from the cartel. No, Leon wasn't about to kill a golden goose, especially one that had promised to move as much stuff as he could supply. He must be worried about turf, and shielding the transaction from any climbers within his organization would prevent them from using it against him in a coup. The one-million-dollar deal, and the few larger deals after that, would probably be recorded as multiple street deals to cover it completely.

Two rings, ten seconds for encryption, "Yes?"

"Cole please," Clint said in monotone.

"Speaking. Have you had contact?" Cole asked.

"Yes. The first buy is tonight. Same place and time. Leon is handling the transaction personally. What do you make of that?" Clint responded.

The audio void indicated Cole's reflection on the twist of events. Every field agent fully expects unplanned actions and reactions. People are not machines, they are driven by emotion, greed and lust. So, the experienced agent cultivates a mental chessboard of possibilities, moves and countermoves. They learn from the choices made, building a deeper composite of their mark and factor in the new choice to guide their reaction to it, much the same way as the FBI and CIA use artificial intelligence computer programs.

"Clint, I take it as good news all round. If they suspected a rat and you were to be planned for termination, the muscle end of his organization would be handling the buy. So you're clean there. I think he is too smart, or better said, not stupid enough, to pocket the cash and leave the cartel out. My guess is he is worried about where you're going to sell the stuff and whose turf is going to take the hit. The stuff can't be traced, but a large deal would be suspect. He'll probably break the deal into three or four street buys in the records to shelter it, but keep it within the cartel. That's critical for us, because the last buy must get you exposed to the cartel. Better they know something about you now through the smaller buys," Cole reasoned, happy that things are progressing quickly.

"Listen, Cole, I think we need to…"

"Yeah, I know what you're going to say," Cole interrupted. "No men, no technology that could screw this up and land a bullet in your head."

"Thanks for understanding Cole," Clint said. "Any news from back east?"

"Yes, Meceli has busted her ass and had a break. She found the source in Johns Hopkins. Seems a grad student with a thing for older men had a brief affair with a South American businessman. He did meet her in the lab once and has not contacted her since. That must be when the research was copied. They're running a physical description on him now. Hopefully we will know who we are dealing with within ten to twelve hours," Cole reported. "And, Clint, I think Meceli has special motivation."

"Thanks again, Cole." Clint said as he closed the special cell phone. Special motivation?

Clint dressed in sneakers, an old SCU tee shirt and a clean pair of blue Umbro shorts, and started his run. He decided on at least five miles this morning to provide time to clear his head and ready himself for tonight. Odds were that everything would go smoothly, but he had to be prepared for the holes. He had to be ready for the unexpected. Certainly, things would not go as expected. What if the police were on to Leon and have him under surveillance? What if he has done this before and the cartel is watching him? What if a rival breaks up the deal? What if, what if, what if. The actions and reactions planned and counter-planned. Around in circles, one picks up where the other leaves off. Circles.

Familiar territory is a weapon. Clint took the same memorized route to Captains in Marina del Rey. This time, he did not stop to observe the building. That was a non-factor, so as he drove down Pacific Avenue he looked for what was new, out of place or missing. With the exception of a few boats back in their slips, and still others out to sea, everything seemed quite normal.

California's trademark weather, he thought. Almost 7:00, the sun beginning to set and the temperature still in the 80s. A gentle sea breeze blew through the open windows of his Porsche 911, bringing in a little dust, covering his briefcase, and he slowed to a stop. The white Cadillac was nowhere to be seen, but Clint — Ricardo Marcus — walked to the front entrance, briefcase in hand.

"Hey, Ricardo!" Ricardo heard from behind him. As he turned he saw Leon, in his white linen suit and blue shirt, standing on the fly bridge of a large yacht, birthed stern in. From there he could see the entire length of Pacific Avenue, as well as the entire yacht club. Good choice, Clint thought as he walked toward the boat. Very good choice.

"Come aboard, Ricardo," Leon said. "Let's go fishing."

Ricardo scanned the boat. There was no one else visible, although there could easily be a dozen men in the cabin of what appeared to be at least a 45-foot Chris Craft. Clint went into emptiness and scanned the boat for life signs as he walked the pier, but was interrupted by the roar of the yacht's twin engines.

"Free those lines and let's get under way," Leon ordered.

Ricardo tossed the mooring line off the bow before stepping aboard, then went aft to free the boat entirely. Immediately after the last aft line was free, Leon eased the yacht out of the slip. He handled the large yacht with ease, obviously having done this many times before. I wonder how many times the yacht returned with one fewer occupants, Clint thought as he climbed the ladder to join Leon on the fly bridge.

"Glad you could make it, Ricardo," Leon said not taking his eyes off the waterway. "Is that for me?" pointing to the briefcase.

"I hope it is," Ricardo said implying that it was his only in exchange for the stuff.

"Spend much time on the water?" Leon asked making small talk.

"Not much," Ricardo responded thinking of the years of training and BEL work as a Navy SEAL, and then briefly flashed into the PBR during training while he rubbed his shoulder. Refocusing, he asked, "Where are we going?"

"We goin' fishin'," Leon sung out rap style. "Fishin' for privacy. No prying ears or eyes. Ya know?"

"I like it. Makes me comfortable. Are we alone on this boat?" Ricardo asked.

"Why, a little nervous, Ricky?" Leon said smiling, and for the first time looked at Clint. They were out of the waterway and Leon was increasing to full cruising speed. The crafts twin diesel engines roared to life and the boat began to plane while it reached cruising speed. The tiny launch that was being towed was being thrashed about in the boat's wake. "Good, I like that. Shows that you're not cocky and overconfident. A little worry keeps you breathing, ya know? Yes, we're alone."

Clint looked aft to see the harbor getting smaller, and for a moment related to the small, motorized launch in tow as it bounced uncontrollably. He looked forward and noticed that Leon was heading directly for a marine layer that was moving toward land. As he entered the layer, Leon throttled back, turning aft to insure the marine layer completely enveloped the boat. No one could see in, we couldn't see out. He then turned on the boat's stereo, placed an unknown jazz CD in and turned the volume up.

"No prying eyes and no prying ears," Leon said and, and as he turned he pointed the gun directly at Ricardo. "Come a little closer, let me pat you down."

"I've got a gun under my left arm, no wires. I'm going to keep the gun," Ricardo stated clearly while he was being frisked.

"Okay, you're clean. Keep the gun," Leon said looking down to holster his weapon. When Leon looked back up, he flinched when he saw Ricardo pointing his gun directly at him.

"Your turn, Leon. Come a little closer so I can pat you down," Ricardo demanded.

"Mother fucker! You don't trust me?" Leon yelled sarcastically.

"I've lived this long by being extra careful, hopefully I'll live a longer life if I continue," Ricardo said while frisking Leon. "Okay, you're clean. Nothing personal Leon, but I don't want to end up as some guy's love slave in prison," Ricardo said as he holstered his weapon.

Leon was looking pretty pissed off, staring directly into Ricardo's eyes with a "don't ever fuck with me again" look. Good. He bought it. It was just enough to give me the credibility I need for the next buy, Clint was thinking.

"I didn't come out here to talk trash with you Leon, let's get this over with," Ricardo said with a hint of exasperation. "Did you bring the stuff?"

"Did you bring the cash?" Leon said looking at the brief case.

"Yeah, one million. Nothing larger than a hundred," Ricardo said opening the case. "Did you bring the stuff?"

"Take the cash out of the briefcase and put it into this duffel bag," Leon said while handing him the dark blue canvas bag.

Ricardo, pondered this for a moment. Not to figure out why Leon had asked to have the money transferred. That was obvious. The money may not be traceable, but the briefcase could easily have a bug or homing device buried within it. No, he was appearing to ponder, for Leon's sake if he should do that when he hadn't seen the stuff yet. It was what Leon would expect. After he felt he had paused long enough, he then started to place the cash into the bag.

"Okay, the cash is in the blue duffel bag. Now what?" Ricardo asked.

Leon grabbed the briefcase and threw it overboard before answering. "That's a stolen launch we have in tow. The stuff is in there. Hop in and motor back by your lonesome."

"Cute, Leon. How do I know the stuff is in there?" Ricardo responded.

"You don't trust me yet, Ricky?" Leon said sarcastically. "I'm hurt, really hurt! Listen, you said you handle all the stuff I could supply. Still true?"

"Very true," Ricardo said.

"Let's plan one, only one more deal. Can you handle a very large single deal? Cash?" Leon asked.

"How large?" Ricardo asked, noting that this was a hole he hadn't considered.

"I can arrange a deal for eight million dollars. Can you have that much in cash?" Leon said.

"Why only one more deal, you going out of business or something? Remember, I need a steady source of supply," Ricardo added for credibility.

The marine layer was becoming denser and it was condensing on their skin, making it reflect the boat's running lights. Leon was considering telling Ricardo something, and then said, "I am able to provide only one last shipment. After that, I'm changing my business. Simple as that. Now do you want it or not?" Leon said, thinking that he would be pocketing the eight million and after a few weeks of White Ice sales, disappearing to enjoy his wealth.

"Okay, but two conditions. One, you and I are the only two involved…"

"You do trust me Ricky. I'm touched!"

"…And two, you introduce me to another source of supply, to pick up where you left off. Hey, I've got an organization to feed," Clint added in a stern voice, indicating that without this, there would be no deal.

Okay, I'll just introduce him to Carlos and his boys and they take care of him, for the good of the operation, Leon thought. "Deal. Be at my boat tomorrow, same time. The first million is in the launch, don't worry. Just tie it up at the end of the pier, take the case with the stuff and leave."

Leon looked at the ship's compass and then turned to give Ricardo a bearing, pointing due east with one hand, as he untied the launch with the other. Clint pulled the outboard motor to life and headed due east back to the harbor, thinking about this newest hole. One buy, not two. His intuition told him that was good news. When he was out of the marine layer and out of sight, he stole a quick look in the canvas bag. It was filled with plastic bags of cocaine.

He's actually pretty smart. Arrange the transaction out in the ocean, under the cover of a marine mist layer, and then throwing the briefcase overboard. There is no linkage of the transaction to him. If I am caught, I would be assumed the thief who stole the launch. Leon is clean and a million dollars richer.

Clint motored back to the harbor without any curious onlookers, tied the launch to the end of the first pier, and walked toward Captains. There was little sign of life on the pier, but Captains was beginning to demonstrate why such a large parking lot was required. Looks like the yacht set liked to party.

He waited until he was on the 405 South before he lifted the cell phone out on the door pocket and dialed the memorized number. Two rings, ten seconds for the encryption to lock in and then, "Yes?"

"Cole please," Clint said.

"Speaking. How did it go?" Cole asked with a little sigh of relief to hear Clint's voice.

"The transaction was completed on his yacht, on the ocean in the middle of a marine layer mist. Not so dumb. He says he's getting out of the business and will make only one last deal, but it has to be a big one, eight million dollars. After that, he's going into a new line of work," Clint reported.

About two minutes went by without a word. Clint didn't break the audio void, sensing, correctly, that Cole was processing the new information.

"I don't like it. The timetable is to our benefit because it gets us deeper into the organization more quickly. My sense is that it is moving too quickly. Damn it, it just doesn't feel right. Shit! When is the last buy set up for?" Cole asked pensively.

"Tomorrow, same time, same place as today. My intuition is that he is interested in one last score, for his personal bank account. But it's his show. We don't have a choice. If I don't go along, my take is that he will fade out and we've lost our entrée. If I do go along there is a distinct possibility that there will be a bullet awaiting the eight million, not coke. Unless you've got something better, we have no choice. He did agree to introduce me to a new source of supply, once he has changed professions," Clint added.

Cole thought pensively about their options. There were none, he knew it, Clint knew it and Leon knew it. It was indeed Leon's show. But we need something, anything to give Clint some edge. Wait a minute, "Clint, didn't you say he agreed to make an intro to a new source of supply?"

"Yes, he agreed, although I don't believe him," Clint responded.

"Clint, think about it. If Leon did that he would be exposing the private transaction and place himself on the cartel's shit list. He won't do that, ergo your dead as soon as he gets the $8 million," Cole reasoned. "Our only chance to save your ass as well as the mission is to make the deal with the new source, not with Leon."

"Impossible, Cole. Leon is not going to walk away from the eight million dollars. But if I can convince him it's with the new source or nothing, because the risks are too high for a one-shot deal, then maybe he'll cut in his source for half, figuring four million is better than none," Clint spoke as the strategy came into focus.

"Clint, your odds aren't great. This is a 'Hail Mary' option and I hope you can jump. I won't ask you to do this. It's your decision. If it were me, I'm not sure I would do it," Cole said, expressing justifiable concern for Clint's life. But, if Clint didn't do it, the distribution of the synthetic would surely take place, killing hundreds of thousands of Americans.

"I knew the risks when I committed to this mission. My life is over without this closure and you know it Cole. But, thanks for your concern. Next contact after I go on a shopping spree with eight million. Out," Clint said as he drove the powerful Porsche south on the 405 toward his home in Laguna Beach.

Immediately upon arriving home he went to the mahogany bar, lifted the telephone receiver and called Leon. To his surprise Leon answered the telephone.

"My package is already on its way to Japan. Tomorrow, same time, same place but your replacement source must be with you or no deal. I've got mouths to feed. If I don't hear from you I'll assume it's off." Clint then quietly replaced the receiver and prepared for another run to refresh his mind.

Running at night was his least favorite time. The air was hotter and filled with carbon monoxide and other toxins that interfered with proper breathing. He needed the release though, tensions were building just like it was before going BEL. Once it started, the tensions were replaced with adrenaline, and adrenaline could be focused to help where tension only sapped energy and diverted attention. In twenty-four hours the circle should grow larger, and is a real sense, much smaller. Intuition told him he was right, but there was uncomfortable confusion in his thoughts.

***

The President was fidgeting at his desk awaiting the arrival of Director Douglas. Agent Meceli had arrived three minutes earlier and was seated in front of the nervous President in the Oval Office. The President broke the awkward silence, "Meceli, what do you think Clint's chances are of stopping the synthetic distribution and coming out alive?"

"Mr. President, those are two questions I have been grappling with for days now. First, if you're looking for a sound bite, maybe one in ten. But, Clint is a most unusual man, probably the most unusual man I have ever met. Of anyone I am familiar with, or even have read about, he is the most likely to succeed," Meceli responded. "Sir, I am aware of your special fondness for Clint, and understand your concern for him, and for the success of the mission."

"Meceli, do I sense a little more than admiration for Clint in your words?" The President asked.

"Yes, sir, I think you do," Meceli answered without thinking, and then wished she hadn't. But Director Douglas was escorted into the office by Ms. Turcott before she had a chance to backtrack.

"I am very sorry for keeping you waiting these few minutes, sir. I know that three minutes can seem like three hours at times like these. But, we have good news all around to report," Douglas said as he took his seat in front of the President's massive desk.

"First, thanks to solid old-fashioned police work by Agent Meceli, we now know who we are hunting. His name is Carlos Ortega, a general in the Peruvian cartel. A very dangerous and capable man. This is a recent photograph. He is forty-seven years old, five feet eight inches, speaks Spanish, English and French fluently, with passable Italian. He, and he alone, runs the American drug organization for the cartel. Every single gram of cocaine, heroin and ounce of marijuana the cartel markets in North America is touched by Carlos Ortega. He…"

"That's the best news I had in some time. Let's find him and arrest him," the President interrupted.

"Sir, we should absolutely do that, but not yet," Douglas replied.

"Why? We know he is the guy. The physical evidence can't be far behind and I can't risk the synthetic hitting the streets. Not to mention he is the one who threatened the lives of my family, and me!" the President barked back, his index finger stabbing the air in front of him.

"Yes, sir. We can arrest him, assuming we can find him, for threatening the President's life, a very serious charge. But if we do, we seriously risk losing the link to the chemist, the stock piles of lethal synthetic drugs, and the cartel itself," Douglas said carefully.

Taking a deep breath, and looking at Meceli for reassurance, the President asked, "What do you suggest, Eric?"

"Thank you, sir. That segues into the next bit of good news. Clint Bear has completed his first buy and has upped the pace to complete one more transaction. An eight-million-dollar transaction. He has made it a requirement that with the transaction he be introduced to the next level of command, to provide insurance of a continuation of supply. Mr. President, we believe the next level of command is Carlos Ortega…"

"Jesus Christ, this is moving too fast. I don't like it; it doesn't feel right!" Meceli spoke up, interrupting Douglas's flow.

"I have mixed feelings about this as well," the President added. "The speed with which Clint has infiltrated the organization is unprecedented, but have we had time to back him up with proper planning, Douglas?"

"Frankly, no, Mr. President. However, we don't have the time to slow the infiltration pace. The synthetic could be released to the streets any time: yesterday, today, tomorrow... who knows. We have one supreme weakness. Time," Douglas replied. "Sir, I'm not being callous here, but what do we have to lose at this point? We don't know the whereabouts of Carlos Ortega. Therefore, we cannot yet prevent the synthetic distribution and the loss of life that will surely follow. The very worst that could happen now is Clint fails to make contact with Carlos. Then we have the option of an all-points manhunt and arrest him on a wide assortment of charges. We will easily get the details from him with... our techniques. The best that can happen is that Clint does make contact and continues his infiltration within the cartel while transmitting the synthetic details to us to enable us to stop the distribution," Douglas said clinically.

"No, the very worst that can happen is Clint is killed, we don't catch Carlos and the synthetic is distributed!" the President countered. Meceli would have said the same thing, but it was far better coming from the President. But, she knew that the Director was right. Clint's life became expendable, by his own free choice if not the dire circumstances, when he volunteered for this assignment. It was the mission that the Director must think of, first and foremost.

"Sir, if we don't get the formula, and those who know the formula, this situation will repeat and may be so wide-spread that it becomes unstoppable. We've got to stop it once and forever," Douglas stated knowing he was right, and knowing the President agreed.

Sleep was an experiment in discontinuity, the telephone ringing just another disruption. "Hello?" Clint said in a groggy voice. "What time is it?"

"It's 3:40 AM. That leaves you just four hours and twenty minutes to pack and meet me at Meadowlark Airport. It's about twenty miles north of you, just east of Sunset Beach. You wanted the intro, so we're going to him. That's my condition to your condition," Leon said and then abruptly hung up.

Clint sat up in bed, and rubbed his face with both hands. He thought about another run, but he needed to conserve his energy. Meadowlark Airport, probably a small local airstrip. They were going to him. Well, even a small jet could have a range of about fifteen hundred miles, that could place him in Canada, Mexico or anywhere west of the Mississippi. However, based on where Paul Cudson was found, Clint reasoned that he'd be going to the Rocky Mountains.

After calling Cole and bringing him up to date, he tried to get another hour's sleep, and knowing it would not come, began to meditate instead.

He headed north on Route 1, taking a left on Bolsa Chica Street when he reached Sunset Beach. The airport catered to small light aircraft, mostly private owners. Leon was standing in the doorway of a twin propeller engine aircraft that looked like a Short Takeoff and Landing plane. Putting two and two together, this was probably the plane that had landed in the Rockies at the druggie's camp. He must be going to meet Carlos Ortega himself.

Clint parked by the chain link fence, grabbed his bag and the oversized bag containing the eight million in cash. It was heavy and awkward to carry, so he threw it over his shoulder as he approached the plane.

"I didn't know if you'd show, Ricky," Leon said once he was within earshot.

"Remember, I've people to feed," Ricardo responded as the engines began to rotate and then roared to life. The black richly sweet smoke rose from the JP12 diesel-like fuel, being pushed far behind the engines' exhaust ports by the propellers swirling gusts.

"Times a wast'n'," Leon said as he stepped aside, allowing Ricardo to enter the aircraft. "Hands out to the side, you know the drill." Ricardo lifted both arms so Leon could frisk him, knowing he would not find anything but his Smith & Wesson.

"Today I got to look in both bags. You know, orders. Got to take your gun too, a little extra security," Leon said. Satisfied that there were no wires or tracking devices, he used the intercom and told the pilot to get underway.

Leon sat facing Clint in one of the four seats, two on either side of the aircraft's interior. He had to duck way down when entering the cabin, and stay hunched over until seated. Clint estimated the interior height to be less than five feet.

The takeoff was due west, over Route 1 and Sunset Beach. The pilot began a wide turn to the right while climbing to their cruising altitude. The plane straightened out after completing a 180-degree turn, now heading due east.

"We will be flying for a couple of hours. There's some food and cold drinks in the refrigerator. I don't drink coffee, gets me too hyper, ya know? But help yourself if you want to make it," Leon said. "The galley is over there behind the sliding panel. No flight attendants on the airline!"

"Maybe later," Ricardo said. "Leon, mind me asking… why are you going out of business? Seems like business should be better than ever?"

"Look, I came up from the street. Not many brothers make it this far. Now, you know I'm careful, but I'm getting tired. I know it 'cause I know myself. Too much longer and that one mistake will be my last, ya know?" Leon said. "I got plenty of money and two last big scores will set me up for life. I'm gunna buy me a bigger boat, get me a couple of women, ya know the type that like each other too, and sail off into the sunset. Shiiit… can't wait!"

Clint got up to get some cold water from the refrigerator while he pondered "two" last big scores. He must be talking about the synthetic drug distribution. He couldn't just ask about the other big score, in this business you kept your nose out of other people's business. Maybe a less obvious tact will provide more information.

Clint postured very carefully, "If you're going out of business, how about selling me your Los Angeles operation? I know the business and it would solve my problem by providing me an uninterrupted source of supply for my Japanese operation. That is, if someone else hasn't already moved in."

Leon considered Ricardo's proposal. If he said no immediately, it would appear the operation itself was folding and he would suspect something is up. If he said yes, he might expose him to the White Ice and the distribution strategy. "If you know the business so well, how the hell would you deal with my guys? They're loyal to me, and don't know you from shit?" Leon said thinking the middle of the road was the best direction.

"You're right, but if you still owned the operation, and I simply ran it for a percentage of the take, you could have your retirement and safety with me taking the risks and still have a handsome cash flow," Ricardo countered.

Thinking it sounded like a workable idea, Leon hated to derail it, but knowing he must, said, "Look Ricky, I got one last big score to make with a… new blend of coke. It's more profitable for me. I'll hit that and be gone. My operation will be left to the guys that covered my ass for years. They deserve it, they took care of me, so I'm taking care of them. End of discussion."

Well, Clint was thinking as he sat back down with a bottle of spring water, that confirms the synthetic drug distribution strategy. A single strike means they are pricing it the same or higher than coke, will make a huge profit, quickly, and then they will get out. That also suggests that the drug will need to be stockpiled in every major city to allow for rapid deployment. The element of surprise is critical. All cities will release the drug simultaneously to reduce the chances of it being reverse engineered and manufactured by a competitor in time to take any market share. Therefore, there is a chance the he can stop the drug from hitting the streets. All he has to do is find and neutralize the chemist, acquire the list of all distribution locations, transmit the information to the Collaborative and coordinate multiple simultaneous drug busts across America. And, Clint thought, the good news is, I've got four… no more than five days to complete the assignment.

The plane began reacting to the thermal turbulence common to mountainous areas signifying they were approaching the Rocky Mountains. The turbulence awakened Leon who had fallen asleep a half-hour after takeoff. Clint was taken back twenty years to a time where the turbulence was caused by the flack of shells meant to stop their approach. He had the same bile erupting up to his throat then as he did now, intuition telling him there would be a hole soon to be encountered that had not been considered.

"I hate this part. He lands this like a not-so-controlled crash. The frigg'n' thing comes down like a stone," Leon said, realizing they were close to landing.

"You're not thinking this is the mistake that will cost you your life!" Ricardo said kiddingly.

"Hey, screw you Ricky!" Leon spat back, realizing he had shown unnecessary weakness, breaking the cardinal rule of the street.

The field landing was textbook perfect; the pilot was probably a Vietnam vet given his age. Once on the ground, the plane taxied for another three hundred feet and both engines were left running. Leon pushed the intercom and asked the pilot, "What's going on?"

"The pilot responded that Mr. Ortega will be arriving tomorrow evening from the east and I need to refuel and do a little maintenance. I am flying out immediately."

"Mo-ther fuck-er!" Leon shouted. "I've got business back in L.A. I can't wait around here for a couple of days." Turning to Ricardo he said, "Look, the stuff is right here," pointing to three duffel bags under the opposite seats, "Carlos Ortega is the next in command and he'll be in tomorrow. You wait if you want to meet him and I'll make the intro by telephone, but I've got to go back."

Clint considered it carefully. Was this the setup he had feared or was it just what they're saying it is… a delay in the time schedule for the meet? He reasoned, What choice do I have? If I return without meeting the new source of supply, Leon will suspect I set him up, and if I wait here I may find that bullet. Either way I risk my death and the deaths of hundreds of thousands of people. Finally, out of the lack of choices Clint responded, "Okay, it's not what we agreed to, but Okay. Throw me those bags. You keep the money bag," Clint said as he labored under the bag's weight while walking down the stairs.

Clint watched as the plane circled. There was no tower to give take-off clearance so the pilot just opened the throttles full, and in a mere ten seconds the plane was airborne. Clint turned to see a big greasy Mexican with one missing tooth standing with an AK-47 pointed at his chest.

"Mr. Ortega won't be back until tomorrow night. You can use that tent while you wait, gringo", Jesús said, spit dripping from his chin. Hey, gringo, don't try to leave the camp. Comprende?"

Ricardo replied in Spanish, "First, I am not a gringo, my name is Ricardo Marcus. Second, I am not a prisoner in this camp. And, third, you'll show me a little respect or you'll be missing more than one tooth. Do you comprende?"

Jesús was not sure if he should roll over and take this shit, or shoot this fucker. His slow thinking was interrupted by a voice coming from his right, Ricardo's left, "He's lying. What the fuck are you doing here?" Tommy — who was actually Art, Clint's half-brother — screamed as he lunged at Clint's throat with his hands.

Jesús was slow on the uptake, and by the time he was certain something was wrong, the other two guys had come out of the mess tent and had started to break up the fight. Art kept screaming, "He's not Ricardo Marcus, he's Clint Bear, he's lying!" Clint had no choice but to fight, as opposed to merely protecting himself at this point.

José and his friend had run out of the mess tent without their weapons, but José pulled a large Bowie knife out of his boot. Art was still attacking Clint, preventing Jesús from getting a clean shot when José moved in. Clint easily countered, sending José hurling backwards, landing on his shoulders and neck. His friend dove in for Clint's feet at the same time José lunged again at Clint. Art suddenly moved to the left and caught José's knife in the small of his back. It was thrust hard, clean through and out his stomach, severing his spinal cord in its travel.

Art fell limp instantaneously, his face emotionless, his eyes locked on Clint's. Motion stopped but for a brief second as Clint watched his brother Art release his last wheezing breath. Jesús used this diversion to bring the butt of his AK-47 down hard on the back of Clint's head and unconsciousness prevented pain.

***

Carlos did not want to return to Washington D.C., however he had no choice. No one knew who he was, he was not being hunted, and he was not connected to Robert or to the deaths of the women in the Rockies. Everything should be all right, but this is the last time, he promised to himself. I must know how much they know; should I move into distribution now, or wait until this last batch is completed and in Houston? Houston is a big market, worth forty to fifty million in White Ice sales, so it would be worth the wait if possible.

Sheila should be able to handle one last hit, he reasoned to himself, and I will enjoy her to the absolute fullest. I've an interesting night planned for her, after she has given me the information I need, he thought as a broad grin enveloped his face. He picked up the phone and called her, "Sheila, oh, darling I have missed you. I was so sorry to have cut short our weekend. Business has a way of tempering our lust!"

"Honey, I've missed you too. Are we still meeting for dinner in Baltimore? I can drive there in a little over an hour," Sheila asked hopefully. Her hand was shaking so that the telephone receiver was banging against her jaw. She thought it was simply nervous anticipation. Carlos knew that she needed to be very careful with their public displays in the District of Columbia. As the Secretary to the President, Sheila Turcott was very well known and easily recognized. So, when he suggested an out-of-town rendezvous, she knew what it meant, and the anticipation was enveloping, almost controlling her.

"I can hardly wait to taste you, my sweet," German replied, finding he would miss using this name.

Sheila had no way of knowing that her mind and body were hooked on White Ice. She had never been so much in love, so to her it was simply lust and love that she needed so badly. She also had no idea that tonight her life was to be permanently and inexorably changed, and not for the better.

She packed carefully, but efficiently. It was 5:50 PM and the beltway would be murderous. Dinner was planned for 7:30 and she would need to change at the hotel. She selected a red body-hugging knitted dress, with a plunging neckline and mid-thigh hem. She selected a faint black pair of hose with matching garters. And she threw in her favorite black rubber dildo, the size most men would have you believe they are, just in case German wanted a show.

Carlos Ortega had checked into the Sheraton, a businessman's hotel, with his assumed name German Aldamado, the man that Sheila was in love with. He had guests arriving later that evening and would not look unusual in the Sheraton's businessman environment. He had selected a suite to allow for extra room. None of his clothes, nor any personal items, remained in the room. The knock on the door signaled the start of the evening.

"You look ravishing, my darling," Carlos said after opening the door.

"You must want something, hopefully me! I must look a fright. The beltway was clogged and I was almost in two accidents trying to get here in time for dinner," Sheila said while she directed the bellboy to place her suitcases on the master bed.

Carlos tipped the boy generously, and turned and looked longingly at Sheila. To his surprise, this required no acts of deceit. He actually was looking forward to this night. He planned to give Sheila many smaller portions of White Ice over the entire evening to see the effect. His guess was that it would make her "drunk-like" passionate, building her to the large-dose climax he planned when the guests arrived.

The door closed and they embraced tenderly, their lips finding their mates. Carlos only concerned himself with the answer to his one question, and manipulating Sheila into providing the answer. It would mean the difference of up to fifty million dollars in White Ice sales, almost that much in profit.

"Honey, our reservations are for 7:30, so you must change quickly," Carlos said smiling broadly.

"I've brought a dress and accessories that should please you, my darling," Sheila exclaimed with a slight giggle. "I thought that might bring a rise in your temperature," she added.

"I'll open the Champagne while you dress. We'll toast our first evening away as husband and wife-to-be," Carlos said calculatingly, thinking, keep her fully engaged in the deception; no suspicions now. I'll get the information I need, have a little stress relieving fun, and be gone.

"Oh, German, I told some of my coworkers about our engagement. They can't wait to meet you. Of course the Secret Service guys only want to complete the required security checks. Maybe next week we can have a dinner party and let me show you off!" Sheila said as she was slithering into the tight red dress.

Alarmed, Carlos casually asked, "I thought we were going to wait until I relocated the business before you threw me to the wolves, oh, I mean your friends," he said light-heartedly. He needed to know how much they had been told.

"Don't worry, I haven't spoiled the surprise. They only know you as my tall, dark and handsome husband-to-be," Sheila said. "I'm almost ready, just let me fix my face."

Carlos put only about twenty percent of a typical dosage into the Champagne glass. The fact that she would ingest the White Ice would make it last two to three times longer than smoking it. If that was not enough, he would just give her another dose at the restaurant, and another yet if needed. He just wanted her drunk-like, happy and inhibition free, what the college guys would call a loose woman.

Carlos was struck by her beauty when she made her entrance. Sheila bore no resemblance to the demur administrative secretary she was during the day. She had a talent to dress, accessorize and act the part, and I will miss that, he thought. Sheila was dressed in an expensive fire-engine-red silk and wool-blend spaghetti-strapped dress with a neckline that exposed just enough of her ample breasts to imply sex. Her dirty blond hair was lightly curled and draping the smooth, flawless bare shoulders. The red spiked-heel shoes contrasted the sheer black hose. But, it was the grin filled with mischief that pleased him the most. He thought for a moment that she could be spared, and come with him, but the thought was quickly abandoned as impossible.

Handing her the glass of Champagne and raising his to offer the toast, "To Sheila, the only woman who has ever taken my heart." They clinked their glasses and drank, she to their love, he to deceit. They talked a few moments and enjoyed another glass of Champagne. Realizing it was time to leave, Sheila retrieved her matching jacket to brace against the fall evening chill.

In the elevator she found herself becoming more amorous and reached down to German's ass for a little satisfaction. Rubbing her breasts on his arm helped, but what she really began craving was explicit sexual contact. Wow, she thought, does this man get to me! The cool gentle evening breeze helped settle her down as they awaited the next taxi.

German told the taxi driver, a young black man with loud rap music playing on a portable radio, "Teo Pepe's please." Teo Pepe's was a Spanish and Mexican restaurant on the better side of Baltimore. It was frequented by professionals and executives as well as the wannabes. There were mostly cozy little booths in a darkened Spanish motif of darkly-stained timbers in between sparkling white stucco. Ceiling fans spilled the cigar smoke from the bar, while real green plants strained to oxygenate the stuffy interior. The olive-colored leather bench seating in their booth gave that low chirping sound, indicating it was real leather, as they slipped into the booth. In a departure from their norm, German chose to sit opposite Sheila, "to admire her beauty."

The waiter, a man in his late twenties dressed in Spanish-looking attire, provided menus and asked if they cared for cocktails. "What would you suggest?" German asked back.

The waiter, taking full advantage of his perspective standing above them, drank in Sheila's partially exposed breasts and responded, "Sir, ma'am, I would suggest that nothing less than the finest Champagne would do," taking his eyes briefly off her chest to make contact with theirs.

"Son, you have an eye to sum up a situation quickly. I agree. Mumm if you have it," German added.

Sheila loved Champagne. It was the one thing she looked forward to with all those Washington political and social functions. In truth, he didn't like the headache brought on by the gas and the aftertaste that inevitably followed more than three or four glasses. But, tonight he would make yet another exception.

The Champagne was just arriving when Sheila excused herself to the powder room. Carlos suggested pouring even though the "lady" was away and placed the bottle in the chiller. As the waiter turned to look after another table, Carlos added another portion of White Ice to Sheila's Champagne.

"Sheila, darling, our waiter seems to be taken by you," Carlos said lifting his eyebrows in a devilish way.

"I think he is more taken with my breasts than with me," Sheila said laughing as she pulled the neckline even lower. "Let's have some fun, shall we?" she added as she pulled her dress hem in the other direction. "I just love men seducing me with their lusty stares, and I love that you, the first man in my life who understands, encourages me," Sheila said as she drank the Champagne.

The waiter returned to take the dinner order and nearly lost his balance. Sheila, seeing him approaching, slid a knife off the end of the table and began to bend over to retrieve it. She met the waiter, who was also bending to retrieve the knife, when she was fully bent over and most exposed to his direct view. He flushed a little and stood up quickly to hear, "Thank you. I'm sorry, I don't remember your name," Sheila asked.

"Yes, uh, my name is Alex. Would you care to order or sit a while longer with the Champagne?" Alex asked.

Sheila gracefully took his hand and caressed it sensuously. "Alex, we will place ourselves in your capable hands," Sheila said as she slowly, but deliberately brought his unresisting hand to her left breast. "You did so well with the Champagne," she added as she kissed his hand before releasing it.

"Sir, I sure didn't…" Alex began apologizing.

"Alex, seems my fiancée is quite take by you. She is very affectionate, and I'm quite liberal. If you take care of us this evening, see to our — Sheila's — every need, you will be quite amazed with your tip," Carlos said to settle his fears. He was happy to see Alex's enlightened face as he left to place his order.

Soon the word spread and the additional and varied attention began. Busboys, other waiters, the headwaiter, even the restaurant manager all came to experience the beautiful "loose woman", and all were secretly rewarded with eye candy. Finally, Alex was presenting the appetizers, along with an exotic looking middle-aged woman with chestnut brown hair and golden tanned skin. "Hello, my name is Belva, and I will be assisting Alex this evening," she said while arranging the tableware for the appetizer. Twice her arm brushed Sheila's breasts, the first time more lightly that the second. Their eyes met, briefly, and with no resistance nor objection expressed, a smile leaked from Belva's lips.

"Your appetizer this evening is a shrimp, scallop and muscle medley in a delicate lime sauce, served on oat toast points. No, sir, we will prepare your napkins for you," Alex said as he placed the large scallop dish in front of Sheila. He then reached for her used linen napkin, resting comfortably on her lap and massaged her thighs as he removed it. His excitement grew when he saw the tops of her garters fully exposed. Shaking a fresh linen napkin, he bent over far more than necessary, to place it, his shoulders roughly rubbing Sheila's breasts without protest. Sheila whispered in his ear, "I doubt that you are enjoying this as much as we are."

Belva watched with envy and then presented Carlos's appetizer with little flare. Just as they were about to leave and see to the other tables, Sheila asked with a hand motioning to her chest, "Belva, I don't want to spill on this dress, would you mind placing another napkin?"

Beaming with excitement, Belva responded with enthusiasm, "Certainly, ma'am. I would be pleased to help you." She shook out another napkin and slowly tucked it in around the plunging neckline. All the while, Sheila and Belva's eyes were locked, pleasurably flinching only when Bleva found Sheila's stiffening left nipple.

Carlos was becoming aroused and wanted more. The appetizers gone and the sorbet dishes yet to be collected,

Sheila again went to the powder room. Belva had been waiting for this opportunity, but was stuck at another cozy table just beginning to take their order. Carlos doubled the prior dosage in Sheila's wine, thinking that this was yet another product in a highly cut form. No, he was out of this business, but he knew the formula and would continue to reproduce his own private supply.

The entrée arrived as Sheila finished her first glass of wine. It was artfully presented, rack of lamb with wild mushrooms, sculptured potatoes and thin asparagus. Sheila, slowly and seductively licking her lips said, "This food is making me hot." Carlos wasn't sure if Sheila was speaking to him, Alex or Belva, but knowing White Ice, she was speaking to everyone.

Alex was far emboldened and, when placing Sheila's fresh linen napkin, actual began to finger her very wet womanhood, staying longer than prudent to the encouragement of her moaning. Sheila, about to climax, did accidentally knock her fork to the floor under the linen table-clothed table. Belva immediately offered to get it and disappeared for a short moment. The ecstasy on Sheila's face was the only clue that Belva was pleasuring her. When Alex had placed Carlos's entrée, Belva, having retrieved the fork, stood up and presented a clean fork to Sheila. There was an electrically charged aroma in the air, all focused on Sheila.

By the time the entrée was completed, Sheila was almost in animalistic heat. The cumulative effects of the ingested White Ice were showing. Thinking it could get out of control, he decided that desert would have to wait. No more pleasure, he said to himself, until I have the information I need. It was nearing 11:00 and the restaurant would be closing soon. He left both Alex and Belva each a two hundred and fifty dollar tip, and a note.

Sheila was uncontrollable in the taxi on the way back to the hotel. She needed unrestrained sex, and a lot of it, now. She stripped off her dress in the hotel elevator and walked brazenly down the hall to the room completely exposed, looking unbelievably sexy in red shoes and black gartered stockings. She stopped by the door and began to unabashedly pleasure herself.

Carlos pushed Sheila to the bed as he heard the door close. He jumped on top of her roughly and began kissing her neck. "I don't want this to go to quickly, my love. I have a surprise for you. Let's warm up by finishing the Champagne we started earlier this evening." Leaving her momentarily on the bed, Carlos went to get two glasses of Champagne, one different from the other.

Carlos emptied the full contents of the plastic sack into Sheila's drink and waited momentarily as it dissolved. His eyes were met with an awesome view as he reentered the bedroom. Sheila had found her rubber black phallic replica and had it buried deeply within her, rubbing it roughly in circular motions as she moaned and whispered in guttural language. She took the Champagne down in one gulp, while the other hand was continuing the motion. The knock on the door interrupted his viewing pleasure.

"I hoped you would come," Carlos said to Belva and Alex. "Sheila is in the other room, getting ready for you both. Why not relax with a glass of Champagne for a few moments?"

Carlos poured two more glasses after opening another bottle. He emptied a full sack of White Ice, splitting its contents evenly between both glasses. After presenting the glasses and suggesting they get "more comfortable", he rejoined Sheila with another glass to get the information he needed.

Carlos gave Sheila the glass, indicating that she should drink it. As she drank, without stopping, Carlos lowered himself and nuzzled into her pubic hair, pleasuring her around the engulfed dildo. "Sheila, what's new with the Robert situation?" he asked knowing she was beyond control.

"They… they can't locate Carlos Ortega," Sheila said in between passionate heavy breathing and moaning.

Carlos was stunned cold. He couldn't understand how they would have identified him? Where was the connection? What had he missed? Could the cartel know about his White Ice? He needed to know more, anything that would help. "Sheila, what's happening with the Martial Law Drug Plan? Is it going forward as planned?" Carlos asked softly, not wanting to alarm her out of the drug-induced trance.

"They're going ahead… ahead as planned and hope to find Carlos Ortega before he kills the President's family. German, take me, take me now!" Sheila said as she began to peak.

"Good God," Carlos said aloud. They knew about him, had connected him to the threat of assassination, and there would be no delay in the Martial Law Drug Plan implementation. He would have to move without Houston… he'd have to break camp tomorrow afternoon and push the GO button. "Sheila, I have a surprise for you!" he said as he walked toward the other room.

Carlos handed Alex and Belva the five hundred dollars he had promised them in the note he left with the check at the restaurant. Alex pocketed his immediately, but Belva returned hers, saying it was going to be her pleasure. Noticing that the Champagne glasses were emptied, and seeing the lust in their eyes, Carlos said, "Sheila is a little drunk, and she can't wait for the two of you to take her." Then he added as he escorted them into the master bedroom, "Take her any way you please."

Alex and Belva left the hotel room some ninety minutes later, leaving Sheila in a deep sleep. Before the morning maid entered to make up the room, White Ice would have claimed its first victim.

Clint was tied about the hands and wrists with nylon rope and placed in an earthen pit about eight feet deep and six feet wide. The back of his head had an open gash that would under different circumstances require fifteen to twenty stitches to stop the bleeding and begin the healing. There were sharp pains, increasing with every heartbeat, both at the gash and in his temples. He tried to stand but his dizzy head and the bound feet made it impossible. He knew the symptoms related to a not-so-mild concussion.

He assessed the rest of his physical condition, and with the exception of the concussion, he was okay. It was then he remembered his brother Art dying in his arms as the blow to his head came. Art was dead, another step in Old Bear's vision now a reality. Brook, Cabris, Old Bear and now Art. The parent bear and three cubs.

What was Art doing here? Why did they call him Tommy? Art was a bit of a wild man, but he would not be involved in something like this, of that Clint was sure. Still, he had known about the deaths of Brook and Cabris and had identified the bodies before Clint. How did he know about them, and where they were?

After nearly an hour of concentration, made more difficult by the pounding in his head, Clint assumed that Art was trying to make a big score and use the money to improve his status within the tribe. How he'd networked into this group is a mystery, and he probably did not know that they were responsible for his sister's death.

Clint shook off his current thoughts of family and focused on his mission and what to do next. He was well bound and in an earthen pit that would be difficult to escape from without the binds; with them impossible. He had to get them to release him, but how? Carlos would be coming back mid-day tomorrow. He looked to the sky and estimated the time to be about 6:00 PM. He had been unconscious for nearly six hours.

His strategy now determined, he looked carefully around the pit until he felt a root protruding from the earth wall. It had been cut with the shovel and the needle-sharp end would be perfect. Clint pushed his forearm into the root and moved his arm in a circular motion to making a clean round hole. He repeated the procedure, making another hole about one half inch to the right. Next, Clint began the inner control, relaxing his body first, then slowing his heart rate. When he had reduced his heart rate to one beat for every twenty seconds, his need for oxygen decreased. Next he worked to reduce his respiratory rate to about one breath per minute. He knew he needed to go deeper. He was only a third of the way there and food should arrive soon.

At 6:30, José came with some food in a bucket and rope to lower it into the pit. He dropped the bucket on Clint's stomach to wake him. There was no movement. José called out, without response. He fetched a flashlight to see more clearly. He could not see any breathing and could not get a response from Clint. He called for Jesús, who made the assessment and then lowered the makeshift ladder. "You keep him covered while I check things out," Jesús said to José while he awkwardly stepped down on the first rung of the ladder.

Once down in the pit, Jesús called for the flashlight. "Looks like he's dead. But how?" Jesús said and then noticing the snake bite on Clint's forearm. "Shit! He's been bit by a snake!" Jesús said as he hurriedly jumped to the ladder, momentarily afraid he might be bit as well. "Let's get the body out of there and bury him away from the camp. Ya know, just in case," Jesús added. "I'll tie the rope to his legs and we'll pull him up. Then you and your friend take him into the forest and bury him. Got it?"

Clint was conscious and aware of his body being raised from the pit, but his body was as if deceased. Total dead weight, flesh becoming cold and looking pale. He was too heavy for José and his friend to carry far. They were tired of digging holes and stopped when the hole was a mere three feet deep. José dragged Clint's body face-up into the shallow grave while his friend was shoveling cold dirt on top of his body. The mound of dirt protruded above the surrounding area as Clint's body displaced earth. José found a few large rocks and placed them on the earthen mound to camouflage the site. Satisfied, they began their short walk back to the camp.

His body was cold, both from the moist earth surrounding him as well as his prolonged hibernation-like state. Clint knew he had to wake himself from the trance quickly, or risk this really being his grave. There was precious little oxygen, he was still suffering from a severe concussion, and hypothermia could set in any time. He had to time his awakening with a massive thrust upward to allow a first breathing gasp to be filled with the cold mountain air, not the cold mountain dirt. Clint began to summon his intuition to "feel" the grave. Where will it be the easiest to burst through?

Two large rocks were placed on top of the dirt mound. One above his feet, the other above his thighs. Control, he said to himself. Control. His weakness for closed-in places began to flood him with fear. Control. I'll use the added weight to leverage an abdominal push while using both hands, now laying on top of my chest, to burst through the earth. I've only one chance, he thought. If I gasp and fill my lungs with dirt, I'll choke and slowly die. This is not my purpose. He focused all his psychic and physical strength, and in one powerful upward motion broke through the earth and gasped the cold mountain air.

José thought he heard an animal and picked up his pace back to the camp.

Clint sat, covered in dirt from the chest down, straining to regain full consciousness. His breathing began to normalize, as did his heart beat, and a chill came over him. He clawed at the two large rocks, pushing them off the mound. Then, shaking, he lifted himself out of the grave. He cleaned himself as best he could, picked the dirt from the still-open head wound and pushed the earth back into the grave, replacing the rocks in case anyone came back to inspect.

He needed rest, water and food. His body temperature was still too low; the hibernation recovery being hampered by his concussion. Clint moved west more steadily now that his oxygenated blood was feeding his tired muscles. He was still dressed in the clothes he wore on the plane, blue jeans and a white, now brown from moist dirt, cotton shirt. His leather rubber-soled boots were helping him move without sound. He found a small circular inlet cut in the rock hillside by a river millions of years ago. Clint collected the driest wood, mostly hardwood for a fire. He would warm his inner body core and then find water and food. The rocks he was placing in a circle around the fire would be used later to encircle his sleeping area to keep him warm.

Tomorrow morning, with the first light from the rising sun, he would take the camp.

***

The maid screamed and began yelling for help in Spanish, shortly before 7:30 AM, when she found the sallow, naked body of Sheila Turcott sprawled on the bed. The hotel manager called the Baltimore police, and the police, trying to learn the woman's identity, electronically sent her fingerprints to the FBI shortly after 9:00. Stephen Shultz, the head of the President's Secret Service, was notified within the hour. Shultz had Suzanne McGee, the most senior secretarial aid, tell the President he needed a few minutes of his time for a national security emergency. Shultz knocked, and without authorization from within, opened the door to the Oval Office and walked in briskly.

The President was sitting at the desk and was just hanging up the telephone for intra-White House communications. "Sir, I have bad news, very bad news. Sheila Turcott was found in a hotel in Baltimore, dead," thinking that the state of the body could be disclosed to the President later. "Sir, I have had the chopper dispatched to bring the body to Bethesda for an autopsy. And, sir, I'm very sorry."

Bill Covey removed his glasses and began to wipe the tears building in the corners of his eyes. He spoke with a voice that conveyed his fatigue and emotions, "When you said national security, I assumed it would relate to the Martial Law Drug Plan and asked for Director Douglas to join us." A knock on the door announced his arrival. "Please bring the Director current, Steve," the President said wearily.

"What have you not told me, Shultz?" Douglas asked.

"Mr. Director, this can wait," Shultz responded.

"No, Stephen. No, I'm afraid it can't. Please tell us all that you know, now," Douglas demanded.

Aggravated at being treated in this way, but sensing there was more to this than what he knew, added, "She was found naked, and there are clear signs of sexual intercourse.

There was no evidence of resistance, no scratches, cuts, bruises or blood. There were two bottles of Champagne and four glasses, three of which have an unknown residue in them. That is all I know at this point. And Mr. President, I'm sorry to have reported this in, well, this way," Shultz said.

Douglas was beginning to put the logical pieces together and asked, "Please divert the chopper to the DEA labs and have the Baltimore police department express all the physical evidence to the lab as well. I'll advise Ken Turner to expect the body and the physical evidence. And we need to keep this airtight. Can you handle that on your end, Stephen?" Douglas asked, not wanting to be seen involved.

"Yes, I have contacts there at the Baltimore PD and DA's office. Given who she is, there should be no difficulty in taking jurisdiction. I can radio the chopper en route and divert it to the DEA. Now, Mr. Director, what do you know that I should know? If it has anything to do with the safety of the President or his family I'm required to know by law," Shultz said forcefully.

"There is nothing we can tell you now, but we will bring you in soon," the President said, responding for Douglas and watching Shultz reluctantly accept his explanation.

The chopper landed on the DEA headquarter's roof where Dr. Ken Turner and Cole Cunningham were anxiously waiting. They wheeled the stretcher to the chopper's side door, holding the body bag from being blown away by the rotor blades' wash. The two Army Corpsmen placed the body bag on the stretcher's mattress, supported by a shiny chrome chassis. Ken took the back and Cole guided the front of the stretcher into the DEA roof door as the chopper lifted off. Once in the lab, Ken immediately took a blood sample and placed a small portion on a glass slide, and placed it under a high-powered microscope. Later, he would do a careful analysis, but Cole wanted an intelligent guess immediately. Looking carefully into the microscope and adjusting focus while changing magnification, Ken finally breathed out.

"It's the synthetic, ninety-five percent sure," he said to Cole after what seemed an eternity. "I'll need to do a battery of tests to be one hundred percent confident. Give me another twelve hours. But, I would not be surprised to find the concentration level to be ten times the dosage needed to get high, and if so, this would be the first murder with the synthetic."

Cole's head was awash with the ramifications of Sheila Turcott being the synthetic's first victim. Was it a message to the President that Carlos Ortega was serious? Would the President's wife and daughter be next? Had Sheila turned? Could she have been Robert's accomplice? Would America's morgues soon be flooded with the hedonistic dead? What did it all mean? Then he remembered that Sheila had a "new man in her life" and it brought a question, "Ken, what would be the effects of the synthetic if it were ingested?"

"Well, similar sexual stimulation, I'd imagine. Probable last for triple the time though," Ken responded. "Why do you ask?"

"Didn't you tell me that there is a euphoric feeling as well as being lost in the sexual high?" Cole asked.

"Yes, yes I did. I think I see where you're going. Once the drug has taken effect there is the basis for the victim to be mentally probed without resistance or remembrance. I would theorize it to be similar to Sodium Pentothal. Ergo, it is possible that Ms. Turcott could have been a leak without her knowledge…"

Cole interrupted, "And without her knowledge, Carlos could have done incalculable damage to the nation, the Martial Law Drug Plan, the President and his family. But she is dead, I suspect not by accident but because she is of no use to Carlos now. That tells me that the synthetic distribution is about to start. Ken, if Clint doesn't complete the mission within the next twenty-four hours, you'd better prepare the medical examiners in every major American city for an onslaught of bodies. Making matters worse, Clint is overdue to report on his progress."

The sun would rise within the next ten minutes, and Clint was ready. The sleeve he cut from his cotton shirt had stopped the blood flow from the head gash, his rest was surprisingly sound, and he was now supremely focused. José and his friend first, Jesús next, and then to his cellular phone to report in what he had learned.

The camp was sleeping. No movement, no one on guard. Amateurs completely relying on inappropriate technology. It took Clint seconds to disarm the laser alarms as he approached the camp. Keeping to the shadows toward the outside perimeter of the camp, Clint floated closer to José's tent. He could see and hear the raccoons entering the mess tent, but they were unaware of him. The prowler raccoons would be clumsy and make noise soon, he thought. Time to move.

Clint was thankful they hadn't found his boot knife and cut a small hole in the tent's rear wall to check the interior. Both José and his friend Chico were sleeping on cots on either side of the tent, their heads to the rear. The front flaps were tied. Moving quieter that the morning mist, Clint encircled the tent, cut the ties and entered. José's friend felt the cold draft of air and raised his head about ready to verbally assault José, when he saw Clint. He pulled a large knife from beneath the sleeping bag, but before he could lunge, Clint countered his right forearm, broke his wrist and noiselessly cut through his throat, severing the carotid artery. His death was silent, but the gurgling blood awakened José, who did not have the time to reach for a weapon before Clint hammered his esophagus with his right hand, fingers bent at the middle knuckle leaving half the fingers extended and now pushed into José's throat. José's face was in shock, his mind racing as he thought. How could you be alive? I buried you… am I having a nightmare? The blow came before his eyes could even blink reactively. He lost consciousness first, and then suffocated silently.

Clint was now at the rear of Jesús's tent. The sunrise flooded the camp, illuminating the mist, creating an eerie mystical stage. Clint floated to the front of the tent, grabbed Jesús by the feet and yanked him onto the floor.

Jesús didn't know what happened, and took a few moments to orient himself. Then rage overcame him as Clint allowed him, actually encouraged him to stand and attack. He had no weapons. They were in the tent. He called for José. "They're both very dead, and you may be next," Clint said leaving a window of hope for Jesús.

"What do you mean, may be dead, you're the dead motherfucker," Jesús said, trying to appear tougher than he was. His eyes darting around the camp looking for his out, a weapon, something, but nothing.

"You tell me what I want to know, and you'll live to see another sunrise. You don't and you're dead. Simple. Oh, it will be a very painful death, just like those women you and Julio raped and murdered," Clint seethed out. It was taking all his heritage and training not to mutilate him slowly right now, but he needed more information about the synthetic distribution strategy.

"Hey, fuck you gringo. Ya, you're a gringo cop. Right?" Jesús spat out.

"Wrong answer, asshole," Clint replied as he kicked down on Jesús's left knee, feeling the pleasure when he heard the crack and saw the pain reach his face. "I can stop here, and the worst of it will be the limp... you'll always have it as a reminder of me and those women. Now, let's try again. Shall we?" Clint said.

Jesús, rolling on the ground in severe pain, pushed the envelope again saying, "Fuck you!"

"Wrong answer again, asshole," Clint said as he knelt down beside Jesús and placed his right index and middle finger near Jesús eyes. Swiftly, Clint swung his fingers down to Jesús's side and plunged them into his kidney. "Now, that's got to hurt." Clint did it another two times and added, "Now, I'm through screwing around. Are you going to answer my questions?"

"Fuck you," Jesús whispered out in between convulsions.

"Your choice, asshole. But, thanks. I'm going to enjoy this. You see, asshole, you and Julio murdered my fiancée and sister," Clint said as he moved to Jesús's feet. Jesús was in too much pain to move and could only whisper his objection. Clint slid his boot knife from its sheath and knelt on Jesús's right leg to prevent it from moving, cutting off his large toe in a single motion. "Gee, now you'll have a limp on this leg, too. Such a pity," Clint added while Jesús rolled involuntarily in the dirt.

"What do you want to know?" Jesús cried out in panic.

"Where is the synthetic drug made?" Clint asked.

"Synthetic drug, you mean White Ice?" Jesús replied, spit drooling through his missing tooth.

"Yes, White Ice," Clint responded, now knowing what it was called.

"I make it here. Now is that it, gringo?" Jesús now unsuccessfully trying to hold his left knee and his right big toe.

"Who has the formula?" Clint continued.

"I do. So does Carlos."

"Where is the formula to White Ice, Jesús?"

"It's in the production tent, hung on the tent post."

"Where did the formula come from, Jesús? Who devised it?"

"Carlos, you asshole. He's a chemist, ya know!"

"Now this is a very important question, Jesús. If you don't answer me fully and accurately, I'll cut your ear off. Do you understand me?" Clint said in Spanish to emphasize the question's importance. With Jesús nodding, Clint asked, "Where are the staging locations for White Ice and when is it scheduled for the street?"

"You're gunna try to stop it. No fucking way. I get five mil when it goes. NO - FUCKING - WAY, gringo!" Jesús said, making his last stand.

"Very wrong answer, Jesús. I thought we had an understanding. Guess not," Clint said as he pulled back Jesús's greasy, stringy black hair and, holding his right ear, slashed his boot knife downward severing it cleanly. Blood erupted and instantly began to pool under Jesús's head. Just as Jesús was going to cry out, Clint stuffed the severed ear into his open mouth. "One more ear to go before I start working on your balls. You want to answer the question now?" Clint added.

Crying uncontrollably from equal mixtures of pain and fear, Jesús agreed. "They're listed on a clipboard in the production tent, and Carlos said he was going to start releasing it this afternoon."

Clint stood and walked to the tent where his duffel bag containing his cell phone was last. It was still there. He dialed the memorized number, heard two rings, waited ten seconds for an encryption lock and heard, "Yes?"

"Cole, please," Clint responded.

"This is Cole. Where have you been? Are you all right?" Cole fired staccato style.

Clint was walking toward the production tent to dictate the formula and distribution locations, glancing at Jesús who was entering shock. "We don't have much time. I've taken the camp. The most senior gorilla had the information we wanted, but I had to get a little rough. The formula was devised by Carlos, who's a chemist. He and the gorilla are the only ones who have it. The synthetic is called White Ice and it's scheduled for distribution this afternoon. Carlos is coming here to start the selling process. There are three dead and one prisoner in need of medical attention. One of the dead is my brother, Art. He was killed trying to... defend me."

"Clint that is great news, about the mission that is. I'm very sorry about your brother. There have been some developments here as well. Sheila Turcott has been compromised by Carlos, and is the first White Ice victim. Carlos must now know we know that he is behind this, and is probably cutting his losses and running. I think we can handle the bust on the distribution centers, and if you can get Carlos we will have White Ice compartmentalized. It's not over yet, but thanks to you, we may actually resolve this crisis. Clint, you've infiltrated the cartel higher than any agent. We can't stop at the White Ice - we've got to go for the cartel cocaine and heroin ring," Cole said thinking on his feet.

Several minutes passed as both Clint and Cole mentally played out different strategies. It was Clint that broke the subtle static silence, "I have to terminate the prisoner. My brother will be positioned as the infiltrator. I will have broken up the fight between Jesús and Art, but Jesús died soon after. I stayed to report to Carlos, my loyalty substantiated by the eight million dollars in cocaine, the formula, distribution sites and chemicals all still here. It should work, especially since he hasn't time and needs the help."

"Just remember, you don't know anything about White Ice. Concentrate solely on the cocaine. Since Carlos knows we know about the synthetic, it will give you additional believability. We're going to do multiple hits on those distribution sites. No matter how tight we keep this, there may be a leak to the press that Carlos or the cartel picks up on. Stay on guard. Be sure to place your credit card encrypted transmitter somewhere in the camp so we can come in later and pick up the pieces. Now I'm activating the recorder, dictate the formula and then the distribution sites," Cole said anxiously.

As Clint walked toward the tent he sensed motion from within. Opening the tent flap slowly and quietly, he saw two women, one older that the other, ankle chained to the floor where they were sitting and filling small sacks with White Ice.

"Mr. President, we have made significant progress," Douglas intoned. "The synthetic is called White Ice, and it's what killed Ms. Turcott. We have the formula and the distribution sites…"

"That is unquestionably the best news I've had — no, the American people have had — since this ordeal began," the President breathed out, interrupting Douglas.

"Yes, it is good news, but there is more," Douglas went on, "The formula is known only to Carlos and one of his men, who is in our custody. Cole is coordinating a multi-site drug bust, seventeen sites to be taken simultaneously. Clint's mission is now expanding to include the cartel cocaine and heroin organization. He plans to befriend Carlos Ortega to do it. Clint is at the point of no return. If he tries to go back, they will terminate him. Going forward is his only option. The next twenty-four hours will be the toughest."

Clint had passed the point of no return with his destiny weeks ago.

The Point of No Return.

CHAPTER 8:
THE BEES

Their motion was repetitive, mechanical, machine-like, executed without thought to a silent cadence. The two women, one older than the other, filled sacks with the crystal known as White Ice. Their legs were clamped to the ground with padlocked leg irons. Their faces devoid of emotion and drained of color. Their eyes telling of the fear and horror that they have and expect to continue to experience. Another hole to be filled in his on the fly planning.

He had a decision to make, and it was an easy one. Let these women continue filling the sacks and die, or un-cuff them and hope they wouldn't blow his cover. There was no decision to make, really. Clint went around to the front of the table. The women didn't even flinch, not even a quick glance at him. They simply continued their robotic motion.

"My name is Clint Bear. I'm an agent with the DEA and I'm undercover. Those sounds you heard resulted in the deaths of your captors; one is hanging onto a thin thread of life. I'm going to take your leg irons off and help you escape to where other DEA agents will meet you. But, I need you to do something for me," Clint asked, watching both their heads turn slowly to meet his eyes.

"You mean it, you're not screwing with me and my daughter?" the older woman said hysterically. "Show me your ID!"

"Ma'am, I'm undercover. I can't carry an ID. But, think about it. Would I let you go if I wasn't who I said I am?" Clint responded calmly, hoping reason could be found even though they were petrified and exhausted. He began by unlocking their leg irons with the keys from Jesús's pocket. "You have been through a terrible ordeal, and you both are very, very lucky. You will live to tell about it. There are thirty-two other women, including my sister and fiancée, who were not so lucky." He finished by handing them a canteen with fresh water.

They were both free now and ran around the table to hug each other. Mom comforting daughter and daughter comforting mom. Both whimpering and crying in spurts. They had privately thought they were going to die here. Die a horrible death. They did not know how accurate those thoughts truly were. Slowly they began to assimilate the situation and the mom turned to Clint and asked, "You said we need to do something for you. What is it? We want to get the hell out of here as fast as possible."

Clint took a deep breath and handed her Jesús's gun, hoping they would feel more in control and trusting of him. She took it, handled it with little experience showing. Finally, she gripped it and pointed it toward Clint, not knowing the safety was still on. Only after she had control of the gun, control of her and her daughter's lives again, did he respond, "You were both kidnapped to fill these sacks with a new synthetic drug called White Ice. It's lethal and cheap to make. Your captors were waiting for you to complete the task and then planned to rape and severely physically abuse you until they tired of you both. Then they would have killed and buried you in a shallow grave just like they did to the thirty-two women before you. I suspect your worst possible fears over the past several hours would have come true, and then a whole lot more." He was being completely honest and very blunt because the plane would be arriving in a few hours. Time was a commodity in short supply.

They lost the color in their faces that had just moments ago started to return. A captive always hangs on to the hope that they will be freed. They need to continue that hope against all odds to survive the ordeal. Hearing that their inner worst fears were more than true almost caused them to faint.

"These sacks need to be filled… they are expected to be filled by the leader of this group of maggots. He will be coming back by plane in a few hours. If they are not filled, and you are both gone, my cover is blown and I'm dead. If they are filled and you're both gone, I can tell them that the task was completed and Jesús and his buddies raped and buried you. He will expect that because that is exactly what has been done to the other women."

"Now look. I'm sorry I have to be so abrupt. I know you both have been through more than a lifetime of terror. But I can't complete filling the sacks alone, and I will not allow another woman to be hurt by these scumbags. You should know one more thing. The synthetic drug is staged and ready for the street and will absolutely and positively kill hundreds of thousands of people. We don't have much time, ladies… will you help me?" Clint asked passionately. "Please."

Mom and daughter never left their supportive hug through Clint's impassioned plea. They now had a gun, felt more in control and wanted to get as far away from here as possible. The daughter, Bonnie, a recent UCLA Berkeley graduate, spoke first, "Mom, I want out of here. But I couldn't live with myself if I ran from this and other people died. We're safe now. Let's fill these sacks quickly and get the hell out of here."

"Where are the other DEA agents? Why can't they help? It's their damn job!" Susan, the mother yelled irritably.

Clint took out his wallet and removed a credit card-sized radio. "When we are done, and it looks like another hour's worth of work for the three of us, I'll take you down the old mining road and activate this. It's a homing beacon. Here, press this with both thumbs when you are ready. It is being monitored twenty-four hours a day. The DEA agents will be there to pick you both up in less than two hours. I'll return here and meet the leader scumbag."

Susan and Bonnie exchanged looks, reading each other, and in unison turned toward Clint and nodded.

Susan added, "I'm keeping the gun."

"You better switch off the safety when you want to use it," Clint responded. "Here, I'll show you. It works like this."

The STOL aircraft was halfway between its El Paso departure point and the new camp in the Colorado Rockies when the squawk box buzzed. Carlos had forgotten that it was still activated. Curious, he thought. With Robert in custody, how would someone even know this box code number? Maybe Robert had broken more quickly that even he had predicted.

Carlos reached over and picked up the receiver bringing it to his ear and the buzz immediately stopped. The unrecognizable voice said, "Sheila took the fall for everything. I am in the clear. Photos of Clint Bear being sub-transmitted with this message. They have had no further progress. Be careful. Out."

The fax paper began to exit the side of the squawk box with the image of Clint Bear while Carlos began to assess the credibility of the message. Robert could have been turned and transmitting disinformation to lead me to believe that I'm secure. Still, it could be true, that the government could have found Sheila and concluded that she was the mole and, deeply remorseful, committed suicide. Both options were possible, but how would he know which was the truth?

"Mr. Ortega, we are circling for the landing site. Please make sure your seatbelt is on," the pilot said over the intercom.

"We are finally having some good luck," the President said to Douglas in the late afternoon status report. "What do you think the odds are that Ortega will bite on the disinformation?"

"That depends on Clint now. He will have to silence the wounded druggie and position Art as himself," Douglas said.

"Why position Art as himself? I don't understand." the President shot back.

Agent Meceli jumped ahead of Douglas, "Mr. President, the photos we sent along with the disinformation transmission were not of Clint but of his brother Art. Carlos will identify the dead body as Clint Bear and, hopefully, will assume that Robert is out and back in business because the information transmitted is accurate. This, coupled with Clint's story of the camp being attacked by Art, should tie it up neatly."

"Yes. It has to be played out slowly so that Carlos can discover it. Not be told. That would be too easy and cause suspicion. Clint needs to gently lead him to these conclusions, at most, for Carlos to accept the story. But if he does, odds are Clint is in further than we could have hoped. Our next step is to organize the simultaneous hits on the seventeen White Ice master distribution centers and, since Cole Cunningham is planning that operation, I asked him to deliver the report personally," Douglas added.

As if on cue, Cole was announced by Ms. Cronwell, the President's temporary secretary, and escorted to the winged chair to the President's immediate left. Ms. Cronwell then went to the side bar to fix him a strong black coffee before leaving the room. He looked as if he hadn't slept in days.

"Cole, I have briefed the President with the exception of the White Ice recovery mission. I have left that for you since you have more details than do Agent Meceli and I. Cole?" Douglas lifted his hand as a signal to start the briefing.

Cole took a long pull on the hot, rich black coffee, then rubbed his eyes, cleared his throat, and began his briefing. "Mr. President, Clint has neutralized the White Ice production camp and determined that the new drug will go to mass market as early as tomorrow. He has also uncovered the White Ice formula and the exact location of the White Ice that has been staged and ready for the street. There are seventeen locations. All the large cities including Los Angeles, New York, Philadelphia, Chicago, Dallas, Miami, Toronto, San Francisco… you get the picture. In approximately ten hours, at 03:00 hours tomorrow morning, timed to limit civilian and press exposure, there will be multiple coordinated recovery missions initiated. We will hit every site at the same time to prevent a warning communicated to one site by another site or to Carlos."

Cole paused briefly to drain the coffee cup, feeling its warmth and caffeine begin to kick in. "Mr. President, we need your personal help on this one. You see, sir, we have no jurisdiction in Toronto. But, we can't let any site have the ability to alert Carlos. And we don't want to alert the Canadian authorities before the fact and allow another potential leak. It is vital that we keep the compartment tight, very tight."

Douglas interrupted, "Sir, we think that a personal secure call to the Canadian Prime Minister is in order to ask for his personal involvement. Every recovery mission must be identically timed. As importantly, the White Ice must come back to us, not to Canadian drug enforcement. We simply can't run the risk of a cowboy taking a sample and eventually reverse engineering the formula. We would be right back where we are now."

"Jesus Christ, Douglas, do you know what you are asking? This could spawn an international incident," the President shot back.

"Yes, I know. But sir, there is simply no other way. That is why I think a personal secure call is the best chance we have. I would suggest you describe the situation as accurately as possible, as honestly as you are able, while asking for his agreement in keeping this private. And, sir, he may be enticed by your commitment to include his and the Canadian government's support in the next MLDP publicity release." Douglas was concerned about his next and final request.

"Mr. President, we must convince the Prime Minister that Department C operatives handle the recovery. Only in this way will we know that there has been no skimming for reverse engineering. He won't like that at all. It puts him in a position of not believing and supporting his own," Douglas concluded and waited for the President's reply.

President Covey sat silently digesting the requests and their logic. Maybe he could find a compromise that could work. No. There was no compromise available. The logic was irrefutable. His challenge was to provide the same information to Prime Minister Marstens. He was a good man, and an effective leader. There was a solid foundation to their relationship, just how solid he was about to find out.

"Leave it with me and I'll let you know by 19:00 this evening. Assume it's a go and have your team ready, Agent Cunningham," President Covey replied and then added, "Douglas, what are the odds that Clint will make it through this alive?"

"Significantly higher if you are successful with the Prime Minister, Mr. President," Douglas replied, using the concern for added motivation for the President. It was not entirely true, and was unfair, but fairness was the least of his problems now.

"When can I go public with the progress we have made? It will be a huge boost to the MLDP," the President asked.

Douglas knew this question would come on the heels of such good news and was prepared for it, "Assuming we take out the seventeen distribution sites without incident, the public won't know that anything has transpired. Carlos may not either. We need to give Clint at least three days to identify the generals and the balance of the coke and heroin operation. Sir, we need to hold on a press release until that time. The premature release could endanger Clint's life."

"Three days then, or until Clint is out of danger," the President closed with the conviction of his office.

Clint walked over to Jesús's motionless bloody body in the camp's hub. He was propped up against a tree in the center of the camp with bandages covering his foot and head. Hearing the plane beginning its approach set the timing. Clint straightened the end of a rusty coat hanger he had retrieved from the tent, lifted Jesús's shirt and drove the slim rod straight into his heart. The very slim diameter of the rod would cause death from internal bleeding, but not for another ten minutes or so, and in the condition Jesús was in, he won't be able to talk anyway. It would not be easy to detect and the puncture wound was too small to bleed. Jesús had gone into shock after he accidentally swallowed his ear and remained in shock through the balance of the day.

The plane was touching down, so Clint went out to meet it, and Carlos, and his destiny. He knew this was a critical moment. Carlos might decide it wasn't worth it, not seeing Jesús, and turn around and take off. Or, he could get out and cut Clint in half with an automatic weapon. I'll know in a few minutes, he thought, as the plane taxied over to where Clint was standing.

The engines remained idling while the man in the rear cabin looked all around the camp. Carlos didn't know the guy standing in front of the plane with his hands held straight out like a scarecrow. He could see Jesús in the center of the camp with bloody bandages on his head and foot. He looked like he was alive and could tell him what had happened and who this guy was. Carlos picked up his 9mm and cautiously cracked opened the door.

"Get on your fucking belly and don't move! Don't even fart or you're hamburger! Move!" Carlos spat out. Not until the guy was on his stomach did Carlos open the door completely and begin to step out.

"Keep your arms out straight and hands palm up. Keep your face to the dirt and your legs spread wide. And don't move a single muscle," Carlos commanded as he walked slowly toward –Clint, gun pointed straight out. Periodically his eyes darted about the camp, still not sure what had happened here.

"Jesús, you okay? Can you hear me, Jesús?" Carlos yelled without response.

"Okay, asshole, who the hell are you?" Carlos yelled over the sound of the aircraft's engines.

"I'm Ricardo Marcus. Leon had to leave early, but I stayed to keep our appointment. Big mistake. Almost cost me my life," Clint responded.

"Yeah, it still might be a big mistake. You're the guy who had a 'large important' deal. Yeah, I remember. You come into my camp and look what happens," Carlos yelled out while looking around for more clues to what happened to Jesús and the others.

"Okay, turn over on your back, but keep your arms straight out and put your hands palms down."

Carlos moved and stood over Clint's head with his 9mm pointing straight at his throat. "Now, tell me Ricardo, what the hell happened here?"

Shaking the dirt off his face, Clint responded, "I flew in yesterday morning with Leon. The pilot said he couldn't wait because he had another run. I assume to pick up you…"

"Don't assume, just keep talking and it better fit," Carlos seethed out, the 9mm not moving.

"Leon couldn't wait. Business. He hopped back into the plane and I waited for you. I've got people to feed, ya know? Well, I go to take a piss and hear gunfire on my way back to the camp. Your guy Tommy is trying to take out the camp. I don't know why. And I'm not assuming. I sneak up behind him and plant a blade in his back, but not before he took out José and Chico and did some serious damage to Jesús. I bandaged up Jesús, did what I could do for him, but he doesn't look good. You should get him to a doctor. Then I waited for the plane to return, and here you are. That's all folks. And, hear this, I don't want any fucking part of this!" Clint responded.

"Where are the other bodies?"

"Behind the center tent. As you can see, Jesús is in the center court of the camp."

"Get up slowly, very carefully, and show me," Carlos ordered.

Rising first to a sitting position and brushing off some dirt, then standing, Clint finally walked to the center tent. As they rounded the tent's corner the three bodies were lined up head to head, foot to foot. Carlos asked Ricardo to turn Tommy's head toward him while he pulled the faxed photo of Art out of his pocket. He looked from the fax to Tommy's face numerous times, and then, finally, lowered his gun.

"That guy isn't Tommy. His name is Clint Bear, a DEA agent. Who killed him?"

"I already told you, I did, but I didn't know he was DEA. Shit. I told you I didn't want any part of this," Ricardo responded, hiding the sorrow at seeing his brother's body again.

"Let's go and see about Jesús," Carlos said while spinning on his heels and heading toward the center court of the camp in a trot.

Carlos was letting down his guard, allowing Ricardo to follow him as opposed to leading him at gunpoint. It's not over yet, Clint said to himself, but we are well on the way. Carlos bent down to talk with Jesús. "Hey, what's your name again?"

"Ricardo Marcus," Clint said.

"Ricardo, help me get him to the cot in that tent," Carlos said while pointing to the tent with one cot.

Jesús was still breathing shallow breaths and sweat dripped down his forehead. Infection was setting in on top of the coat hanger hole in his heart. There wouldn't be much time left before Jesús stopped his suffering. Clint was thinking that America had won, because he'd had a much more painful and lengthy death planned for Jesús. Jesús died before regaining consciousness, unable to rebuke Ricardo's story.

Carlos walked over to the production tent and whipped open the flap. His gun remained in his hand, hanging down by his side. The sacks were completely filled and neatly lined in rows in the cardboard boxes.

"You must be real stupid or very smart. There is over fifty million dollars of product in here. Why didn't you just take it and run?" Carlos asked testing Clint again.

"Look, I came here with eight million in cash to make the first of many buys. I'm not looking for a quick score; I need a reliable source to feed my organization. After what happened here, I'm not convinced of your reliability, and I'm certain I don't want any part of this," Clint added.

"I just might kill you and take that eight million in cash. Clear profit for me," Carlos added while gesturing with his 9mm.

"Yeah, the thought crossed my mind you might think that way. But, my organization in Japan can use eight mil a week, maybe more. That's four to five hundred million a year. A lot to turn your back on, wouldn't you say?" Clint postured carefully.

"No one risks bringing the coke into the U.S., then risks bringing it out of the U.S. and into Japan. They go directly into Japan. This doesn't play!" Carlos said with his suspicion building.

"You take the risk in bringing it into the U.S., not me. I have a foolproof way of getting it out of the U.S. and into Japan. Virtually risk free," Clint positioned carefully, knowing this was the hook.

"You've got sixty seconds to live. Convince me of the foolproof system, or you're a dead DEA agent!" Carlos commanded.

Waiting a few seconds for effect, Clint finally responded, "It's simple. I own an hourglass manufacturing plant in L.A. We blow the glass and manufacture the sculptured wooden cradles. They are very high end and very expensive. The bleached white sand in the hourglass is really coke. The consistent crystalline structure makes for the glass keeping perfect time. The sealed glass of the hourglass structure prevents even the dogs from detecting the coke. It's perfect and foolproof."

Carlos quickly assimilated the system. It was foolproof and ingenious in its simplicity. The best plans were the simple ones. Just like the best machines were the ones with the fewest moving parts. The fewer parts, the fewer breakdowns. Ingenious. He tucked his 9mm into the belt of his pants.

"Ricardo, help me move these boxes into the plane."

Clint had done it. He was in.

Cole took personal charge of the recovery mission in Washington D.C. He had handpicked all the recovery team leaders for the other sixteen missions. Each team consisted of fifteen men and women. The leader and seven team members were DEA or Department C agents. The remaining eight team members were a Counterterrorist Navy SEAL team who had trained with each other for months. Each member of the recovery team had their job, and were the absolute very best at it.

The recovery mission was a simple plan and identical for each of the seventeen missions. At precisely 03:00 CST, the electricity and telephone lines going to each building would be cut. The cellular telephone towers in the area would be temporarily disabled. All digital satellite communication lines would be delayed by thirty minutes.

Every member of the team would be dressed completely in black and use silenced weapons. Their communication would be through voice activated encrypted FM perimeter radios with a range of one thousand feet. The local police would not be alerted. The compartment would remain within the recovery unit.

Each team's mission was simple. Terminate, with extreme prejudice, all occupants of the building and recover the White Ice and any other drugs with no unsilenced gunfire. They were to take the bodies out and leave no trace of the recovery team. Simple. Leave the area clean, devoid of human trace. Devoid of drug trace.

Cole, waiting to start his mission command in Washington D.C., watching the second hand sweep through twelve, ordered the recovery mission, "Go." Simultaneously, sixteen other recovery mission leaders did the same in other parts of America, as well as in Toronto.

The building was in the lower west side of Washington D.C. in a warehouse district. It was a red brick and wooden structure that had seen its fair share of use twenty years ago. The blueprints obtained at the assessor's office were eighty years old but gave the team the basic structure layout. The logical location for the White Ice was on the top floor of the four-story building. With the power cut, night vision goggles gave the team another advantage.

As they expected, a battery-operated lantern was activated in the right rear room of the top floor. Other than that light, the building was engulfed in total darkness. Cole was comforted that they knew where the druggies were, and where they were not, and immediately radioed this information to all agents. Squad Four would need to remove their night vision goggles prior to going in that room.

The silence was deafening. It was 04:09 EST. Agents who had secured the first and second floors had reported in. They reported hearing silenced gunfire and thuds on the third floor. Finally, the third floor was secured with three druggies down. One male and two female bodies were on the shoulders of Navy SEALs being noiselessly carried out to the nondescript van.

Cole was alarmed to hear an unsilenced gunshot and see the flash through the fourth-floor window. It was quiet enough that it shouldn't draw any attention. The druggie who was lucky enough to get a round off was quickly taken down. At 04:13, the agent reported the floor secured, White Ice and cocaine located. Four dead bodies, all male, were being carried out when the request came for all team members to help with the drugs. It took over an hour for the fourteen Agents and SEALs to carry all the drugs down to the vans. Cole logged the booty in and estimated the street value to be fifty to sixty million dollars.

One down, sixteen to go, he thought, as the last van drove away. The power came back on as if by magic and everything looked as it had at 03:59.59.

Cole reached for his satellite phone and with a single push of one button was connected to the II4C control center. "Director, this is Cole. Number one is secure. No incidents. All product in hand. Any word from the others?"

"Yes, numbers two through nine are secure as well. Number ten had an incident. A local cop doing a routine check. McClausky told him it was a DEA exercise and was just finishing. He will write it up and someone will complain about not being notified. Not serious. Numbers eleven through fifteen are all secure. Number sixteen is almost done, and no word from number seventeen yet."

Number seventeen is Toronto, Cole thought. He didn't have a good feeling about this, not good at all.

When the last box of White Ice had been loaded on the plane, Carlos had a decision to make. What to do about Ricardo. He reasoned that Ricardo would be better than

Jesús, more believable. Clint had the ability and experience to set up the White Ice operation and he could make the cartel believe it. That was always his big fear, when people started to die how the cartel would respond. The White Ice cash flow wouldn't hit his foreign accounts for five to seven days after it hit the streets, and he would need to stay around until then. With Ricardo on the team, Carlos would be able to position him to take the fall and he could walk out free and clean. Clint will be his fall man, and much, much more believable than Jesús. Perfect!

The new source of coke revenue would continue his cash flow for the cartel, making them suspect him even less when the White Ice began to hit the street and take coke business away. All in all, a blessing in disguise. Even more perfect.

He told Ricardo to get in the plane and he would drop him at the El Paso airport, and he could make his own way back to California. The next contact would come through Leon.

Prime Minister Peter Marstens was accommodating, to a point, but didn't want to let this be another American bully job on Canada. He listened carefully to Bill Covey and knowing he was not an alarmist, took the situation for what it was — deadly serious.

In the end, Marstens agreed to allow the fifteen-person recovery team quietly in the country, fully armed. His only condition was that the team must be commanded by a Canadian and appointed Richard Fontaine, the head of the Canadian Security Intelligence Service. Fontaine was Special Ops prior to joining the CSIS and had seen action in the Gulf War before that. He was experienced, loyal and thorough. And, he was not going to let America come onto his soil and run an operation. Period. Hole number one for Toronto.

But Marstens had been very specific. Fontaine was there to observe and assist where necessary, but the Americans were to handle the tactics unobstructed. Just in case, Fontaine had three of his best CSIS agents stake out the likely escape route, should any of the drug runners make it out of the building. Hole number two for Toronto.

The team waited in their respective nondescript vans while the squad leaders went with Marshall, the U.S. Team Commander, to do recon. Black matte-finished binoculars with antireflection-coated optics were trained on the distribution center from a hill three hundred and twenty yards away. The building was on the extreme south side of the city, near an abandoned and dilapidated railroad repair station. There were seven automobiles in the protected yard and no indication of any people. The windows in the building were painted inside with flat black primer, allowing no light in or out. It also prevented any visual indication of internal movement.

The night was uncooperative. A light mist falling added to the chill in the air. Clouds covered the moon's light, and the mist interfered with the night vision goggles adding a blurred image. All combined, it added to Marshall's unease.

Infrared scanning equipment showed there were at least sixteen people in the building. Some moving about, most remaining perfectly still, most probably sleeping.

The plans showed a clean entrance to the front of the single-story brick structure, not the gated, fenced and barbed wire fortress that Peter Marshall, Special Agent in Charge was now looking at. Sensor tests confirmed the fence was electrified and alarmed with a closed circuit battery-powered system. The power would be cut off so he was not concerned about the electrified fence. The battery alarm system would need to be bypassed. however. Hole number three for Toronto.

"Cudworth, you have eleven minutes to determine where the alarm system power source is and neutralize it," Marshall ordered. "Let me know the instant it is out."

"Collin, the fence can't be an obstacle. Figure it out but don't take any action until I give you the word. You've got less than ten minutes to be in ready state," Marshall said, getting ready to give his next set of orders.

"Fontaine, got any ideas why we didn't know about these 'minor' issues before arriving?" Marshall spat out, letting his irritation show.

"Hey, you're the Big Bad American DEA. Thought you guys knew everything. And, yeah, I've got a few ideas I'll use when you guys finish screwing this up!" Fontaine fired right back. His smirk added to Marshall's already high level of contempt for Fontaine.

"Don't count your money before you leave the table. Big mistake. We can do this without you, and with that attitude we will. Now get the hell out of my way. Now!" Marshall seethed out as he took off toward the communications van.

"Squad Leaders, listen up. Cudworth and Squad One will take out the perimeter alarm system. No one is to move to or past the perimeter fence without hearing the alarm has been neutralized. Next, Collin and Squad Three will remove the fence as an obstacle. Collin will advise us how to enter the perimeter grounds. Once in, the plan remains the same. Acknowledge in order," Marshall ordered.

Each Squad leader signified his and her understanding of Marshall's orders by speaking "Acknowledged" followed by their squad number. Each did so in unison. Each of the fifteen team members heard the complete transmission as they sat in ready for the assault.

"Team, this is Cudworth. The alarm system has been bypassed and is no longer a threat. Out."

"Team, this is Collin. The fence has three gated areas, two on the south side and one on the east side. All are being opened now that the alarm has been neutralized."

"Okay, team. Infrared systems tell us there are sixteen people in the building, four movers, twelve sleepers. You all know your jobs. Let's move out," Marshall said at precisely 04:00 with Fontaine at his shoulder.

The team began to converge on the building from three sides, north, south and east. There was a chilled mist in the late night air, now lightly blowing from north to south and there was no ambient noise to blend into the assault. Marshall waited in the command van and stayed attentively tuned into the communications between squads. Agent Moser was the first to confront a moving target. She neutralized the moving target instantly but her silencer burst with the first discharged round. The noise awakened another six targets.

"Move, everyone move. Take all targets out immediately," Marshall ordered and adding, "Shit!"

No one gave witness to Fontaine placing a small lead cap from a hollow point bullet into Moser's silencer during the briefing. Had he known that she was a firearms specialist, and it was completely improbable that her equipment would malfunction, he would have chosen someone else to cause the screw up.

The silencer's bursting had awakened six of the sleepers. There were now nine movers to contend with, and with Moser not able to use her weapon, her effectiveness was severely reduced. Fontaine was loving every minute of this, replaying in his mind the press coverage that a fucked-up American DEA operation on Canadian soil would garner and the added power and respect his department would gain by salvaging the fucked-up operation.

His fantasy glory bathing was short lived as he watched the infrared thermal imaging monitor showing the nine movers falling one by one, and the sleepers remain motionless. Not another sound was emitted thanks to Marshall, who suspecting sabotaged equipment due to Weapons Specialist Moser's silencer bursting, and ordered a fifteen second weapons check before continuing.

The building was secured in sixteen minutes thirty-seven seconds. All sixteen targets neutralized with the bodies being placed in one of the nondescript black vans, the White Ice and cocaine secured in another white van.

Fontaine was internally furious with the operation's success and was trying desperately to hide it from those around him in the command van. He was impressed with the precision and capability of the DEA team, but he would never, ever, share this thought with anyone.

Marshall turned the wind up over to Collin and reached for the secure telephone to report to Cole Cunningham. As he reached behind him for the phone, his eyes and Fontaine's eyes locked, and with no words spoken Marshall had confirmation that Fontaine had known about the electrified fence, known about the battery backed-up alarm system and placed the debris in the silencer of Moser's weapon — Fontaine had tried unsuccessfully to sabotage the operation. Marshall needed to make his decision before Cole answered the secure telephone.

"Cole, this is seventeen. All secure. No casualties. We are pleased with the assistance of the Canadian government. Out."

Marshall stood and turned to Fontaine, placing his face squarely in front of his and then leaned a little closer to his ear, whispering, "By not telling us of the fencing and alarm system you, personally, endangered the lives of my team.

By placing debris into the silencer of our weapons specialist you endangered the success of the operation and Moser's life, and that was your undoing. Only an outsider would not know how thorough she is and how impossible it would be for her weapon to malfunction. You are stupid, self-righteous and pig-headed and I should kill you where you stand you fucking son-of-a-bitch. But we will handle this properly and let the Prime Minister see to it that you are very properly rewarded." Then Marshall brutally pushed Fontaine aside and exited the communications van, the last sound he heard coming from Fontanne's body as it bounced off the van's floor.

Cole sat in his government-issued steel gray poorly cushioned chair in front of his steel gray well-used desk, supporting yet another large cup of black coffee. He couldn't believe that all seventeen sites had been neutralized without incident. No local police, no press, no civilian involvement. God must certainly be on their side. He had hoped, but experience told him that they would be fortunate to have had only four incident-ridden operations since they were planned so hastily. The Navy SEAL antiterrorism team along with the DEA SWAT teams worked incredibly well together. No one would have guessed it.

His thoughts were now with Clint. The last two women had activated the credit card location transmitter and were picked up within sixty minutes. They directed the DEA team to where the camp was. He was thinking that the onsite status reports were overdue from Agent Sam Forrest when his government-issued telephone rang.

"Cole Cunningham," Cole intoned.

"Hi, Cole. Sorry to be a few minutes late. It's a bit harried here," Sam responded assuming that Cole would recognize his voice.

"Here's what we've got. The camp is abandoned just as we were told. There were four dead bodies that have been positively identified as Art Bear, Jesús Pinos, José Cervantes and Chico Ramos. Jesús Pinos has been marked and is the only known suspect. The field team has already found one shallow grave with two more female bodies, white, mid-thirties, time of death uncertain, and one smaller empty grave. The synthetic that was destined for Houston was right where Clint said it would be and there is evidence of production. The lab is going over everything with a very careful eye. The tire prints on the grass runway are consistent with those found on STOL aircraft. The green Plymouth Roadrunner has prints all over it and the lab says it may take several days to lift the back seat area. Oh, there were no window or door handles in the back, must have been how they abducted the women so easily. The bruising found on the bodies must have come from the leg irons we found in the tents where the production and packaging was done. The outer perimeter was poorly protected by two laser diode intrusion detection systems, the fools. That's all I've got for now. My guess is that the lab will finish in two days," Agent Forrest said and immediately began taking a long breath.

"Sam, did the women indicate which way the plane was headed when it left?"

"Yes, due south," Sam responded, feeling foolish for not including it in the status report.

Cole thought, Due south. They could be heading for Peru, Columbia, Mexico… and all would require one or more fuel stops. He will have the likely locations covered. There was a suspected distribution site in Texas; east of Eagle Pass, a border crossing from Mexico's Piedras Negras, about one hundred miles northwest of Laredo. I'll send a SWAT team there with photos of Clint and instructions on how to take him out. But if the plane leaves the country, Clint will be on his own with no more than a day before all hell breaks loose when the wholesaling sites don't report in.

"Cole, anything else?" Sam asked.

"Yes. I doubt that anything here will go to trial, but just in case make sure the evidence is not compromised in any way. And Sam, take personal charge of the synthetic and personally, with your own hands, see to it that it one hundred percent gets secured."

"Got it. That is how we've been handling it. Out."

The STOL aircraft was flying beside mountain ranges and through crevasses to avoid radar detection, routine operation for Carlos. The thermal and wind currents made for a bumpy flight where sleep was difficult to find.

Only another day till the White Ice reaches all locations and then he would order his wholesalers to start selling to the street operation. I'm going to bump the price to fifty percent above cocaine, he thought, and that should net him a hundred dollars an ounce, about sixty-five million dollars from each of the seventeen locations, all in his accounts within five to seven days.

Carlos thought, I am going to live like a god! Maybe Ricardo can be of more help than I originally thought. Yeah…

"Pilot!" Carlos spat into the plane intercom system.

"Yes, Mr. Ortega?" the pilot responded.

"How long to El Paso?"

"We are beginning the final approach now. I expect to be at the general aviation terminal in about twenty minutes."

"Good. We will switch to the Gulfstream. Our guest, Mr. Marcus, and I have urgent business to attend to in Peru. Please notify them of our expected arrival time," Carlos said as he slowly turned to meet –Clint's curious eyes.

Was this the hole that would lead him to his death or the break he needed to get to the hive, Clint pondered, and then decided that he would know only when he knew. The best use of his time now would be to develop a series of contingency plans for the most likely scenarios that awaited him in Peru. He closed his eyes and began to group the contingency plans within the scenario headings of: I'm Carlos's fall guy, how do I get Carlos back to the U.S. to be arrested, my cover has been compromised, etc.

The Gulfstream jet would make the thousand-mile trip to Peru in less than three hours. By then, the cartel's inner circle will be waiting for Carlos to inform them of his "urgent business" and new guest, Ricardo Marcus.

The trip from the regional light aircraft airport in the central coastal region of Peru to the exclusive Northern coastal residential area of Paraiso took only twenty minutes, helped by the well-known black Mercedes limousine that stopped at no traffic lights, for no pedestrian in a cross walk, and obeyed no speed limit. The driver, who appeared to be incapable of speech, seemed to be looking for the pedestrian who would challenge his authority.

The lush deep-green vegetation, the tropical flowers, the well-groomed divided streets presented to a tourist the picture of paradise, and that is what Paraiso is — Spanish for paradise — providing you stay well clear of the drug business that consumed the area and its inhabitants. Drug money controlled the politicians, police, local militia, schools, hospitals, fire departments — making it impossible to stay clear of the drug business in Paradise.

The wrought iron gate was supported by stone guard stations on each side, the Armani-suited guards armed with MAC-10 automatics and supervised by a more heavily armed third guard station elevated some thirty feet in a stone light house-like structure. The mansion was not visible through the dense plantings and broad-leafed trees. The Mercedes was carefully inspected by three men, each assigned an area of the automobile. One was under the hood in the engine compartment, another used mirrors to inspect the undercarriage, while the third looked through the contents of the trunk. After the three reported it was safe the gate was opened, tire breaks lowered so as not to puncture the bosses' tires, and the limousine waved through.

The drive to the mansion took another four minutes. Clint felt the tension begin to build in his body as the car neared the mansion. It was a three-story sprawling beam and stucco style building with an impeccably manicured several acre lawn, tennis courts to the right, a large L-shaped swimming pool to the left, and straight ahead an eleven-door garage with attached living quarters. The steps to the mahogany double doors seemed to fluidly flow out of the structure to meet you… no, to get you, Clint thought. His reconnaissance was interrupted by Carlos.

"Mr. Marcus, come with me, would you? There are a few people I would like you to meet," Carlos said as the door was opened.

"I don't really have much choice now do I, Carlos," Clint responded with an appropriate level of anger and fear for having been taken into this situation. "Care to tell me what this is all about?"

"You will know soon enough." The language had switched from English to Spanish.

They were coldly greeted at the door by Alfonso Fassure, a lieutenant for the head of the cartel. It was obvious that Alfonso did not like Carlos, and by extension Clint.

"Hello Carlos. He is waiting in the library. I will stay with Mr. Marcus," Alfonso spat out in monotone.

Carlos walked through the grand foyer toward the double doors that must eventually lead to the study.

"Ricardo Marcus," Alfonso said over and over while standing in the foyer. "I know that name from somewhere. Have we met?"

"I don't think so. You don't look familiar and I can't place your name," Clint said, speaking in Spanish.

"I'll make some inquiries. It will come back to me. It's my trademark — I always remember faces and names."

Shit. He has probably met or somehow interacted with the real Ricardo Marcus and can't associate my face with the name, and it's only a matter of time before he realizes that I'm a fake... Clint's thoughts were interrupted by Carlos returning from the library.

"Ricardo, come with me. There are people who would like to meet you," Carlos said, gesturing that he should follow him.

"Wait a minute Carlos, I haven't cleared him yet!" Alfonso countered.

"Well, what have you been doing all this time, playing with dolls?" Carlos responded eloquently. "Do now what you should have done immediately and you will find that I have already cleared him."

Seething with very obvious hate for Carlos, Alfonso efficiently patted down Clint for weapons and wires and, satisfied that there were none, walked in the opposite direction without another word spoken. Clint could see that Alfonso had a 9mm semiautomatic holstered under his well-tailored linen suit jacket and a small earpiece that was probably listening to all security-related communication within the mansion and on the compound.

As they walked to the library, Clint could not help but think of the old movie *Gone with the Wind*. The circular staircase to his right could have Rhett Butler and Scarlett O'Hara doing their famous scene.

The library doorway was flanked by six very well dressed and serious men, three on each side of the door. No introductions were made. Their eyes penetrated Clint as he walked into the library on Carlos's right. Carlos turned and, using both hands, slowly slid the mahogany double doors closed.

The air was filed with the aroma of Cuban cigars mixed with vintage single malt scotch whiskey. One man was standing, and four were sitting on expansive dark brown leather chairs. The dim lighting amplified intermittently by the burst of flame from the relaxing fire. The thick oak shelves rising two stories on all four walls supported countless books, giving way to lighted original oil masterpieces by Monet, Picasso, Miró and van Gogh. The room reeked of wealth and power, as was its intent.

"Mr. Marcus, may I present Santiago Cero," Carlos said as he motioned to the man standing.

Clint confidently walked closer and extended his hand, saying, "I'm very pleased to meet you, I think? Mr. Cero, I am not here entirely voluntarily, as I assume you are aware. Would you be so kind as to tell me why I am here?"

"I am sorry you have been inconvenienced and we will hopefully make it up to you. Carlos has indicated that you have made an unusually large purchase of product and that your operation can support continued purchases in similar or larger quantities. Is this correct, Mr. Marcus?" Santiago inquired.

"Yes, it is correct. I assume that Carlos has told you about my operation."

"Yes he has, generally, but we would like to hear more, the details. It is important that we, all of us in this room, understand your operation. You see, we represent the

Peruvian cartel. We are smaller than the Colombian cartels and our focus has been product distribution in North America only. So come, sit, and tell us, will you Ricardo?" Santiago said, gracefully pointing to the vacant leather chair in the semicircle's center.

Clint had worked through this contingency on the plane here. This was one of the better scenarios for him and the Department C operation. He had decided to provide all the details they would need to understand that his operation was not a threat, but a market expansion opportunity for the Peruvian cartel.

"I started in the business when I was just fourteen years old, first as a courier and then selling product on the streets of Mexico City. The typical ounce purchase in Mexico netted a whopping twenty-five American dollars — a tough way to make money. The same product sale just north of Mexico City in San Diego would net twice that, all with less risk since the laws are easier to leverage. So I set up my own street operation there."

Clint paused to let the cartel absorb the transition to America and for him to organize his thoughts. His Spanish flowed completely naturally now.

"The market was always fertile, no problem on the selling side. The supply side has always been problematic since I was a competitor to the larger organizations. So I carved out a niche that was uniquely mine, the up-market professionals who had the money and couldn't afford the risk of a street buy and would pay more for the security. The added sale price helped me offset the margin lost with my purchase from the large street operations who always took their cut."

Now Clint had to transition to the Japanese market, and this was the critical point. If the cartel accepted this, the final operation would be an easy sell.

"My street organization prospered and so did the area. Thousands of Japanese were immigrating with temporary work visas to get the required American business experience before moving to the next level of management back home in Japan. The dollar/yen relationship gave these guys outrageous buying power and they were buying product like it was really candy!" The last comment was greeted with belly laughs from most of the cartel. They were enjoying the story, believing it to be the truth.

"Their problem was that the supply was not as plentiful nor as inexpensive when they returned home. Their buying power fell nearly by a factor of four in Japan. Several asked me to set up an operation in Japan. A few offered to help, and that's how it started. The problem was how to get the product into Japan. As you may know, Japanese Customs are extremely thorough, and more so with shipments and luggage from Latin America and third world countries. However, the U.S. has just as thorough a Customs process, and the Japanese, knowing that, are far less stringent on shipments and luggage from the U.S. So, since I had access to the product in the U.S., all I needed to do was to find a secure method to get large quantities of product into Japan through the less watchful eye of the Japanese Customs Authorities by originating through the U.S."

Clint was looking at the men, studying their faces, memorizing and cataloging them for future reference. Two were nodding their understanding and agreement, one was smiling and the other was emotionless. Santiago was pensive, still processing when Clint continued.

"The key to getting past Japanese Customs is to get past the dogs that can smell product through just about anything. These dogs can smell through Ziploc bags, vacuum packaging, coffee grounds, everything. So, I set up a manufacturing company north of Los Angeles. Bottled Time is its name and we produce hourglass timers. We blow the glass, manufacture the wooden cradles, fill and calibrate the glass and then heat the glass to seal the fill hole. Even to the trained eye and the best drug dogs, the hourglass is just that, a collectable, beautiful hourglass. But it is a foolproof way to move four pounds of uncut product. The hourglasses are shipped to our distributor in Japan, a company set up by the Japanese businessmen who offered to help. They open the hole and replace the product with refined bleached sand and sell the hourglasses to retailers. The product is cut and wholesaled, with some kept for personal use. They make a very respectable profit on the hourglass sales as well."

Clint stopped and waited for what he had told them to settle in. The questions that surely would follow would tell him how well his story was accepted. Everything should check out, including the Bottled Time Corporation, which was part of the cover that Cole had set up for him a few weeks earlier. The first buy of one million dollars and the latest for eight million should add to his credibility.

"Ricardo," the voice from the emotionless man in the far right chair, "What was your prior source of supply?"

Clint, knowing this was a weak link and also knowing that Cole had no choice, there simply was not enough time to set up a more penetrating cover, responded, "That has been a problem, as I indicated earlier. Joey was my best source of supply in San Diego, but he was… retired, just when I had finalized the expansion of my operation in Japan. I still have a small group of other suppliers, but combined, they could not provide what my operation demands. Before Joey retired he made arrangements for me to meet with Leon in L.A."

Carlos was very pleased with Ricardo's litany. The cartel was focusing on this new business opportunity, brought by him, and not focusing on daily business. That would help when the sales of his White Ice started to eat into product sales tomorrow. He took the opportunity to suggest that Ricardo be excused to shower and enjoy dinner after his long flight.

"Ricardo, as Santiago said, we apologize for inconveniencing you, and we will make amends. But, now you must be tired after your journey so we have arranged for fresh clothes and a fine meal. We have a well-stocked wine cellar here. If you would like, the steward will offer a suggestion." Turning to escort him to the double doors, Carlos called out abruptly for Alfonso to escort him to his room.

Alfonso led him up the circular staircase to a room in the center of the mansion without speaking until he roughly opened the door to the room. "Ricardo, you will find a robe near the shower. Fresh clothing and dinner will be brought up after you shower."

Clint entered and quickly surveyed the room. Small, windowless, and secured with a sentry no doubt at the door. It took a moment, but finally he saw the surveillance camera in the sculpted molding in the upper left corner of the room, placed where the entire room could be monitored. Nothing more to do except shower, eat, rest and await the cartel's reaction to his story. He mused, I will either be executed or really in business in the next twenty-four hours — time being his enemy, the longer the wait the more likely their decision would be execution, fortified by the lack of communication from several of their key North American operations.

***

Alfonso got the call he was hoping for forty-give minutes after escorting Clint to his room.

"Listen, this can't be verified, but I believe it's true. Ricardo Marcus was killed in an FBI drug bust eight months ago in South L.A. It's a pretty tight circle, sealed records and all, so something stinks. Watch your ass and don't call me here again!" The call from within the LAPD was abruptly terminated.

Alfonso whispered to himself, "We've got a fed on our hands and Carlos let — no invited — him in. He's not going anywhere so I'll have to time this to totally screw over Carlos. This will get me into the inner circle... even better, replace that scum bag Carlos.

It was after 9:00 PM before consensus was gained that the cartel should supply Bottled Time with product for a piece of the action. Consensus was that Ricardo should report to Carlos, and that he should oversee the operation from America as he did the other cartel business. The knock on the door came just after the toasts of success with aged, rare single malt scotch whiskey.

"Come in," responded Santiago.

"Please excuse the interruption," Alfonso said, continuing, "I'm growing concerned. It's after 9:00 PM and the only major North American operation to have checked in is Houston. This is highly unusual."

All eyes, alarmed, immediately went to Carlos, who had the responsibility for North America.

"I'll check it out," Carlos said, noticing the shit-eating grin on Alfonso. "It is probably just an added security measure not to communicate as regularly in response to President Covey's Martial Law Drug Plan. It's a smart move. I left the U.S. earlier today and everything was fine.

I'll check it out tomorrow when I'm back in the States... we don't want too many calls from here now, do we?" Carlos replied in as casual a tone as he could muster to demonstrate his confidence and lack of concern. "Alfonso is overreacting, as usual." Inwardly, Carlos was anything but confident.

Santiago and the rest, a little more relieved that everything was fine, agreed. But, Alfonso didn't agree and left to check out the coincidence of the Fed upstairs and the operations incommunicado, hoping to find the last nail he would use to seal Carlos's coffin.

When the door closed, Carlos continued, "I'll go and present our conditions to Ricardo and let you all know his decision."

That prompted roars of laughter from the entire cartel. No one tells them of their decision, they either go along or die. Simple as that. Most everyone goes along.

The knock on the door interrupted Clint's rest. He wasn't sleeping, but was restfully meditating and reinvigorating his tired body while lying flat on the oriental carpet near the bed's footboard.

"Come in," Clint said, responding to the knocks.

"I trust the accommodations are to your liking?" Carlos said as he closed the door behind him.

"First Class, and without a reservation, how do you do it, Carlos?" Clint irritatingly replied.

Carlos ignored the sarcasm and curtly stated, "We will take fifty-one percent of Bottled Time and supply you all the product you can move at fifteen percent less than you were paying before. Bottled Time profits will be distributed according to shareholdings on a monthly basis."

"Pretty steep, don't you think?" Ricardo shot back. "What if I say no?"

"You won't. Period. You'll work for me. Get some rest, you will be leaving in the early morning," Carlos commanded as he left the room, closing the door quietly behind him.

Clint had succeeded in penetrating the cartel, and very quickly. His major concern now was Alfonso. If he was able to dig anything up that would blow his cover, all progress would be lost and he'd be dead. Clint moved to the bed for a more complete rest.

It was just after 11:00 PM when Alfonso burst into Clint's room, awakening him fully from a restless sleep. The language had switched from Spanish to English — not a good sign. He had two other heavily armed men with him.

"Get up and come with me, motherfucker, and don't move a muscle except to walk where we tell you to or you're a dead man," Alfonso commanded.

"What's this all about?" Clint questioned, hoping for some clue as to how this would play out.

"Shut your fucking mouth and move," Alfonso spat back.

They walked down the "Gone with the Wind" staircase and into the formal dining room where the cartel sat finishing their dinner with another cigar and brandy. The unwelcomed intrusion was painted on the faces and voiced by Santiago.

"Alfonso, there had better be very good explanation for this. We have decided to invest in Mr. Marcus's business. He is now associated with us."

"Mr. Cero, I checked more deeply as to why we have not had contact from most of the operations, checking through our Mexican operation. The U.S. operations, with the exception of Houston, aren't answering their cell phones and no wholesale business activity is apparent in L.A.,

Chicago and Dallas, where our Mexican operation has resources to verify. Every indication points to our major wholesale operations being taken out," Alfonso reported.

"That's bullshit and you know it Al," Carlos countered. "We have confidential security measures that kicked in when the President stepped up the surveillance for the Martial Law Drug Plan!" But privately, Carlos knew that what he'd just said was a cover only, but hoped it would buy a few days' time.

"My name is not Al, its Alfonso. And, there is more Mr. Cero. I have a source in the LAPD who confirms my remembrance that Ricardo Marcus was killed in a FBI drug bust eight months ago. With the operations potentially taken out, and the appearance of a dead man in our headquarters, who is in all likelihood a Fed, I think we need to relocate quickly!"

Santiago Cero was not a man prone to knee-jerk reactions. He considered the options, uninterrupted by the cartel. Carlos and Clint were doing the same when Santiago broke the silence with a question to Ricardo.

"Ricardo, what do you have to say about all this?"

"Well, I'm obviously not dead am I, so Alfonso's source must be wrong. If Alfonso had thought to ask for a faxed photograph you would have the proof you need. Strange that someone who pretends to be so thorough didn't think to ask, don't you think?" Clint volleyed, thinking quickly on his feet.

Carlos jumped in and played on the turning momentum, "Is this yet another feeble attempt to discredit me? I told you I had Ricardo thoroughly checked out before bringing him here!" Privately, Carlos was very concerned that he had indeed brought a federal undercover agent into the inner circle.

"Alfonso, did you personally attempt to contact any of the operations directly?" Santiago asked.

"Of course I did, Mr. Cero. There were no responses to any of my cell or satellite calls at any of the major sites. We could be taken out next!" Alfonso replied.

"Well, we have a conundrum," Santiago said. "It is indeed highly unusual for there to be no contact by our operations within a twenty-four-hour period. But there has never before been a Martial Law Drug Plan offensive to contend with, has there. Before us, we have Ricardo Marcus who has offered the cartel a unique profitable business opportunity for which it appears has little to no risk. Alfonso would have us believe these two disparate occurrences are directly related, and if true, we must retire Mr. Marcus and take the necessary defensive actions for personal safety. If false, we will have thrown away a very profitable business enterprise and ended a potentially mutually beneficial long-term relationship with Mr. Marcus. We can't just sit here and wait, because if Alfonso is correct we may be retired right here this evening."

"Yes, that's exactly right. We should move to the alternate residence immediately!" Alfonso stated louder than necessary, his propensity to overreact very apparent.

"What do you think, Mr. Marcus?" Santiago asked.

"I think that moving is not necessary. The U.S. Government has no authority here, so what's the problem? But, if you feel you must move, go to the last place in the world where the Feds expect you to be and then monitor those places where they would expect you. That will tell you everything," Clint postured.

Looking carefully into Ricardo's eyes, and without losing eye contact, Santiago said, "Disarm Alfonso and tie his hands. Tie Mr. Marcus as well. We will leave immediately on both jets. Carlos, you take Alfonso,

Ricardo, and five men and fly to the last place the Feds would expect, our distribution site in South Texas. The rest of the cartel will join me on my jet to our private retreat. Carlos, I will radio instructions based on what happens in the next twenty-four hours. You will either retire Ricardo Marcus the Fed or Alfonso the snitch. Either way, make it professional and immediate."

"And Carlos, while you're in Texas awaiting my instructions, find out what's going on with MY OPERATIONS!" Santiago barked.

The Gulfstream circled the Texas distribution site until sunrise. Before making the landing on the old crop duster landing strip, the pilot did four flybys in each coordinate direction as slowly as the aircraft could safely fly without stalling. Each flyby created a dust cloud that required nearly fifteen minutes to settle before the next flyby could be executed. There was no sign of anyone, any car or truck, nothing but the abandoned building they routinely used for breaking down their product shipments and sending them on their way in planes, cars and pickups.

Carlos ordered the pilot to land so they could get some fresh air and stretch their legs. Clint and Alfonso sat on opposite sides of the plane, hands bound and pensive, both individually confident that the other would be shot.

The landing was unusually rough with the airstrip only half-remaining and the balance simply dirt and sand that easily blowed in the wind. As the corporate jet came to a stop near the vacant building, the dust it had raised began to encircle the aircraft, making visibility nearly impossible. The pilot was trying to shut down the engines to prevent damage from the excessive dust and sand when Carlos ordered the door open and three men to inspect the building and surrounding area.

The remaining occupants of the plane started coughing as the dust blew into the aircraft cabin and the pilot slammed his security door shut to prevent the dust from damaging the instruments and thereby prevent takeoff.

Less than ten minutes later the three men walked casually back to the plane through the settling dust cloud and reported to Carlos that the area and building were secure. There was no one in the area and no sign that there was anyone had been here recently.

"Okay, everyone out for some fresh air now that the dust has settled. You two keep watch over Ricardo, and you and you keep watch over Alfonso," Carlos ordered while pointing out the men for the various tasks. "You lose them, I lose you!"

The early morning temperature was less than eighty degrees, but by 9:00, a mere three hours from then, it would be over one hundred. Everyone was walking around the plane, stretching their legs, enjoying the fresh air and waiting for the radio communication from Santiago Cero when there was a "hissing" sound obvious to everyone.

Clint had seen the red laser dot on the tires a few seconds before the shot and prepared himself. His cue was when the commotion began; training told him always take advantage of the first few seconds of confusion.

"They're shooting out the tires, grounding the plane, then they will come for us!" Clint yelled. "Carlos, head to the building, now, the plane is useless!" He used his body to push Carlos to the building when the first bullet hit Clint's shoulder, right upper side. The impact blew him back several yards, nearly hitting the building. Clint struggled to his feet unsteadily, shook his head to orient himself, and looked down to his right shoulder to see the blood begin to flow.

Carlos stopped momentarily to see Ricardo struggling back to his feet and the bloody shoulder wound. He took out his 9mm and began moving to the building when he saw the second bullet hit Ricardo on the left side of his chest. This one lifted him off his feet eventually landing flat on his back, raising a dust cloud in the process. He ran to Ricardo in a crouch, and reached down to check his pulse. It was weak and slow, Ricardo was dying.

"Ricardo, I must know, did you sell us out?"

Ricardo responded in a faint whisper, "Take care of Bottled Time, she'll make you a lot of money. The people are loyal, too. I think Alfonso is after you, no? He's a fucking... snitch." And then just, before the last of Clint's air wheezed out of his lungs, he pressed the two buttons on his watch twice fast before his eyes went lifeless.

Carlos crawled into the building where everyone else was and found Alfonso. Without a moment's hesitation, he raised his 9mm and shot him in the head, again in the heart and again in the stomach. Then he spat in Alfonso's dead face and kicked him in the balls. Alfonso just had enough time to inhale the air that was to be used to protest, but not enough time to form the words.

Breathing heavily and near insane rage, Carlos collected himself, took several deep breaths and said, "Okay, here's the situation. These are Feds. They were tipped off by our fucking snitch here before we left the mansion. They killed Ricardo, Pepe and Theo. There is no way we will win this fight. We either take as many of them out as possible and go out doing it, or we try to fight this in the fucked-up American court system. Odds are even that we can beat in court, 1000 to 1 that we'll beat them here."

Then, a loud, high-pitched shock wave filled the building. He was stunned as were the others, dropping to their knees not knowing what had happened. Bom Bom's toy didn't impact Clint who was unconscious from the bullet wounds.

Carlos recovered and waited but the decision was obvious. They dropped their weapons, raised their hands high over their heads, and followed the white handkerchief in Carlos's right hand out of the building.

Men and women dressed in tan camouflage canvas survival fatigues appeared out of nowhere and from all directions. There must have been sixty agents scattered about and when Carlos's men originally surveyed the area they had seen one. Incompetence, Carlos thought.

Carlos, the pilot and the three remaining men were kneeling, facing the van with their hands bound behind their back with heavy-duty nylon cable ties, watching the bodies of Ricardo, Alfonso, Pepe and Theo get body bagged and taken away. It was a memory that would stay with them all for a long while. Large thick-walled black plastic bags with a zipper-sealed top and handles on the four corners to aid the movement of dead weight.

Carlos wasn't thinking about the dead, he was thinking that the White Ice would be on the streets today and the proceeds in his accounts in five to seven days, and he would be able to buy his way out of anything. He was unaware that Alfonso was dead on with his assessment that the major wholesalers had been taken out, the White Ice and cocaine taken by a new group, Department C. He was unaware that he would never be a free man again.

Five, four, three, two, you're on.

"Good evening, fellow Americans. I am pleased to report that the Martial Law Drug Plan has made significant progress in the fight against the trafficking of illegal drugs in America. Early this morning, Federal Agents arrested the North American head of the Peruvian drug cartel, Carlos Ortega, in South Texas. Carlos Ortega's organization is responsible for more than forty percent of the cocaine traffic within North America, representing a street value of more than sixty billion dollars each year. Yesterday, in the very early morning, Federal Agents raided the wholesale operations in seventeen major cities and arrested or eliminated those trafficking in drugs without casualties to our agents. I would like to offer special recognition to Prime Minister Marstens of Canada, who fully assisted and supported the multiple simultaneous raids. The Peruvian cartel has been literally put out of business in North America. It is not the end of the MLDP, merely a start that proves we are moving the right direction," President Covey announced while sitting at his White House desk as he donned his serious face for the camera's benefit. Then, nodding slightly and sliding the paper notes to the side to reveal the next page of notes, he continued.

"In the process of implementing the Martial Law Drug Plan, I have formed a new organization to investigate and enforce America's laws where cross-border and cross-responsibility efficient agency action is required. It is called Department Collaborative and is being permanently headed by the former Director of the CIA, C. Eric Douglas. Department C's charter is not limited to illegal drugs only, although that is their focus currently, but will be expanded to include specific types of terrorism, gambling, internet crime, human trafficking, and weapons and munitions traffic. The Department will have a substantial permanent and rotating temporary force recruited from the Departments of CIA, FBI, DEA, ATF, State, Defense and Secret Service. In essence, a Collaborative of existing well-trained government agencies with broader responsibility and authority. Director Douglas will be providing you more details in the coming days and weeks," Covey said, pleased that the Department C announcement could be dovetailed into a major success. It would add a great deal of grassroots support.

"There is still a great deal to do. We have had a major success, but it only reduced the illegal cocaine traffic by an estimated forty percent and the funds it created for terrorists. There is still the sixty percent, with a street value of one hundred and forty billion dollars to deal with. In addition, there is still heroin, marijuana, crystal meth, prescription drugs sold illegally, and more to stop. We can and *will* stop illegal drugs in America. We have sent a very clear message to the drug lords and to the world that we are determined to end drug abuse in America. Department C is the tool to move more quickly and efficiently to ensure the Martial Law Drug Plan's success. People of America, sleep just a little more comfortably tonight. And, I say to those involved with illegal drugs within America, stop now. There are clinics staffed to help those of you who use drugs. And those of you who traffic drugs, know that there is a jail cell ready and hard time, very hard time, is very certain. Good night and God bless America."

"Cut!" the White House communications director said, adding, "We are off the air, Mr. President."

Santiago Cero was back in his primary residence enjoying breakfast on the stone-inlaid patio, the fresh humid morning air accented by the orchids, when the servant brought a tray holding a silver coffee decanter, a bone China cup and saucer, and the morning newspaper. Santiago reached for the paper resting on the tray's corner while the servant poured the coffee.

The headlines interested, but didn't shock Santiago — Local drug lord enforcer Alfonso Negro's family is found brutally killed.

Santiago had nothing to do with the killings, but was certain that Carlos did. It was how lessons were taught and learned in his world. Alfonso's wife, daughter, son, father and mother were lessons to others in the organization that loyalty is paramount. He neatly folded and put the paper down while looking out over the luxuriant green sprawling manicured lawns for answers that didn't come. He needed to form a new North American wholesale operation, but wasn't sure where to start.

His thoughts were distracted by the bees that were collecting the orchid's nectar, moving from flower to flower, skipping over the dead dried-out orchids. Interesting, he thought, how bees are like us, someone dies and we move on to the next in line.

CHAPTER 9:
THE HONEYCOMB

Department C had moved into permanent offices, once a secure CIA operation headquarters in Washington D.C. that had become redundant with the budget cutbacks, now made secure again. It was in close proximity to the other agencies and the White House, and had all the necessary technology linkages. It was a seven-story brick building surrounded by poorly landscaped acreage attempting to hide the barbed wire canopy on the chain link fencing and guarded parking lots. The various dish antennas on the roof gave the correct impression that this was not just another office building.

In one of several windowless briefing rooms located in the building's core on the fourth floor, C. Eric Douglas, Director of the Collaborative, was addressing a spirited small group of men and women. Among them was Agent Meceli, Cole Cunningham, Sam Forrest and Navy SEAL Lt. Commander Bob Garret.

"This next phase of the MLDP will take place off American soil. The Peruvian cartel has suffered a severe blow to their North American operations, but they are still able to rebuild, and that must be prevented or all we have done is temporarily impeded the cocaine supply," Douglas lectured seriously.

"We have organized a covert operation using the same techniques, equipment, and HumINT that is used in BEL ops. The mission is to enter Peru, covertly, assassinate the remaining members of the Peruvian cartel and their lieutenants and make it look like it is the work of a competing cartel. I have selected someone with extensive BEL experience to command the operation, Navy Captain Clint Bear, and will turn the briefing over to him," Douglas said as he opened the briefing room's side door, letting the newly recruited and promoted Clint in and then quietly leaving the room, closing the door behind him.

Several in the room thought Clint had been killed in the taking of Carlos Ortega's plane in South Texas two days ago. Cole and Meceli both knew that the marksman responsible for taking Clint out was using rubber blood bullets that severely hurt the mark, but didn't penetrate the body. They were designed to roll when the tip, containing real goat blood, exploded and therefore converted the forward motion of the bullet to deflected motion. It was one of Bom Bom's special designs and it allowed Ricardo Marcus to be dead, and Clint to assume his new responsibilities. Clint's severe shoulder and chest bruises would heal in time, as would the slightly restricted arm motion due to the deep muscle damage.

Clint started the in-depth briefing as he moved to the front of the room.

"This op, code name Apache, will take the focus as a counter-terrorist op, with a few alterations. Plan accordingly. First alteration is we will not be on American soil, therefore, there will be absolutely no American identifying ordinance or effects. The men and women selected for this mission have been appropriately screened. Second alteration is if you can't carry your wounded out, they are to be left." Everyone knew what left meant... left without the ability to be tortured into revealing the team's identity.

Clint pushed a button on a hand-held device similar to a television remote control and the large high-resolution screen illuminated a map of the coastal region of Peru.

"We will rendezvous at 1600 hours on helicopter pad six. Have your teams in full counter-terrorist readiness. We will chopper to here," using electronic laser pointer on the projection screen, "where we will be dropped at sea and make our way to the Aquarius, under the command of Captain Preston Cornwell, at approximately 2310 hours. Our underwater transport will take us five miles off the coast of Peru, surface here, at 0200 hours, where our teams will raft ashore."

"There will be four teams. Our mission to terminate, with extreme prejudice, the remaining three cartel generals, the cartel head, and their lieutenants. The hits must appear to be gang-style: the head, the heart and the stomach. A cover story will be strategically placed to make it appear that a rival cartel is moving in on their business, assuming weakness from Carlos Ortega and the seventeen wholesale site hits. Questions so far?" Clint asked, waiting a few seconds and making eye contact with each person in the room before moving on.

He looked over the group and saw a lot of pensive faces, but with no questions forthcoming, he continued.

"The four groups will be headed by SEAL Commander Weisman, Team One, SEAL Commander Foley, Team Two, Special Agent Meceli, Team Three, and I will head Team Four. The teams will have two hundred and ten minutes from time of departure to time of recovery.

Sunrise is our enemy. The Aquarius cannot be seen, period. The briefing reports in front of you describe an alternate extraction should you miss the sunrise deadline. Please leave the reports here when you leave. Make no written notes; commit everything to memory," Clint added.

"Questions, please?" Clint asked one last time.

"Yes, Agent Meceli."

"Sir, I command the backup team. I wait with the rafts, monitor our secure radio traffic and dispatch help wherever and if needed. With three active teams, it is possible that backup will be needed by more than one team at the same time. Is there a priority to be followed?" Anne-Marie Meceli logically asked Clint.

"Tough question, Agent Meceli," Clint responded while taking a deep breath.

"Yes, there is a logical priority. Since the goal of the mission is to prevent the cartel from reforming their distribution, the organizational structure is the priority. The team assigned to the cartel's head man, followed by the generals and then the lieutenants. Any more questions?"

"Yes, Commander Foley?"

"Sir, how serious were you regarding bringing our own out, should they become injured?"

"Commander," Clint addressed without hesitation, all business like, "I'm one of you. You know that, and you know the rule to never leave your own behind. However, my order stands. If you can't carry them out, you are to leave them behind and ensure their silence. No exceptions. Anyone who cannot handle this, leave now." Clint was hoping that the order would create an extra incentive to ensure everyone's safety. The prevention of casualties is the most effective means to this end.

"Okay, that's it. Remember, this op is voluntary. If you have second thoughts now is the last time you have to withdraw. See you in full readiness at 16:00," Clint concluded as he pushed the remote to turn off the projection screen. "Meceli, would you stay behind for a moment?"

Clint didn't know why he had asked Anne-Marie to stay behind. Maybe it was the comment that Cole had made before he went undercover, "Meceli may have special motivation." Maybe it was that he was beginning to see her for more than just a team member.

It was an awkward moment, both wanting to say something, both not knowing what to say. The silence after everyone had left the room was deafening. And then, intuition took over and Clint reached out to Anne-Marie, pulled her unresisting body toward him in a warm and strong embrace. No words were exchanged, the embrace speaking better than they could. Several minutes later, a knock on the door, followed by it slowly opening, ended the moment. It was Douglas's assistant, asking Clint to see Douglas before leaving. Anne-Marie walked slowly to the door, and side-stepped past Douglas's assistant without turning back.

Nervousness should always be present before a major mission. It helped focus the mind, giving the chance to review the data, think through the contingencies and find the holes. Anyone who said they were not nervous and or absent of anxiety was either a liar or certifiable. Either way, they were not who you wanted covering your back while on a mission. The Apache team members were all nervous, all reviewing the mission data and checking their ordinance. A healthy and expected sign.

Each member was dressed in canvas black bodysuits with soundless plastic zippers and buttons to aid in dressing. The standard equipment consisted of a Kevlar bullet and knife-resistant vest, black hood, night vision goggle, Smith and Wesson .357 matte black Model 66 pistol, double magazine MAC-10 submachine gun with silencer, two incendiary bombs, two bricks of C-4, six grenades, a matte black finish survival knife, compass, water pouch, thirty feet of black nylon rope and a wireless secure communicator with ear clip.

All of the equipment could be purchased on the open market. Nothing was used that was U.S. Government issue, but all was top of the line, just what a drug dealer would purchase. The mission language will be Spanish in the unlikely event that the communication was overheard or compromised.

Each member of the team had studied the maps well enough to make their way to their assigned marks three different ways in total darkness without the aid of night vision goggles. They were not expecting more than light resistance, but the teams were prepared for a heavy counterattack. With the mission data reviewed and ordnance checked countless times. Most team members were lying on their beds, eyes wide open, finding whatever rest would come and waiting for the 16:00 rendezvous.

"Thanks for stopping by, Clint," Douglas said from behind his new antique desk while reaching into the drawer and turning off the recording device that taped all conversations in his office. "I needed to share with you one more element of the mission. The President is unaware of this mission, and it needs to remain that way, for his sake."

"Director, thank you for sharing that, but you needn't have troubled yourself. I, and everyone on the team, know we are breaking a dozen American, Peruvian and international laws by executing this mission," Clint said tiredly. "I have been over it dozens of times, and I can't see a better way for us, Peru, or the world to rid ourselves of this menace. I'm sure that every member of this compartment has done the same soul searching. There just isn't another way to cut out the cancer and bring back a healthy society.

"Mr. Director, the President must always have deniability. I know that as well as you do. Going back to the BEL missions, you and I knew the need for deniability. But back then you, as my black control, kept the distance between us. I didn't know who you were. Now, you and I operate slightly differently, but with the same noble purpose."

"Son," the Director said, opening his mouth to say something and then nodding, closed his eyes and chose to say nothing, his mood heavy.

There was nothing more to be said.

The two Air Force transport helicopters, jet engines roaring, rotors beginning to spin, were loaded with two teams each with rafts, ordnance and supplies. The pilots, assuming a training exercise, were given orders to transport the teams to Andrews AFB. From there they would be transported by an Army jet to Lackland AFB in southern Texas. A separate specially equipped Navy over-water transport would then carry them to specific coordinates in the Pacific Ocean. None of the transports were aware or connected to the others and all believed that this was a routine training mission. Keep the compartment tight.

During the various flights there was little talking and no banter. The team members had their game faces on, and they would remain on until the mission was over.

The helicopter's fuselage was being assaulted by thousands of raindrops, their sound effects increased by the chopper's speed. Midair fueling was a challenge but all went well. The red illumination aided night vision by allowing the pupils to fully dilate, but cast a baleful glow that no one acknowledged, having been there before.

The chopper flight from Lackland was turbulent, with both the external weather and internal thoughts in a state of unrest. Clint had not been on a BEL-type mission in over twenty years and he hoped, privately, he was up to the task. Where are the holes? What could go wrong? What are the contingency plans? Will the team stay together? Questions without any new answers.

Meceli, noticing Clint doing what she referred to as the mental checklist for the umpteenth time, slid over next to him.

"Clint?" Meceli asked just above a whisper so as not to disturb the others.

Clint looked over as if he was awakening from a deep sleep, said, "Ya?"

"How about dinner tomorrow night? I have a hankering for Italian," Meceli asked placing her hand on his right knee. "Man doesn't live by counter-terrorism attacks alone!" she added humorously.

Smiling, and knowing what she was doing, he responded, "I'd like that very much, more than you may know." Clint added, "It is like I never left the battle field. I lost men, close friends, men with wives and kids. Maybe if I…?"

Meceli cut him off, "Maybe if you what, had a crystal ball, could change the past? Don't go there Clint. I have a confession to make. I went through your files and I was blown away by your accomplishments. In war, people die. But far fewer people died on your BEL missions than on any other in recorded history. That means there are more Afghanistan vets that are husbands and fathers as a direct result of you. You Clint, and Bill Covey is one of them. And I'm proud to be on this mission with you and under your command."

Clint was very touched. His confidence was boosted and he no longer questioned the details of the mission… but now found that he was beginning to question his feelings about Meceli.

The pilot announced over the intercom, "Ten minutes to drop zone." On cue, all team members began to assemble their gear and made ready to jump into the frigid waters of the Pacific Ocean. Wetsuit hoods and gloves were put on but fins and masks would wait until splashing to ensure they were not lost and didn't create injury during impact. They will be jumping from over twenty feet, an altitude high enough to ensure that errant waves didn't swamp the helicopter, low enough to help reduce the potential of injury on impact. The result is an impact roughly similar to an eight to ten-foot jump to solid ground.

Clint picked up the intercom phone and buzzed the pilot, "Has the Aquarius checked in?"

"Yes, Sir. About seventeen minutes ago. She will be surfacing in seven minutes thirty. Everything is going as the training mission coordinator planned," the pilot confirmed. "And chopper two is right on our tail at seven o'clock."

The pilot brought the chopper down to about twenty feet above sea level. The sea swells were eight to ten-feet high, but he needed a margin of safety, as one large swell could flood the compartment and bring down the aircraft.

The Aquarius could be seen surfacing about four hundred feet to the starboard, a safe distance away should one of the helicopters lose control. Chopper two was about four hundred feet further starboard.

The blinking red door light signaled it was time to disembark. In full gear, each of the team members began jumping feet first into the frigid waters. The choppers kept a three to five knot forward speed to prevent the team members from landing on one another. The last team member pushed the two large ordnance parcels encased in floatation devices out and then jumped.

The team members were each making way to the Aquarius and being tossed about with ease by the eight to ten foot swells. The crew of Aquarius were climbing on deck with lines to pull the men, women and ordnance on board, with chopper one from the port and chopper two from the starboard side, observing.

11:18 PM. The Aquarius was topside for seven minutes and twenty-six seconds and with all team members accounted for and ordnance stowed, was diving and making way for the coast of Peru.

Director Douglas and Cole Cunningham had painstakingly organized and then reorganized the transport over the last day. Everything had gone perfectly, a very good sign. It had been organized with three branches of the service and one agency — all within twenty-four hours. Clint was thinking that this was one of the many benefits of Department C, the ability to cut through the red tape and get things done.

Both teams were sequestered in the officers' mess and it was a little cramped with twenty-four people where there would normally only be ten. Still, it was important to keep the Aquarius crew out of the compartment. Clint had requested hot breakfasts with strong black coffee, fruit and water for the team. They may or may not be hungry, but the diversion would help ease the building tension.

Some of the team were beginning to joke around a bit, just a bit, another good sign that the team also thought the mission was proceeding smoothly. Clint's observations were interrupted by a loud rap on the bulkhead and a voice asking for Captain Bear.

"Yes, Chief, I'm Captain Bear," Clint responded to the boat's Chief Petty Officer as he walked to the bulkhead opening.

"The Captain would like a word when you have a moment. If now is convenient, I'll escort you to his cabin."

Looking around at his team eating and relaxing and then turning to the Chief, Clint responded, "Now would be fine."

Clint had not seen Captain Preston Cornwell since they met, by happenstance, during his training at the NSA camp in central Virginia, but he would never forget the tragedy that had befallen his family. The loss of twin sons for simply being in the wrong place at the wrong time, drug dealers warring over territory, and then his wife, unable to endure the loss, taking her own life. The side effects of a drug-centric society. Clint, lost in remembrance of their meeting, neglected to bend his six-foot-three-inch-frame low enough and banged his head as he followed the Chief through yet another in a series of bulkheads. The Chief, out of respect, pretended not to notice.

The Chief finally stopped and wrapped on the door leading to the Captain's cabin. From inside the cabin, Captain Cornwell bellowed, "Come in."

"Thanks, Chief," the Captain said as he rose to shake Clint's hand.

"Captain, good to see you again," Clint said warmly. "I didn't expect we would have the pleasure again."

"Well, to be candid, I volunteered for this assignment," the Captain said.

"How did you know about it?" Clint asked with a little concern showing.

"Clint, I've been in the Navy for nearly forty years and in that time you make a lot of friends. Douglas and I go way back. Way back."

"Okay, that helps put it together," Clint said in relief.

"Wait a minute Clint, I'm not in the compartment. As far as I know this is a training mission, and nothing more, so don't develop loose lips on me now. Hear?" the Captain stated with Clint nodding in acceptance.

Captain Cornwell lowered his voice a bit and in a tenderhearted tone, looking into Clint's eyes and placing his big hands on Clint's shoulders, continued, "Clint, you learn a lot in forty years. I know intuitively the intent of this mission, that's why I volunteered. You see, I need to be part of this, I need to do something, for my family's sake. They were good kids, they helped in the St. Augustine Catholic Mission, they were honor roll students, good kids. They looked after their mother when I was away on tour, they were never in any trouble. Never. Then, dead, at seventeen, both of them dead, and I didn't even get to go to their funeral and say my goodbyes, all because of damn filthy drug dealers!"

The big weathered Captain was hunching over and crying unabashedly, "I need to do something! You know how I feel. You, of all people, know the pain, the emptiness, the nothingness that envelops you," The Captain spewed out, his hands shaking, muscles tensed to the point of snapping.

Clint knew all too well what the Captain was feeling, the pain and anguish, the loneliness and fear, the hatred toward the drug dealers and users, the lost sense of his life's purpose. Intuition told him to stay with the Captain a little longer.

01:53 AM

The phone on the officers' mess wall was answered by Meceli who hung up, turned and said to the teams, "Ten minutes to surfacing. It's a go!"

The Aquarius was three nautical miles off the northern coast of Peru. The seas were only two to three feet, the rain had stopped and there was only a quarter moon. Radar had reported no local shipping traffic except an oil freighter steaming due north seven miles away with her stern to the Aquarius. Perfect.

Some of the team had benefited by a few hours' sleep, others simply by physical and mental rest. Everyone were now wearing the black canvas camouflage suits, in full readiness, and staging themselves and ordnance near their assigned hatch.

"Up periscope," the Captain said.

Carefully, methodically, the Captain surveyed the water's surface for any sign of life. Slowly, he completed a 360-degree turn before smacking the periscope handles up into the column and saying, "Surface!"

The horn blew several times and the boat could be felt inclining rapidly as she made her way to the dark Pacific's surface.

The Captain turned to Clint and extended his hand saying, "Remember, sunrise is at 5:56 AM. I'll surface here again at precisely 5:30 AM. God speed and good luck, Clint."

All four teams disembarked in two minutes forty-six seconds, benefiting from the few hours of rest and the calmer seas. The Aquarius was topside for five minutes and eleven seconds, leaving four teams paddling in as many rafts silently to the Peruvian coast.

2:47 AM

The teams assembled in the same location, a small inlet hidden from the ocean side by a protruding cliff and from the landward side by the dense vegetation growing up to and over the cliff. The four black canvas-covered rubber rafts were secured with adequate line to allow for the incoming tide to ensure their return ride. One team member scaled the cliff and secured four lines to aid each team's assent. Meceli's Team Three waited at the crest of the cliff and monitored communications, alert for any team needing backup.

The dank night air laid heavy, thick enough to cut with a machete. Vision was aided by a starlit sky, with several fast moving clouds intermittently blocking the quarter moon. The teams heavy black canvas suits, needed for camouflage and to carry their gear, hastened their dehydration due to the poor breathing.

Clint, heading Team Four was en route to the mansion. He had chosen the mansion because of his personal familiarity with the security, the grounds and the mansion layout. He had assigned Teams One and Two with Foley and Weisman to the outbuildings where the muscle and lieutenants were likely to be found. They should be in sight of the mansion's main gate in six to seven minutes, the added time consumed by using paths behind other homes in lieu of the streets.

Clint could make out the glow of the mercury lighting that illuminated the gate area of the mansion and signaled the team to crouch and wait while he reconned. Clint, in a crouch, moved closer, and then in a crawl moved within two flowering shrubs where he could see the entire gate area.

The massive stone pillars that supported the gate were, as before, used also for the guards' shelter from the elements and potential intruders. Hole one, security had been increased. Where there had been one guard on either side, there were now two. The small building to the left probably housed additional men as well. The thirty-foot stone tower, as intimidating as before, contained unknown armament and personnel, but still remained the team's first target.

The plan would remain unchanged. A frontal assault on the gate would be suicidal, so Clint reasoned that the gate guards must be taken from within the compound. Therefore, all teams would await Team Four's notification that the wall alarm system had been eliminated. Teams One and Two would move over the wall toward the large garage and outbuildings while Team Four would take the tower. Once in the tower, Team Four would support the elimination of the gate guards from within the compound. By that time, Teams One and Two should have the outbuildings secure and would move to support taking the mansion.

Clint reasoned that now, both time and defensive numbers were the enemy, and radioed for the alarm system specialist to begin his work.

3:19 AM

"Team Four: Perimeter alarm deactivated."

"Team Leader: GO."

"Team Three: Acknowledged," Meceli said, her pulse rate beginning to increase.

The night was still, dank and heavy, the only occasional sounds coming from the indigenous bird life. The locals were unaware that eighteen men were moving through the compound aided by mercury lighting. Each knew that there could be alternate alarm systems and were cautious when moving branches and stepping through pathways.

Clint reasoned that the tower entrance would not be secured since it was within the compound and was pleased to learn he was right. Three men, Clint one of them, waited at the bottom while the other three snaked up the stone circular stairway to the perch doorway. Not a sound was heard until two and a half minutes after "Go Mission", when the confirmation was radioed.

"Team Four: Tower secured. Three down, all up," which meant that there were three guards killed, and the team had suffered no casualties. From the perch, within seconds, they easily took out the four gate guards. The sound of one guard falling alarmed one of the additional guards in the small building, who came out to investigate. Clint was already close to the door and took one out with a single silenced shot to the head, the three remaining in the building were eliminated by the other two SEALs.

Hole two, the guard station telephone was ringing. Clint almost picked it up, but thought better of it and let it continue to ring. Surely, someone will be down to investigate soon.

3:56 AM

"Team Two: Clear. Proceeding to mansion. Seven down, all up."

"Team Three: Acknowledged."

"Team Four: Gate area secured. Proceeding to mansion. Eleven down, all up."

"Team Three: Acknowledged," Meceli thought that things were going very well so far. Twenty-one down with no casualties was excellent results.

Clint was aware that Weisman's Team One was overdue to check in, but communication security was to report only the conclusion of an assignment with the results, or to request backup. Each communication must be preceded with their team number for identification.

Team Four was moving up to the mansion in the shadows of the main road. The results of hole two was four Uzi-armed men walking the center of the main driveway. Clint signaled to take them from behind as an added advantage. Four spits were heard and the heads whiplashed from the bullets' penetration. The bodies fell in unison, followed by the roar of unsilenced Uzi fire as the finger of one guard was pushed into the trigger by his dead weight.

Hole two caused hole three. Lights began to come on within the mansion, signaling the inevitable added resistance they would face when taking the mansion.

"This is Weisman. I need some help by the garage."

Clint, knowing this was a breach of communications security, and also knowing that Weisman would not breach security, knew this was a trap. He had to acknowledge quickly before Meceli acted.

"Got you Weisman, all others dead, I'll be there in five."

Meceli put together what was happening and ordered four men to the mansion in support, one to remain with the rafts and monitor the communication. She went in support of Clint. She ordered a change of plans for the mansion.

"Wiggens, tell Foley it would take too long to secure a 'live' mansion, room by room. Gather the incendiary bombs and place them at all four corners of the main building and under the main gas line. Use the C-4 grenade style to implode the structure, it will also stun the occupants for several minutes to allow the flames and smoke to do their work. Position the team around the structure and take out anyone who escapes and wait until the mansion is in full flame before evacuating. Now double-time it! Go!" Meceli said as she broke into a full run to Clint.

4:11 AM

All team members had earpieces and had also concluded what was happening. They also knew that there could be no further radio communication until Clint radioed properly that the situation had been secured.

Clint had made it to the garage area in less than three minutes. He could move more quickly, knowing that the tower had been secured. During his run, he had heard two unsilenced gunshots coming from the direction of the garage. When he peered through the brush, he was horrified to learn why.

"¡Entregar! ¡Entregar! ¡Venir fuera!" the guard was screaming: Surrender! Surrender! Come out! Two men from Team Two were lying facedown with a pool of blood around their heads. The other four were bound, hands behind their backs tied to their ankles. The guard had his pistol to one of their heads while seven other men guarded the perimeter.

"¡Entregar! ¡Entregar! ¡Venir fuera! ¿No?" he fired another shot and the SEAL fell on what had been his face before the bullet exited.

Clint felt a part of his resolve bleed out of him as he watched the blood gush from the SEAL's head. He screamed for them to cease, "¡Cesar! ¡Cesar!" as he walked out of the underbrush, hands held high, having left his MAC-10.

Meceli had made it there in time to see Clint walking from the underbrush into his captor's hands. All eyes were on him, giving her a very short-term advantage. She raised her MAC-10, ordered her shots and pulled the trigger. The silent bursts had killed three guards before the other four knew what was happening. Another went down as they looked for the muzzle fire.

Clint had crouched and retrieved his pistol, placing three bullets in the head of the guard that had shot the three SEALs. One of the two remaining guards, having taken cover within the garage, fired a round into Clint's leg causing him to drop his pistol. MAC-10 fire pierced the garage wall, preventing the guard from aiming again.

The last guard made it into the underbrush and was moving toward the last burst of MAC-10 fire. Clint pulled out his boot knife and was moving toward the three SEALs to cut them loose. Weisman was alarmingly darting his eyes toward the brush to see Meceli coming out cautiously. A little movement to her right and the last guard jumped out, ready to fire. In a single fluid motion, Clint threw his knife spanning the thirty feet in an instant and finding the guard's throat. The guard fell back and Meceli put three rounds into the body.

4:38 AM

The thunderous explosion caused the Clint and Meceli to glance in the mansion's direction. While cutting the three SEALs free she had told Clint of the change in plans. The mansion was ablaze, its flames lighting up the countryside. Soon help would arrive.

"Team Leader: Garage secure. Seven down. Three not up. Report!" Clint barked partly as a result of his accelerated adrenaline flow and partly due to his gaping leg wound. Meceli was field dressing his upper thigh to help close the wound and stem the blood flow.

"Team Two and Four: Mansion down. All secure. Evacuating. All up," Foley filling in for Clint's absence in Team Four.

"Team Three: Acknowledged"

"You four, back to the cliffs," Clint ordered pointing to the three SEALs and Meceli. Then he grabbed Anne-Marie's arm, pulling her back to him, and kissed her warmly, lovingly.

"Where are you going?" Meceli asked.

"I need to check the mansion with my own eyes. It's not over until I do," Clint snapped as he struggled to his feet.

"Then I'm going with you. Period. Court-martial me later, but I'm going. Period." Meceli ordered back. Her resolve complete.

Clint, surprised with her attitude, paused and then nodded in agreement. "You three, back to the cliffs and don't wait for us. Repeat, do not wait for us. If we are not there on time, leave without us. Understand? The sub surfaces at 0530, be there! Go!"

4:49 AM

The pain in his leg was intense and Clint was having

difficulty mentally isolating and controlling it due to the continued blood flow brought on by the run to the mansion. Meceli could see that he was slowing, and slowed her pace accordingly. The light from the fire was aiding their progress by making it easier to chart their course several hundred feet in advance.

They could literally feel the heat coming from the mansion before they could actually see the burning structure. The heat was becoming unbearable with their black canvas camouflage suits and the ninety-degree ambient temperature, and similar humidity. Breaking through the last of the underbrush, Clint and Meceli gave witness to the engulfed mansion. There were several bodies near the large mahogany double front doors, including Santiago Cero and the three other cartel Generals. Soon the mansion's once sound stucco and beamed structure would be collapsing to ashes and mark the end of the Peruvian cartel.

5:11 AM

The full teams' complement, less three and Meceli and Clint, were paddling three rafts out into the still dark Pacific Ocean. One member kept night vision goggles on, looking to the coastline hoping to see Clint and Meceli. Another kept a Global Positioning System in hand to pinpoint the Aquarius's surface location.

Meceli and Clint were en route to the cliff, moving as fast as they could, aware of the time. They decided to take the same back paths and avoid the serious eyes of the public coming out of their homes to see the burning mansion, even though it would take a few minutes longer.

Clint's black canvas pant leg and boot were completely permeated with his blood, his dizzy head confirming it before his eyes. They still had more than a half mile to the top of the cliff, in his condition, easily another five to seven minutes. He had lost a significant amount of blood and the energy consumed to stay conscious was consuming the energy he needed to continue running.

"Meceli, you go ahead, I'm slowing you down and someone needs to report," Clint ordered unconvincingly.

"I never leave my own, especially someone I'm in love with!"

"What am I going to do with you, Anne-Marie?"

Meceli took his arm over her shoulder to prop him up and support the weakening leg. It helped pick up the pace, but the added weight was quickly exhausting her. They lost their balance several times, and tripped over each other's feet several times more. The last time they fell, Meceli fell on top of Clint in a rather compromising position, and they both laughed uncontrollably.

The tension eased and unexplainably rejuvenated them, and they made the last thousand feet to the cliffs edge in about two minutes. Meceli handed Clint her water pouch, and he passed her his. They both drained the eight ounces in seconds and gathered as much strength as they could to repel down the cliff.

5:22 AM

The Teams had reached the surface coordinates, still without signs of Meceli and Clint.

Meceli cut the two lines that they were not intending to use, letting them fall the thirty feet to the rocky shore below.

"Meceli, can you make it?" Clint asked, joking.

"Maybe you could help me, big man!" Meceli shot back, thankful that Clint found a way to cut through the building tension. A thirty-foot fall to the rocky shoreline below would result in certain death, either by the fall itself or by the inevitable capture when the extraction sub couldn't be reached.

They both put the rope through the metal belt hooks, slid over the cliff's ledge and started easing themselves down. Meceli was exhausted from supporting the much larger Clint, and fell unrestrained the last twelve feet. Clint moved at a snail's pace due to the double-wrapped hook and didn't realize Anne-Marie had fallen until he was on the stony shore.

"Clint, I think I've broken my ankle!" Anne-Marie shouted over the pounding surf, crying from the pain and from the perceived failure.

Clint's intuition told him that the Aquarius was surfacing, three miles off the coast, and that there was no possibility that they had the ability to paddle to it before sunrise. But, intuition told him to keep moving anyway, so he reached for the raft, cut the tether and pulled it closer to Anne-Marie. Where the strength came from, he didn't know, but he simply lifted and placed Anne-Marie into the raft, pushed off and began paddling.

"Come on Meceli, we can still make it! Pick up a paddle, and by the way, your treat at the Italian restaurant tonight!" Clint screamed over the pounding surf.

5:30 AM

Captain Cronwell snapped the periscope handles up and yelled, "Surface! Prepare for casualties." He was hopeful that Clint was in one of the three rafts.

The Aquarius surfaced within thirty-five feet of the three rafts, and had men and ordinance onboard in less than three minutes. Foley had reported that Clint and Meceli were seen just beginning to paddle, obviously both had sustained injuries.

It was clear to Captain Cronwell that Clint and Meceli would not make it to the sub before sunrise and his orders were equally clear, submerge and leave the stragglers. Well, he thought, there is a first time for everything and this will be the first time he would disobey a direct order. No moment in his Naval career would be remembered with more pride.

"Chief, launch the motorized skiff and you, personally, go out to get them!" the Captain ordered. "We don't leave our own! Ever."

"Way ahead of you Captain, the skiff is already topside. We never leave our own."

"Thanks, Chief. Navigator, bring me as close as possible, and then a hundred feet closer, but keep us on the surface! Exec, take the helm!" The Captain barked.

"Aye Aye, sir."

Seconds later, the skiff's engine roared to life and the tough Chief could be seen between the spray heading to a small dot close to shore. He had a tether attached to the bow wrapped around his wrist to hold him steady as he bounced airborne off the wave tops.

The Aquarius had moved to within three quarters of a mile and the Chief was nearly back to the boat, raft in tow.

5:47 AM

Just nine minutes to sunrise and certain detection.

"Exec, turn the boat to a heading of 010 degrees. Get ready to haul our asses out of here," the Captain ordered.

"Aye Aye, sir."

By the time Clint and Meceli had reached the boat, they were both unconscious, Clint from the massive loss of blood and Meceli from the excruciating pain of her broken leg, not ankle, being continuously pounded by the surf while in tow.

Any Peruvian who was so inclined to be looking at the glorious sunrise that morning may have seen the Aquarius's antenna, but then would have dismissed their findings, as with the next blink of their eye there was nothing.

Orders broken, multiple times. Losses less than anticipated. Mission successful.

Clint awoke first. The sub's sickbay was small, white and sterile. Unknown to Clint, Meceli was in the rack to his right, but behind a white curtain. He was weaker than he had ever felt before, even with the chest wounds sustained while saving Bill Covey's life in Afghanistan more than twenty years ago.

Captain Cronwell was sitting there, waiting for him to regain consciousness.

"Meceli is fine, just a broken leg. She'll be good as new and dancing the newest dance in six to eight weeks. All but three of your team are on board and accounted for. You, my boy, have lost a lot of blood, most of which has been replaced by the donors within your team, but other than that, you're going to be fine. We are heading back to the southern coast of California," Captain Cronwell reported, knowing that a mission commander always wants the status first thing.

"Preston, thanks," Clint said more deeply and seriously than the thanks for a mere status report. "I'll never forget what you've done, for me and for the country. You have made the difference."

Smiling the Captain began to walk away, heading for the bridge, feeling, for the first time in years, a sense of purpose again, when Clint called to him.

"Oh, Captain. I need a favor. Can your Mess Chief cook Italian?"

www.ingramcontent.com/pod-product-compliance
Lightning Source LLC
Chambersburg PA
CBHW020250200626
46816CB00001BA/218